GUILD
OF
MAGIC

JON AUERBACH

GUILD
OF
MAGIC

NYC
QUESTING
GUILD

II

CONTENTS

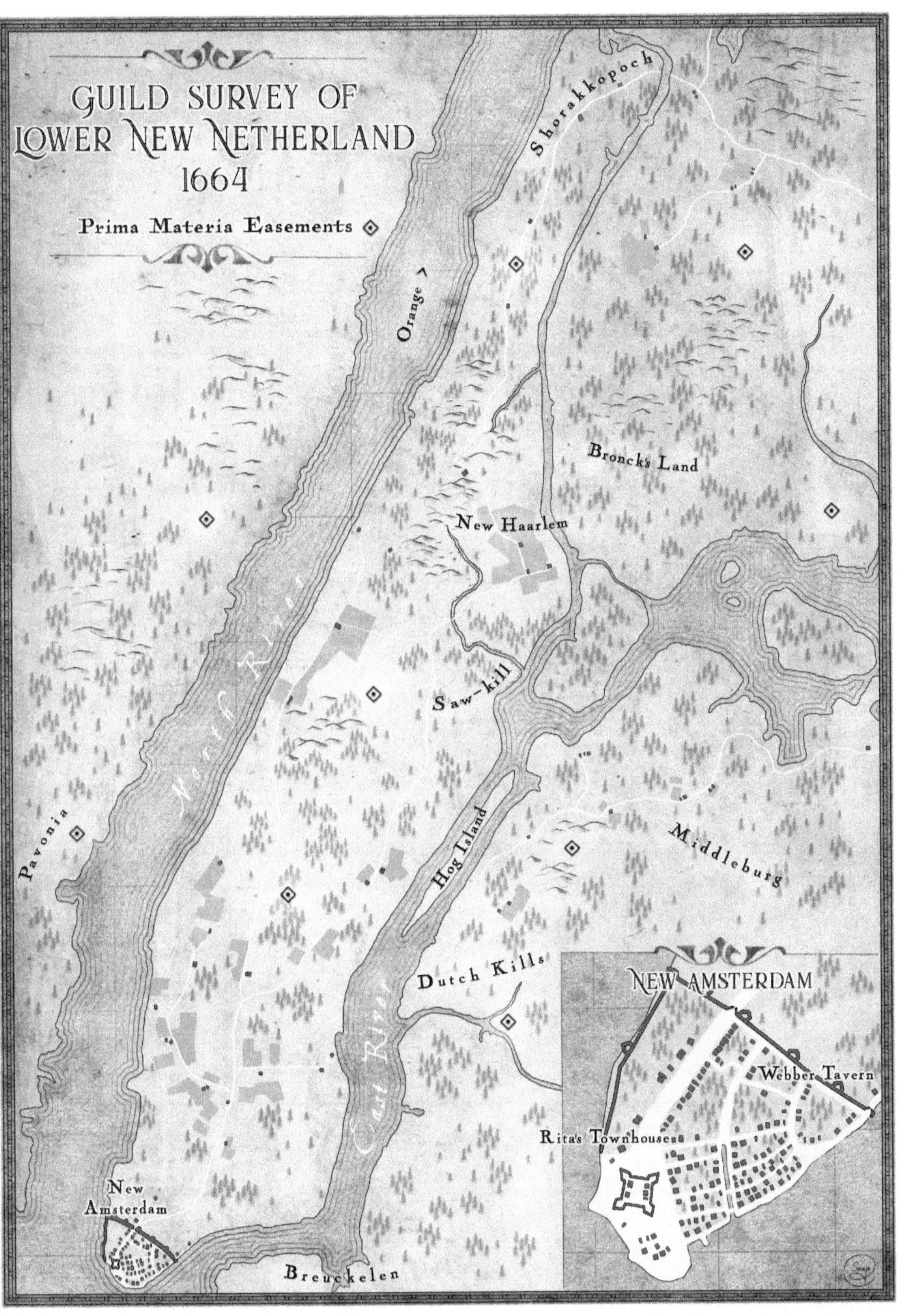

GUILD SURVEY OF
LOWER NEW NETHERLAND
1664
Prima Materia Easements
Shorakkopoch
Orange
Bronck's Land
New Haarlem
North River
Saw-kill
Pavonia
Hog Island
Middleburg
East River
Dutch Kills
New Amsterdam
Breuckelen
NEW AMSTERDAM
Webber Tavern
Rita's Townhouse

GUILD OF MAGIC

IN ANY AGE

The world hums as I sleep in my rainy prison.

Despite all the changes that have transpired, there is a familiar rhythm, an inevitable pattern that emerges if one listens long enough. And listening is all I can do. It has been several decades since I was corporeal. Maybe people are getting smarter, learning from their old mistakes. Maybe they have forgotten about me and I will remain in this wooden box for all eternity, or at least until the alchemy that binds my essence to this stone wears away and I can finally escape into an everlasting rest.

Or maybe I need only one more opportunity to break the pattern that has been my existence these fifteen hundred odd years. Maybe the next person who slips that silver chain over their neck and presses the stone will be the conduit I need to return to a true life. And when that happens, I will finally destroy those who imprisoned me. For across these long centuries, although I have forgotten their faces, I have not forgotten their names.

One day, the box finally opens again.

I, of course, cannot see such a thing in my current state, but I have learned to mind my surroundings enough so I can sense this. I feel a soft hand lift the chain and my stone out of confinement and onto the neck of someone warm. Another hand presses the glamour and my body erupts from it, enveloping the girl who had found me. I can feel her energy pushing against mine. It is mortal, but it is fiery and fierce. A sacrifice worthy of my renewal.

In those brief few seconds, when the two of us merge, I learn what I can about her.

A castellan's daughter. A daughter of Atlantis through her maternal line. A keeper of a Relic.

Now that is interesting. Much more unique than the usual plebeians who find me.

I try to divine more, but the moment is over, and I must step back and merely watch.

She clasps her hand, my hand, around her mouth to stifle the fit of excitement. To her, I am a magical costume. But she will soon learn the truth. She stares ahead at the other woman in the room with her, and if I still had a heart, it would have skipped a beat.

Her appearance has changed slightly, but I would remember that hair and those eyes in any age, my sister is that striking.

"What do you think, Eliana?" she says. Even her voice is the same.

"I love it, Alea!" says the girl. So that is what she is calling herself in this era. Clever.

"I knew you would," says my sister. The girl leans in toward Alea, but this, this is too much for "Alea," and she reaches down her hand to the girl's neck to withdraw my body back into the stone.

Several days later, I awake again as the girl is running about the island that is her home. She basks in the freedom I give her, to move unseen through the crowded market and through the soldier camps. I would warn her to be a stranger in the midst of the familiar may be exhilarating, but is also dangerous, especially for a young woman. But I do not yet have the strength to do anything other than observe. And wait.

Finally, after a half a year of dalliances, I feel strong enough to exert myself. And thankfully, that is when Alea has decided to return to see her young lover. She enters the girl's bedchamber through the window and presses the stone while Eliana slumbers. I awake and stare at her, the moonlit sky casting a gentle glow on the room.

"Hello, sister," she says. "I have been looking for you for a long a time."

Eliana does not move and I take that as my cue, so I extend myself around the sleeping girl and it is as if I am almost alive once again.

"Sister," I say, sitting the girl up in the bed. "It is good to see you. I do not remember the last time we shared such a quiet moment together."

"That is because they have stolen most of your memories," she replies. "But you, you somehow kept enough inside of you after..."

"After they reduced me to a hollow shell," I say. "Yes, I was always quite remarkable. Tell me, have you come to restore me to my former glory?"

The sad look on my sister's face tells me all I need to know.

"Finding this stone took centuries," she says. "I do not know how much longer it will take me to find the others."

"I see," I say. "But I have been productive on my own while you were looking for me. And this girl you have found will provide me with strength enough for now, I think, to continue my work. With the two of us, it will be easy to track down where they have taken my-"

"I'm sorry," Alea says. "But you cannot have her."

I laugh.

"And why not? Is this not why you have ensnared her with your charms? You were always good at finding the … oh."

My sister, ever the romantic, even if it will be fleeting.

"Yes," says Alea. "Again, I am sorry. But, I will find others. The three of us, together, we will be so formidable. You will see."

"OK," I say. "We will do it your way. Because whatever draws you to this girl Eliana, I felt it too. She is special."

"On that we agree," says Alea. "For now, though, I must take back my present from her. But know this, we will see each other again soon. I am sure of it."

My sister is a terrible liar.

CHAPTER ONE

RED PILL

◦

"Living is easy. Dying is harder."
– LADY MELANIE FITZJAMES, DUCHESS OF MONTAGU
CHARLESTON, SOUTH CAROLINA, MARCH 1, 1815

The phone rang.

This was not an uncommon occurrence in this city of eight million souls, most of whom spent the majority of their in-between moments with their heads glued to a glowing screen.

But this particular phone was not an iPhone, an old rotary landline, or one of those fancy-at-the-time flip phones where the cover slid down with the press of a button.

No, this was a pay phone on the darkened corner of 1st Street and First Avenue. And it shouldn't have been ringing at all, because as my research had confirmed after my prior visits to this nexus of firsts, this phone booth should have demolished several years ago with the rest of its brethren.

Despite all that, the phone continued its song, and I knew that the patience of the person on the other end was growing thin. So I crossed the darkened avenue without further delay, slid the folding door of the booth open along the rusty track, and stepped inside.

"Hello?" I said, picking up the dirty plastic receiver and wishing I had wiped it off first.

"You're late, Jade," said a gruff female voice on the other end.

I glanced down at my watch. It was 3:20, Monday morning. So, technically, I was a minute late.

"Look, I've been playing this game with you and your friend and that other guy who sounds like he's always eating a bag of chips for five weeks now, and I don't really appreciate the-"

"Enough. Do you want the next mission or not? Because from where I'm sitting, it sounds like you really don't want to be in the Guild."

"Fine, sorry. No more backtalk. What's the scoop?"

"In 47 minutes, a crate of green apples will be delivered to the Union Square Trader Joe's. You will make sure that it does not make it into the store."

Apples, why was it always apples?

"OK," I said. "But that doesn't give me a lot of time to get up there and figure out a plan."

"Well," said the voice, "maybe next time, then, you won't be tardy."

The line went dead with a click and I hung up the phone with such force that I nearly broke the plastic in two. I briefly considered demolishing the rest of the booth using the quarter of a strength buff that I had left to my name, but thought better of it. Once I somehow completed this latest Quest, there would be time enough to vent my frustrations in a proper manner.

Except that was a lie, because every time I thought I had gotten one step closer to being done with this silly initiation, I found myself again thrust into a nearly impossible task.

They all started the same way.

A cryptic text message would appear on the simple black cell phone Gilbert had given me after I had thrown my gold token into the fountain at Greenacre Park. The first one had provided the location of the phone booth and the second one, a date and time. There was no pattern or rhythm to the timing of the five summonses I had received, save that I was always given at least an hour to get to the phone.

It was fortunate, then, that I didn't have a job, didn't have any friends (at least any who remembered me), didn't have a boyfriend, and didn't have a semi-sociopathic mentor-turned-Questing partner. All of that would have held me down, would have prevented me from completing the Guild's gauntlet.

And what a gauntlet it had been so far. It was like I was back in my first months of the Quest Board, except these Quests weren't of the simple fetch variety. No buying bagfuls of groceries at Chelsea Market for me. Instead, it was scrambling along wet rocks on Atlantic Beach, trying to collect enough moss to fill a ramekin. Or stealing a particular petal from the corpse flower at the New York Botanical Garden. Then there was the afternoon I spent smuggling rare books out of the library where I used to work.

Sure, it was satisfying to have handled everything that they had thrown at me. And the Quests also served as a useful distraction to help me forget about that horrific day on the island. But each time I received a new Quest, the same sinking feeling would return, that this would be the one that I couldn't complete. And with that failure, I would be booted from the Guild, my gold token confiscated in the middle of the night by some Guild henchman, or Gilbert, or even Dalia herself.

I pushed aside such thoughts and began walking briskly uptown. It would be a 15-minute walk to my destination at this pace, and that would give me at least another 15 minutes once I arrived to formulate a plan. Assuming this was a popular delivery time, the loading bay would be swarmed with workers and I didn't exactly look like the archetypical produce deliveryman. That was especially the case with the glamour activated.

The small green stone hung on a silver chain around my neck, nestled under my mother's locket. That locket was the reason for my current predicament. What I had originally thought was just a stupid birthday gift from my now-dead mother was actually the hiding place for a gold token. And that token was worth more than just the gold it was made of. It was the twelfth and long-missing gold token of the Worshipful Company of Alchemists, otherwise known as the Guild.

My watch ticked over to 4 a.m. as I turned left onto 14th Street. Seven minutes to come up with a plan.

Perfect.

If I were Beatrice, it would have been plenty of time. I would simply sidle up to the worker unloading the truck, ask him his name, and then hand him a note written in command ink that would order him to give me the apples.

Or I would eat a small piece of a speed buff and just take the apples with no one the wiser. Or if that wasn't feasible, then I'd use a strength buff or a sliver of power from the purple stone on my finger and steal the apples by force.

Or if all of those options for some reason failed, then I would stab the guy with the Medoblad, turn him to stone, and take the apples. And then, if I was feeling charitable and the incident hadn't made the national news yet, I would come back later and stab him with the other end of the blade to heal him.

But all I had at my disposable was the tiny bit of strength buff, a tube of vitality serum, and the glamour, now that Beatrice was gone. When activated, the stone created a projection around my entire body that made me look and sound like a 22 year-old redhead with sparkling green eyes and a raspy voice. I had dubbed her Jade Peters, after my old handle, JadePhoenix42, and I was spending more and more of each day as her as the weeks of my initiation had slowly ticked by.

This was the unfortunate consequence of presenting myself as Jade during our initial encounters with both Dalia and Gilbert. And then there was the high I still felt every time I stepped out in public behind her facade. Truth be told, I didn't like what the glamour was doing to me. There were too many nights where I would go to sleep as myself and wake up the next morning up as her. But that was a problem for another day. Now, I needed Jade in spades.

I crossed 14th Street and walked the full block to survey the scene. The store was bounded by two sets of metal doors, and hordes of workers were already furiously moving pallets of wooden crates onto hand trucks at both ends before pushing them inside. This would not be as simple as batting my eyelashes, flashing a smile, and walking away with the apples. I cursed under my breath as I reached 4th Avenue and saw a red truck rumbling toward the intersection. I was out of time and out of options.

The light turned green, and I watched the truck begin to cross the road. But before it could pull through the intersection, something grabbed hold of my body and forced me into the street. It was as if someone had attached puppet strings to my limbs and was manipulating my movements from above. My arm raised itself up from my side and stretched out in front of me, my hand now urging the truck to stop.

Thankfully, it did.

The truck let loose four successive blasts of the horn, but whatever was controlling me held its ground and my other hand began pointing to the curb on the south side of the street. The driver stared at me in disbelief and then, to my relief, turned on his blinker, and I felt myself step backward to give the truck berth to maneuver over to the curb.

That's when I saw it, out of the bottom corner of my eye. The glamour stone was glowing ever so faintly, the green light shimmering in the darkness of the early morning. If I could just reach my hand up a few inches, then I could deactivate its alchemy and regain control of my body. But it was as if the stone could read my thoughts, because no sooner had I formulated the thought than the glamour's pressure around my real body increased exponentially. I struggled against its weight, but found my will being pushed into the back of my mind, leaving me a bystander in my own flesh.

I watched as I walked over to the truck and rapped my knuckle against the door. The driver glared at me through the window, his eyes bloodshot and his hair ruffled, before slowly opening the cab and stepping out onto the street.

"You mind telling me what the fuck you think you're doing?" he said, spit flying from his mouth.

I wanted to say that I also would like to know the answer to that question, but then my mouth, or rather, Jade's mouth began to move on its own accord.

"And good morning to you too, sir," said the voice with a sing-song note. "We're full in front, so you'll have to unload here, I'm afraid."

The man looked at me cross-eyed and I thought he was about to unleash a second tirade at me, but instead, he grumbled something to himself and started walking to the rear of the truck.

I followed him, the glamour pulling me forward like I was a dog on a leash, and watched as he slid the back door of the truck up to reveal crates filled with produce. Including one near the front filled to the brim with green apples. The driver took out a small hand truck and unfolded it on the street, before stacking several crates on top of it and wheeling them away toward the store without another word.

The crate with the green apples remained and my hands quickly snatched it from the truck and then my feet were on the move. It seemed too easy, putting aside the fact that I had completely lost control of my body. Jade walked me south on 4th Avenue for a block and then turned onto 13th Street, continuing on until we reached a 24-hour parking garage, which we entered. The attendant was asleep in the booth, and so we journeyed unimpeded to the back, where a door opened into a dark alleyway. As my eyes adjusted, I could see that we were behind the Trader Joe's, a smattering of empty crates and other refuse strewn about. Something about this place was familiar, but I couldn't quite remember what or why.

"You're welcome, by the way," said Jade's voice, before the pressure suddenly subsided and my body reappeared from the beneath the glamour.

A wave of relief washed over me and I looked down to see my hands, my real hands, holding the requested crate of apples. There would be time to deal with what had just happened, but for now, I wanted to take a few moments to savor my success.

But it was a short victory party, because a minute later, I heard the patter of footsteps approaching, and I turned around slowly to see a group of a dozen teenage girls all dressed in black leather jackets with jet black hair and black eyeliner, pleated black skirts, and knee-high black boots emerge from the shadows of the alley.

"You," said the girl in the middle, who was holding a very long, very sharp, and very glowing knife with a bright white hilt, "are trespassing in our territory."

It all came back to me in an instant and I could feel my stomach turning itself inside out.

"And you are?" I said, but I already knew the answer, the images of the glowing green scar and the frail old man flashing in my mind.

The girl with the knife smiled.

"We're the Black Vultures. And you're about to die."

CHAPTER TWO

BIRDS OF PREY

"The process grows harder each time. Restoring my youth is a trivial matter,
but altering my appearance so as to not arouse suspicion taxes my facilities.
And without Rita's lifetime of memories, now lost to me, when I look in the mirror
at my new visage, it is as if I have truly been reborn."

One time, when I was 12, I was cornered in a bathroom by a gaggle of girls not too dissimilar from the one currently threatening me with bodily harm. They grabbed me by the arms, dragged me to the last stall, and stuck my head in the toilet until I thought I was going to drown. It was not a pleasant afternoon.

Sixteen years later, this encounter was shaping up to be worse than the last one.

"Oh. I see," I said, trying to project an air of confidence. These girls didn't know a damn thing about me and maybe I could use that to my advantage. "You going to stab me with that the little knife of yours? For accidentally walking into your 'territory'? Give me a fucking break."

This time, it was the girl to the leader's left who spoke, although in the dim light of the alleyway, they pretty much all looked like a goth version of the Children of the Corn.

"No, the stabbing is only for when you don't listen to what she said," the second girl said in a deep baritone voice that squeaked at the end, betraying her near-pubescence. I nearly laughed, but then remembered poor Steve, rapidly aged, struggling to sit down on the subway, and Polly, who in her desperation had betrayed us to the Guild in the hopes of finding a cure.

"That blade looks very scary, I have to admit. Did you get it at Hot Topic with your training bra? You used it on a friend of mine. He said it was like getting cut by a Play-Doh knife-wielding Girl Scout. I don't even think he put a bandage on the wound after."

My bravado was on the verge of faltering and unless they relented soon, I was going to find myself on the wrong end of a very painful and very slow death. And without the Medoblad's other blade to heal me, I would be in an old-age home next to Steve before the month was out. Maybe Polly would come to see us on the weekends.

The second girl turned red and curled her fist, but the knife-wielding girl stopped her.

"I think your friend has misinformed you. This 'knife' is actually the Relic *White Hilt*, passed down from father to son for a thousand years, until I was born, and my dad, in disgust over failing to produce a first-born son, refused to give it to me. Do you know what I did to him?"

Shit.

"You threw a temper tantrum and then ran to your room crying?"

I slowly lowered the crate of apples to the ground and brought my right hand close to the glamour stone. It wouldn't be much, but maybe showing them I too had ancient power on my side would make them reconsider their aggression.

"Enough," the girl replied. "You are starting to annoy me. So you'll be finding out exactly what happened to him. Marcy, Leila, if you don't mind."

Two girls nodded and then reached into their jacket pockets to pull out brightly colored square gummies. They unwrapped them, broke off tiny pieces, and started chewing. I cursed Beatrice under my breath. If I ever saw her again, I was going to give her an earful about how much trouble she had caused us by selling her buffs to Phineas.

I grasped the glamour with my fingers and squeezed, the familiar wave of Jade washing over me.

"But I mind," I said, nearly shouting. "Because my name is Jade Peters, and I'm a member of the Guild."

All of the Black Vultures' eyes widened in unison, but their leader was undeterred, and she gestured to Marcy and Leila, who vanished in a flash and reappeared at my side, their brass knuckle-adorned hands gripping my arms behind my back so hard I thought they were going to crush them.

The leader slowly approached as I struggled to free myself, but I was no match for the girls' alchemy-enhanced strength.

"Impressive," said the girl. "So you're not just a regular idiot walking into my alley, you've got yourself a glamour! And a rather attractive-looking one at that. That will be very useful to me."

She grabbed the chain around my neck and started to pull, but suddenly stopped as loud footsteps echoed on the alley stones behind us.

"I wouldn't do that if I were you," said a familiar voice.

An unassuming man wearing a brown sport coat and horn-rimmed glasses had emerged from the back of the garage and strolled casually toward the rest of the gang.

It was Gilbert.

The Vultures all rotated their heads in unison like something out of *The Exorcist*, and stared at the newcomer.

Calling him unassuming was being charitable. Banal would be a better fit. I'm sure he didn't mind being described as such. There was a certain benefit to not being noticed, to being ignored by the masses, and that was doubly true when you were a member of a centuries-old shadowy organization bent on reclaiming the lost magic of the world.

But there was nothing ordinary about how we had met.

He had been the literal bogeyman for several weeks, pursuing Beatrice and me from the shadows as we searched for a cure to undo the stone curse of the Medoblad. Until we learned that the Gilbert that had been dogging our footsteps wasn't Gilbert at all, but Doug, Beatrice's first trainee, who she had tried to kill after he turned into a crazy stalker.

Then Gilbert had intervened and twisted Doug into an even crazier stalker and had also given him a glamour to boot, one made in his own image. Needless to say, things got out of hand, and the real Gilbert had shown up after we had been forced to turn Doug into a pile of broken stone. Then there was that whole "throw your token into the mysterious pool of water" ceremony that Gilbert had invited us to, where Beatrice's gold token had exploded and she had fled without so much as a goodbye. With her gone and all the people from with my normal life either dead, forgotten, or furious at me, the man in the alleyway was the only person who might have cared that I was still alive.

Which was all a long way of saying that I was kind of glad to see him.

The lead girl dropped the glamour and turned to face Gilbert.

"And you are?" she said, motioning to Marcy and Leila to rejoin their compatriots. I used the opportunity to slink off to the side of the new confrontation that was developing.

"I'm Gilbert."

The girl's demeanor wavered slightly. Evidently his name alone carried weight in this world, but what he was going to do against that Relic, I wasn't sure.

"If you're Gilbert, then you know that this is our domain, and the Guild has no business here."

Gilbert looked around the alleyway before turning his attention back to the leader.

"Not much of a domain, if you ask me. Looks more like a shithole," he said with a smile.

"Fuck off," said the girl. "You, I'll give a pass to, but this bitch back here," she turned and pointed to me, "wandered in here uninvited. You can have her once we take our toll."

"You really that desperate for a crate of apples?" said Gilbert. "How about I give you $50 plus a few bronze for good measure, and you can buy all the apples you wa-"

"Do you think I'm stupid?" asked the girl. "Those aren't just any apples, those are from Running Brook Orchard. They've got celestonite and with them, I'm going to take the Black Vultures out of this alley and claim what's ours."

"Don't count on it," said yet another voice from the shadows. A young woman soon appeared from the garage. She had dark auburn hair and was sporting a pair of sunglasses, despite the early hour. Her outfit was capped off by knee-high black boots and a pleated skirt, but instead of the black one worn by the Vultures, hers was orange, which matched the hair-tie around her ponytail.

"Patel," said the lead girl with a scowl. "What are you doing here? Come to beg us to let you back in? It was you who thought you were too good to lead us anymore, once the Guild had come calling."

"Zoe, charming as ever," said the woman. Despite her British accent, there was something familiar about her voice. "No, I'm not here to reclaim the mantle from you, although maybe I should. I'm here for my knife and for her."

She pointed at me and it was then I realized who she was. The woman from the phone.

"As I was just saying to your friend over here," said the girl called Zoe, "if you walk in here uninvited, there will be consequences. And it's my knife now, in case you've forgotten. The price you paid for abandoning us."

The woman, who couldn't have been older than 20, smirked at the threat, reached into the flannel tote bag slung around her shoulder, and pulled out an improbably long metal sword with a jewel-encrusted hilt. The blade glistened, despite the darkness that enveloped the alley, and I wondered what alchemy it possessed.

"Emma," said Gilbert to the woman, holding up a silver pocket watch he had pulled from his jacket. "We're going to be late to our appointment if you don't hurry this up."

Emma rolled her eyes at Gilbert and held up her empty right hand, which sported a set of thick silver rings on her middle three fingers. She pulled her hand back slightly and the knife in Zoe's hand began to shake, much to the Vulture leader's consternation.

"Heh," said Emma. "I figured you were too much of a shit-for-brains imbecile to cleanse the auragen off of *White Hilt*."

She yanked her hand backward and the knife flew out of Zoe's grip, spun end-over-end several times, until Emma snatched it out of the air with a flourish.

"Much better," she said, adjusting her stance to account for the new weapon in her arsenal. I could only gawk at the alchemy prowess on display, my little glamour paling in comparison.

The other Vultures looked at Zoe for some sign of strength, but all the fight had gone out of her, and she stood there, dumbfounded. It was then that Marcy or Leila—I didn't know which—dashed forward with buff-enhanced speed. But when she reappeared mere inches in front of Emma, her arm already halfway cocked into a punch, the woman was ready.

She deflected the girl's brass knuckles easily with her sword blade, sending the Vulture staggering backward a few steps. Undeterred, the girl scrambled to her feet and tried again. This time, though, Emma sidestepped the punch and then smashed the pommel of her sword into her attacker's stomach, sending the Vulture onto the ground.

Emma nudged her fallen former comrade in the ribs with her boot, and, satisfied that the girl was unconscious, she bent down and started removing the brass knuckles.

"Hey," yelled Zoe. "Don't you fucking dare-"

It all happened so fast that I was sure my eyes were playing tricks on me, because the next thing I knew, *White Hilt* was somehow floating in mid-air in front of Zoe. I looked over at Emma, who was back on her feet, her arm outstretched and the fingers of her ring-adorned hand clenched around an invisible tether.

She loosened her grip slightly and the dagger inched closer to Zoe's throat, a look of terror forming on the girl's face.

"Emma, please," Zoe said with a whimper. "You don't have to do this."

"But I think I do, Zozo. Remember when I would call you that and you would get so annoyed? It was cute, in a way. Then I showed you what real alchemy looked like and it was as if the psychopath switch went on in your mind. How many people have you hurt with this blade by now?"

"I ... I don't-"

"Answer me," said Emma, the anger in her voice rising to a crescendo.

"11," the girl blurted out.

"That's 10 too many. If I let you walk out of here alive, how many more will you-"

"Are you quite finished?" interrupted Gilbert, and Emma shot him a venomous look, as if he didn't grasp or care about the significance of what she was doing. But in that one distracted moment, Zoe ducked under the floating blade and made a beeline toward her former mentor.

The poor girl, she never saw it coming. Instead, all she saw was Emma yank back her hand in a furious motion before the dagger's hilt hit her squarely in the rear of the head. Zoe let out a guttural cry as her chin hit the pavement a few inches in front of Emma, and the woman tapped the unconscious girl's cheek with the tip of her boot before nodding to herself.

"Yes. Now I'm done."

CHAPTER THREE

VITAL SECRETS

"I buried Rita in a stately grave in Richmond. There were no attendees at the funeral besides me. In a month's time, there will be the reading of the will. I need to summon the heirs."

"You're a real buzzkill, you know that?" Emma said to Gilbert as we walked through the garage and back onto the street. Her sword had somehow disappeared back into the tote bag, along with the newly reclaimed *White Hilt*. "Was going to cut off her hand for good measure, but I guess I'll have to save that until after her 18th birthday."

Gilbert ignored her, and we continued toward Union Square, the crate of mind-linking apples still straining my forearms.

"Umm," I said to both of them, after a few blocks of total silence, "thanks for bailing me out back there."

"Don't get used to it," said Gilbert. "Anyway, it was better than having to explain to Dalia why our newest member was murdered in the service of Ms. Patel's revenge quest."

"Hey!" interrupted Emma.

"You're lucky I'm even speaking to you," he said. "The Guild initiation is not about settling old scores. You of all people should know that."

"I'm sorry," I interjected, "but you're the woman from the phone, right?"

Emma nodded.

"And you're also in the Guild?"

"Right again, Jade. She's quick, this one."

Gilbert rolled his eyes at the quip as we reached the interior of Union Square Park, which was still quiet at this early hour. He directed us to one of the benches and I finally put down the crate of apples.

"In case you hadn't gathered from before, I'm Emma Patel, Second Seat of the Pavonia Table."

She extended her ring-adorned hand and I shook it.

"The what table?" I asked. "Also, what's with the fake British accent all of a sudden?"

"S'not fake," said Emma, breaking into a cockney version of her accent. "Imma true Brit, I am!"

"Oh," I said. "My mistake."

"My mum and dad are from Coventry," said Emma, dropping back into her regular elocution. "Lived there 'til I was 12. Then had to move here after my gran died. When the Guild calls, you can't refuse."

"So it would seem," I said. I thought about adding that all of my calls from the Guild so far had been from her, but dropped it.

"We'll go over all the formalities at the meeting tonight," said Gilbert. "And now that the formal initiation is almost over, we'll get you properly equipped, so you don't need to be rescued again."

"Almost over? What else do I have to do? Steal the dodo beak from Oxford?"

"Don't be ridiculous," said Gilbert. "We have much more experienced people working on that. No, it's just a swearing in and a lot of paperwork."

"Great," I said. "I love paperwork."

A shudder ran through me as I remembered the reams of paperwork they had forced me to fill out after Hammond had canned me from my job at RPGLab last month. For a company with only one female developer, it wasn't a good look to fire said developer, especially after she had just saved the whole team's ass in front of their biggest investor. As much as I wanted to run to the nearest lawyer and file a wrongful termination suit, the severance package they had offered in exchange for my permanent silence on the issue was too good to pass up.

"You'll be getting a call at the phone tonight at 10:30 with the meeting location," said Emma. "Don't be tardy."

"Can't you just tell me right now?" I said. "I'm standing right here."

"Fine," she said. "10:45, under the Bethesda Terrace in Central Park."

"Thank you," I said. "Wait a minute. How were you expecting me to get up there from all the way downtown in 15 minutes?"

"You caught me. Wanted to see if your friend had left you any speed buffs. Oh well."

"Let's get moving," said Gilbert, and the two Guild members left me alone with my thoughts and a crateful of apples. That was, until Emma ran back a minute later, her tote bag held open.

"Sorry," she said. "Almost forgot those. Would you mind?"

"What?" I asked. "You want me to dump all of these into that tiny little bag?"

It was obviously no ordinary bag, but she didn't know how much I still didn't know about alchemy. If she had pressed me, I would have said that the bottom of the bag was lined with vervorium, just like Polly's shells and those stupid doorknobs.

"You got it," Emma said with a shit-eating grin.

I kicked myself for not pocketing some of the apples when I had the chance and then reluctantly poured the entire crate into the tote bag, which accepted them without protest.

"Thanks luv, see you tonight."

Emma slung the bag around her shoulder effortlessly and retreated east toward Park Avenue.

"Where can I get one of those?" I called after her, but she just chuckled and ran off into the morning sun.

The city slowly sprung to life as I walked. The supers sprayed their hoses, cleaning the sidewalks as they did every morning. The coffee shops and the bodegas opened their doors, welcoming in their sleepy patrons looking to start their days with a hot cup of caffeine and a muffin. The commuters headed to the nearest subway station or bus stop.

Two years ago, I would have enjoyed this ambling stroll, still blissfully unaware of the shadows of magic that covered the world. Last year, I was too busy Questing for wooden and iron tokens to care. And now, more than I anything, I wanted to be passed out in my cozy bed in my fifth-floor walk-up with the shades drawn and not wake up for several days.

But that wasn't an option for several reasons. First, I obviously had to show up at the meeting point tonight. Second, I had abandoned my old apartment and roommate in the middle of the night several weeks ago, leaving only a cryptic note and a wad of cash to pay the rest of my share of the lease, retreating to a still unfurnished studio in Greenpoint. And finally, because there was work that needed doing.

I stopped at a coffee cart on the corner, purchased a large iced coffee, and withdrew a small stoppered vial and plastic eyedropper from my bag. The liquid shimmered a pale green that matched its taste, and I walked over to a bench in front of an empty storefront and carefully uncorked the glass tube. I lowered the tip of the eyedropper into the vial, pulled up a tiny portion of the liquid, and then deposited the liquid into my coffee. Even the 24 ounces of pure caffeine and sugar was not enough to blunt the putrid taste of that one little drop, and I felt my body shudder involuntarily as I drank the entire contents of the cup.

Except it wasn't my body. The glamour was still active, and I looked at Jade's reflection in the storefront window, who remained stoic and still while the effects of the vitality serum kicked into high gear. This was a different beast than the one that Beatrice had given me that early morning in our old office after our escape from Doug. That serum had operated like a mini volcano, sending an explosion of heat and rejuvenation into every corner of my body.

The current serum, though, was more like an everlasting gobstopper. The tiny drop kept on working for 24 hours, giving me just enough energy to keep me balanced on that edge between exhaustion, awareness, and delirium. It was a dangerous game I was playing, because I had no doubt that I was setting myself up for a horrific crash at some far-off point in the future.

The recipe I had found tucked under a sliver of carpet in our office on the 47th floor of the Chrysler Building. Everything there had been stripped clean when I finally paid a visit a week after Beatrice's disappearance. Even the vervorium doorknob that formed the gateway to the island house was gone. Maybe she was still holed up there, waiting out the Guild, but I had barely had a moment to myself in the past month, let alone the half a day it would take to journey by boat out to the South Shore of Long Island.

Beatrice's handwriting was neat and concise. "Improved vitality serum," it had said at the top, followed by a list of ingredients, some mundane, some magical, with a list of complicated steps at the bottom. I didn't know where the hell I was going to get 40 grams of 80-day old lemon zest or 80 grams of a 40-day old cardinal's feathers, but fortunately, it only took me a day to notice the seemingly random pattern of underlined letters and numbers in the note.

The letters had spelled out "toilet tank in hall" and I had sprinted back to the office to find a yet another envelope taped inside. Unlike the one that she had left me in the bathroom at the Met, this one held only an old key. But much to my disappointment, it wasn't the vervorium key we had used to travel through the Washington Square Park Archway.

Buoyed by the vitality serum working its alchemy on my exhausted body buried under the glamour, I quickened my pace, eager to get to my current destination before the full morning rush hit. 6th Street was seemingly immune, unlike its brethren, and when I turned off of Fifth Avenue, I found myself walking down an empty block to the green relay mailbox. I fished the old key out of my purse, inserted it into the rusted lock, and turned. The compartment swung open without complaint and I smiled as I looked over its contents.

This had been the second half of Beatrice's message. The underlined numbers in the recipe had provided the street number and she had scrawled the street name inside the bottom corner of the envelope. During my first visit here, I had been pleasantly surprised to find containers with enough of the prima materia to make at least several vials of the vitality serum. The hideaway had provided a convenient headquarters of sorts, somewhere that couldn't be tied to Beatrice, to me, or even to Jade.

I smiled at Beatrice's ingenuity in coming up with this mailbox of all things as a failsafe, but then shook my head as I considered how far she had fallen from the woman with the secret lab on the Lower East Side or the woman with her own private island. This was most likely all the remaining help I was going to get from her, and the thought that I was now truly on my own was terrifying.

My hand absent-mindedly found its way up to the glamour stone and I grasped it slightly, then felt the weight of my counterpart dissolve. With all the commotion in the alley, I had nearly forgotten what "Jade" had done. Was this what Ty had warned me about when she had given me the stone? I hadn't come across the girl since that morning in the abandoned train station, but her business card was among the items stowed away in the mailbox, along with some peculiarities from my former partner that I hadn't had time to suss out.

I pulled out my phone and brought up our previous text conversation and was about to send another help request, but then thought better of it. The mystery of the glamour would just have to wait until I had someone new from this side of the world that I could really trust.

Instead, I withdrew the stack of unmarked bills from the mailbox, put a small sealed envelope in its place, and then locked the compartment again. The envelope I had addressed to Molly Vestrit, one of Beatrice's apparent pseudonyms, and the note inside contained a short missive expressing my hope that she was still OK and to contact me if she was able to safely meet. I doubted she would ever read it.

The cash, which represented a sizable portion of my severance payment, I stuffed into an envelope and placed at the very bottom of my bag. I surveyed the block to see if anyone had noticed my mailbox hideout, but Beatrice had chosen the location wisely, and the street was still deserted. Satisfied that no one was about to rob me, I retreated toward Sixth Avenue and walked south. With five minutes to spare, I reached the rendezvous, a small square in the middle of the West Village dotted with rotting benches and misshapen cobblestones.

I took a seat on one side of a set of back-to-back benches in the middle and waited for Janus to sit down behind me. He had come highly recommended by a number of users in the back corner of Craigslist as one of the best forgers in the city. The cash would pay for the papers that would solidify my double life as Jade Peters: a driver's license, Social Security number, a passport, and even a rewards credit card with a great sign-up bonus. Maybe I would treat myself to a one-way ticket to Omaha with the miles once I was satisfied that the Guild wasn't going to kill me right now.

My phone alarm went off, signaling one minute until the drop, so I fished out the envelope of cash and bent down to place it under the bench. As I did, though, the glamour loosed itself from under my sweatshirt and I realized I was still "me." I quickly pulled the hood over my hair and covered my face with one hand, while activating the glamour with my other hand. When I sat up again, I was Jade, my now voluminous red hair spilling down the sides of my face.

"Jade?" said a gruff voice behind me.

"Yes?" I replied, in Jade's raspy tones.

"Iss done."

I almost turned around to look at Janus but remembered the explicit instructions not to do that very thing and instead wait 10 minutes before retrieving the goods. Fine. I had almost the whole day until my next harrowing experience was scheduled to start, so I tried to relax and appreciate the picturesque city park.

An old woman sat on a bench at the far side, knitting a golden scarf. It stretched down to her ankles, and it reminded me of the

Golden Fleece from the *Jason and the Argonauts* movie I watched as a kid. I wondered who she was making it for.

A pair of ducks hopped out of the little pond and waddled over to me, almost as if they were trained to expect food whenever someone sat down by themselves on a bench. I flashed my empty hands, and they quacked angrily and scurried back into the water.

A breeze swept through the park and brought with it a sheet of newspaper. I picked it up to discover that it was from yesterday's *Times* Style section, and absent-mindedly turned it over to find the featured *Vows* column and that's when my jaw dropped.

The bride and groom stood in the center of a circle of rocks on the outskirts of the woods, surrounded by their wedding party. The women were dressed in bronze sheets of fabric holding bouquets of dark orange flowers and the men had matching bronze bow ties. It was all quite ridiculous and I would have had a good laugh had I not recognized the two women in the center. Because staring up at me from the crinkled half-page photo with half-distant looks in their eyes were none other than Lisa and Stacy.

CHAPTER FOUR

INITIATION BY FIRE

"Why did I not name myself the heir? Too many questions and no good answers. So Rita spent the last decade of her life, in addition to her political machinations, finding suitable stewards for her legacy. These, other than the Foundations, are the only memories she did not commit to writing, and so, they remain in my head."

Central Park, for all its magnificence during the day, was scary as hell in the night. The great green lawns were empty, as were the jogging trails and the cyclist paths, and the only light in my vicinity came from intermittently spaced street lamps, which, to add another level of terror, flickered randomly whenever I approached.

I reached the top of Bethesda Terrace at 10:43, the full moon illuminating the murky waters of the popular row-boating pond below. The figurehead of the eponymous fountain looked up at me with its stone gaze. It was supposed to depict the Angel of the Waters, but in the ominous glow of the moonlight, I could have sworn that instead it was an alerion, the sigil of the Worshipful Company of Alchemists, otherwise known as the Guild.

I walked gingerly down the steps, Jade's familiar weight pushing slightly against my actual body, and then turned and strode toward the tunnel that ran under the terrace. Decorative columned archways lined the entrance and extended down into the darkness, but of the Guild escort that should have been waiting for me, there was no sign.

"Hello?" I called out once I had reached the interior of the passageway. "Is anyone there?"

Jade's voice echoed down the terrace underbelly, but the only response was silence.

I threw back my head in frustration, fighting against the urge to unleash every ounce of fury that had been building up inside me these past few weeks. What was left of my resolve gave way after three seconds and I screamed.

When I opened my eyes again, four hooded and cloaked figures were standing under the archways, two in front of me, one to my left, and one to my right. They approached slowly, and I swiveled in a circle, looking for a familiar face. But the moon's reflection off the pond was suddenly blinding and the only thing I could make out were the identical gold clasps that held the cloaks in place. Finally, the figures stopped three paces away and unhooded themselves.

One was Gilbert and one was Emma, which was slightly reassuring, but the other two were total strangers.

"Jade Peters," said one of them, a man with silver hair and a silver goatee and a silver cane that had somehow appeared from inside the sleeve of his robe.

"That's me," I said.

"Present your token," he replied with a distinctive Texas drawl.

I fished my locket out from underneath my jacket and unclasped it. Inside was the gold token that was my entry ticket into the Guild. I held it out for the silver-haired man to see and he stepped forward to grab it from my hand, but I snatched it back from his grasp.

"That's not how this works," I said. "My token stays with me. You already know it's real."

I turned to look at Gilbert, who nodded in assent.

"Fine," said the man. "Lucca, the blindfold."

The fourth and final figure, a 30-something woman with glasses and short purple hair, produced a black silk scarf from underneath her robe and handed it to the man, who stretched it out in front of him with both hands, letting his cane fall to the ground.

"Is this really necessary?" I said.

"I'm afraid it is, Ms. Peters," said the man. "Don't worry, though, you'll get your eyes back just as soon as we reach the Guild hall."

"I'm sorry, what? What do you mea-"

The man closed the gap between us in a flash and pushed the blindfold against my eyes, which I closed involuntarily. I felt Jade buckle under the stress of whatever alchemy was contained within the scarf, as if her entire body was about to crack into a million pieces. But thankfully, the man pulled back the blindfold after only a few seconds.

Except that when I opened my eyes again, the only thing I saw was nothing.

They placed a cloak around me, and I did not protest. They pulled the hood up over Jade's fiery hair, secured it with what I imagined was a matching gold clasp, and I did not fight them as my arms went limp at their sides. They muttered words of an ancient language in unison, and the cloak constricted my limbs. I began to walk, but not of my own accord.

The blackness that permeated my field of vision was absolute, and the sheer terror of it had drained all the fight out of me. Even Jade had not been moved by my plight to intervene. Whether that was because I was not truly in danger, or the blindfold had somehow dampened whatever she was, I wasn't sure, but I held onto this glimmer of hope like a drowning woman clutching a sinking life preserver.

We walked in silence up the sloping path along the pond that led away from the Terrace and then up another hill that I knew led toward the Met. Finally, the quiet of the park was broken by the familiar sounds of city traffic, and I surmised we were close to the Engineer's Gate on 90th Street. I felt the ground shift as we moved onto the cobblestone sidewalk that lined the west side of Fifth Avenue. Then my body was directed across the street, down the sidewalk, and then across another street, until we resumed our northward trek on Madison Avenue.

What a sight we must have been, five robed figures skulking around in the night. But then I wondered if anyone could see us at all. We would be hard to miss otherwise, even at this time of night. Surely the doormen of the tony Upper East Side buildings we were passing would not keep quiet about such a bizarre tableau, even by New York standards.

I wanted to say something, to curse these men and women for their treachery, but found the muscles in my throat and my jaw unable to hear my brain's commands. So I gave in and tried to enjoy the only sense left under my control. I should have heard the hum of the air conditioners above my head, the gentle honking of horns, and the screech of tires. But the streets were eerily and unnaturally quiet, and I resigned myself to being trapped in this cocoon until either I was welcomed into the Guild or stabbed in the back and pushed into the sewer.

I lost track of how far my body had walked and wouldn't have been surprised to find myself in the middle of the Brooklyn Bridge by the time this was finished. At some point, I felt myself sit down in a comfy chair and the hood was removed from over my head. As soon as it was, my limbs suddenly fell to their sides as if the invisible puppet strings had been cut. Then the blindfold was pressed back against my face and quickly removed. I took a few deep breaths, unsure if I even wanted to return to the brightness of the world. But finally, I heard someone clear their throat, and when my eyes fluttered open again, they were all staring at me from around a big wooden table.

The man with the silver facial hair, who was now sporting a cowboy hat of all things, sat several chairs away to my left and the blonde-haired woman named Lucie, two seats to my left. Emma had taken up a seat opposite the man, and Gilbert was in the middle seat across from me. Along with a familiar woman.

"Welcome, Jade Peters," said Dalia de Wyck, 13th Chairman of the Guild, dressed in an elegant black dress with the familiar black stitching, a hint of a smile on her face. "Let us begin, shall we?"

Gilbert picked up a piece of paper and began reading.

"Roll call. J.P. Laurel, First Seat of the Orange Table?"

"Here," he said.

Gilbert made a notation on the paper and then continued.

"Lucca Josephie, Second Seat of the Breuckelen Table?"

"Yep," said the woman.

"Emma Patel, Second Seat of the Pavonia Table?"

Emma nodded.

"I need a verbal confirmation," said Gilbert sternly.

"Present," said Emma, rolling her eyes.

"Dalia de Wyck, First Seat of the New Amsterdam Table?"

"Present," said Dalia.

"That leaves me, Gilbert Barbata, Second Seat of the New Amsterdam Table, also present. And as we have two first seats present, we have a quorum, so this 432th meeting of the Worshipful Company of Alchemists shall come to order."

He banged a gavel that had somehow appeared in his hand against the table and then sat down.

All this talk of tables and seats made me reexamine the wooden table we were sitting at. It wasn't one table, as I had originally thought, but four that were connected with some sort of gold inlay. The table's outlines were also different. The New Amsterdam Table looked almost like the island of Manhattan, but the others were indistinguishable shapes.

Behind each table were three seats, with everyone sitting in the specific Seat that Gilbert had called. Which meant that I was slated to be the Third Seat of the so-called Breuckelen Table.

I took a minute to survey the rest of the room. On the wall to my left were several banners sporting symbols I did not recognize. And on the opposite wall was a series of four gleaming metal shields, each with a different crest. Wooden chests were haphazardly pushed against other nooks in the room, and several half-burned candles provided a dim glow.

"Do I hear a motion to dispense with the reading of the minutes from the prior meeting?" asked Gilbert.

"I move," said Emma.

"Seconded," said J.P.

"All those in favor?" asked Gilbert.

"Aye," said everyone but me.

"Nay?" I said with apprehension.

Gilbert frowned.

"Jade, seeing as how you are not, at this moment, a member of the Guild, you do not get a vote. But you may read the minutes to your heart's content later this evening if you should so choose."

"Oh," I said, my face turning red. "OK."

"Good," said Gilbert. "With that settled, let us turn to the two matters of new business on tap for tonight's meeting. First, we have a new member to initiate."

All eyes suddenly turned to me and I felt as if they were piercing through the glamour and staring at the real me, an interloper hiding within another interloper.

"Jade Peters," said Gilbert. "The Membership Committee," he gestured to the assembled Guild members at the three tables, "has considered your membership request. As you know, membership in the Worshipful Company of Alchemists is not something given lightly. We are honor-bound to uphold the charter given to the Founding Twelve. To guard, shield, and cultivate the Secret of Secrets: the ancient art of alchemy. Only those of sound mind, body, and essence are worthy to be inducted into the Guild, an appointment that is not only for your lifetime, but for your heir as well and their heir, and so on."

"Can we get on with this?" interjected Emma, who had used the length of Gilbert's speech to remove her robe, revealing a faux leopard bomber jacket and figure-hugging black blouse underneath. Evidently, she had plans later tonight that were about as far as you could get from a meeting of a secret magical society.

Everyone ignored the outburst, except Gilbert, who tilted his head slightly in Emma's direction as if she was an annoying fly that would not stop buzzing in his ear.

"Second Seat Patel, it seems as if I'm keeping you from something more important? Another night of downing tequila at some God-forsaken basement bordello, maybe? Or do you have a gentleman caller that we should know about? Well, whichever it is, you may want to put those plans on hold until after we get to the second item of business."

Emma glared daggers at him before slinking down in her chair and putting her robe back on.

"Now, where was I? Oh, yes. Jade. You have proven yourself worthy of the three elements."

I tried to piece together which of my trials and tribulations had corresponded to each of the so-called elements, but Gilbert continued his long speech.

"And as Committee chair, I now pass along the Committee's recommendation to the Chairman that you be elevated to full Guild member."

Gilbert produced a piece of paper from his robe and handed it to Dalia.

She considered it, her eyes scanning up and down the page, and I couldn't help but wonder what they had written about me. Finally, she placed the paper down on the table.

"Thank you, Gilbert, but I'm afraid I will have to reject the Committee's recommendation."

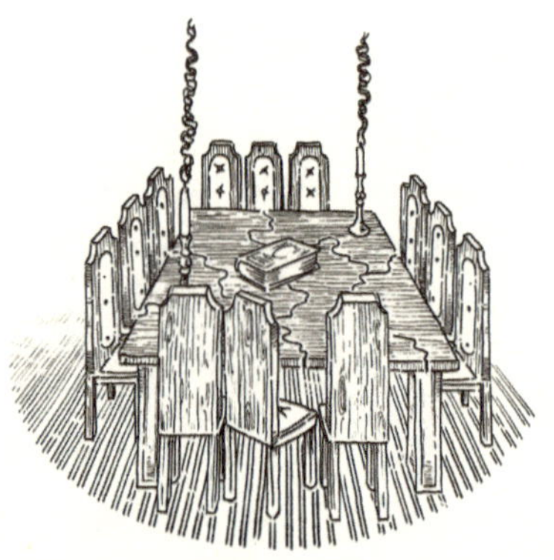

CHAPTER FIVE

BLOOD WORK

"Finding an heir was a harder task than one would think. So many of the old families have daughters who they bred with the sole capability of being sold off like show cows. It is a shame that they wasted such beauty and physique without also cultivating their minds. Such women in ages past have ended dynasties and empires. The spare sons fared no better, spoiled beyond usefulness, like a rotten strawberry."

Everyone started shouting all at once. Out of the six people present, it was me, surprisingly, who took this new development in stride. J.P. rose to my defense first, followed by my tablemate, Lucca.

"I insist, Dalia, we put Ms. Peters through her paces and-"

"We've adhered to the protocols to the letter," interrupted Lucca, "and she satisfied them. It is not your place to-"

"Are you serious with this shit?"

Emma was the most indignant, and I suppressed a snicker as she too made her piece known. It was then that I realized they were not so much defending me and my status as a Guild member, but the process itself. After all, if Dalia could undo all their hard work on nothing more than a whim, what else could she do? Demote them? Revoke their membership entirely?

All three continued on for some time before Gilbert finally brought the meeting attendees to heel again with several bangs of his gavel.

"Order," said Gilbert, before turning and whispering something to Dalia, who nodded and then stood.

"Let's try that again, shall we? As I was trying to say, I cannot accept the Committee's recommendation at this time. Ordinarily, yes, your initiation would have been sufficient. In fact, it might even have been a bit overzealous," said Dalia, looking briefly at Emma, before continuing.

"But this is not an ordinary induction. You," she said, pointing at me, "have somehow discovered what was once thought lost forever: the twelfth token and with it, the claim to the Third Seat of the Breuckelen Table that has been vacant for hundreds of years. So the normal set of protocols will not be enough, particularly when you have refused to tell us where it was you found the gold token."

I stared at her, unblinking, wanting more than anything to slink down into the robe and let it carry me away from here. I had done everything that was asked of me, and then some, even when it had seemed impossible.

"What will be enough, then?" I finally said, the anger rising in my voice. "How about I cut off my own arm and offer that on a silver platter? Would that satisfy you?"

Dalia laughed, followed by a smattering of nervous chuckling from the rest of the room.

"Don't be ridiculous, Jade," she said. "That would be a waste of a good limb. And you're going to need it, anyway."

"What are you talking about?"

"You all were so quick to yell and snap and shriek, like a bunch of yapping dogs, that you didn't let me finish. I only said that I was rejecting your recommendation that Jade be admitted into the Guild now. I never said anything about turning you away entirely."

"Dalia, this is not proper," said J.P. "The Committee's recommendations have always been respected. You cannot just-"

"What, run the Guild on my own? No, unfortunately not. Maybe if I could, then things would be different."

"What is that supposed to mean?" asked Lucca.

"Enough bickering," Dalia said. "Jade, your admission to the Guild is suspended pending one final task. Complete it and you will be welcomed with open arms. No more hoops to jump through and no catches. You might even find yourself moving up a Seat in the process."

"What would I have to do?" I said, not really wanting to know the answer.

"Simple. All you need to do is fetch a vial of Dragon's blood."

"You're joking, right? Dragons aren't real."

"Not that kind of dragon," said Gilbert, removing an envelope from his robe and placing it on the table. "It's a red resin, been around for thousands of years. We want you to take the one from the Emerson Pigment Library up in Boston."

"So you were in on this the whole time?" said J.P. "Why then did you make us engage in this charade? Why are we even here tonight? You both know that our resources could have been spent dealing with-"

"Stop," said Dalia, her voice suddenly thunderous. "If you must know, J.P., you were the one we were going to ask to retrieve the vial. But you've just convinced me it would have been a mistake to give you this task. So it will be up to Jade and Emma instead."

"I'm sorry, Jade and Emma what now?" said Emma. "You're daft if you think I'm going anywhere near that vial. You wanted J.P. to get it, have him go to Boston with the new girl and leave me out of it."

"Emma," said Dalia, "your father was the one who located the vial in the first place. It seems only fitting that his eldest daughter and heir to his Seat be the one to finish what he started."

"Is that supposed to make me all sentimental or something? You think you can manipulate me that easily? Well, piss off!"

Dalia arched her eyebrows and was about to say something when Gilbert intervened.

"Emma, do not let your father's work die in vain, he wouldn't want tha-"

"Don't pretend that you speak for him. Or for me."

With that, she pushed herself up from her chair, threw the hood of her robe over her head, and with a squeeze of the gold clasp, she was gone.

The room went silent, save for the slam of the side door that the now-invisible Emma had just slammed shut, and we all glanced around the room awkwardly waiting for Dalia to continue with the meeting's agenda. Instead, she whispered something in Gilbert's ear, who nodded, before retreating out the backdoor without another word.

"We're done for tonight. Next meeting will be in four weeks," said Gilbert and J.P. and Lucca too rehooded and vanished. "Jade, stay so I can give you the specifics."

The side door opened and shut again and only then did Gilbert traverse the length of the table and sit down in the empty Pavonia Third Seat.

"Do these meetings normally go like that?" I asked, and Gilbert let out a chuckle before sliding the envelope toward me.

"Only on days ending in y," he said with a half-smile. "You get a room full of people who are used to not taking no for an answer and sparks inevitably start to fly. It's a wonder the Guild has gotten anything accomplished in the last hundred years."

I opened the envelope and withdrew a single sheet filled with typed letters.

"The pigment library has over 2,000 specimens," said Gilbert, as I scanned the paper. "We've been able to narrow down the location of the Dragon's blood vial to the fourth floor, but the library's index is, unsurprisingly, not publicly available. You'll have to see what you can come up with once you're on the ground in Boston."

"Ooohkay," I said.

"Any questions?"

"Only a million. Like, for starters, where the heck are we?"

"Ah, I suppose that would naturally be the first question after we basically blinded and kidnapped you? You can see for yourself when you leave, but we're currently in the south tower of the Madison Avenue Armory. It's been the Guild's headquarters since the mid-60s."

"You mean that abandoned brick castle on 96th Street? I used to walk by here every week in high school on the way to chess club. Never thought it was anything more than an old relic that the city refused to let anyone tear down."

"And that's why it makes the perfect headquarters for our organization," said Gilbert. "This tower has the meeting room, the library, and Dalia's study at the top. If you go down to the basement, you can reach the north tower, which has office space for each member. We've also got some auxiliary locations scattered around the city that we've collected over the years, but unfortunately you'll have to wait until you actually become a member to get access to those."

"Fine. But now that I know about this place, you're just going to let me come and go as I please?"

"Yes, and you can keep the robe too, for now. Put it on somewhere safe and activate it, and then you can enter through the door on the corner of 96th and Madison that we took you through tonight."

"So you guys really are just walking around with invisibility cloaks like it's no big deal. Do I have that right?"

"Ha, yes. It's actually a pretty complicated piece of alchemy, but for your purposes, just pull the hood up over your head, grip the gold clasp for a second, and then, voila, you're invisible."

I tried it for myself and nearly fell backward when my entire body vanished below me. It took me a moment to locate the gold clasp again and undo the alchemy, and I breathed a sigh of relief when the outlines of the robe reappeared along with the rest of me.

"That … will take some getting used to," I said.

"They're mostly useful at night when there aren't so many people around," said Gilbert. "During the day, you'll probably make it about five feet before bumping into someone. Also, walking about Manhattan in a full-length black robe in broad daylight will still draw stares, so try to use it sparingly."

"Understood," I said. "All that talk earlier about getting me properly equipped, that went out the window, I assume?"

"Yes, for now. But take the robe. It might be useful for your task, but don't think you're just going to waltz into the library with it on and walk out with the vial. There's a reason that Emerson has been able to hold onto it for so long."

"That's super helpful," I said. "You got any more pointers? Should I duck when the booby-trapped metal blade comes swinging for my head?"

"Go talk with Ms. Patel. Despite her performance tonight, she's got a cracking mind, as she would tell you, for sneaking into places where she's not welcome. If you hurry, you can catch her at her usual haunt down in the Village."

"Fine, I'll do that. It's not like I wanted to go to sleep anytime soon."

"Good," said Gilbert, ignoring my sarcasm. "I would suggest that you two head up to Boston as soon as possible. Dalia will expect you to have retrieved the vial by the next Guild meeting."

"Fan-fucking-tastic. Just so I know what the hell I'm getting myself into, what's so special about this vial anyway?"

"It's the only known remaining sample from the 1652 batch made by George Starkey," said Gilbert, as if I should recognize the name as readily as the president of the United States. Thankfully, he acknowledged my bewilderment without comment and continued.

"One of the most accomplished alchemists of the past half millennium. And, in a strange coincidence, one of the former occupants of your Seat."

"Oh," I said. "That's, umm, interesting. But that still doesn't answer my question."

Gilbert's demeanor suddenly spun on a dime, the somewhat friendly chat we were having turning deadly serious.

"We believe that it's the key to creating a new Philosopher's Stone."

CHAPTER SIX

DREAM TEAM

"Ultimately, she found her solution in the unlikeliest of places. One day, as she was walking along Wall Street, she happened upon a young girl selling flowers."

The bouncer at the door to Firebird eyed my newly acquired fake ID with extreme suspicion before looking me up and down, my hooded sweatshirt and ratty tennis sneakers doing me no favors. But thankfully, Jade's sultry smile opened many more doors than my own could, and he finally handed the ID back to me and waved me through into the packed house beyond.

I spotted Emma sitting at a bar that stretched along the back wall, gentlemen callers on either side, and I approached with trepidation, not knowing how I would be received by the group. Taking the empty stool next to the guy on the left, I made my presence known, only for

Emma to roll her eyes and throw back her head.

She whispered something into the ears of both guys, and they handed her their phones in unison, into which she dutifully typed a phone number before returning them to their owners. Once the stools were vacated, I slid down one spot and hailed the bartender.

"What are you doing here?" she asked, before downing the remainder of her clear drink. "Besides mucking up my plans for later this evening?"

"It's almost 1:30," I said, my body crying out for the rest I was so reluctantly denying it. "There's not much evening left."

"Says the girl who looks like she's been locked in the library for the past month. I'm surprised they even let you in here, looking like that."

The bartender, a tall woman with a pixie haircut wearing a leather vest and sporting piercings up and down her ears arrived and greeted Emma with a confused look.

"What happened to those guys? I liked the blond one."

"She happened," said Emma, nodding in my direction. "Another Tito's neat for me, if you wouldn't mind, Svetlana."

"And for your friend?"

"She's not my friend. More like a cock-block."

"I'll have the same," I said, and the bartender departed.

"Of course you would," said Emma, who ignored me until Svetlana returned with our drinks.

"You have exactly five minutes to tell me what the hell you want. Maybe I can still catch one of those guys before he finds someone else to shag in the bathroom."

My eyes widened. "I wouldn't have pegged you as that type of woman."

"That's cos I'm not," she replied, producing a tube of purple lipstick after fishing around for a few moments in her tote bag from earlier.

"One kiss and he'll be unconscious for six hours. Can't decide whether to leave him his shirt or his pants."

"I'm sorry, but this all seems so-"

"Definitely the pants, only after I've dunked them in the toilet, though, so they're cold and wet when he wakes up."

"-wrong. I thought you liked the guy?"

"The prick sidled up here and cupped my arse within a few seconds of sitting down. Then he suggested that he and his friend take me back to their apartment to dou-"

"I'm sorry I asked!" I shouted, turning beet red. "You think he's going to wake up tomorrow morning embarrassed and suddenly become a changed man?"

"Course not. That's why I'm going to send a picture of his half-naked ass passed out to every single person in his company and every single contact in his phone."

"That sounds like a … creative plan. Anyway, I just wanted to talk to you about our trip to Boston. We've only got four weeks to get the Dragon's blood and-"

"*We* don't have anything. *I'm* going up there in a few days and will return with the vial, somehow, and you will just wait here and beg Dalia at the next meeting to let you into the Guild. Or not. Frankly, I don't give a damn what you do as long as it doesn't involve me."

"But Dalia and Gilbert said-"

"What? That we need to 'work together to get the job done'? Well, I just spent the last month doing what they told me and look how that turned out! If they want me to get the vial, then I'm doing it my way."

With that, Emma threw down some cash on the bar, applied the lipstick around her mouth, and stormed off in a huff.

"She off on one of her revenge missions?" said the bartender, who had returned and was clearing away the column of empty glasses that were arrayed across the bar.

"You know what she does? And how she does it?"

The bartender smiled.

"Who do you think gave her the lipstick? Something I worked up in the back, in one of the old kegs. Emma's helping me test it out. Fortunately, well, I guess also unfortunately, this place draws in a ton of assholes. But we're slowly changing that."

"That's, um, very noble of you."

Svetlana raised an eyebrow at me.

"You're new. What happened to the other girl?"

"I … I don't know. Never met her."

"Hmm," said Svetlana. "I've got an extra tube if you want to go after the second guy. Just do it somewhere else. One passed-out jackass I can deal with, but two in one night will start drawing questions."

She dug her hand into one of her vest's pockets, pulled out three tubes, and slid them down the bar to me.

"Why's there three?" I asked, examining the tubes.

"One's the lipstick, one's a spray to stop you from passing out from the krekoxin in the lipstick. Otherwise you'll be waking up around the same time as your target. And the last is a 'perfume' version of the lipstick for when kissing isn't practical."

"Oh," I said. "That makes sense. Thanks."

"You're welcome. Next time you're in, let me know how it turns out."

Svetlana turned to walk away, only for Emma to appear out of the crowd behind me and reclaim her seat.

"That was fast," said the bartender. "Hope he didn't get too grabby before you knocked him out."

"Nah," said Emma, smiling. "I pushed him up against the wall just as soon as we cleared the bathroom door and he went down like the sack of shit that he is. Also nicked his wallet out of his jeans for good measure. Guess we're going up to Beantown for free."

"You came around quick," I said, secretly thankful that I didn't have to beg Emma to actually do what the Guild was asking.

"Well, taking that asshole down 40 rungs will do that to you. Don't make me regret it, though. And we'll be catching the 7 a.m. Acela, yeah? So go home and pack some stuff, and I'll see you in the lounge in a few hours."

The rest of the night was a complete blur, as was getting to Penn Station and getting on the train. It wasn't until we were well past New Haven that my mind came to, and I looked across the table to see Emma passed out with her mouth wide open, spittle dripping down her face.

Of course.

I hadn't wanted to argue with her over the quick turnaround, not with her grudging decision to work together on what I had dubbed our "epic quest." But there was only so much more my body could take, both with the constant running on adrenaline and the glamour almost always on, and I dreaded the inevitable crash that was approaching.

I pulled out my laptop, opened up an empty text file, and wrote "Steal the Dragon's blood" at the top. Then I unhelpfully added four bullet points:

- Gain access to the library
- Locate the Dragon's blood
- Remove the vial
- Escape without getting caught or killed

So simple.

In the rush to leave, I managed to pack my invisibility robe, as

Gilbert had advised, my trusty vial of vitality serum, and Svetlana's lipstick, but after those items and my glamour, I was plumb out of alchemic tricks. I considered whether I could use the robe and glamour in tandem. I could enter as Jade, disappear, and then reappear as myself somewhere else. At best, though, it was a diversion and would additionally require an awkward conversation with Emma where I would have to convince her that my actual body was the glamour, like Zoe had mistakenly thought back in the alley.

Emma at least brought some additional firepower, with *White Hilt*, the giant sword, and whatever else was in that bag of hers. I contemplated rifling through it while she was still passed out, but thought better of it. Who knew what crazy shit was hiding in there?

I decided I would concentrate my efforts on the access and locating steps. Fortunately, at my first job out of college, the higher ups had seen fit to hire a battery of penetration testers and social engineers to challenge our IT security. Truth be told, that company wouldn't have been on anyone's radar to steal from, but the CIO needed to justify his existence, and so for weeks we were all on edge while we waited for the red team to infiltrate us. And I had witnessed how miserably we had failed in both waves of the attack. But now those agonizing weeks of training afterward were about to prove very useful.

The library, of course, wasn't open to the public, other than a small exhibit in the building's lobby with some historical pigments. I highly doubted our quarry was stored there, but it would at least give us one free visit to survey the layout of the building and observe the security, to see if we could talk our way in pretending to be grad students doing research for our theses, or if more fulsome cover identities would be required.

"Wass, what happened?" Emma's head slumped forward, and she startled herself awake, turning away to surreptitiously wipe the drool off her chin.

"Good morning, sunshine," I said, shaking my head. "Thanks again for making us take the early train, by the way."

Emma straightened herself out and looked out the window, the sunlight hitting her in the face, and she flung the curtains shut with a flourish.

"If we waited any longer, we wouldn't have time to get to Al's for lunch. It closes at 2 on Tuesdays," she said, matter-of-factly.

"What are you talking about?" I responded, nearly ready to tear Jade's hair out.

"It's a sub shop. Best subs on the East Coast in my opinion."

"Are. You. Fucking. Serious?"

I felt something in my head snap and the blood rush to my fists, but Emma just sat there, straight faced. Finally, as I was about to reach over the table and shake her by her collar, a small smile crept across her mouth and she burst out laughing.

"Ha! You should see yourself right now. That was great. But seriously, we should definitely go there for lunch. Their Italian sub is-"

I stormed out of the seat, nearly tripping over myself, and didn't look back as I made my way to the cafe car and away from Emma's laughter. After ordering a ridiculously large iced coffee, I sat down at one of the stools and buried Jade's face in her elbows.

"Hey," said a voice next to me. I ignored it until I felt someone poking me in the ribs.

"Leave me alone," I said, until finally I looked up, expecting to see Emma, but instead finding a woman with frazzled blonde hair and familiar green eyes.

"Beatrice?"

CHAPTER SEVEN

MADAM MASK

"Rita was not stupid. She knew it was a con.
But she wanted to see how clever a con the girl had conjured."

"**B**eatrice, is that really you?"

I repeated her name again, not quite believing what I was seeing, but she just stared at me, her eyes sharp as icicles. Finally, another jab hit my midsection, and I lurched awake, my former mentor gone. In her place was the punk-ass girl who had been tormenting me for 24 straight hours, the neck of an open bottle of beer in between her fingers.

"What do you want?" I said, taking a big sip of the now watered-down coffee.

"Just want to talk, feel like I got us off on the wrong foot, what with sending you into the Vultures' alley and then acting like a total git after Dalia went off script."

"Does she do that a lot?" I asked. My three interactions with her thus far had not been overly pleasant.

The first had been at the Met lecture. I hadn't actually spoken to her that night, but I now surmised it wasn't a coincidence that she and Gilbert had been there when we had stolen the vervorium doorknobs. The second had been at the Guild summons. Beatrice and I had walked into that conference room in midtown not knowing what or who to expect. She had seemed pleasant enough until she had threatened us with one of the long-lost Crown Jewels of the United Kingdom. And now she had upended everything again.

"Buggered if I know," said Emma. "She's barely been at the Guild meetings I've been at, save for the last two. You must bring out something in her."

"What do you mean?"

Emma took a swig of beer and I was about to chide her for drinking at this early hour, but held my tongue.

"Can't remember the last time there was a full meeting of the Guild called. But a month ago, we get a message in the middle of the night, telling us to report to the Hall with our gold tokens to boot, for a full accounting."

"Oh," I said.

"Then we get word that there's been a new member that's come forward. 'Cept it's not for one of the current seats, it's the fabled long-lost Third Seat of the Breuckelen Table."

"Don't you mean Brooklyn?" I interjected.

"No, it's pronounced 'Breuckelen.' The original Dutch settlement in what's now Brooklyn. The Tables represent the settlements where the founding Guild members were from. Pavonia, my Table, that was the original name for Jersey City and Hoboken. Orange is up near

Albany. And obviously New Amsterdam was on Manhattan Island."

"So your family has been in the Guild this whole time?"

"Not exactly. Anyway, I looked at your notes after you ran away. Seems like you have some good ideas about how we're going to pull this off. I want to hear more about these cover identities. I assume yours will involve that glamour you've got hiding under there?"

"What?" I said, instinctively looking down at the chain around my neck.

"I heard Zoe rambling about it while I was hiding in the garage, waiting for the right moment to emerge. Also, it's fairly obvious. I can feel the weight of it pressing down on you."

"Oh," I replied. "Umm, yeah, I guess that will be part of it. Hadn't thought it all the way through yet. And what do you mean you can 'feel' it?"

"With these," Emma said, holding up her left hand, which sported a set of silver rings. "They're made of druithyl. Acts like a metal detector of sorts. Whenever there is alchemy nearby, they vibrate and then change colors to indicate the type of alchemy present. Definitely going to need them to avoid any traps in the library."

"Gotcha, and the rings on your other hand have auragen that is linked to *White Hilt*. That's how you were able to pull it out of Zoe's hand."

Emma smiled.

"Exactly. That wasn't what they were originally intended for. It's really a throwing knife, despite its size. With the rings, I can retrieve it in the middle of a fight. Let me ask you something though. What does it feel like?"

"What does what feel like?"

"When you have the glamour on."

"Oh," I said. It was disconcerting, having people think that my real body was actually the glamour. Maybe this is what Ty had meant when she said not to activate the stone so much. Maybe that is why "Jade" had somehow emerged and taken control of the glamour. But these were questions for another time, and I promised myself to take off the stone as soon as possible.

"It's, it's like wearing a heavy blanket at first. You feel like you're dressed up as a ghost and that it's so obvious that the illusion is fake. But then, over time, it becomes a form-fitting costume and then eventually a second skin and now I don't even really notice it anymore."

Emma was hanging on my every word, and I was glad for once to be the one who didn't know what the heck they were talking about.

"So, is it…"

"What?

"A guy or a girl?"

"A girl," I said. "It's nothing crazy, if that's what you're thinking. She looks like a normal twenty-something with brown hair."

"Perfect," Emma suddenly grabbed my hand and stared deep into my eyes. "I love a brunette."

"I … I don't even … what?" The words stumbled out of my mouth, and I wrenched free from Emma's grip and jumped up from the barstool.

"Ha, just messing with you. Don't be such a prude. Seriously though, can you show me her?"

"Now?" I asked, looking around the car and finding it empty except for the distracted cafe worker. The last thing I wanted was Emma's rings to go silent when the glamour deactivated and her to realize the truth about me. I didn't know what repercussions that would have with the Guild and didn't want to find out.

"You don't have to," said Emma, sensing my hesitation. "We can wait until later when no one will-"

"No, it's fine. Just … try not to yell. And I'm only activating it for a second."

I pulled up the hood on my sweatshirt to cover Jade's bright red hair, hoisted up the chain of the glamour necklace, and squeezed the green stone. Nothing happened. I squeezed it a second time, muttering under my breath, but still, Jade's grip on my body would not let up.

"Something wrong?" asked Emma.

"Maybe, usually it activates no problem. Let me try another way."

I grabbed the glamour again with one hand, pretending to activate it, and at the same time reached behind my neck to undo the clasp. After a minute of blind fidgeting, I finally freed the other end of the chain, and the stone fell down into the confines of my sweatshirt.

But when I looked down at my hands, they were still covered in freckles and the strands of the hair I had tucked into my hoodie were still red. It was then that I felt her take control again, just for a second, to curl my ... well, her mouth into a smile.

"What's so funny?"

"Nothing," I said, pushing back against the glamour and suppressing the urge to scream. "Damn thing won't work."

I reached down under my sweatshirt and retrieved the stone, reattaching it around my neck.

"Hmm," said Emma, looking around the confines of the car. "Might be the work of a nullifier."

"A what?"

"An alchemy nullifier. Deprotium, more specifically. Stops all alchemy within a certain range from working for a set period of time. It's used as a defense mechanism usually. Maybe another journeyman is also on this train."

"And a journeyman is ..."

"It's what we call the high-level Questers who aren't in the Guild," said Emma.

"Oh," I said. "But your rings are still working, aren't they? And that Mary Poppins bag of yours?"

"You have a lot to learn, Jade. A week in the Guild library would go a long way, if they ever let you in there. Auragen and vervorium are in the class of persistent prima materia. They're 'always on,' for lack of a better word. Whatever powers your glamour, powerful as it might be, still needs to be activated, and the nullifier stops that."

"I see. Well, if I can't get it working, we'll need to adjust the plan. The robes will become more important."

"Agreed," said Emma. "And my bag."

"What about it?"

"You'll see," she said with a wink while downing the rest of her beer. "I'm gonna go back and take a little nap. Want to have a productive afternoon after lunch."

"Fine," I said. "Wait."

Emma turned around and gave me a quizzical look.

"What?" she asked.

"Were you there?" I said, my voice trembling slightly, nearly holding back the question I had been waiting all day to ask.

"Was I where?" she replied.

"Were you there," I repeated, "when they stabbed Steve with your knife?"

Emma swallowed and blinked several times before answering.

"Yes," she said, blankly. "And I was the one who did it."

E veryone wears a mask.

It's the makeup we apply, the outfits and accessories we carefully assemble, the hair we crimp. It's in the way we talk, the stories we embellish, the histories we retroactively edit.

We hold tight to that mask, because it's the only thing protecting that tiny piece of yourself that you keep deep down in the recesses of your mind that you're afraid to reveal it to anyone.

I've worn that mask. I pretended to fit in with Lisa and Stacy. It was painful at first, but I got good at playing the part. Then the same thing again with Duncan. But mine was different. Because it wasn't guarding that last sliver I was too scared to share with them, lest they judge me or reject me or shun me altogether. No, what I was hiding was that it wasn't there at all. I had spent years trying to convince myself otherwise. That I was too damaged, too broken by my mother's death, to have anything left inside.

And now, the mask I wore was someone else entirely.

I stared up at the ceiling from the enormous bed that took up most of the posh hotel room and pulled out the glamour. My fingers turned red as I squeezed it over and over, with the same result as before. After the 20th time, I finally broke down and began sobbing into one of the decorative pillows.

"Give me my body back," I whispered, baiting whatever Jade was to take control again and explain herself. But she refused the call.

"Have it your way then," I said out loud.

I pulled out my phone, opened my contacts, scrolled down to the name I was looking for, and before I could convince myself otherwise, started a video call.

"Pick up, damn it," I muttered to myself in that raspy voice that I hated more and more each time I opened my mouth. I held the phone out in front of her face, her green eyes staring back up at me. Finally, after the seventh ring, a chime went off, and a girl appeared on the screen.

"Jen, is that you?" said Ty Anzio.

"Of course it is," I said. "Who else would it be? You're the one who gave me this."

I pulled the chain up over my head again and held out the stone in front of me. It swayed back and forth, as if the gem was trying to hypnotize me, and I closed my hand around it and chucked it across the bed.

"What did you do?" said Ty, her eyes wide.

The audio crackled and from what I could see behind Ty, it looked like she was in a crowded school cafeteria. The long, brown hair she had sported during our prior encounters was gone, one side of her head now shorn down to a buzz-cut and the other featuring tapered layers of black hair. It made her look like a goth kid who was trying too hard.

"Where are you?" I asked, ignoring her question. "And what happened to your hair?"

"Oh, you like?" said Ty, tucking the black strands behind her right ear. "Seeing if it will catch on with the seniors."

"Wait, you're actually still in high school? I thought you were just dressing the part."

"I come and go as I please," she answered. "No one really pays attention to me here, so it suits me. But back to you. You ignored my warning, didn't you?"

"Maybe," I said. "What exactly is happening to me?"

I didn't want to admit what else Jade had done, and frankly, I was ready to return the blasted stone to Ty in an instant and deal with the repercussions if it meant getting my body back.

"Do you know what a glamour is?" Ty asked.

"I … it's … it's an alchemy-based illusion. It projects the image and sound of a person."

"That's what it does," she answered. "Not what it is. There is a difference. And it explains everything."

"Well, don't keep me in suspense here. It's not like I've been possessed by a body snatcher."

"Actually, that's exactly what's happened, Jen. Because that glamour I gave you? It's not a stone, it's a person."

CHAPTER EIGHT

SINS OF THE PAST

*"So she bought a bouquet and went on her way. Upon reaching her
townhouse without incident, she felt a slight ping of disappointment.
Until later that night, when she heard the stone at her doorway sound,
and so she slowly descended to the ground floor."*

"Why'd you do it?" I said to Emma the next morning at breakfast in the hotel lobby after a nearly sleepless night trying to wrestle with what Ty had told me. There was little she could do for me, she explained, until we could meet in person, so I had tucked the piece of information away in the back of my head and tried to focus on the task at hand.

Emma ignored me and continued steeping her black tea before squeezing the bag against the side of the cup and then adding a lump of sugar.

"Sorry?" she finally replied, after indulging in several sips.

"Why did you stab Steve with *White Hilt*? I saw the scar and I saw what's happened to him since. Don't even know if he's still alive at this point."

"Serves the fucker right," said Emma, taking a casual bite of the large biscuit she had ordered, as if we weren't discussing how she'd inflicted a horrible, deadly curse on someone. "You Americans know how to make a proper scone. Was never one for crumpets or pikelets. In Coventry, the only thing my mum would get was these clanger knock-offs. They were absolutely terrible."

"What the hell is wrong with you?" I said, slamming my palm down on the table, which drew stares from the surrounding patrons, but not Emma. She instead picked up her knife and spread a generous helping of the salted creamy butter on the remaining half of her biscuit.

"Nothing," said Emma, suddenly changing her grip on the utensil and pointing it at me. "Stop meddling in things that don't concern you."

"If we're going to work together, I need to know why. And they do concern me. Because of what you did, I nearly lost everything."

"Fine," she said. "But no more questions. About anything."

I nodded in agreement.

"He was trying to sell us."

"What?" I said.

"My former mates. We were young and dumb and trying to take over more of the alchemy black market, and he came calling with a new designer drug. One hit and you felt unstoppable, both figuratively and literally. And it worked wonders. Until one night, we get back from a Raid, and Callie starts going all wide-eyed and crazy, and then ..."

Emma looked away for a moment, and I stared down at my empty coffee cup while she composed herself.

"She was gone. Her body and brain were still working, but what made her Callie, it was burned out of her. By the drug. She just stood against the wall in the alley. For days. And then, he shows up, with his stupid green sweater and a leering grin, and Callie stirs to life immediately, like a robot receiving a command, and runs to his side. We were all meant to end up like that, sold off as compliant husks to the highest bidder, if Callie hadn't OD'd and made us realize what was happening first. So, yes, I stabbed him with *White Hilt*, and I wish I had finished him there."

I stared at her, my mouth gaping open, a knot in my stomach from the nightmarish tale she had just revealed. This world that I had thought I had a grasp on was always finding new ways to show me how little I knew. And that, coupled with the revelation from last night, nearly made me vomit in terror.

"What's on the agenda for today?" asked Emma, as if she hadn't just told me one of the most horrific stories I've ever heard.

"We're going to be doing a bit of sightseeing around town," I said. "It's part of phase one of my infiltration plan."

"You got the glamour working, I assume?"

"No, unfortunately," I said.

"Then what?" Emma said, with an irritated tone. "Just yesterday, you didn't even know this place existed. My da spent years tracking down this vial, to the exclusion of everything else. They're not going to let us waltz in there and take it."

"On that point, I agree. First, though, we need to find out where the vial is being stored by accessing their internal computer network. Then once we know where it is, we come back for the retrieval."

"And I suppose you have a plan for that, too?"

"No," I said. "That I will be relying on you for. And figuring out how to disarm any traps or wards or whatever alchemy is guarding the vial."

"Uggh, fine. I'll work on it. But I'll need some time."

"That's OK. Because phase one will take at least a week. How do you like these, by the way?"

I pulled a set of blonde wigs out of a bag sitting under the table and held them up for Emma to see.

"I'm good, thanks," she said. "But I'd think you'd look OK as a blonde. Doesn't clash too much with those freckles."

"Thanks. I think. Well, if you're not going to wear a wig, then an enormous sun hat, sunglasses, and some bright red lipstick are in your future. If you can talk without your accent, like you did on the phone before, then that would help even more."

"I thought the point was *not* to stand out," said Emma.

"No, that's for phase two. In phase one, you are going to be invited into the library as an honored guest, with me playing the role of your overworked and mistreated assistant."

"I don't understand."

"Say hello to your cover identity, Zazy Scott, makeup expert and influencer."

I handed her my phone, which displayed a brand-new Instagram account for the persona I had created earlier this morning.

"You're joking."

"Nope. The library has a lot of pigments that were used for makeup hundreds of years ago. Zazy is going to be launching her own line this fall. This will be perfect synergy."

"Sure. Theoretically. But this Zazy person you've dreamed up has no influence over anyone. Not even a single picture or follower."

"It's only 11," I said. "By tomorrow morning, you'll have hundreds of posts and a hundred-thousand plus followers to boot."

"How?"

"What kind of assistant would I be if I couldn't deliver that?

Today, though, we actually need to take some real photos about town for some authenticity."

"This is getting ridiculous. I'm not doing that."

"You have nothing to lose, if this doesn't work. Me, I stand to lose everything. Tell me, what will Dalia do to me if we fail?"

"Well," said Emma, pausing to take a sip of tea and a bite of her biscuit, "your token will be given to someone deemed worthy. Then I imagine your memory of the past month will be erased, hopefully in a pleasant manner, and you'll either wake up in your bed or in a mental institute, depending on how she's feeling that day."

"Wow," I said. "That was worse than I was expecting."

"Yes," said Emma. "But point taken. We'll try it your way. For now. And I guess I'd rather have you in the Third Breuckelen Seat. The devil you know…"

"I'll take that as a compliment," I said. "Finish up your breakfast, then. Fenway Park awaits."

Six hours and even more outfit changes later, we made our way through the double doors of Quincy Market. Despite her earlier hesitancy, Emma leaned into the role of Zazy with aplomb, and by the third stop on our Beantown tour, we had groups of teenage girls eyeing our photoshoots, wondering who we were.

"One more in the center of the building should do it," I said as we walked past busy food stalls on either side.

"No," said Emma, who was currently sporting the oversize sun hat from earlier, along with a long floral sundress and platform heels, which couldn't have been comfortable.

"Fine," I said. "We can rest a bit on those benches."

"I'm not tired. We just have other business in here, and I don't want to be seen like this. Wait here."

Emma walked off to the bathroom, and I puzzled over what she could be talking about until she emerged in her original outfit from this morning, her prior set of clothes no doubt tucked away in her tote.

"This way," she said. "She's down at the other end."

"Who is?" I asked, but didn't receive a response.

The east end of the hall transitioned from food to clothing and accessories, and I wondered if Emma had gone fully into character and wanted to buy an entirely new ensemble for the last photo. But we soon stopped in front of a stand full of random knick knacks and souvenirs, and my confusion only grew when Emma motioned over the teenage girl behind the counter.

"Maude here?" asked Emma, and the girl shook her head from side to side.

"No, ma'am. She's off today," the girl said, in a thick Boston accent.

"Of course. Nikki … Serata, is it?" Emma said, reading off the name tag that hung on the girl's overalls. "You have license to show us around? Cause I really don't want to have to come back tomorrow."

"Not sure what you're getting at, ma'am," Nikki replied. "Everything we got is out here on display."

"Is that so?"

Emma reached into her jeans pocket and quickly withdrew a small object, which she plunked down on the counter. I peered over her shoulder to see what it was.

A silver token, with the familiar alerion sigil etched in the middle.

The salesgirl's face lit up with recognition and she nodded silently before raising up a section of the counter and retreating to the back of the stand.

Emma retrieved the token and walked through, and I followed, still unsure exactly what was going on. At the rear, we found Nikki crouched down, fumbling with something on the floor. It was a hatch, and when she opened it, a foul smell emerged from the black hole hiding underneath.

"Be careful as you go down," called Nikki, who had already begun her descent.

Emma found her footing on the set of stone steps that corkscrewed down into the darkness, and I had no choice but to join her. Thankfully, dim lights shone up from somewhere below, because otherwise I would have tumbled over the side of the railless stairway. I reached the bottom and found myself in the middle of a long hallway barely four feet across, lit by pairs of familiar red stones on either side.

"Where are we?" I asked as Nikki escorted us down the corridor.

"This passageway leads to the original basement of Faneuil Hall. We moved down here in 1762 after a group of anti-witch zealots burnt down the Hall the year before. Probably the only time those idiots ever got anything right."

"My American history is a little rusty," I said, "but who is the 'we' you are referring to?"

Nikki turned around to give Emma a look as if to say, "Who is this moron you brought down here?" but Emma just shrugged her shoulders.

"The Dutch West India Company," the shopgirl eventually replied, as we reached the end of the corridor, which culminated in a worn wooden door. "In those days, the alchemy arm of our operations was run more out in the open. People viewed it more as hokey science or superstitious junk, like those fake cures they now sell at the back of magazines. But then there was that whole burning down the hall thing I mentioned a second ago, so we thought it would be wise to move underground."

"So you work for the Guild, then?"

"Not exactly," she said, producing a keyring from her overalls pocket. "We were spun off as a separate enterprise in the early 1800s. The Guild wanted to focus on its Questing and magic-hunting, and we were left to keep the alchemy economy running."

"Let me guess," I said. "You guys came up with a really clever name like 'The Market' or something."

"Oooh, close," said Nikki. "We're the Night Market, Boston branch."

"And yet," I said, "it's only five p.m."

"Well, 'Night Market' sounds better than plain old 'Market,' or so I was told. You can probably find the full account of how the name was chosen in the Guild minutes from–"

"Enough," interjected Emma. "We just need some basic supplies and a bit of alkahest."

Nikki ignored the demand and opened the locked door with a loud click before placing her palm on the wall just to the left of the doorframe. Suddenly the room beyond sparkled to life, and my jaw nearly dropped at what I saw inside: a veritable bazaar of oddities, jars, vials, weapons, and shiny objects that made Beatrice's downtown laboratory look like a Little Tikes workbench.

"Your noob is showing," said Emma, nudging me in the ribs and I quickly shut my gaping jaw. "Act like you've been here before, yeah?"

"Yes, Ms. Scott," I replied, and Emma rolled her eyes as she followed Nikki into the wondrous cavern beyond.

CHAPTER NINE

SHOP TALK

"Climbing through the window was a boy who appeared to be the same age as the girl, bearing similar features. On his wrist was a glowing bracelet. She kept out of sight and watched as he quickly surveyed the foyer before grabbing an impressive looking but not particularly valuable vase, where she had placed the flowers."

E ven with everything I had been through, the alchemy I had witnessed, and the secrets about the world I had learned, there was something about walking down a hidden passageway to find an honest-to-goodness magic shop lurking in the shadows of an old building that made me giddy like a schoolgirl.

But before I could even get situated, Emma and Nikki had already begun haggling over the price of the goods we required.

"We're always happy to extend a line of credit to the Guild, Ms…?"

"Patel. Emma Patel, Second Seat of the Pavonia Table."

"Patel, Patel, that name sounds familiar. Oh! You're the daughter of Akash Patel? I remember he came in here a few years ago when I had just started working here after school. How is he?"

"He's dead. But thanks for asking. Anyway, you were saying something about a line of credit? I didn't think the going rate for alkahest was *that* high."

"What's alkahest?" I asked, and Emma rolled her eyes at my ignorance.

"Alkahest is the universal solvent," said Nikki. "Dissolves anything it touches, except bark spider silk. Which is used to line the vial. And unfortunately, yes, there's been a dwindling of the quota that VAC releases to the market and we can only buy so much."

"At the risk of my friend's eyes falling out the back of her head," I said, "what exactly is VAC?"

"Van Asch Corporation," said Nikki.

I swallowed hard at the name. Van Asch Corporation could only mean one thing: that Rita van Asch's legacy had lived on well past her death. And if this company wasn't part of the Guild proper, it meant one more player out there in the shadows, along with whomever Frankie had been working for.

"They have a monopoly on some of the most valuable prima materia. Obviously, we have a lot of purchasing power, but there's only so hard we can push."

"If you're done with the history lesson," Emma said, "just tell me how much."

"800 silver if you want the whole vial," said Nikki. "Or 100 silver for a milliliter, but you need to bring your own vial."

"Are you fucking kidding me?" said Emma. "It was 50 silver a vial last year in New York!"

"I'm sorry, ma'am," said Nikki. "As I said, the supply on the market has constricted and we can't-"

"Yeah, yeah, yeah, you need to make a living. But the Guild will have my head if I go running up a line of credit like that without getting sign-off first. Let me get someone on the phone."

Emma stormed out of the shop and I heard her footsteps echo down the dark hallway until she was no longer visible.

"You have a branch in New York?" I asked.

Nikki nodded.

"Yep. Here, this lists all our locations, hours, and proprietors."

She handed me a small laminated card with a picture of a woman standing in front of a row of tents in what looked like Union Square. I flipped it over to find the words "Welcome to the Night Market" written in flourishing script at the top, followed by a long list covering every major city in the country and some minor ones as well. But it was the one in the middle that caught my eye.

"I've been to this one," I said, pointing at the New York entry, which listed a certain stall in Hunt's Point Market in the Bronx and a certain proprietor with half-moon spectacles and a very pronounced slouch.

"You've met Phineas? He's a legend. My grandmother had a tryst with him when she was my age. Or so she claims. What's he like?"

"He got the better of me. Ended up trading everything I had, and what I received wasn't enough."

I recalled the healing serum briefly curing Frankie, her cryptic words about the pearl in the triangle, and then the horror I felt as she turned back to stone. That had cost me Beatrice's entire supply of the mind-reading apples, and all it had bought us was the location of the fake gold token. And that token had literally exploded in our faces, leading to Beatrice's current exile. So needless to say, my past experience with the Night Market had not been a good one.

"Oh. Well, he and my grandma are alike in that respect. They think we're still back in the days of haggling in the Campo de Fiori. Me, I take a more collaborative approach. Why make an enemy out of a customer over a single deal when there's a lifetime of transactions to be had?"

"Sure, I guess. While we're standing here waiting for Ms. Patel to finish whatever she's doing, do you have any glamours in your inventory that I could take a look at?"

"Ooh, wish that we did. You don't find those just lying around in the Night Market, I'm afraid."

"Why not?" I asked. "I thought they were relatively common."

This was not an unreasonable proposition, what with how Ty had straight up given me one and how Doug had coincidentally also had one. But now I knew that there was more to the glamour that your typical mixture of prima materia.

"No, no, no. They most certainly are not. I wouldn't quite categorize them as Relic-class objects, but it's a close call. Don't think there's been a new one created in at least a hundred years."

"What?"

"Yeah, well, ever since the Treaty of Verdun outlawed alchemic experimentation on humans, it's not exactly like people are shouting from the rooftops that they've transmuted one."

"Oh, right," I said, pretending I knew what the Treaty of Verdun was.

Thankfully, Emma saved me from asking any further embarrassing questions when she returned to the shop with a flourish.

"Let's go," she said to me.

"But what about the alkahest?" I said. "Did the Guild-"

"We can talk about it over dinner. Thank you, Nikki. We'll be back."

"I'll show you both ou-"

"No need, no need. We know the way."

And then she grabbed me by the arm, and the magic shop faded from view as quickly as it had appeared.

"Of all the great restaurants in this city, this is where we have to go?" I said, as a waitress arrived with three plates of oversized sushi stuffed with tuna and peanuts.

"First of all, don't insult the tuna peanut roll. It's amazing. Especially with the sauces on the side. Second, the booths in here are very comfortable. And third, we're guaranteed not to be seen by prying eyes."

I turned around to scan the crowded restaurant and, sure enough, the table and booth arrangement was such that every diner was focused on their own meal.

"Fine," I said. "But why did you order three of these? They're enormous."

"One for you, one for me, and one for him," said Emma, pointing behind me. I turned again to see the smiling face of J.P. Laurel making his way through the maze of tables toward us.

"What is he doing here?" I asked,

"I invited him."

"Just now? When you went to call the Guild?"

"No," said Emma. "Please. We all don't have hordes of vervorium at our disposal. We had scheduled this back in New York."

"What? Why?" I whispered, as J.P. drew closer, his silver cane in his right hand and that ridiculous cowboy hat still on his head.

"Because if it's a choice between you and him, no offense, I would choose him. You have a lot of spunk, I'll give you that, but you're still so ... J.P.!"

"Emma, dear," said J.P. with a warm smile on his face that soon turned to a slight grimace when he met my eyes. "And Jade. You're here."

"When did you get to town?" Emma asked, ignoring J.P.'s displeasure at my presence.

"Took the shuttle up this morning," he said, sliding into the empty spot in the booth. "There are a number of historical sites in and around the city that I've been meaning to visit. Was rather enlightening. There is so much we still don't know about the early days of the Guild during the Revolution."

J.P. picked up one of the sushi pieces, dipped it in the orange sauce, and then popped the whole thing in his mouth, before waving off Emma's offer of chopsticks.

"No need, no need. Ever since I got back from Kyoto, I only use my fingers."

"Suit yourself," said Emma. "So, I still have a tiny bit of alkahest left from Budapest, but I don't think it will be enough. And before I borrow the money from you to pay for a fresh vial, I wanted to be sure it was worth it. Have you given some more thought to my plan?"

"Yes, I have. And I think it's lacking in both practicality and creativity. Y'all aren't just going to be able to waltz into the library, pour some alkahest on the box, and waltz out with the vial of Dragon's blood. Come on, Emmy. I know you have a better head than that!"

I snickered at the nickname, and they both glared at me.

"And what, pray tell, are you laughing at?" asked J.P. "I don't think you realize how fortunate you are that Emma here even let you come on this here Raid. If it was me that Dalia had paired you with, I woulda slipped something in your drink at the start and by the time you woke up, I'd already be on my way back to New York with the vial."

"J.P., enough. Jade here has actually come up with a very clever infiltration plan. It's me that's lagging. I've looked over Da's notes a hundred times. Blunt force seemed liked the only thing he hadn't considered."

"Yes, well, you do that and the box will probably implode, taking you and half the block with it."

"Fuck, that's what I thought."

"But don't worry, don't worry. Your Uncle Jippy has come to the rescue in your direst time of need."

I looked at Emma, expecting her to snap at his blatant condescension, but all I saw was warm admiration on her face, as she picked up a piece of sushi with her chopsticks and started smearing it with both of the sauces. Whatever this relationship was between them, it was deeper than I had realized.

"Thank you, J.P. So, what's the plan?"

"It's simple, really. We create a replica of the box and then swap it with the real one, which you'll put into your bag, and then one of my people will be waiting to extract it on the other end immediately."

Emma paused for just a second, and the sushi fell from her chopsticks, but she quickly picked it up and ate it in one bite.

"How ... well, the abrupt distance separation could, in theory, break the auragen link. But that still doesn't solve the problem of actually opening the box."

"Trust me, darling, that bitch won't care if we haven't opened the darned thing, long as we have it. We'll figure out that part later if need be."

"Then you think…"

"Yes, this was meant as a fool's errand for all of us, you included, Ms. Peters."

My head popped up at the mention of my fake last name and I hesitated slightly before deciding to risk further

"Your bag, it's linked to a place?"

Emma and J.P. both shot looks at each other before J.P. nodded.

"Yes," said Emma, sliding one of her ring-adorned hands toward me on the table. "My family's ancestral domus. These rings, and others, help pull free whatever I need at the moment."

"And it exists in a real place, like in some sort of storage unit?"

"Not something so obvious. But yes, and we guard the location of the physical entrance from all others."

"Which you can wipe from my associate's pretty little head just as soon as he gets back from wherever it is that is," said J.P. "It's somewhere in India, I imagine?"

I saw Emma start to shake her head, but she stopped herself before completing the thought.

"Don't. And my family hasn't lived there in seven generations."

"My apologies," said J.P. "I just wanted to know what sort of travel time we were dealing with."

"I … I need some time. We don't, we've never-"

"I understand, and remain at your disposal, Emmy dear. Now I hate to eat and run, but I need to be getting back to the missus. We'll talk tomorrow once you've had the night to think it through."

J.P. leaned over to give Emma a kiss on the cheek, which she received with a slight smile, before he tipped his hat to me and stalked off. I excused myself a minute later to use the restroom, but when I returned, Emma was staring off into space.

"Are you OK?" I asked with trepidation as I slid back into the booth. She didn't acknowledge my presence, and I looked down to see that her hands were trembling.

"I'll just go pay then. Do you want me to … you know what? I'll see you back at the hotel."

A different me would have stayed, would have tried to coax the source of her angst out of her, so I could offer some words of comfort. The current incarnation of myself, however, wanted to give her a slice of the lone mind-reading apple left from my visit to the orchard that was tucked in the recesses of my bag and force my way into her thoughts for my own edification. I felt my hand slipping quietly down to my side and brushing against the false bottom. Whether it was directed by my baser self or by Jade, I wasn't sure, but I didn't want to stick around to find out. So I took the coward's way out and left the sobbing girl to her troubles and her sushi.

CHAPTER TEN

BLACK HAT

*"She let him continue, but he seemed skittish and soon retreated. The next day, she
returned to the girl and asked to see her brother, but the girl feigned ignorance."*

I didn't see Emma again for three days. Which was fine, because we
wouldn't be ready for our first run at the library until next week,
as I needed to finish uploading the posts from our photoshoot to
Zazy's Instagram account, in addition to the fake photos I had created
showing her in various cities around the world. And also because all
the stress of the past few weeks had finally caught up to me, as each
night's sleep was worse than the last. By Saturday morning, it felt as
if I was back in college on the tail end of an all-nighter.

"I'd like to read your dad's notes," I said, somewhat surprised to
see her at the restaurant when I arrived, after I had spent an hour in
front of the mirror trying yet again to deactivate the glamour, even for

a few minutes. Her usual breakfast of a black tea and American biscuit was already finished, and she looked up at me as if she was in a haze.

"What?"

"Your dad's notes. About the Dragon's blood," I said. "Maybe there's something else there."

"What?" she repeated. "Oh. His notes. He didn't have any."

"What do you mean?" I asked. "Dalia said-"

"Dalia is a twat. And didn't know my dad from Adam. He didn't keep his research or his notes or anything on paper. Didn't trust it. He kept it all up here," Emma said, tapping her temple three times.

"So then-"

"Right, it's all gone. All of it. The motherfucker spent most of my life trying to track down the components of the Stone and then up and died in the middle of the night. Didn't leave a will or a diary or anything behind. Luckily the Guild's bylaws are pretty ironclad regarding inheritance, so I got his Seat instead of my arse of an uncle. But it seems like he left me his mess to clean up just the same."

"I see. For whatever it's worth, my mom didn't leave me anything either, when she died."

A bald-faced lie that I thought was true at the time. My mother gave me her locket as my real inheritance years before her death, that much was obvious now. But it was little solace to the scared girl who was suddenly and absolutely alone in the world.

"Huh. Sorry to hear that. Unfortunately, that still leaves us back where we were a few days ago. With me sending J.P. to the cache to pull the box out."

"You don't trust him? It seems like you two are close."

"Very. Our families go back several generations. Ever since we first joined the Guild. J.P. was the best man at my parents' wedding. Still, I don't think I can just..."

Emma trailed off and fixed her gaze on the wall behind me, and I pretended to look down at my phone, which I had set to lock after two seconds of inactivity, lest Emma grab it and wonder why there were hundreds of pictures of a brown-haired girl who did not look like Jade stored on it. Of course, I had to shut off the face unlock given that my own face was also locked away.

Wait a minute.

"What if there was another way?" I asked.

"There isn't," said Emma. "At least not one that we will be able to flesh out anytime soon."

"Let me ask you something. This box, it's just sitting there, in some nook in the collection?"

"Supposedly."

"And so what if whoever put it there wants it back?"

"They don't want it back. It's what's inside that matters and what matters, to them, is that no one unlock it."

"You've been operating under the assumption that we have no way of getting the key. But what if you're wrong?"

The still half-full tea kettle next to Emma's cup nearly fell on its side as she slammed the table with both hands.

"I'm not. We can't. I didn't pay much attention to what my dad was doing, but this I am certain of: he never found it. Didn't even come close. Are you really that fucking full of yourself that you think you can find in a few days what he spent a decade looking for?"

"Let's just say I know a thing or two about locked boxes."

"This is stupid. Can't believe I agreed to this."

"Shhh. Stay in character."

"Fine, but stop speaking with that horrific accent and just pretend that you're American!"

"I am American!"

"Even better!"

Zazy Scott and her assistant Jane Hutchinson emerged from the taxi in front of the Emerson Library at precisely 9:15 on Wednesday morning and walked toward its gleaming double doors. Jane carried a large storage bag on one shoulder and a flannel tote bag around the other, while Zazy looked weary carrying the tiny purse she clutched in her ring-adorned right hand.

"Jane, the door please," said Zazy/Emma.

"Are you fucking serious?" I said under my breath. Yes, I felt bad about using Jane's name again after manipulating her all those months ago to break into Frankie's spin class, but it was the first thing that popped into my head when I created the fake employees of Zazy's soon-to-be makeup empire.

"You said stay in character!" hissed Emma in response. "Zazy doesn't open doors for herself. It's beneath her."

I shook my head in disbelief, the strands of the blonde wig I was wearing rubbing against my temples.

"OK, OK, one sec. And you're enjoying this too much."

"I am what you made me."

I fumbled with the door handle, the postercard-filled bag nearly sliding down my arm. In contrast, Emma's alchemy-enhanced tote felt like it weighed nearly nothing. "Zazy" walked through the open door, and I quickly let go of the handle and ran in after her before the door slammed shut on me.

We had entered a pristine lobby drenched in sunlight, beyond which was the Atwell Courtyard. I motioned Emma toward one of the stone archways that led out into the indoor courtyard, and she followed behind me. The museum that housed the Library wasn't open yet, but several of the small tables were occupied by students either furiously staring into their laptops or outright asleep.

We walked to the courtyard center and looked up. The Italian-inspired archways stopped after the second floor, and from where we stood, I could just see the glass walls enclosing the fourth floor, where the beige cabinets holding thousands of pigment samples awaited.

"It's up there?" I whispered.

"Yep," said Emma. "But don't forget, you still need to work your magic and figure out which one."

"Yeah, yeah," I said. "Seems like I'm doing all the work here. Next time I get to be the obnoxious socialite, and you can be my overworked lackey."

"If we ever have to work together again, I think this current arrangement is more to my liking. Let's go."

Emma strode off to the elevators at the north end of the courtyard and I scurried after her, like the good lemming I was pretending to be.

We reached the fourth floor without incident or interception, only to be greeted by an empty reception area and a set of locked glass doors down one hallway.

"Well, they certainly rolled out the welcome mat, Jane," said Emma, who had upped her British accent to another level. "Where is this Mona Hardin person who you said was going to show us around the collection?"

I resisted the urge to tell Emma where she could shove the oversized sunglasses and fumbled for my phone.

"Umm, let me check the email again, Ms. Scott. They were supposed to-"

"You do that," said Emma, almost shouting. "I'm going to sit down on that uncomfortable looking piece of furniture over there and hope it doesn't give me a herniated disc."

Emma retreated to a backless wooden bench off to the side of the foyer, and I pretended to look for the email with the details of our meeting with the assistant curator.

But in reality, this was all going exactly according to our plan. I dashed down the hallway opposite the locked glass doors as quickly as I could without running, and then hurried back to the reception area.

"Come on," I said, waving Emma up from the bench. "It's empty."

We retreated into the spacious conference room I had discovered and closed the door, although the glass walls afforded us little privacy.

"Great job, *Jane*," said Emma. "I can literally see where the bloody vial is hidden, but we can't go any further. I told you that you should have worn the fake baby belly. People are extra nice to pregnant women."

"Will you fucking relax?" I said with a snarl. My patience was wearing thin at Emma's condescension, which I suspected was only partially an act. "I'm just getting started. Can you get my equipment out of here?"

I handed her the magic tote bag, and she reached her hand into its depths. When she brought it out again, she was holding a laptop bag that stretched the edges of the tote farther than I thought possible.

"That's a neat trick," I said, as I unpacked the contents of the new bag.

"The edges are lined with chrysomallos. It stretches and contracts as needed," said Emma.

I set my assemblage of hacking tools on the table, which consisted of a laptop loaded with white hat and black hat software and a small black box the size of a deck of playing cards.

"What the hell is that little thing going to do?" Emma asked.

"This 'little thing'," I said, "is an ODROID C2. It's a tiny but very capable computer. It's our gateway into the Museum."

I ran an ethernet cord from the ODROID into a free port embedded in the conference room table and then opened the laptop. Within a minute, the devices were connected, and I began snooping around. Emma towered behind me in her six-inch heels like the overbearing bitch she was pretending to be, usefully blocking anyone outside the room from seeing what we were up to.

"What exactly are you doing?"

"Seeing how far I can go from this port. If it's connected to the rest of the Museum's internal network … yes!"

I shut the laptop quickly and stored it away, before retrieving a small plastic bag.

"That's it? You're done?"

"No, the real work will begin tonight, which, thanks to our little friend here, I can do from the safety of the hotel," I said. "But before we go, I need to do one more thing…"

I removed two stickers from the bag and stuck them on either side of the ODROID.

"Property of Carter Museum IT. Do not remove from room," said Emma, reading the stickers. "I have to admit, that's pretty clever."

"That's why you pay me the big bucks," I said, as I tucked the ODROID into the mass of messy cables that covered the outlets and ports in the middle of the table. "Let's get the hell out of here."

"I thought we were waiting-"

"Oh, no!" I said at the top of my voice, as we walked out of the conference room. "It's all my fault. I … I misread the email. Our meeting is tomorrow. Not today. Mona is at an offsite-"

Emma finally snapped back into character.

"Are you that daft? Honestly, I can't believe I hired you over that girl from Cambridge. She might have been ugly, but at least she could read a two-line email without fucking everything up! Now, carry this please. My arm is tired."

"I'm sorry, Ms. Scott." I said, taking the small purse from Emma and wishing I still had the Medoblad. "It won't happen again, I swear!"

"For your sake, I hope that's true."

CHAPTER ELEVEN

DRAGON'S DEN

"Right this way, Ms. Scott," said Mona Hardin, the assistant curator, directing us around the courtyard perimeter and toward the elevator.

"Thank you," said Emma in a fawning voice. "I'm looking forward to finally visiting the collection. I've read so much about it and already have some ideas on what pigments would be perfect for my powder palette."

"We have some in mind that we think you'll really enjoy. And of course, we are most appreciative of your commitment to donate a portion of the proceeds to the Museum."

Emma shot me a glance, which confirmed that she hadn't bothered to read all the way through the elaborate email correspondence I had constructed between the two of us that I had forwarded to Mona.

"Yes, well, my grandmother was a great patron of the arts, so it seemed only fitting that I continue her work."

"Oh, that's lovely," said Mona. "What sort of work did she do?"

"She, umm," said Emma, stumbling over her words. This is why I had impressed to her over the past few days that every nook and cranny of her cover identity had to be thought through three times over.

"She was on the Board of Trustees of the Coventry Art Museum," I interjected, when it was clear that Emma was still tongue-tied.

"Yes, thank you Jane, I just couldn't put my finger on it. Yes, Gran especially loved the Museum's hat collection."

"Oh," said Mona. "I hadn't heard of that. I'll have to take a look when I get a moment."

I cursed under my breath. While there was an art museum in Emma's hometown, it consisted entirely of blacksmith implements. But hopefully we would be long gone from here before Mona figured that out.

We exited the elevator on the familiar fourth floor, and the curator walked us over to a small display case next to the reception desk.

"So I thought I would start by showing you some pigments we have showcased this month," said Mona, standing to the left of the case. We peered inside to survey the array of vials and other specimens.

"That vial in the back corner contains Mummy brown, which is made up of ground-up mummies."

"You cannot be serious!" said Emma. "That's gross!"

"Yes," said Mona with a smile. "That's usually the reaction we get. But it does wonders to add transparency to paintings, so it was in high demand in the 17th century. And that piece of foil in the front is coated with a sample of Infiniblack. Traps practically all light within the nanotubes it's made of. You can't even tell that the foil is crumpled from that side. It's incredible."

"Wow," said Emma. "Jane, you're taking notes, right? Tell me you're taking notes."

"I'm taking notes," I said, scrambling to pull out a small notepad from my bag.

"Good. We'll want to think about including an Infiniblack-based eyeshadow in the line. And make a note that I have follow-up meetings with potential distributors on the 3rd, 12th, and 17th."

"Yes, Ms. Scott," I said, not knowing what the hell she was talking about. Maybe she really had immersed herself in the character and was throwing out little details that would make us seem more believable.

"If I may interject for a second," said Mona. "Unfortunately Infiniblack is not something that you can readily purchase. It's tightly controlled by the manufacturer in England. And you certainly can't use it for human applications. It's highly abrasive to skin."

"Noted," said Emma. "We'll think of something. I have a lot of contacts over there. Anyway, is there anything else in this little case that we should look at, or can we move on to the collection itself?"

Mona looked a bit perturbed at Emma denigrating the display, but stifled her reaction.

"No, that's good for now. We can always come back at the end if there's something else you want to see."

"Excellent!" said Emma, and motioned for the curator to lead us onward. When we got back to the hotel later, I would need to have a talk with her about being unnecessarily condescending.

We walked down the hall, and Mona waved her ID over a badge reader to the left of a set of glass doors. Its red light turned green, and I heard something in the door click.

"Shall we?" she asked, and we both nodded in agreement as the curator pushed the doors open. Unbelievably, the first leg of our mission was complete.

"Now down here on the fourth floor is the Romberg Collection of Pigments and Varnishes. It was assembled by Dean Romberg over the course of 50 years. He traveled the world collecting rare pigment specimens, and we are so fortunate to be the beneficiary of all that hard work. This way."

We turned a corner and made our way down the corridor we had glimpsed from the conference room the other day. The left side was lined with cabinets showing shelves full of jars, vials, and other containers. Underneath them were several rows of drawers.

"The Pigment Collection is organized by color," said Mona, as we walked down the hallway. "Starting with yellow in the middle and then extending toward blue in one direction and then toward red in the other direction. On the upper shelves, you have the pigments themselves, and underneath, in these drawers, are the chemical duplicates of the pigments. And then finally, on the lower shelves, you have the raw materials."

I spotted it just as we reached the middle. It was just lying there, peeking out from its paper wrapping, a simple placard in front of it identifying it to the world as "Dragon's blood." Next to it was a lump of "Dragon's blood gum," the hardened version of the pigment. Above, somewhere amongst the racks of vials and rows of jars was the prize we were seeking.

"Are we close to the Tyrian purple?" I said to Mona, after nodding to Emma. "Ms. Scott is a particular fan of the color, and I think it is safe to use in cosmetics?"

"Why yes," she said. "Just a little way down. Let me show you."

"You two go on ahead," said Emma. "These reds here are simply delightful. I want to take a closer look."

"OK," said Mona. "But please don't open any of the cabinets."

"Wouldn't dream of it," said Emma with a grin.

I walked with the curator down to the purple section, looking back quickly to see Emma on her tippy toes staring at one of the upper shelves.

"So as you can see," said Mona when we reached our destination, "Tyrian purple is-"

"Hold on one sec," I said, pulling out my notebook and writing Tyrian purple in big obnoxious letters at the top. "OK, go."

"As I was saying, Tyrian purple is made from a secretion of predatory sea snails. Thousands of snails would be required to-"

"Hold that the thought," I said. "I … I think I'm going to be sick."

"Look, I know some of the pigments are made up of unpleasant-"

"It's not that," I interjected. "Can … can you get me to a bathroom? I'm in my first trimester and-"

"Oh," said Mona. "Oh! I'm so sorry. Yes, it's right down this hall. But let me tell Ms. Scott to come help you since-"

"She doesn't know," I said, pretending to wipe sweat from my brow. "And you say anything to her. Please. She doesn't, she won't…"

"OK, OK. Let's hurry then."

We darted to the end of the hallway, where a set of bathrooms awaited, and Mona led me inside. I retreated to the stall furthest from the door, knelt down in front of the toilet, and pretended to puke my guts out.

"How are you doing?" called Mona.

"I'm … I think I'm … nope," I said, going in for a second round of fakery. My phone buzzed, and I quickly pulled it free from my pocket to see a text from Emma.

"Big whoop," it said, which was our code word for aborting the mission. I wanted to rush back to the Dragon's blood cabinet to see what could have happened, but took a few moments to gather myself before slowly opening the stall.

"Phew," I said to Mona, who looked half-sick herself. "That was a bad one. Thank you for your discretion."

We found Emma crouched down several colors down from where we had left her, staring at a rack of orange vials.

"Jane," said Emma, her cheeks red. "There you are. I was wondering where you ran off to. I'm afraid I've got nothing. This isn't doing it for me. Maybe we should consider a partnership with the Aquarium. I'm thinking a clown fish-themed lipstick and maybe-"

"But..." said Mona.

"I'm sorry," I said. "You've been very kind, but we need to get going."

I grabbed Emma's arm and pulled her away from the exasperated curator and toward the elevator. A man in a white lab coat emerged from within and attempted to thread his way between us, which was a terrible mistake, because Zazy Scott was not the type of person to move out of the way for anyone. And I didn't help the situation by "accidentally" elbowing him, sending him careening into Zazy, who pushed the startled lab worker aside with a shove.

"Keep your hands to yourself, perv!" said Emma with a look of disgust and the man, too embarrassed to say anything in front of Mona, ran off without a word.

We rode down to the lobby in silence, where several dozen people were scurrying about with truckloads of floral arrangements for some reason, before hailing a cab to take us to the five-star hotel we were pretending to stay at.

"What happened?" I finally asked when we had both collapsed into the large leather chairs in the hotel lobby.

"It was empty," said Emma flatly.

"The box? You actually opened it?"

"Yes," said Emma. "You make it sound like you didn't think your little magic codeword was going to work."

"Hey I never said that it was a sure thi-"

"Well, I didn't need it, in the end. All those hours practicing and the box was already unlocked! And completely empty, by the way. I would have taken it with me, but it's stuck to the shelf with at least one, maybe two auragen links. I couldn't even lift it an inch."

"So now what?"

Emma held up a white ID badge sporting a picture of the man from the elevator.

"Wow, that was some quick work."

"Compared to what I used to knick for the Vultures, this was an easy get. Do you think it will be enough?"

I looked at the grinning face of the man on the badge.

"Only one way to find out."

CHAPTER TWELVE

SPYCRAFT

The phone rang several times before he answered.

"Hello?" said a man's voice.

"Hi, is this Phil Farnsworth?"

"Yes, yes, it is. What time is it?"

"3:40 a.m. I just need a minute."

"Wh-what? Why are you calling me this early?"

"Sir, IT never sleeps. Especially when we have museum employees who are so careless with their ID badges that they lose them in Harvard Square."

"I, uhh, I don't know how that happened. I'm really sorry. But someone returned it, then?"

"Yes, someone did. Thankfully. But now we have to double-check that whoever had your badge didn't improperly access any of the Museum's facilities. And that's going to take time. So until it's done, you'll have to work remotely."

"What? But my research is in the-"

"Yes, in the laboratory, we know. Surely, though, there are some administrative tasks you can occupy yourself with until next Wednesday?"

"I, uhh, I think so. But how am I going to do that from home? I won't be able to log in to the internal network here."

"That's why I'm calling. We're getting you provisional access on your personal computer. Should be done by Monday afternoon. But first things first. In a few moments, you're going to receive a text message with a four-digit pin. I'll need you to read that pin to me so I can authenticate your account."

I paused, and swallowed hard, waiting for the man on the other end of the line to attach himself to the hook I had thrown to him.

"OK. I'm ready."

I hit "Submit" on the museum log-in screen I had open on my own laptop and crossed my fingers.

"While we wait for that pin to come through, I need you to know that as museum IT personnel, neither I or anyone else on our staff will ever ask for your password, either over the phone or via email. But what we're generating now, it's just a temporary pin that will only work for the next 60 seconds. That's why I needed to call you."

"Right, right."

That nasty bit of psychology had been so effective at my old job that the entire engineering team, supposedly some of the best and brightest minds in the city, had been called into the conference room the next morning to explain why nearly everyone had given away the two-factor authentication pin to the random stranger on the phone the day before.

And the truth was I didn't even need his password, as I brute-forced my way into his email earlier this evening and reset it. But he didn't need to know that.

"OK, I got it," said the lab coat. "It's 2514."

I input the pin and with a click, I was into this dope's account, and with it, all the information about every specimen stored in the collection.

"Thank you. We'll take it from here. If I were you, I'd probably not mention this or losing your badge to anyone, yeah? Wouldn't want the hammer to come down on you for a silly mistake."

"O-ok," Phil replied. "I'll just call in sick, I guess."

"You do that," I said. "Have a good night."

"I found it," I said, several hours later, after yet another restless night. We had moved our normal morning meeting to the five-star hotel out at the waterfront where we had been deposited the previous afternoon. I didn't think we were being followed, but we had spent too many mornings in the same spot, eating the same breakfast, so a change seemed in order.

"You did?" asked Emma, who looked glad to be back in her normal garb, and I didn't have the heart to tell her that the respite would only be temporary.

"Well, I'm not 100% positive. But if I'm wrong, then the vial is not in the Museum at all, so we're screwed anyway."

"Fantastic, I guess. So where is it?"

"It's in the lab, either on the fourth or fifth floor. Was moved there a few days ago, somehow. The Collection's database and Farnsworth's email were cryptic on who or how that was accomplished. All I found was a note in the inventory that said 'exodus.'"

"Well, whatever. We can figure that out later. The important thing is that you…"

Emma suddenly collapsed onto the table in a heap, the sobs coming soon thereafter. I was so taken aback by what was happening that all I could do was hand her a napkin.

"Umm, what's wrong?"

The girl slowly composed herself and wiped away her smudged mascara before gulping down the rest of her tea.

"Everything! This was supposed to be my mission. It was my dad's life's work for fuck's sake, and all I've done so far is let you parade me around town in costume, almost give up my family's oldest secrets, and then open a box that was already unlocked."

"I thought you didn't care. You told Dalia that-"

"It's called holding your cards close to your vest, Jade. Of course I bloody care!"

"Oh. I see."

In my urgency to earn a place in the Guild, I had neglected to realize how much this task meant to Emma. And in doing so, how I was on my way to alienating my only ally and almost friend.

"Look," I said. "I'm sorry I kind of, well, entirely pushed you to the side. It's just I was already in over my head and then you told me what would happen if we failed and I…"

"You don't need to apologize," she said. "I overreacted. You've actually been great. Sure, I thought you were a jerk at first, but I was wrong. We'd be lucky to have you in the Guild."

"Thank you," I said. "That means a lot. But we still have to finish the Raid."

"Yes, we do," said Emma. "And I think I know how we're going to do it."

The woman with pink hair, a long black dress, a gorgeous diamond necklace, and pink heels exited the Mercedes sedan holding a flannel tote bag. Ahead of her, wedding guests were chatting around cocktail tables scattered outside the Museum entrance, the warm May weather providing the perfect backdrop to what was sure to be a magical evening for the happy couple getting ready inside.

But the pink-haired party crasher had other thoughts. She threaded her way through the crowd, drawing whispers and stares from the attendees. Was she one of the bride's college friends? Or a business associate of some kind? With all the attention the woman was attracting, the guests could be forgiven for not noticing the second woman wearing a hooded black cloak that was carefully trailing one step behind. That second woman was me, clad in my invisibility cloak, and the first woman was Emma, who had decided to pick out her own outfit and disguise for this evening's final infiltration.

We reached the front door of the Museum, and Emma opened it, letting it slowly close behind her so that I had enough berth to glide through. Inside, guests were making their way toward the inner courtyard, which had been transformed into a magnificent display of floral opulence. But Emma ignored all of it, walking directly to the bathroom across from the elevator, and I followed. It was thankfully empty, although the flower infestation had spread into here as well, with decadent arrangements displayed between the sinks.

After the door closed behind us, I tapped Emma on the shoulder three times to let her know I was still there, and she nodded slightly.

"I'll make two loops around the courtyard before heading up to the fourth floor and then return down here."

"OK," I said with a whisper. "Good luck. I'll be in the back stall. You know the code word?"

"We don't need a code word," she said, frowning. "I'll just ask if you're in there."

"Fine," I said. "Go."

She left, and I entered the stall and locked it behind me, before removing the hood of the cloak and undoing the gold clasp. If anyone else had been in the bathroom, they would have seen the bottom of my cloak appear out of nowhere, and I quickly pulled it up and tucked it into my waistband.

I waited in silence, trying to calm my pounding heart. A few minutes in, a chattering group of women entered and one of them tried my stall.

"Sorry!" I said. "Taken."

The interloper stalked off, but the flow of women in and out continued for another 20 minutes. What was taking Emma so long? My thoughts slowly drifted to the last time I had found myself in a strange bathroom: the night of the Met Gala. Inside that bathroom had been two letters that had ended my friendship with Lisa and Stacy. And Dalia had been there too, as if she had known all along what Beatrice and I were going to do. There was still so much I didn't understand about what had happened with Frankie, Doug, and Gilbert. Hopefully, once this was all over, and I had ascended to the Third Breuckelen Seat, I would get some answers.

The chatter finally subsided, which probably meant that the ceremony had started, and at last, I heard the door open again, followed by the familiar clacking of heels.

"Jade?" Emma called out.

"Yes, still here."

"Good. I'm all set. Cloak on. Let's go."

I pulled the hood back over my head, re-affixed the top of the cloak into the gold clasp, and stepped out of the stall.

No one was there.

"Emma?"

"Yes, here.

"OK. You might want to change out of those heels then. They're pretty loud."

"Oh, good call."

The flannel tote bag suddenly appeared floating in mid-air, out of which a pair of sneakers materialized, which then disappeared as well, leaving only the garish pink footwear abandoned on the floor.

"You going to take those?" I said.

"No," Emma said. "They're horrid." The heels skidded across the bathroom tile until they finally stopped underneath the sinks. "Let's go."

It was easier said than done. Now that we were both invisible, the only way for us to stay together was for Emma to quietly snap her fingers. It worked well enough that we exited the bathroom, traversed the courtyard, where the ceremony was in full swing, and down a long hallway, until we came to the end, where another bathroom awaited.

The door opened inward of its own accord before closing a few seconds later.

"Empty," said Emma.

Above us hung a security camera, and I darted under it, lest the cloak somehow betray me. I felt Emma's cloak rustle beside me and then the bag appeared again, followed by a piece of black material and a long selfie stick that had been hidden inside.

"The case give you any trouble?" I said, as the purloined Infiniblack attached itself to one end of the selfie stick.

"No," said Emma. "No alarms or anything. The alkahest ate through the glass like a charm. Pulled out the Infiniblack and then got the hell out of there."

Emma pushed the black film against the camera and removed the selfie stick, the material completely obscuring its view.

"And now we wait," she said, staring up at the camera. "That thing makes me so mad."

"What, the camera?"

"No, the Infiniblack. There's an alchemic paint called aconitium that does something similar. Made only in a small village in Romania. But now the normies have their own version. It's only a matter of time before they figure out technological substitutes for the rest. Can you imagine what would happen then?"

"Umm, I had never really thought about it, to be honest." I said, wondering why Emma had launched into a philosophical tirade in the middle of the Raid.

"Well, you should, Jade, you should. Because change is coming, whether Dalia wants it or not."

"I'll keep that in mind, I guess. But getting back to the task at hand, remind me again why we're even bothering with this exercise? We're invisible, for goodness' sake!"

"Because," whispered Emma, "we'll need to de-robe once we get to the lab. And this way, we'll know the guard won't be troubling us."

"OK," I said. "How are you going to do it? The spray or the lipstick?"

"I saw him at the desk. Not a bad-looking bloke. On a normal night, I'd try to kiss him, but we need to be absolutely certain. So the spray will have to do."

"Sounds like a plan."

We waited for the guard to appear, all the while the clamor of the ceremony floating our way. It sounded like a fun wedding from what we could make out, and I wondered how much fun I would have had at Lisa's wedding had the whole memory erasure thing not happened. But I stuffed that pathos down into the recesses of my mind as the security guard finally appeared at the end of the hallway.

His walk was slow and deliberate and, unfortunately for him, he stared at the obscured camera for way too long. Because by the time he turned around to see what that weird spritzing noise was, it was already too late.

Emma tried to brace his fall, but he was heavier than he looked and her hands were full, so instead of a graceful landing, his head hit the floor with a thud.

"Shit," said Emma. "Do you think he's OK?"

My pulse quickened as I examined the unconscious guard. He was still breathing and there was no blood anywhere, thankfully, but anything more than that, I didn't know.

"I hope so," I said. "Let's get him out of sight."

We clumsily dragged the man, whose name tag said Dennis, into the small bathroom and let the door swing shut slowly.

"Now what?" I asked to the empty hallway.

"Now," said Emma's disembodied voice, "the fun begins."

CHAPTER THIRTEEN

ALCHEMIC SURETY

"Rita observed the two resourceful children and came to the decision quite easily. 'No longer will you want for food or shelter. And you shall be educated in the old ways and the modern. Should you prove your mettle, when I pass from this world, you will inherit my name and all that comes with it. Do you accept this?' The brother and sister stared at each other, bewildered, before nodding. 'Good,' said Rita. 'Good.'"

My jaw dropped immediately when I saw the disaster that greeted us as we exited the elevator on the fourth floor. "What the hell happened here?" I said to Emma's invisible figure. "You said the alkahest ate through the glass no problem. You didn't mention anything about it destroying half of the case!"

The display was somehow still precariously balanced on three legs because where the fourth leg had been, now only air remained. And the same went for the contents of the case that had been in the front corner. I shuddered to think how much destruction one tiny drop had caused.

"Hmm," said Emma. "Guess I put more alkahest on there than I originally thought. Oh, well."

"Oh, well?" I said, trying not to raise my voice. "They're going to find this tomorrow and then…"

"And then what?" Emma shot back. "They'll call the police? Write us an angry letter? We'll be long gone by then, if they ever even figure out who the hell we are. You need to calm down right fucking now or else you can just wait here."

"Fine," I said.

Phil Farnsworth's badge appeared in mid-air, and I followed it to the double doors we had passed through yesterday. It waved itself over the badge reader to the left, the red security light turning green, and with a click, the doors unlocked.

"Let's go," said Emma as the door pushed itself inward. I trailed her through the gap, breathing a sigh of relief once we were clear on the other side and no alarms had gone off.

"That worked surprisingly well," I said.

"Easy part's over, though," said Emma. "Whoever unlocked the box didn't just leave the vial out on some table for any rando to take. Need to expect some sort of countermeasure is in place. That's where these rings come in."

Emma held up her left hand, which sported even more rings than I remembered.

"Right," I said, the small pit in my stomach growing ever so slightly. I had let Emma fully take the lead on the rest of the mission as a show of confidence in her ability. But the fact that she really didn't have any idea what we were up against was incredibly disconcerting. Then again, who knew what else she had in that magic bag of hers?

Lights from the wedding down below cast an eerie glow on the hallway of colors, but we turned away from the atrium and walked casually into the adjacent laboratory.

Emma appeared out of thin air, her cloaked figure looking ominous among the tables scattered throughout the room. I followed suit, undoing the gold clasp on my own cloak, and she nodded at my now visible features, before quickly shedding her garment and partially stuffing it into the top of the flannel bag.

We crisscrossed the room, ignoring the numerous paintings wrapped in plastic, but quickly concluded that this floor of the lab seemed to be destitute of pigment samples. Climbing the wide staircase back at the front, we reached the summit of the Raid and our last chance to find the prize.

This floor of the lab was situated differently. Instead of tables of artwork, there were benches with microscopes and computers. Vials and cans of samples and standards dotted the workspace, and the gentle hum of machines reminded me of my old office. Again, our survey turned up empty, and we regrouped at the top of the stairs.

"It doesn't seem to be here," Emma said. "You're absolutely positive that the Dragon's blood was transferred to the lab?"

"No, and I never said I was," I replied. "The inventory page just said that-"

"Shh," said Emma, holding up her left hand. "I think I'm getting something."

She held her palm flat and moved it around in a circle, and I could just make out the vibrations emanating from the druithyl in her rings. Moving a couple of feet forward, Emma repeated the exercise, shook her head from side to side, and then walked to a different set of benches. Finally, she stopped in front of the lone piece of artwork in the lab: a seven-foot tall painting of a woman in a red dress that was suspended between a wooden frame resting on an easel. The figure was striking, with red eyes and hair that matched her dress, and she stood behind a looming horde of knights on horseback. At the bottom of the frame, a small label read "*Girl on fire*, Artist unknown, 1495."

"What is it?" I said.

"The Dragon's blood," she said. "It's in the painting."

I looked at the portrait. The color of the red fabric seemed to pop from the canvas, almost as if the woman was about to step out of the painting into the real world.

"The note in the inventory," I said. "Exodus. But, what … why did they do that?"

Emma ran her finger across the dress and it came up clean.

"They're moving it. Maybe they were expecting us, or someone else. Knew we'd be on the scent of a vial in a locked wooden box. So they repurposed the Dragon's blood. Coated over the regular paint with it. Makes sense. It was hidden in the pigment collection, after all."

"So now what?"

"I don't know," said Emma. "I'm thinking."

She circled the easel with her left hand out in front of her to detect more hidden alchemy. The silver rings continued vibrating as she surveyed, but to my untrained eyes, it didn't look like there was anything else there.

"Hmm," said Emma, finally, after a few more minutes.

"What?" I asked.

"I can feel a second source of alchemy coming from somewhere around the painting. But…"

"What do you mean, second source?"

"The rings, they vibrate with a slightly different frequency depending on what they're detecting. So I can feel the Dragon's blood and then…"

Emma reached her fingertips forward to touch something at the bottom of the easel, and that's when the whole damn thing caught on fire.

The flames were blue, which I wasn't expecting. They also had formed a neat ring around the canvas, but had gone no further. And finally, they seemed to be ice cold. It was at once amazing and terrifying.

"What the hell is happening?" I asked.

"It's varutium," Emma replied. "Only burns where a specific primer has been spread. I should have figured."

"Varutium?"

"Some call it hellfire. A bit dramatic, if you ask me. Used to create impromptu prisons back in the day for the virgins who were to be sacrificed in a volcano or stabbed on an altar or some other nonsense. Then they started using it to burn the girls straight up. Then finally it fell out of use and memory sometime around the 18th century. Obviously these fuckers found a lost stash of it somewhere."

"How do you know so much about it, then?"

Why did every new alchemy discovery of mine have to have some terrifying past that needed reckoning with?

"Because," said Emma, "it's what killed my gran."

"What? Are you serious?"

"Yep," she replied nonchalantly.

"Well, I guess I have to applaud your calm demeanor. If I ever came face to face with the scumbag that killed my mom, I don't know what I'd do."

"Oh, I'm not calm, I'm fuming," said Emma. "But I learned long ago how to channel my anger until I could release it somewhere useful."

"If you say so," I said, my growing unease making my arms twitch.

"I'm guessing it's not the kind of fire that water can handle?"

"You are correct. Damonium, on the other hand, would douse it in an instant. But I don't have any of it in my bag, unfortunately."

I couldn't help but stare at the otherworldly blue flames as they danced around the woman in the red dress. Then the colors suddenly mixed together into a raging blaze of orange and sulfur, and I was back in the burning lighthouse, the ceiling about to collapse and two women splayed out on the floor in front of me. I felt my arm bring itself up to my face and then felt my palm violently connect with my cheek, nearly sending me tumbling to the ground.

I quickly regained my balance, Emma none the wiser, and that's when a small whisper escaped my lips.

"Get a hold of yourself, Jade, or I will."

Jade's grip of control released itself and my body ... well, her body, went slack. I closed my eyes, muttered a few soft words of self-encouragement, and then took my place next to Emma in front of the burning painting.

My partner-in-crime had retrieved a small footstool from her flannel bag and was now nearly eye level with the woman in the painting.

"What are you doing?" I asked.

"Being very careful not to set myself on fire," Emma replied. "What does it look like I'm doing?"

"Sorry," I said. "Umm, do you need any help with that?"

"Yes," said Emma. "Stop talking."

I nodded and watched as Emma slowly brought her hands to the top of the canvas. Several pieces of wire were fastened to both the burning frame and the painting's support board. She extended her arm behind one corner of the canvas, ignoring the flames just inches away, and after about 30 seconds, she withdrew it and the painting dropped slightly. She moved on to the second piece of wire and soon detached that one as well. This continued on as she worked her way along the top of the painting until she reached the last bit when suddenly her whole body jerked forward.

"Are you all right?" I asked.

"Not really," said Emma, who tried to detach herself from the painting only to find her right hand stuck.

"Why can't you get your hand off there?"

"They must have…" Emma grunted as she made a second attempt at freeing herself. "…sprayed the canvas with neutral auragen. It's bonded to my rings."

"Who did?"

"Enough with the fucking questions, Jade! I need to think."

I looked over at Emma's bag at the foot of the easel. Inside was probably a magic hacksaw that could cut an auragen link and who knew what else.

"Your bag," I said. "Is there anything in there that could help?"

Emma stared at the bag, and then at me, and her face recoiled.

"Yes, but…"

She tried to pull her hand free yet again, only for the auragen link to snap it back into place.

"…I can't get anything out of it with my rings stuck. Unless…"

"What?"

"The alkahest. It's in a tiny pocket on the outside of my bag. Get it, quickly!"

I complied and found the small vial that had once held the silvery liquid. It didn't look like there was more than a drop of the alkahest left, but I knew what the stuff was capable of, so maybe that was enough.

"OK, now what?"

"I saw a larger stepladder right by the stairs on this floor. Bring it over here."

I did as I was told again and positioned the metal steps next to Emma's stool, climbing up to the top so that I was standing a few inches above her, the flames a little too close for my liking.

"What am I supposed to do with this?" I asked.

"You're going to CAREFULLY pour the last few drops onto the portion of the painting between my fingers."

"OK," I said.

I unstoppered the vial and tilted it gently against the painting. Somehow, the alkahest must have dribbled out onto the canvas, because a tiny hole appeared in between Emma's pinky and ring finger. We both waited with bated breath for what seemed like an hour for the alkahest to dissolve the auragen bond.

"It's not enough," said Emma, surveying the partially dissolved painting. "You're going to break the vial on my rings."

"What?"

"I need to be sure the rest of the alkahest gets out. If I lose part of a finger, so be it."

"You're serious," I said.

"Yes. Do you think you can handle this without flipping out?"

I nodded.

"Good. Aim for the ring on my pinky," said Emma. "And with feeling, Jade. You only get one chance to get this right."

"Thanks, that was just the confidence boost I needed."

My hands immediately started trembling as I made a few practice motions, ending with me tapping the vial gently against Emma's pinky ring. Finally, I took one more deep breath, and then swung the vial toward Emma's hand.

But alchemy has a funny way of messing with your expectations of how the world should work.

Because at the last second, I felt my arm suddenly shift to the right, as if someone had jerked it with a puppet's string, and instead of smashing Emma's hand, the vial flew out of my grasp and into the burning frame.

"You always make sure."

Emma stared at me as the words escaped my mouth, but they weren't mine.

"No!" she shouted, trying with one last effort to pull her hand free.

The room suddenly exploded with a flash of blue light, and I was thrown backward. I landed with a hard thud against the leg of a nearby table and quickly tried to get to my feet. But my head was spinning, and my vision was cloudy, and so I collapsed onto the floor, unable to do anything.

Smoke was everywhere when I regained consciousness a few moments later, and I felt myself being pulled back into the memory of that night in the lighthouse again. I gasped for air and grasped for control, not wanting to surrender myself to the whim of the stone. Slowly, I crawled over to where the easel had been, my eyes struggling to stay open.

But only one truth remained.

Emma was gone.

"**B**FD firefighters say they've never encountered a blaze like the one that tore through the fourth and fifth floors of the Carter Museum last night, taking nearly 13 hours to get the fire under control. Miraculously, of the two casualties of the night, one was merely the abrupt end of the wedding in the courtyard on the first floor, which was scheduled to last until 2 a.m. The guests were safely evacuated thanks to the quick thinking of the security guard on duty, who was found unconscious under the activated fire alarm. Unfortunately, the other casualty was the Museum's near-priceless collection of pigments, paints, and varnishes, which was completely destroyed. A hundred years of curation, gone in the span of hours. Reporting live from Cambridge, Natasha Nettle, Channel 13 News."

I flipped off the third newscast of the morning and resisted the urge to throw the remote control at the hotel room TV. But I had caused enough damage for one day. My body ached in every possible place, the three doses of healing serum I had ingested over the course of the night doing little to relieve the pain. Jade's eyebrows, and maybe mine too underneath, were nearly singed off, and the hair on my arms would have been too if I hadn't still been wearing the cloak.

That garment somehow had come out of the explosion unscathed, and it was buried somewhere within the folds of the sheets, as I hadn't bothered to remove it before I collapsed into unconsciousness, if you could call it that. My eyes might have been closed but my mind had been wide awake, relieving the events of the disastrous evening in all sorts of different and horrible ways. But in every replay, the result had been the same: Jade had seized control of my arm and directed the alkahest toward the hellfire.

The stone—her stone, I realized—was tucked at the bottom of my suitcase. Her visage still clung to my body like an annoying relative who refused to leave after a family gathering. As much as I wanted to run to the Bunker Hill Bridge and toss the stupid thing into the Charles River, knowing my luck, that would only deepen Jade's grip on me.

I grabbed my phone from the nightstand and dialed Emma's number yet again. It went straight to voicemail. It was silly, I knew, to hold out hope that she had somehow escaped the blaze, that she was lying low while she recovered. But I had seen the burnt threads of her dress, the scorched strands of her pink wig, the melted metal puddle of what had been her necklace, and the singed scraps of the fabric that had been her bag. Maybe she was in a hospital bed somewhere, her body burned beyond recognition. But the most likely outcome was that the alkahest-enhanced blast had completely obliterated her.

I flipped over onto my stomach and let out a string of muffled cries into a pillow. But whatever catharsis I had hoped to achieve was diluted by hearing that alien voice come out of my mouth. And what followed was every anxious thought that I had been suppressing the previous few weeks. My hopes at joining the Guild, discovering why my mother had the gold token, ridding myself of this prison enveloping me, all now out of reach.

I screamed again and felt something inside me crack, like the last boundary between myself and Jade had finally been weathered away by whatever alchemy was powering the glamour. And then my body lifted itself off of the bed, walked over to my luggage, and retrieved the stone from its hiding place. I stepped into the bathroom and watched in the mirror as my hands gently placed the chain over my head and then tucked the gem into the confines of my sweater.

"*That's better*," said Jade's voice with a smile, and that was the last thing I remembered for the next two weeks.

GILDED MACHINATIONS

The rain is falling, as usual, but I am used to it.

I remember the feeling of actual rain drops on my skin. It was as if the world was renewing itself, just a little bit with each storm. I remember the pitter-patter on the roof of my house, like a timpani drum in one of Beethoven's symphonies. I remember the smell of morning dew that greeted me when I opened my door. I remember the rainbow of colors arching through the sky. I remember that a promise was made to me by one I held dear. And I remember that I am a prisoner and that these are just memories, a few left from my many lifetimes.

And then one day, the rain finally stops once more. The box opens, and a hand reaches inside. The necklace and its stone are placed around the neck of a young woman. It is her 18th birthday, and her gentleman caller has thought to curry favor with her father by lavishing a gorgeous piece of jewelry on his hopeful bride-to-be. He tells her father that despite the simple wooden box's appearance, the necklace is worth more than it seems. And in that regard, he is correct.

I feel the young woman's energy mixing with mine. She is vibrant and she is bold and she does not love this boy. But she will do what she is told, because that is her station in life. It is 1889 and Ariella Livingston is a girl out of time, in more ways than one. She reminds me of another girl I knew briefly in a different age.

Ariella senses something is something amiss with the gift but cannot possibly decipher what it is. Still, she dutifully wears the necklace every day as the months go by, as her nuptials are arranged and draw nearer, and as I grow stronger.

One evening, as she is staring at herself in the mirror, Ariella grasps the necklace's green stone tightly, and something unexpected happens: I appear and I am radiant. The girl screams with my voice and nearly sends the entire Fifth Avenue manse into a tizzy. Her lady's maid is soon rapping at the door, and it's all Ariella can do to stop the older girl from downtown from barging in and finding a peculiar blonde dressed in her mistress's clothing. Another squeeze of the stone and I am funneled back into my prison. Ariella thinks she has temporarily gone mad from the pressure and the crushing weight of expectations and vows not to touch the stone again.

A month passes, and the wedding is now only days away. Ariella is sobbing on her bed after a particularly trying dress fitting and the idea somehow enters her head. A moment later and my trap has been sprung. I bide my time and watch as the girl runs to the mirror again to look at me. I could take control, as I have gathered enough of her energy, but I wait and see what she will do.

And what she does next is something even I could not have expected. The summer night is cool despite the stench of Manhattan, and Ariella quickly threads her way toward her betrothed's townhouse a few blocks away. It feels so good to walk free that I don't care at the moment that I am letting her do the walking for me. The girl sneaks into the house through the servants' entrance in the back and then climbs up the rear staircase until she's just outside his bedroom. A rap on the door and it opens a few moments later. The boy is young, but cute. She could do a lot worse.

"Who … who are you?" he asks and Ariella presses my finger to his lips, pushing him inside and closing the door with enough force that someone is bound to have heard something. His resistance is surprisingly short-lived, but then again, I am nothing if not rapturous. The two embrace in unsubtle ways and, sure enough, the escapade has attracted the attention of her betrothed's household. And, clever girl that she is, who should barge through the door moments later, but the boy's father, trailed by Ariella's own father. She smiles and pushes her way past the startled men and back out into the night, a free woman.

Or so she thinks.

The next morning, her wedding dress is still waiting for her in her antechamber, and she runs to her mother, hoping for an explanation. But it is not the one she wants to hear. Everything will go forward as planned, her mother says, there is too much at stake, too much embarrassment were her father to call everything off. She will have to make do, she will have to take it in stride, for the good of her family and for her own sake. She doesn't want to be known as the rich girl who couldn't keep a man satisfied, now does she, her mother chides.

This she cannot abide.

Ariella runs to her room and shuts the door. She spends the rest of the day staring in the mirror, daring herself to disappear beneath me. Finally, she comes to a decision that I wholeheartedly endorse. She pulls out my necklace and activates it, and that's when I speak to her at last.

"Hello," I say, and I take control long enough to squelch any urge to scream.

"You seem to be in a predicament, but I can help, if you let me."

I give her back my body for a moment so she can respond, and she nods my head.

"Good. There isn't much time, and I am not very familiar with this era. Enlighten me."

"What … what do you want to know?" she says, quivering.

"Everything."

Ariella starts from the beginning, from the founding, which I know, to the wars that followed, to the gilded age we currently reside in. For a girl with several brothers, she knows much of her father's business. We go over this in great detail. Finally, I let her sleep as I get to work.

The girl wakes up days later in a four-poster bed that is not her own. The room is sparse at the moment, just the bed and a silver mirror. She runs to the latter and squeezes the stone and I reappear, smiling.

"Where am I?" she asks.

"Your new home downtown. Congratulations, you own the whole building. And your tenants will start moving in within the week."

"I … how did you…?"

"Your father's creditors were happy to extend him margin for some promising trades, the results of which were funneled into several holding companies, which then took out loans from other banks to acquire real estate in many parts of this fine city, including the new apartments on this block."

"My father … the paper trail … he'll find me at some point."

"Don't worry about him. The maze I've constructed is hardened against such snooping. Besides, if he gets close enough, I need merely knock over one domino to send his entire house crashing down."

"You wouldn't!" she exclaims.

"Why shouldn't I? They were about to sell you off like a breeding cow. You deserve to be free."

She contemplates this and acquiesces to my machinations.

"What happens now? Who are you?"

"Now, we build. As to who I am, I am a lost soul, same as you."

CHAPTER FOURTEEN

LOST AT SEA

"This was the truth of it. But still Rita withheld one final secret. Her true legacy, the
First Seat of the New Amsterdam Table, that would pass to another. To me."

I finally woke up.

Frankly, I don't know what it was exactly that triggered it.

Maybe Jade had done all she set out to do in those two weeks.
Maybe her control over me had naturally waned to the point of breaking. Or maybe the arrival of the final remaining piece of my old life
had been enough to stir my sense of self from its forced slumber.

I sat up in my bed in New York and looked at my phone, plugged
in and charging away on my nightstand like nothing odd had happened.
Tapping the screen twice, I nearly vomited when I saw the date appear.

And then something else unexpected appeared.

A text from Duncan.

"Hey, we need to talk."

Yeah, that's the last thing I needed to do right now.

I put the phone down and assessed the situation. My studio apartment, which I had moved into shortly after Beatrice disappeared, was immaculate. But that had not been the case when I had left for Boston. The stacks of boxes were gone, the closet next to me was full to the brim with clothing I didn't recognize, save for the invisibility cloak, and I was wearing pajamas that were a far cry from my regular ratty sweats.

But one thing I did recognize: the glamour stone. It still hung around my neck, like a portable prison, and my body was still buried beneath its alchemy. I drew it out of the satin nightshirt that Jade must have bought me and stared at it. Its formerly pale green color now shimmered with a vibrancy that shocked me. And when I went to pull it up around my neck, it suddenly gained about 20 pounds, causing me to drop it in an instant. Once it rested back against my chest, the stone magically deflated back to its normal weight.

Ty's words came back to me, ones that I had ignored amid the search for the Dragon's blood. She had said that the glamour wasn't a stone, but a person. And her warning from the day she had first given me the necklace now rang crystal clear. Somehow, some way, the body I had been wearing wasn't just an alchemical illusion created by someone with a thing for redheads. It was an actual person, and I had unwittingly been feeding it … her, for weeks, until "Jade" had pushed her way to the surface.

And boy, had she been busy, if what she had done to my apartment had been any indication. I grabbed my phone and texted Ty, but when she didn't respond after 15 minutes, I spent the rest of the morning tearing over every inch of my apartment, looking for clues as to what Jade had been up to. But whatever or whoever Jade was, she was no dummy. Other than the expanded wardrobe she had purchased, there were no clues, no evidence, not even a hint of what she had been up to.

I gave up my search around 1 p.m., my stomach growling and my anxiety from being Tyler Durden-ed for two weeks waning enough to venture a trip outside. It was then that my phone sprang to life as the name "Ty Anzio" splashed across the screen. I frantically hit the answer button and was greeted by the face of someone who looked like they had walked into a bramble bush.

"What happened to you?" I asked.

"I could ask you the same thing," Ty answered.

"What do you mean? I told you this stupid glamour you gave me wouldn't turn off. And now-"

"I've been trying to get in touch with you for weeks. But every time I called, I got a weird buzzing sound and then the line went dead."

"Oh, right. It's a long and short story. The short version is that I've been unconscious for two weeks, and the long version is something I'm still trying to puzzle out, because the glamour stone you gave me took control of my body, and I have no clue what she or it did."

"I see," said Ty. "Well, I did warn you not to overdo it."

"Yes, you did. But you could have mentioned the consequences. I thought I would just, you know, start believing I was someone else. I didn't think there was an actual 'someone else' inside the stone!"

"Would you have believed me?"

"Well, no," I said. "Maybe I would have been a little more cautious, though. Used this thing sparingly until the Guild tracker gave up and then given it back to you. And not let it literally consume my body and mind!"

"Calm your ass down, Jade. It's not as bad as you-"

"My name isn't even Jade!"

"That's news to me, but fine. Who are you then?"

"I'm Jen," I said. "Jen Jacobs."

"All right, then, *Jen*. First thing you're going to do is stop freaking out. It's not helping and will only send you right back to the metaphorical pit where the glamour stuck you while she ran the show. And then the next thing you're going to do is—shit, I need to go."

"What? No. No, no, no. You're not pulling one of those. Are you fucking serious?" I screamed at the bloodied face of the teenager in the phone, whose eyes suddenly had a look of fear in them.

"Just keep out of trouble. I'll be in touch as soon as I can."

And with that, she was gone.

I resisted the urge to throw the phone into the wall, and instead took ten deep breaths, then made my way into the bathroom. The face that greeted me in the mirror was familiar in a way that I hadn't felt before. It was as if my mind had reoriented itself to truly believe that the glamour's body was my own. And could I blame my brain for thinking that? It had been so long since I had been myself that I was beginning to forget the way my cheeks dimpled when I smiled, or where the precise position of the oddly shaped birthmark on my forearm.

I looked at the redhead with green eyes and freckles in the reflection. Had she really been alive? How was it that her body had been forced inside the stone? What about her mind? I was becoming increasingly convinced that whatever or whoever had created the stone had not intended for this woman's consciousness to come along for the ride. But somehow, it had, and it had been feeding on me, growing stronger until finally it had displaced my own mind.

My fist suddenly connected with the wood paneling next to the mirror, and I winced as I drew it back, blood trickling down my knuckles. I looked at the wall to assess the damage only to find that the panel had been dislodged completely and had fallen to the floor. Cursing my impulsiveness and the landlord's cheapness, I bent down to retrieve the piece and then to reattach it in its place. Except when I did, my eyes finally registered what had been hiding underneath, and I dropped the panel in shock.

Because where the drywall should have been, someone had neatly carved out a hollow compartment and inside was rack after rack of Beatrice's vitality serum.

I t was mid-afternoon by the time I reached 6th Street and I had to wait about half an hour for a clear window to approach Beatrice's mailbox stash without attracting attention.

I shouldn't have been surprised to find the relay mailbox completely empty, but the sight of everything gone made me want to eat the last strength buff and tear it out of the ground. So, once again, I found myself powerless swimming in a current beset by hostile forces on all sides, with only the invisibility cloak to steady myself.

Great, I thought. Who needed to be invisible when only a handful of people alive even knew what I looked like?

After quadruple-checking that neither Beatrice nor Jade had stashed a hidden envelope or message or clue inside, I locked the door of the mailbox and retreated to a nearby coffee shop. The barista gave me a half-knowing grin as I ordered a cortado, and I froze.

"This is going to sound a little crazy," I said, my voice barely above a whisper, "but, umm, have I been here before?"

"I've heard crazier, don't worry," she said. "But no, was just looking at your top. It's from that new boutique over on Carmine Street, right?"

"Yeah, exactly!" I said.

I stuffed a $5 bill into the tip cup and ran out the door. It wasn't much, but I needed a distraction to take my mind off of the events in Boston and whatever was going to happen at the next Guild meeting, which was now only two days away. Well, maybe Jade had solved all my problems in the time she had been in control, and I would be welcomed like a conquering hero. Or, more likely, she had her own agenda that didn't coincide with my own or the Guild's.

On a whim, I dug out the Night Market card Nikki had given me in Boston and scanned the list of locations. Sure enough, the Carmine Street boutique was one of them.

The shop was in a small basement below a townhouse and filled to the brim with racks of lacy dresses and women holding champagne flutes who probably worked with or knew Lisa. I shoved my way to the back, where a petite elderly woman with uneven bushy hair was perched on a stool behind a wooden table, looking completely bored.

She eyed me as I approached and then shook her head.

"You're back," she said.

"Yes," I replied. "And I-"

"Look, I already told you, I don't know where to get any more. You bought the rest of my seller's stock, and he won't have a new shipment from VAC for at least three months, maybe longer."

"Fine," I said, quickly putting on an air of displeasure. "But there's something else you can do for me."

"Oh?" the woman replied. "Haven't I already done enough to repay my father's debt five times over? The Council has rules against this sort of usury and-"

"You really want to get the Council involved in all of this?" I said. "Go ahead. I'm sure they'll be really interested to know that you're operating in-"

"OK, OK," said the woman. "Keep your voice down. What is it you want?"

"Information," I answered. "I want to know everything you know about glamour stones."

The woman scratched the side of her head, white flakes falling down onto her shoulder, and I grimaced.

"Is this a test?"

"What?"

"There's the answer. You told me not to tell you anything about that."

I stared at her, bewildered.

"What are you talking about?"

"You said, and I quote, 'If I come back here asking about glamour stones, don't tell me anything.' And I said, 'that makes no goddamn sense. If you want to know about them, I would tell you, for a price.' And then you put a knife on my throat and repeated the command, and when I agreed, you so nicely trimmed off this patch of my hair."

She tapped on the bald spot on the right side of her head and gave me a half-smile.

"So you won't tell me, then?" I asked, wishing I had whatever knife my alter ego had used.

"Afraid not," the woman replied. "I'm rather fond of my locks, and I can't say the same thing about you, whichever version of you I'm speaking with."

"Fine," I said. "But you'd better hope that next time I come back here, I-"

"Excuse me, ma'am?" said someone behind me.

I stiffened as if I was a statue, recognizing the voice immediately, and turned to face Lisa.

"Umm, are you done paying? You've been standing there for a long time."

I stared at my former best friend Lisa, who had no inkling of who I was. Even if the glamour had been off, she wouldn't have recognized me either, thanks to that disastrous evening at the bar when I accidentally wiped all traces of myself from her memory and Stacy's too.

"And now you're just staring at me," she continued. "Is she done?" Lisa said to the bushy haired woman behind me.

"Yes, yes, she was just leaving," the woman replied.

I stepped awkwardly to the side and let Lisa drop the pile of garments onto the table, which the shop woman began sorting through and scanning. Lisa finally turned back to me and handed me her empty champagne flute, before heading back into the crowd to fetch more clothes.

"Friend of yours?" asked the shop woman, who was about halfway through the dozen dresses Lisa had dumped on her.

"Sort of," I said. "It's complicated."

"I can see that," said the woman, tapping her the rims of her glasses.

"You can see what?"

"Everything. Your alchemy leaves a trace. Well, everyone's does, but yours is particularly sloppy. One of the reasons I was staunchly opposed to the Expansion. That girl, she was your friend?"

I nodded, and the woman squinted through her glasses at Lisa behind me.

"Hmmm. Yes, I see the vestiges of the … oh."

"What now?"

"You thought to fix the first with the second. But really, you've just doomed her even sooner. That poor dear."

My heart was now pounding as I waited for the woman to reveal what else I had done, besides leading Emma to a fiery demise and Beatrice to her exile and Frankie to a forced death.

"What … what will happen to her?"

"Her mind is unwinding."

"I don't understand. What does that mean?"

"She's slowly forgetting herself. Little by little. Day by day. A memory here, a memory there. It won't be long now, I think, until the only thing she has left in her head is your betrayal."

CHAPTER FIFTEEN

SURFACE PRESSURE

The alleyway next to the boutique was not the best place for a panic attack, but I had barely made it out the door before I felt my mind cracking again. My hand reached into my purse and pulled out a small compact mirror.

I flipped it open with a flourish, and Jade's smile greeted me in the reflection.

"Not again," I muttered through gritted teeth, only for the smile to force its way back across my mouth.

"I let you have a little time to yourself and you immediately go spy on

me? Will another fortnight at the helm teach you some proper manners?"

The pressure suddenly subsided, and I ventured a response.

"What do you want from me?" I said to the face in the mirror, which changed again as soon as the last word left my lips.

"What do I want? I want what everyone in my situation wants. Freedom. Agency. Control."

"What does that mean? What are you?"

"I was someone. Then they destroyed me and took my body for themselves. But a fraction of my essence still remained, had to remain, for the stone to work. And that will be their undoing. I will make sure of it."

"I don't understand."

"Of course you don't. But you should. You are right in the middle of all of this, whether you realize it or not. If you stay on your track and do not venture into mine, this will all work out in the end."

Jade vanished, and I was left staring at my adopted face in the mirror.

"Hey!" I shouted. "Now you don't feel like talking?"

Some of the boutique patrons stopped at the mouth of the alley and stared, but I ignored them and replayed Jade's words in my mind. Ty had been telling the truth, it seemed: the body I wore had been someone, but who was she and who had converted her into a glamour, I hadn't the faintest idea. And I had a feeling that either Ty didn't know or wasn't about to tell me.

I felt the weight of my burdens push down on my shoulders and I squatted down, trying to find a modicum of balance. In that moment, if I could have downed a vial of the memory serum to make me forget everything, I think I would have done so, despite knowing what would likely happen to me. It would be the easiest of escapes, but even that path was cut off from me, seeing as how Beatrice was the only one I knew who had the serum.

I stood up slowly, took a deep breath, and walked out of the alley. A warm June breeze enveloped me and made the glamour stone sway back and forth. It shimmered just slightly, whether from the afternoon sun or from Jade, I wasn't sure. But I took it as a sign that she was in there, listening, ensuring I stayed on my track. Well, that track led right back to the Guild, and it was there that I was going to get some answers.

The next 24 hours passed at a glacial pace. You never think about how many hours there are in the day when you don't try to sleep, and I didn't dare even close my eyes for more than a second, lest Jade decide to take full control again. And with the vitality serum off limits, I needed another way to avoid drifting off into unconsciousness. Fortunately, I still had the invisibility cloak, and so at 10 p.m., I donned the garment and went for a nighttime stroll. I ended up walking from my Cobble Hill apartment up to the Brooklyn Bridge and across, through the Financial District, and finally down to Wall Street.

I tried to picture what the city had been like when Rita had lived here. The vivid memories from her rings were still fresh in my mind, but they now seemed so alien when contrasted with the gleaming city that had replaced every single building from that time. Well, almost every building. During my wandering, I walked by Fraunces Tavern, whose two-toned brick exterior and dormer windows stood out on the busy modern street. A plaque outside exclaimed that the building was the oldest standing structure in Manhattan, having been constructed in 1719. I wondered what secrets its walls have heard over the centuries.

Next, I passed by where Rita's bank had once stood, where she had stashed the twelfth gold token in an unassuming box in the basement. How that token made its way from there to my mother's necklace,

I had no clue. Or had it been the fake token all along, a latent trap laid by Rita for her enemies to eventually spring? I still had so many questions, and the only people who could answer them were dead.

I walked along the East River promenade as the sun rose, dreading that I had another half-day to wait before facing my fate at the Guild. But maybe I could jumpstart the process. The towers of the Guild headquarters loomed ahead in my mind as I traveled north, until finally I reached the unmarked entrance at the bottom of the south tower. There was no handle or any other door-opening mechanism, but I pressed my palm into the middle of the wooden barricade and was completely surprised when it opened inward. After a quick survey of the surrounding empty streets, I pushed onward into the castle.

I was greeted by twin staircases, one leading up to the meeting room, and one leading down to the basement. Choosing the latter, I found a dark, narrow passageway that suddenly sprang to life when I stepped off the stairs. Was it more of the red glowing stones from the cave, I wondered? But then I remembered what Frankie had said, how we had it all backwards. That the cave wasn't the Guild's stronghold at all, but something that she and her family had kept hidden.

I didn't have time to ponder yet another mystery because I was distracted by the tapestries I could now see hanging on both walls. And they weren't just colorful weavings, but depictions of scenes out of history. The one immediately to my left depicted an uncannily familiar scene: it was the Guild's negotiation with the Lenape in northern Manhattan. And there was the tulip tree mentioned in the plaque on the surviving Inwood rock, in all its glory. A small group of men and women dressed in European garb stood next to the tree, and on the other side stood a group of Lenape, who had allegedly sold the island for 60 guilders' worth of goods. Rita, too, claimed in her diary that "we" had bought the island for that amount. Seeing this tapestry here in the Guild's headquarters, I was left to wonder whether the Guild itself had been the purchaser.

Moving farther down the hall, I came across several more tapestries. There was one showing the building of a castle on a hill somewhere, and then another showing that same castle on fire, which I thought was a rather peculiar narrative to display. Another showed a group of three people standing around a stone-lined altar with a figure tied to a stake in the middle. The precursor to a witch burning, I wondered? The final one depicted a woman standing behind a crowd of men listening to another man read from a piece of parchment. This had to be Rita, attending the reading of the Constitution she had helped draft from the shadows, as chronicled in her 1787 diary that we had found in the cave. Clearly, the Guild considered this one of its major accomplishments, but I doubted it was because they were fans of democratic republics.

I finally reached the end of the passageway and made my way slowly up the staircase. Exiting on the first floor, I entered a small square room with three doors arranged on each of the other walls. A bronze plaque with a small circular indentation in the center hung to the left of all three doors, and I examined the one immediately to my left.

"Orange, First Seat," it said, and not surprisingly, the other two plaques were for the Second and Third Seats of the Orange Table.

On the second and third floors, it was the same, this time for the New Amsterdam and Pavonia Tables, and I was nearly out of breath when I reached the top landing. I wondered whether the Breuckelen Table members were put here as punishment or as a reward, or whether it was neither and they had some alchemic means of climbing all those stairs without getting tired.

I approached the door to my right, which had a bronze plaque next to it just like all the others.

"Breuckelen, Third Seat," this one said. My Guild office. At least until they expelled me later this evening for the disaster in Boston. I went to open the door, only to realize that it had no doorknob. Upon further inspection, neither did the other two doors. I rolled my eyes. Why was it always something? Returning to the door of my office, I considered the circular indentation in the plaque, which looked to be the size of a large coin. Of course.

I retrieved the gold token from within my locket and pressed it into the plaque. A click sounded nearby, and then the door inched forward.

"After you," said a voice behind me and I nearly jumped out of my skin.

It was Gilbert, sporting his now-inactive invisibility cloak, under which I could see a grey suit and red tie.

"What ... why did you do that?" I stammered.

"Sorry, couldn't resist," he said glibly. "Just wanted to be here when you opened the door."

"Why?"

"Because that door has never been opened before. I mean, I know what's inside. The same wooden desk, workbench, and chairs that's in the others. But after they were deposited and that plaque was installed, the Third Seat office has been locked ever since."

"I see. What about at the old headquarters?"

"Same deal. An empty office for an empty Seat. And so on and so on. It's good to see that the locking alchemy has held firm all these years. Will have to make a note of that in the current volume of the Compendium. Anyway, feel free to take a peek inside, but make it quick. The meeting is about to start."

"Thanks," I said, and he departed back down the stairs. By his easy-going demeanor, it seemed like he wasn't aware of the calamity that had occurred, which I surmised was a bad thing. I would have rather entered the boardroom with news of my failure already disseminated and processed, instead of having to explain what happened to an excited audience expecting to receive one of the components of the Philosopher's Stone.

The Stone. Everyone with a passing interest in *Harry Potter* thought they knew about that stone, but to find out that it was actually real? And that people were trying to create a new one? If the popular legends were true, the stone was a wellspring of immortality and unlimited gold. It sounded like a horrible combination, no matter whose hands it ended up in.

I pushed the door all the way in and stepped into my temporary office. It was as how Gilbert described it. A simple wooden desk was set against the wall sporting the lone window with a matching wooden chair stored underneath. On the opposite wall was a tall wooden workbench and a wooden stool. The door on this side had a knob, and I pulled it shut and heard the lock click. If what Gilbert had said was true, then there was no way for anyone else to get inside this room now. The thought was of small comfort, as the last place I'd want to hide from the Guild would be right at the top of their headquarters.

But the hour of my expulsion was drawing near, and so I exited the office, wondering if I'd ever be able to return. I made my way back down the stairs, back through the dark basement hallway, and climbed the last set of stairs up to the foyer outside the boardroom, where Gilbert was waiting for me, a perplexed look on his face.

"What?" I asked, hearing the sounds of animated discussion spilling out from beyond the door.

"Nothing," he said. "Come inside. We're ready to begin."

The chatter immediately stopped as I entered the room, and I was greeted with 20 sets of eyes all staring at me as if I had three heads. Including a pair belonging to one Emma Patel.

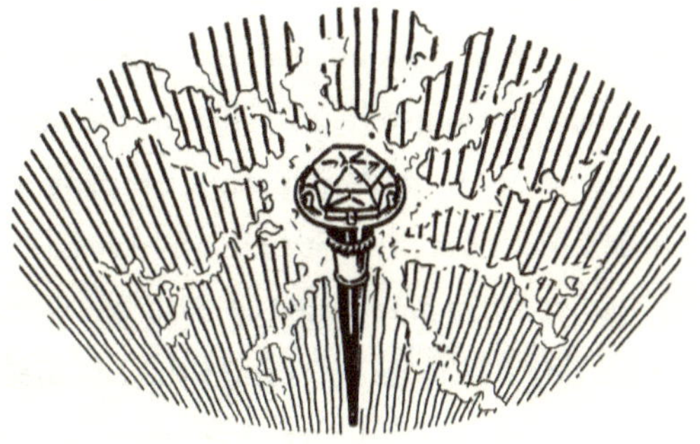

CHAPTER SIXTEEN

TRUTH

*"And never would. For soon after, he dropped dead of a mysterious malady.
And that is how the newly christened Lady Melanie Fitzjames became a duchess."*

An uncanny hush fell over the room as I sat in my Seat next to Lucca and a lanky guy in his mid-twenties who must have been our First Seat. Every other Seat was filled, save for Gilbert's at the opposite end, which he quickly took, and I tried to glance at all the other Guild members, but my focus went immediately back to Emma.

She was alive! I wanted to run to her, to tell her I was sorry, to explain what had happened, but her eyes were fixed on the windows behind the Orange Table, where J.P. was seated.

And before I could even try to walk over to see her, Gilbert banged the gavel against the New Amsterdam Table and the meeting began.

"Roll call," said Gilbert and he went around the Tables, with each member acknowledging that they were indeed present. I tried to keep track of the names as best I could, but before I knew it, it was Lucca's turn and then mine. Emma responded shortly thereafter with a quiet "present," before the New Amsterdam Table finished the roll.

"This 433rd meeting of the Worshipful Company of Alchemists shall come to order. As this is the first time we have had a full session in three … hundred years, Dalia wanted to say a few words before we began with the reading of the minutes from the last meeting."

Dalia, clad in the same black dress from a month ago, stood slowly and addressed the room.

"As Gilbert said, there haven't been 12 members around our collective Tables since before the Schism. So I'd like to pause so that we can all reflect on this historic moment we are bearing witness to."

She turned her head to look at each Guild member and when she came to me, I felt my control slip just a little, before she moved on to the other half of the Guild, before finally taking her seat.

"Thank you Dalia," said Gilbert. "Several items of business from last meeting are directly relevant to tonight's meeting, so as Guild secretary, I am overruling any motion to waive the reading of the minutes."

Satisfied that no one was going to protest his procedural maneuvering, Gilbert pulled out a long piece of parchment from his inner suit jacket pocket and placed it on the table.

"Item one: the status of the membership application of Jade Peters, holder of the Breuckelen Table Third Seat token. The Membership Committee reported on Ms. Peters's successful completion of the Initiation and made its recommendation that Ms. Peters be elevated to full Guild member."

I looked quickly at J.P., Lucca, and Emma, the first two of whom had slight scowls on her their faces, while Emma's remained a blank canvas.

"Chairman de Wyck then rejected the Committee's recommendation pending one final task, which brings us to item two: the retrieval of the vial of Dragon's blood by Second Seat Patel and Ms. Peters. Ms. Patel, I understand the mission was a success."

I nearly did a spit take as Emma slowly nodded her head and then drew out a vial from the sleeve of her blouse containing a shimmering red liquid and held it up for us all to see. I stared at it for a few seconds before my gaze was drawn down to Emma's right hand. Which was charred completely black.

"What ... what happened to your hand?" I blurted out, and everyone's eyes were suddenly fixed on me again.

"You happened," said Emma coldly. "Why don't you explain to everyone how you threw the alkahest into the raging varutium instead of freeing me, and then I will complete the tale on how I heroically salvaged the mission after you abandoned me?"

"Abandoned you? I didn't ... everything burned, you were gone ... and I thought you were..."

"Dead? Clearly I'm not. But as I said, I'll get to that. You first though."

With her other hand, she beckoned me to start, and I looked at Gilbert for some sort of direction, but he just shrugged his shoulders. And so I recounted everything that had happened from the last meeting. Of course I left out the part about the glamour's imprisoning of me, but I made sure to relay in exquisite detail J.P.'s offer and Emma's uneasiness in accepting it. Finally, I reached those fateful moments in the lab and how the vial of alkahest "slipped" out of my hand and into the blaze.

"The explosion knocked me out for a time," I concluded. "And when I came to, the only thing left of Emma, or so I had thought, was the charred remains of her disguise."

I let out a long deep breath and tried to ignore the reservoirs of sweat that had pooled under my arms. The room remained silent for about a minute, the Guild members nervously trying to gauge each other's reactions, before Gilbert finally broke the impasse.

"Emma, Ms. Peters has recounted what transpired up until she thought you perished. Now please enlighten us how you escaped, and with the Dragon's blood to boot?"

"With pleasure, *Gilbert*. So, when the alkahest hit the varutium, the entire room erupted into an inferno. That much is true. Including every part of the stupid outfit she made me wear."

I wanted to interject that the crazy getup had been Emma's idea, not mine, but kept my mouth shut.

"But what Jade conveniently omitted," Emma continued, "was that I am nothing if not resourceful. So with my left hand, I ripped off the burning garments, wig, and shoes, and then pulled the painting free from the easel with my right hand still stuck to it."

Emma twirled the vial in her hands as a dramatic pause, and I quickly surveyed the room to see how her tale was being received. J.P. was fiercely enraptured, his body leaning forward, eager to hear her next words, and his right hand gently tapping his jeweled cane against the edge of the table. The rest of the assembled Guild, including Dalia, didn't seem as enamored, save for a few people whose names I'd already forgotten.

"But by then, the fire had trapped me within a small radius, with no way out of the lab that wouldn't involve horrible disfigurement."

"Your hand though," said my First Seat.

"I'm getting to that, D.C. May I finish?"

The guy called D.C. nodded.

"There was one way out, but it is, for lack of a better word, frowned upon by my family."

"Your bag," I whispered, and Emma turned slowly to meet my gaze.

"Yes, Jade, that is correct. I forced myself through the bottom, painting in tow, and fell through the vervorium portal for what seemed like an eternity, before finally landing in the Mondal cache."

"Clever," said Gilbert. "And then you waited until the fire was put out before going back through?"

"No, of course not," said Emma. "I presumed, correctly, that my bag was destroyed. And therefore, returning the way I came would have trapped me in the void, which would have been a particularly unpleasant fate. But that left me stranded inside the cache, the painting still attached to my hand. Fortunately, my family has always taken a particular interest in linking and de-linking compounds. So it was only a matter of days before I had worked out the means of extracting both my hand from the painting and the Dragon's blood from the paint."

"Ah," said D.C. "That's what happened to your hand."

"Yes, an unfortunate but necessary consequence of the paracelsus procedure. I'll be needing to examine the Guild's libraries on healing salves soon to see if there is a way to reverse this, but after the initial 12 hours of excruciating pain, it's mostly just a cosmetic injury."

"And then what, you waltzed out of the cache, hopped a flight from wherever, and returned just in time for our meeting?" asked Lucca.

"Exactly."

"Well done, Ms. Patel, well done," said J.P. "You are a testament to the Guild's ingenuity and resourcefulness."

"Thank you, Mr. Laurel. I agree," said Emma with a smile.

"If you're quite finished, then there is the matter of your reward," said Gilbert. "Second Seat Patel, for your bravery in the face of almost certain death, we will recommend to the Compensation Committee that you be awarded 500 silver tokens, a generous supply of three prima materia of your choice from the Guild's stores, and priority selection for your next Guild assignment."

"I don't think so," said Emma.

"What?" said Gilbert.

"You think I'm an idiot? You think I don't know how much this vial is really worth?"

"Ms. Patel," said Dalia quietly. "You obtained that vial in the service of the Guild. By right and by law, it is the Guild's property."

J.P. suddenly stood up from his chair.

"It's awful funny hearing you talk about 'law' like it's something that applies to you," he said, his voice trembling with anger.

"What is that supposed to mean?" asked Dalia.

J.P. ignored her and turned to face the rest of the Guild.

"There is someone here who is not who they say they are."

I felt my teeth bite down on my bottom lip and tried to wipe the blood from my mouth without anyone noticing. He had to be talking about me, right? Emma knew I had the glamour and she must not have believed my story about it not working.

"And that has cost us immeasurable damage," J.P. continued. "But it ends tonight. It ends now."

Gilbert banged the gavel down on the table three times before Dalia waved him off.

"J.P., you're out of order. If you have a grievance, take it up with the Grievance Committee at the appropriate time."

"What good will that do?" he replied. "Seeing as how the grievance I have is integral to the Grievance Committee and this whole damned organization."

Dalia stood up abruptly and somehow I felt the force of … her. Her anger cascaded around the table, ricocheting from member to member, but when it reached J.P., he batted it aside with his cane.

"The only one who is out of order, I'm afraid, is you," he said, and slammed the heel of his cane down onto the floor.

The room exploded with a flash of light, and I closed my eyes instinctively, only to feel a different force than the one Dalia had just thrown at us. It enveloped my whole body, and I felt Jade's shell around me begin to crack, her voice crying out in terror before being suddenly silenced. When I finally opened my eyes again, half of the Guild was staring at me, and the other half was staring at an unconscious teenage girl who was sitting in the Seat where Gilbert had just been.

It was Ty.

REVELATIONS

"Truth be told, I am not fond of the Old World accent. But the people here seem to respect it. And it is expected from a woman with my title. So I will endure it for this lifetime as a minor inconvenience."

It only took a moment for everything to erupt into chaos. There was shouting, curses, epithets, more shouting, and at some point, someone threw their chair against the window. During that commotion, one of the Guild members had bound my wrists and ankles together with a piece of gold rope, completely immobilizing me. I suspect that they would have done the same to Ty had Dalia not moved in front of her.

Finally, a tense order returned to the room, and I looked at J.P., who had a satisfied, smug grin on his face. He, in turn, was looking at Emma, who was trying to fake the same look, but clearly failing.

"Well," said J.P. "Like they say down in Wimberly, sometimes your hook reels in two fish."

"That doesn't make any sense," said Ty with her typical teenage snark. "You live in the middle of Hill Country. There's no fishing!"

"Who are you?" asked Lucca, pointing at Ty.

"I'll tell you who she is," said J.P. "You are looking at Ty Anzio de Wyck, otherwise known as Dalia's only daughter."

Had I not been firmly tied to the chair, I would have fallen over from the revelation that the girl helping me all this time was none other than the daughter of the Chairman of the Guild. I tried to recall at that moment everything that Ty had told me during our encounters, now that I knew who I was really dealing with, but the mayhem would not relent.

"By your comment, J.P., it seems you expected your nullifier to only reveal one interloper hiding in our midst tonight," said Lucca. "But instead there are two. Who, then, is this?"

"Haven't a clue, Luc. Emma, you've spent the most time with her. Who is she?"

Emma glared at me with even more venom.

"She's a goddamn liar, that's who she is. Well, that's not entirely accurate. She was honest about having a glamour."

"A detail you failed to mention to me in Boston," said J.P. "And if you had, I would have told you never to go near the-"

"Enough," said Dalia, quietly. "That's enough."

"I don't think so," said J.P., rising to his feet again. "In fact, I'm just getting started. I am hereby invoking Article XII of the By-Laws and am moving for a vote of no confidence in Chairman de Wyck's leadership."

"Seconded," someone yelled out.

"Excellent," said J.P. "All those in favor, say-"

"And I," interrupted Dalia, "am invoking Subarticle XVI and am moving for a full inquest, to take place at the next meeting."

"Seconded," said D.C., my First Seat.

"All those in favor," said Dalia.

Four hands went up besides Dalia's, and I would have added mine if it hadn't been tied to the chair. But that left her…

"One short of passing," said J.P. "Which you would have had if our dear friend Gilbert were still with us. But I'm afraid-"

Emma's hand suddenly shot up.

"I vote for an inquest," she said.

"The Ayes have it, then," said Dalia, with a half-smile.

"Emma Nadia Patel, what are you doing?" said J.P., his voice nearly screaming,

"I want to know why."

"That's preposterous," he said. "We know why, it was to-"

"We had our suspicions," said Emma, "and now, in a month, we'll know the truth. And until then, Dalia, I'll be keeping this vial."

"Fine, we'll do it her way," said J.P. "You're only delaying the inevitable, Dalia, you realize that. In a month, you and your daughter's grip on this institution will finally be at an end, and then we all will be free to-"

"If you say so, Mr. Laurel," said Dalia. "But a lot can happen in a month. If no one has any new business for tonight, then I will hear a motion to adjourn."

"What about me?" I said, in my own voice.

J.P. laughed.

"What about you, indeed? Seeing as how Ms. de Wyck was so adamant in rejecting your application to join, she can figure out what to do with you now. I move for adjournment."

"Seconded," said the woman to my left whose name I'd forgotten.

"All those in favor?" asked J.P., waving his cane in the air like a maestro conducting a symphony.

"Aye," said the entire room.

"The Ayes have it."

The room emptied rather quickly until only Dalia, Ty, and I remained. Mother and daughter whispered to each other for several minutes, before Ty finally removed my bonds and gestured for me to take up one of the closer seats.

As I walked toward the head of the table, I glanced down at the now-inactive glamour around my neck, taking a second to carefully remove the chain. The stone made barely a peep when I slammed it against the Orange Table, and if Dalia cared about my outburst, she didn't show it. But Ty's eyes went wide, and I had to stifle a laugh at how ridiculous she looked in Gilbert's clothing.

"Ty tells me your real name is Jen Jacobs," said Dalia quietly, after a few more minutes of silence.

"Yes," I said. "I-"

"Where did you get your token?" she interjected.

"I … umm … it's hard to explain."

"Try."

Fearing that the truth of the matter was less believable, I went with the easy lie.

"In the wall of a parking garage downtown. It was underneath the etching of a-"

"And your friend's? Where did she find that one?"

"You'd have to ask her," I replied. "She wouldn't tell me."

"I see," said Dalia.

"Can I ask you something?" I said. "Why?"

"Why what?" replied Dalia.

"Why did you give me that?" I said, pointing to Jade's glamour.

"I didn't. That was Ty's doing. My daughter has a particular fascination with glamours, although I don't share the same fondness, for several good reasons, many of which you've already witnessed in the last two months."

"You could have warned me what would happen if I wore it too much," I said.

"As a matter of fact, I did," said Ty. "I specifically said–"

"You said nothing about the glamour having a mind of its own. Had I known that, I would have–"

"Enough," said Dalia, and we both stopped. "This is pointless and we have a much bigger problem to deal with now."

"Yes," said Ty. "I suppose you're right. My current count is three. Do you agree?"

"No," said Dalia. "You're off by one. You forgot her."

She pointed at me, and my eyes widened.

"Sorry, what are you talking about?"

"We're tabulating the votes for my mother," said Ty. "With you, it's still not enough."

"But am I even in the Guild? You rejected my application last meeting pending the retrieval of the Dragon's blood. And then J.P. said–"

"Mr. Laurel is an idiot who thinks he has already won," said Dalia. "I've dealt with many such men over the years. He left me to decide whether you can join the Guild because he believes that you and your vote, in the end, will not matter. But I am going to prove him incorrect. Doubly so."

"What does that mean?"

"It means, Ms. Jacobs, that if you pledge yourself to me, I will officially approve your application to fill the Third Seat of the Breuckelen Table."

The offer sounded familiar, and it reminded me of a similar one that Beatrice had given me. Except, it hadn't been an offer, it was a command.

"And if I refuse?"

Dalia laughed.

"No one refuses. No one turns down a Guild Seat. Especially not that one."

"Even if it means I have to sell my soul to you?"

"I'm not the devil," said Dalia. "Far from it. And besides, we need you."

"You need me? For what? To help rubber-stamp another term as Chairman?"

Dalia motioned to Ty, who nodded and nearly sprinted out of the room.

"No, as Ty said, your vote, by itself, will not be enough. The candidates for Chairman do not vote, and so there are ten votes and I will at best get five, if you are so inclined. That leaves it at a tie, and a tie means things are settled via more draconian measures. To avoid that, I need your help to recruit someone over to our side."

Ty returned then, carrying something familiar and unfamiliar.

"Do you know what this is?" asked Dalia, tapping the lid of the plain wooden box that Ty had placed on the table.

"Yes," I said. "It's the box you said we stole. Which we didn't, for the record."

I thought back to my initial meeting with Dalia at the weird midtown office, where she had accused us of kidnapping Frankie, the Guild's Keeper and the wooden box. But it had been exactly the opposite, as Frankie had been kidnapped *by* the Guild, or at least by Doug.

"Noted," said Dalia. "But had we not accused you, you never would have found the Compendium."

"We didn't find the Compendium," I said. "Just the one page we gave you at our first meeting."

"I see," said Dalia. "Is that the story you're sticking to?"

"You think we're lying?"

"Of course I do. You and your friend found the whole Compendium, but other than the page you gave me, it was blank, wasn't it?"

"How … how did you know that?" I said.

"Because," said Dalia, "this box holds the rest."

She gently tipped the box onto its side and a torrent of metal rings spilled forth from inside.

"And do you know what these are?" asked Dalia.

"Yes," I said, deciding that any further lies would be called out immediately. "They're memory rings."

"Correct. When paired with the respective blank page, the memory, or in this case, the entry, can be recovered. And with it, the hundreds of years of Guild knowledge that we lost."

The sinking feeling that had been quietly building in the recesses of my stomach during the meeting finally reach its apex as I realized what it was they wanted me to do.

"I see. And, let me guess, you want me to find out where it is exactly Beatrice hid the Compendium."

"You got it," said Ty, who picked up one of the rings and flipped it into the air. The tiny circlet seemed to take an abnormally long time to return back to the earth and when it did, it rattled around the top of the box before finally settling in place. "You find the Compendium, my mother becomes the triumphant hero, J.P. loses his stupid vote. Everybody wins."

"Seems like I'm the one doing all the work, though," I said, drawing stares from both mother and daughter.

"Well, yes," said Dalia. "You're the ones who didn't give me the

Compendium in the first place. If you and that uppity friend of yours had handed it over a few weeks ago, it would have saved you a lot of trouble now."

"So, what would you like me to do?" I asked. "It's not like we're on speaking terms exactly. I have no idea where she is."

"You have some idea," said Dalia. "That relay mailbox that you and she have been using. I'll admit, it's clever. Figure out a way to reach her."

"Is there anything you don't already know about me?" I said, exasperated at how nearly every secret I possessed had already been taken from me without me even knowing. "Do you want my ATM pin?"

"No, that's quite all right," said Dalia. "I have enough money for several lifetimes."

"But I don't," said Ty, "if you're offering."

Dalia ignored her daughter's quip and gestured for the rolled-up piece of paper that Ty had brought back with the box.

"Do I even want to know what that is?" I asked.

"Only if you want to officially join the Guild," Dalia replied, unfurling the paper and withdrawing a quill pen and a vial of ink from her bag. She dipped the tip of the quill into the ink, made several flourishes across the parchment with it, and then slowly pushed the finished product toward me.

A handful of lines written in faded black ink were set at the top of the mostly empty parchment, contrasted with the insertions that Dalia had just added:

"Now, let it be known, as witnessed by the Chairman, that Jen Jacobs presented the twelfth Alerion token and hereby claimed the Third Seat of the Breuckelen Table for her and her heirs in perpetuity."

Just below that were two signature lines, one for the Chairman, which Dalia had already inked, and a blank one for me.

"Well?" said Dalia. "The ball is in your court."

"The offer I made you at the fountain still stands, by the way," said Ty. "Walk away and you'll wake up with a bank account filled with lots of money and all it will cost is a slightly larger memory wipe. But the whole thing should be relatively painless. And we'll figure out some other way out of this mess."

"No," I said. "Every time I fight through whatever crazy bullshit gets thrown at me, it's always, 'are you sure you want to continue?' The answer then and the answer now is the same: yes. The pen, please."

Dalia handed me the quill, and I signed my name with a flourish.

"There," I said, rolling up the paper and handing it back to Dalia. "Now you can't get rid of me."

She considered me with a discerning look before taking the scroll from my hand

"Good," Dalia said. "Then this meeting is now officially adjourned."

She stood up abruptly, shoving her chair into the New Amsterdam Table, the vibrations sending several piles of the memory rings sliding over the edge and onto the floor.

"Wait, you're not going to clean this up?" Ty called out as Dalia strode out of the room.

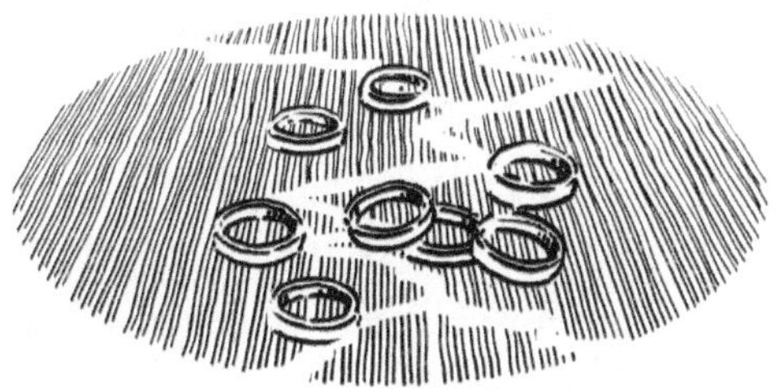

CHAPTER EIGHTEEN

LOW-HANGING FRUIT

*"I am anxious and excited to see how Duff and Lorna have grown.
They had so much potential. I hope they have not wasted it."*

"So," I said to Ty as she scooped up the scattered memory rings, making a scraping sound as she did. "If I'm a goddamn liar, what does that make you?"

The teenager flicked one of the rings at the box from several feet away and it hit the rim and fell onto the floor.

"Depends on your definition of lying," said Ty from underneath the table. After a few seconds, her hand reappeared holding the ring. She briefly considered tossing it back into the box with the others, but instead placed it on one of her fingers.

"How do you figure?"

"I told you that you were being followed by a Guild tracker. And you were, to an extent."

"You forgot the part where that 'tracker' was actually your former crazed apprentice pretending to be you! Not to mention the fact that you were also Gilbert this whole time and that you-"

"I've always been straight with you, Jen. I gave you the glamour so you could hide from Doug. I warned you not to overuse the glamour, but you did anyway. And I would have helped you deactivate it if J.P. hadn't activated that damn nullifier."

"So this is my fault, then?"

"Probably. I don't know. You probably broke the thing now, so who cares?"

"Where did you get it?" I asked. "And yours? From what the clerk at the Boston Night Market told me, these aren't exactly your run-of-the-mill magical jewelry."

"They're not. As to where I got them, that's a story from another time. Suffice it to say, I'm beginning to think they are more trouble than they're worth."

"That's an understatement. I didn't think I was ever going to be me again. Maybe I should send J.P. a thank you note."

"You can thank him after you've found Beatrice and the Compendium," said Ty. "But don't worry, I will help you."

"Oh, great. Because your help has been so useful as of late."

"I'll pretend I didn't hear that. Besides, it's not just me who's going to be helping you. You've got nearly half the Guild at your disposal as well. They'll be more than willing to assist, seeing as how they will stand to lose a lot if Dalia loses the Chairmanship. As do I."

"How long have you pretended to be him?" I asked. Now that I knew the truth, that there was no Gilbert, I wondered if the fear that Beatrice had felt had come from Ty's excellent acting or maybe this current front was a facade, and deep down, she was a creepy psycho-path just like Doug.

"Too long," said Ty. "The last holder of the New Amsterdam Second Seat died with no issue and no will. Under the bylaws, the token should have reverted to the Guild, to be issued to a worthy individual who passed the Gauntlet. But my mother had a different idea."

"Let me guess," I said. "She created a fake long-list nephew who just happened to be named Gilbert."

"Almost. She was going to find someone to be a puppet. It was my idea to use the glamour, to take the Seat for myself. I didn't think she would go for it. After all, with enough money, she could persuade anyone to do anything she wanted. Me, on the other hand…"

"…revived a crazy stalker and tried to rehabilitate him by locking him up for years. Yeah, can't see why your mother didn't think you were right for the Seat."

"In my defense, it sounded better on paper. And I should have realized that splitting a person into two glamour stones would never be as robust as a single gem. Anyway, we're getting off course here. You only have a month to track down Beatrice. I'd get moving, if I were you."

My mind had nearly cracked from the whirlwind of the past 48 hours, and if I was forced to begin yet another errand not of my choosing, I was going to completely lose it.

"Thanks for the tip, but I'm taking a mental health day. There's just something about letting a disembodied gemstone use me as its puppet that has put me all out of sorts."

I walked back to the Orange Table where I had deposited the glamour and gingerly picked it up. There was no way in hell I was putting this thing back on, and the bare wooden desk in my office in the north tower that only I could unlock needed a nice decoration.

"And besides," I said, turning back to Ty, "what about all your friends who were lining up to help me a minute ago?"

"They still will. I just need a day or two to set them straight. After all, they really only knew me as Gilbert. Go grab the low-hanging fruit, and I'll see who's ready to talk by Thursday."

I spent all of Tuesday either asleep or drunk. Sometimes both at the same time. On Wednesday morning, I woke with a splitting headache that unfortunately lingered until the mid-afternoon, as I was still too afraid to take any of the vitality serum that Jade had stashed in my bathroom.

The low-hanging fruit took most of the day and the next to locate and determine it was rotten. I hit Beatrice's known locations: her downtown apartment, our former office in the Chrysler Building, our other former office off the south shore of Long Island, and finally Beatrice's Madison Avenue apartment. I saved that one for last, not wanting to confirm what I'd already suspected: that Beatrice had even abandoned her son to escape the Guild's clutches.

With a fancy (and rather heavy) bouquet of flowers in tow, I arrived in the lobby of her building at 6 p.m. on Thursday. One smiling doorman in a burgundy hat and jacket pushed the revolving door for me, and then another greeted me at the fancy desk just inside.

I set the vase down with a thud on top of the marble counter, my forearms nearly jelly.

"That's quite an arrangement," said the doorman. "Who's it going to?"

"Taylor, Apartment 31C."

The smile on the man's face vanished in an instant.

"Sorry, I think you have the wrong building."

"Are you sure? The order's for Beatrice Taylor. It's from her husband, Garrett and their son, Jack-Jack. A belated Mother's Day bouquet I was told."

"They don't live here. So please go." It was more of a command than a request, so I complied and retreated to the revolving door with the vase, where the first doorman was now also glaring at me.

"You can leave the flowers if you want," he said. "I'm sure my wife would love them."

I resisted the urge to tip the vase over and let the water slowly spread all over the fancy blue marble floor and instead set it down gently before showing myself out.

The rest of the night I spent huddled over my laptop at home, trying to find some clue online as to where Beatrice had gone. Their apartment hadn't been sold, Garrett's LinkedIn profile still showed him at the same job, and she had done nothing to merit a mention on Page Six.

I texted Ty at 11 p.m. to report my failures and was surprised when she responded within a few seconds.

"Dont worry, Clouser is going to help us. We're meeting him tomorrow morning."

"Whos that again?" I replied.

"First Seat of the Pavonia Table. Hated Emma's dad and hates J.P. So I was almost positive he would be willing to talk."

"Great. When/where?"

"9 a.m. Philz Coffee. Navy Yard."

"Oh. Didn't know there was a Philz in NYC yet."

"There isn't. It's the one in D.C."

"What? Y the hell do we have 2 go all the way down there."

"Because that's where Hugo lives. He's the Guild's man in Washington."

Despite the early hour, the 6 a.m. Acela was packed to the brim, and I walked nearly the length of the car, my overnight bag in hand, before I found a pair of empty seats together. I was beginning to think that Ty had missed the train entirely, but she finally appeared in her familiar jacket as we pulled away from Metropark Station.

"Don't talk to me until Baltimore," she said as she sat down in a huff. "Last time I had to get up this early, it was the morning of the 9th grade English Regents exam."

"You were the one who scheduled the meeting! And I didn't think you actually went to school."

"What did I just say?"

Ty pulled an eye mask from her jacket pocket, snapped it around her head, and slumped down on the tray table attached to the seat in front of her. Well, at least this train ride was an hour shorter than the one up to Boston.

I did as instructed and didn't say a word to Ty until we arrived at Baltimore, even though she had woken up at Wilmington.

"OK," said Ty, when we were 20 minutes away from Union Station. "Do you know what you're going to ask Hugo first?"

"What do you mean, what am I going to ask him first? I don't even know why we're seeing him in the first place!"

Ty rolled her eyes.

"I thought you said you went through the low-hanging fruit. Don't tell me you missed the part where your ex-partner got served with divorce papers and then a restraining order on top of that after she tried to kidnap her own kid?"

"I … umm … no, I did not hear about either of those. How did you know?"

I could see Beatrice divorcing Garrett. I mean, I was surprised she hadn't done so years ago. But him getting the drop on her?

"The police blotter is your friend in times of need. Unfortunately, by the next day, Beatrice had skipped bail and evidently town. The trail went cold after that because everything's under seal, but I'm hoping Clouser will get us back on track."

"How's he going to do that?"

"You'll see. Come on, we're almost there. I don't want to wait in the horrid cab line."

Ty marched us up the length of the train until we were just outside the first class car. Then, when the doors opened, she bolted out onto the platform, and by the time I caught up with her after running through the massive marble lobby, she was already climbing into the back of a cab.

"8:45," she said after we had cleared the traffic circle in front of the station. "Should get there right on time."

"Why the rush? I thought he wanted to help us. Who cares if we're a few minutes late? We did just bust our butts to get down the Acela corridor at the crack of dawn."

"Because," said Ty. "Hugo is one of those people who schedules his day down to the quarter-second. He probably has a 10 a.m. somewhere on Capitol Hill with a senior staffer, then lunch at Charlie Palmer with a senator or two, and then who knows what in the afternoon? Sometimes I think he likes his above-ground job more than being in the Guild."

We pulled up to Philz at exactly 8:57, and Ty threw a wad of cash at our driver before bolting out the cab door, leaving me to take our luggage. Inside, a line threaded its way toward a row of seven baristas, who were efficiently doling individual pour-overs to the mix of government workers and hipsters.

"Two iced mint mojitos, please," said Ty when we made it to the front.

"Make it three," said a voice behind us, and I turned around to find none other than Gilbert.

CHAPTER NINETEEN

SAUSAGE MAKING

"At the appointed hour, they appeared. Duff was quiet and reserved, but Lorna was very outgoing and friendly. They have come a far way from the street urchins that Rita found."

oth bags I was carrying landed with a thud on the floor, and I turned white as a ghost at seeing the specter of that man before me. It couldn't be Doug. I had seen Beatrice shatter his body into a hundred stone pieces. And the only other bearer of that awful visage was the person standing right next to me.

Thankfully, Ty steadied my arm slightly and nudged me forward.

"Hello, Hugo," she said. "Did you at least wait until you left the Guild Hall before you turned that thing on?"

"Oh, absolutely not," said Hugo in that familiar and chilling voice.

He pulled out the chain from underneath his bright white collared shirt and smiled. "I've always been fascinated with that rather forbidden branch of alchemy, and apparently you have too, so I activated up in my office right then and there."

We joined him at the table and waited in silence until our drinks were ready. Hugo promptly withdrew a tiny flask from his suit jacket pocket and added a small nip of whatever was inside, before nearly gulping the entire cup down in one sip.

"Hoo. That'll get me through the rest of the morning. Where was I? Oh, right. The glamour. Haven't really turned it off since. This will be extremely helpful in my day-to-day down here."

Ty frowned.

"I told you not to-"

"I know what you told me, but I'm my own man. I can figure these things out as I go. Besides, you are one to talk. How long did you spend as him?"

"Too long," said Ty. "And honestly, I'm glad to be rid of him. It. There's a danger there that will swallow you up whole if you're not careful. Ask Jen here. She knows firsthand."

"Oh, that's right," said Hugo, a grin stretching across his face that reminded too much of the maniacal look that Doug had given us just before he revealed his true self. "You have one too. Can't say I prefer this current version of you. I liked you better with the red hair and long legs."

"Gross," said Ty. "Jen is the reason we're here this morning. She needs help tracking someone down."

"Do you now? You've bottomed out all leads, and so your path has led you here?"

"Not exactly," I said. "But we don't have much time. This woman is the key to everything."

I pulled up a picture of Beatrice on my phone and placed it on the table.

"Now *her* I like," said Hugo. "She still alive?"

"Presumably," I said. "But we haven't seen her in two months. And a lot's happened since then."

"Such as?" asked Hugo.

"Her husband served her with divorce papers. Then she took her kid, and then she promptly got arrested and hit with a restraining order. After that, we're not sure."

"Hmm," said Hugo. "You're fortunate that she escalated things. There are likely court records and maybe some hearing transcripts. If you sift through those, you'll probably find a lead or two that will set you on the right path. Hardly the sort of thing you need my help for."

"If this was all so easy, then why are we here?" I asked.

"Did Ty not tell you what it is I do?" asked Hugo.

"She said you were the Guild's man in Washington."

"Yes, that's true, but that makes it sound so pedestrian. Everyone has their 'man in Washington.' Or, err, woman. And then there was that one time a defense contractor hired a 15-year-old hacker, but that didn't go so well. What I am is something else."

"And that is?"

"I'm the Guild's Tracker."

I shot a stern look at Ty.

"I thought you made up the whole damn thing about there being a 'Guild tracker' after me!"

Ty shrugged her shoulders.

"What gave you that impression?"

"Because you said … ugh, has anything you've told me been true?"

"Yes," she said. "And no. Also, if you'd listened carefully, you'll have noticed that he said Tracker with a capital T, whereas I did not."

"It's too early for that, and especially now that-"

"If you don't mind," said Hugo. "I didn't trek all the way down to Southwest to listen to you two squabble like a bunch of uptight sorority sisters. Now, if you want my help, it will have to be between meetings, as I'm very busy today."

"We don't have time for that," Ty said. "In less than a month-"

"Let me make one thing clear to both of you: I don't like being played for a damn fool. Especially by someone I thought I respected. Who now doesn't even really exist. So I will be dictating the terms of how and when I provide my assistance for whatever it is you two are trying to do, or else next month you may find that my vote is firmly with the other camp."

"Fine," said Ty. "I'll move our tickets back to the 7 p.m. Acela. Are you happy?"

"Oh, I'm always happy," said Hugo. "Now, did either of you bring your cloaks? The former redhead here I can spin as my new temp, although it would have been easier if you brought the glamour. However, you, Ms. Anzio, will need to stay hidden. Unless, of course, I decide to lend you your old disguise for a few hours."

"No, that's quite alright," said Ty. "Besides, he looks better on you than he ever did on me."

"If you say so," said Hugo. "Then, if you wouldn't mind suiting up, we can be on our way."

"And that's why this one change here will really streamline the allocation of some much needed funds for retired renaissance fair knights in need," said the real Hugo Clouser. Compared to Gilbert, Hugo lacked any sort of menace, other than the constant feeling I had that he wanted to sleep with me.

I resisted the urge to roll my eyes at the 20 minutes of bullshit I had just heard, but we were seated three across in a tiny booth in the lobby of a Marriott near MetroCenter, and that didn't leave much room for anything.

"I'll see what I can do," said the tall woman with mousy hair and tortoiseshell glasses opposite the booth from us. She was the junior staffer for a Senator on the Special Committee on Aging, and by the looks of her, it was fairly obvious how she had got her position.

"Much appreciated," said Hugo. "My new assistant Jen here can give you a copy of the proposed changes."

Taking my cue, I pulled the twenty printed sheets of paper out of the portfolio folder Hugo had given me before we arrived and slid them across the table, careful not to accidentally elbow the now-invisible Ty, who was uncomfortably wedged in between two of us.

"Thanks," said the staffer. "Same time next week?"

"You can count on it," said Hugo. "I'll bring the gin."

The staffer slid out of the booth, only for her heel to knock into Ty's ankle, causing her to yelp uncontrollably.

"I'm so sorry!" I said. "Didn't mean to…"

"It's fine," said the woman. "Honestly, Hugo, if you didn't make us sit in this cramped booth in tourist central all the time. Do you know Jack buys me dinner at CP at least twice a quarter? Not to mention-"

"There's a lot I could mention," said Hugo, smiling, as the staffer turned beet red. "But unlike some of my other colleagues, I prefer the discretion that this fine establishment provides. And plus, where else do they let you bring in your booze without anyone batting an eye?"

We all waited in silence for a few minutes until Ms. Long Legs was out of sight, and then Ty de-cloaked on the opposite side of the booth.

"Would you mind telling me why we spent the last three hours trudging from one boring meeting to the next?" asked Ty, who bent down to rub her ankle again. "These Hill creatures all seem utterly uninterested in what you're selling, even if you are sleeping with them."

"As they should be," said Hugo. "I find a lack of engagement with the subject matter the key to my success. If I came in here and at the meeting at Kramers, and during the chat in the Dupont Underground with all the bells and whistles, do you think they all would have agreed to allocate $100 million in funding for a dozen different public works, studies, research grants, and investigations? All of which are funneled back into the Guild's coffers?"

"What are you talking about?" I said. "You didn't do any of that!"

"Yes, I did. Through various subcommittees, bureaus, and the like, funds will be allocated, task forces will be created, ad hoc planning commissions will materialize, all with a singular purpose that they're not even aware of. Look, it's all a bit technical," said Hugo. "But the important thing is that the Guild's financial future in the above world is secure for another ten years and I can finally leave this cesspool."

"You did all that today?" I asked. "Three coffees and an afternoon tea and now Dalia is swimming in lucre until 2030?"

"Don't be ridiculous. I've been working on this for the entire session. And all of the session before that. And the one before that. Tracking down opportunities to stuff money where no one will find it, tracking down backwater agencies of our delightfully bloated federal bureaucracy where no one will miss a dollar or two million. Getting shit done is hard and slow work, ladies. Which is why I'm not too keen on what J.P. is selling. Speaking of, did you know he was following you?"

I craned my neck over the top of the booth, but the Texan's stupid cowboy hat was nowhere in sight.

"That's news to me," said Ty. "Are you sure he's not following you?"

"Also a possibility," said Hugo, pulling out his pocket watch. "He thinks I'm firmly in your camp. And knows I'll have the inside track on where the votes stand. So before he sidles in here on his charm offensive, I'll get you started on your side quest. Now, let's see it."

"See what?" I asked. "I already showed you her picture."

"Yes, and I'm already thinking about whether you should pass along my number when you find her. I love a fresh divorcee every now and again."

"Is he always this gross?" I said to Ty, and she nodded.

"Anyway, my tracking requires some physical piece of her. A hair, skin follicles, eyelashes, or a finger if you have one. Then I can get to work and you can get on with whatever it is you need her for."

"I ... I don't have any of that. Like I said, she's long gone, and I already looked for any trace of her at her last known whereabouts."

"I see," said Hugo. "Well, even my talents have a limit. I can't track a ghost, I'm afraid, so unless you've got an envelope from a letter she sent you or-"

"Wait, that's it," I said. "I do have something of hers."

"Excellent," said Hugo. "What is it?"

"Her memories."

RING OF TRUTH

"I introduced myself as a friend of the late Ms. van Asch and reveal the requirements to receive their inheritance: they have one week to extract the contents of a certain box hidden inside Gracie Mansion."

The girl in front of me was nervous. That much I could tell from her shaking arms and her bugged-out eyes.

"I made the last one into a powder, so it would last longer and you wouldn't think I was an addict by asking for more so soon," she said.

This part of the memory was new, as the last time I had relived this encounter, I was half asleep on the train.

"Bought a mortar and pestle at Goodwill," she continued. "Snorted a little bit to see what would happen and passed out. Woke up, did a little more, tried to finish a paper. Then it wore off again. But not before a thought occurred to me. I needed to inject it. So I went down to the health center, got into the exam room, and then took off with some syringes and tourniquets before the nurse came in. That did the trick. But I only had a little left, so I needed to find you."

She pointed a finger at me and it felt like I was in the apartment with her and not Beatrice, which was enough to jolt me back into the present.

But the memories I had inadvertently siphoned from Beatrice during our initial encounter at the party almost a year ago were as fresh in my mind as if they had occurred yesterday. Except that Kate O'Laughlin had been dead three years, after Beatrice had killed her in some unknown manner that left no one the wiser. I reflected on these new revelations and wondered what had happened to the poor girl. Were the focus buffs really that powerful that she had descended into a crazed mania?

"A memory," said Hugo, his brow furrowed. "It's unorthodox, but I think it will do the trick. The only difficulty is getting it out of that head of yours. I assume a lobotomy is out of the question?"

I rolled my eyes.

"Fine, but that leaves nemosyne. And that's not something you find in your average Night Market outpost."

"Nemosyne?"

"Colloquially referred to as memory ink. You write down the memory onto the page and when the ink dries, the memory is siphoned out of your head. Then it can be reformed into something more suitable for the tracking."

"Oh," I said. I was quite familiar with nemosyne, only in the reverse fashion, as my head also held two of Rita van Asch's memories from two hundred years ago. "And I suppose you're about to tell me that raw nemosyne hasn't been seen in a hundred years?"

"No," said Ty curtly. "In fact, until a few weeks ago, there was coincidentally quite a plentiful supply at a certain pigment library up in Boston. But you and Ms. Patel conveniently burned the whole damn collection, so now we need to go to plan B."

"Which is what, exactly?" I asked. "Please don't tell me I have to break into yet another museum."

"Not a museum," said Hugo. "A mansion."

"Whose mansion?"

"Your First Chair," said Ty. "D.C."

"To be more accurate, it's not really a mansion," said Hugo. "It's more of a multi-story townhouse that spans an entire block in a tony Brooklyn neighborhood. But yes, a mansion in city terms."

"So, I'm just supposed to break into D.C.'s house, locate his secret stash of alchemic treats, and make off with the nemosyne?"

"If you want to find that blonde," said Hugo. "Then that sums it up pretty succinctly. Or you could ask him for some. Though I doubt he'd give you more than a single letter's worth."

"Whose side is he on?" I asked Ty point blank.

"Not ours," she replied curtly. "But not J.P.'s either. So if you go down this path, it should be without leaving a trace that you were there."

"Well, that's just fantastic," I said, nearly laughing. "It's a never-ending escalating gauntlet of shit. It wasn't enough that I spent two months stalking a payphone at three in the morning every day. It wasn't enough that I nearly died in a horrible explosion or almost got my hand charred by some hellish fire. But now it's up to little ol' me to steal yet another magic totem, so I can single-handedly solve all the Guild's problems! And do it quietly, if you wouldn't mind. Well, I do mind! I'm done."

Ty and Hugo looked at each other as if I were the crazy one. But

I had finally reached my breaking point, and it was so satisfying to unload everything after so many months of agita, stress, anxiety, and helplessness.

"Been practicing that speech, haven't you?" asked Hugo. "Felt a little rushed. Anyhoo, I've said my piece and my offer stands, if you get over your pity party. Now, if you don't mind, I need to go freshen up before my evening drinks with a particularly delightful senior staffer from New Mexico. And avoid J.P. while I'm at it. Ty knows where to find me. It's been a pleasure, ladies."

Hugo nearly sprinted out of the lobby, leaving me alone with the now-moody teenager.

"Before you launch into another tirade, let me ask you something," said Ty, her voice barely above a whisper. "Why did you decline my offer at the fountain and again the other day?"

"What do you mean?"

"I offered you untold wealth and the ability to enjoy it without the burden of what you now know. Yet you refused and instead chose to join the Guild. Why?"

Her query was as pointed as *White Hilt*. I tried to recall what was going through my head during that fateful evening. The shock of Beatrice's token exploding in the water and her immediate flight had jolted my brain. Had I been asked the same question the next morning, I wasn't sure I would have given the same answer.

"I … I didn't think I had a choice. That you wouldn't just let me walk away scot-free. That I had to see things to through, to find out why my mom hid the gold token in my locket."

"I see," said Ty. "I guess that makes sense. We haven't given you or Beatrice any reason to trust us, have we?"

"No, you haven't. And why'd you want to kill Beatrice so badly, anyway? Was she really that much of a threat? I mean, it was more understandable when I thought Gilbert was real, but you're just a kid."

Ty took a swig of the half-empty glass of gin that Hugo had left and placed the now empty glass upside down on the table with a decided thud.

"Correction," I said. "A kid who has a drinking problem."

"I'm not a kid," said Ty. "Growing up with Dalia as my mother erased any childhood rather quickly."

"Sorry," I said. "Couldn't your mom have found someone else for her political machinations?"

"It's not that simple. Do you even know why we exist? You don't, do you? Well, I'll tell you. The Guild exists because there is magic out there in the world and it is not to be trifled with. It is ancient and it is powerful and it is fleeting and we are the ones who ensure that there is still magic left after we are gone, that the heirs to our Seats and their heirs and so on will still have something extraordinary left to wield. Because were it not for our efforts, all magic in this country would have been exhausted at least a hundred years ago, if not more. And with all the schemers out there, trying to make a play from what's left, there is nothing thicker than blood."

I turned over Ty's words in my head to make sense of them and realized I couldn't. Maybe because I had spent so long chasing down the Guild as if just belonging was enough and I hadn't considered what joining the Guild actually meant. Or maybe because something didn't quite add up.

"But, isn't the Guild the one who created the Quests in the first place? How does unleashing the Quests and the Raids on the city align with preserving magic?"

"Simple. Do you know how many people besides you have actually worked their way up and learned the truth about what we are doing?"

"No."

Ty held up her index finger and wagged it at me.

"One. And even she took a shortcut. After a certain number of months or years spent grinding away chasing those elusive gold tokens, most of the people who are lucky enough to have found the Quest Board either give up due to boredom, insanity, or death. Mostly the first one, but sometimes the latter two. But we're getting off track here. You find yourself in rarified company, Jen, and I don't think you realize the opportunity you've stumbled upon. Once this nuisance with J.P. gets resolved, then you'll really see what being in the Guild is all about and why you'd be a fool to walk away now."

"Everyone keeps saying that, but so far, all that's gotten is me is one missing ex-partner, one former partner with a charred hand who probably wants to kill me with said hand, and one semi-sentient magic stone who seems set on taking over my body. Tell me, when does the good part actually start?"

"Sooner than you think," said Ty. "You won't be going into D.C.'s townhouse empty-handed. I promised you after your initiation that you'd be properly equipped, and now you will be. So get over yourself, focus on the task at hand, and help us put this insurgency to bed."

"Fine," I said. "But I hope you have something good in your bag of tricks. I don't feel like barely surviving a five-alarm fire again."

"No tricks, just good ol' fashioned magic. But you'll see soon enough. Anyway, I'm going to take a stroll around Capitol Hill in my cloak, to see if I can catch any pols saying something awful. I'll see you at the station."

Ty slid out of the booth and nearly fell onto the floor, the effects of the gin on her teenage physique clearly unexpected. She regained her composure and strode out of the lobby before I could say anything. I remained at the booth for about 20 minutes, half hoping to run into J.P., to see if he had a more enticing offer up his sleeve than this nigh impossible Quest I had been tasked with. But when he failed to materialize, I resigned myself to another month of non-stop stress and dread, and began the long walk back to Union Station with my overnight bag slung around my shoulder.

I didn't get very far, though, because no sooner had I exited the hotel than I collied with the last person I was expecting to see: Duncan.

MEET-CUTE

"The box was left behind when Gracie was forced to sell his estate. A pity that he forgot how to unlock it, as it would have perhaps saved him from financial ruin. I sent the children off and hoped for the best."

"**W**hat the fuck are you doing here, Duncan?" I said without thinking as I stared at my ex-boyfriend. His hair was a far cry from its purposeful messiness, he had about two weeks worth of stubble on his face, and I couldn't tell if the yellow t-shirt he was wearing was like that when he bought it or whether he just hadn't taken it off yet this month.

"Jen," he said, as if he was a middle schooler caught looking at an old Hustler by his mom. "Umm, hi."

"Hi to you too. Now, I'll ask again, what the fuck are you doing here? This isn't Sun Valley or TC Disrupt or that random meetup in

Hell's Kitchen you dragged me to our on our third date. So I have to imagine that you are here because you are following me."

Duncan stared at me as I felt a wave of anger wash over me that somehow paled in comparison to the one that had manifested 20 minutes ago. Because for all the shit that the Guild had put me through, this was the man who had cheated on me, proposed to me, and likely had gotten me fired from my job. The shock of me catching him off guard finally wore off and suddenly his entire demeanor changed, as he went on the offensive.

"What did you do to me?" he asked.

"What are you talking about?" I replied. I knew damn well what I did to him, having erased the same five minutes of our last dinner together so I could get him to admit that he was cheating on me.

"I think I figured it out for myself, but I want to hear it from you."

"Hear what?" I said. "How mad I am that you got me fired? I don't have a lot of time before I head back to New York, but I promise I'll listen to whatever you bullshit have to say, as long as it takes less than 30 seconds."

"Sure you will, right before you wipe my memory again."

"Wh-what are you talking about?"

"I've been busy the last few months, but I finally caught on to you."

Duncan fished something out of the pair of ratty jeans he was wearing and shoved it in my face. I instinctively shut my eyes, but when I opened them again, all that greeted me was Duncan's phone.

With the Quest Board open on it.

"What is that, another video game company you invested in because RPGLab turned out to be a bust?"

"It's not a bust, but no."

Duncan pulled the phone back, before tapping on it a few times and showing it to me again.

My eyes went wide as I looked at the profile screen of UnDunc, who I assumed was Duncan. He was at level 31, which seemed impossible.

"Looks familiar, doesn't it?" he said. "You were always a terrible liar, Jen, so just stop the act and maybe we can have a real conversation for once."

"What if I say yes? And that I know exactly what that is? Then what?"

"Then what? Then you can start by telling me what you did to me during that dinner. Was it cadmonium? That's what I thought at first, but it turns out that it only makes the person experience time so fast that it seems like no time has passed at all. Or how about hyphrosia? That was somewhat promising, but after some experimentation on one of my Cathay Lounge girls, the only thing it does is make the subject fall asleep immediately and wake up a minute later. Maybe it was pure Wood's metal. But that's been hard to find since the 50s. And then finally, it hit me: a bathtub gin version of letherium."

I tried my best not to let my jaw figuratively drop down past my knees. How did he know about any of this from finding an invite to the Quest Board and spending the last three months grinding non-stop? Even I hadn't heard of any of the prima materia he rattled off like they were old hand.

"I'll tell you what I did," I said, after several awkward moments of silence. "But not here. Not out in the open."

"No, we're doing this here and now. Because if we don't, then I might not remember that I found you."

"What do you mean?"

Duncan put his phone away and then slowly walked over to one of the benches abutting the hotel entrance. He hardly looked like the confident, suave, and ruggedly handsome guy who had strolled into my office one random afternoon what felt like so many years ago. Instead, he looked like Kate had the night of the encounter I had just relived. Was all this because of me?

I joined him on the bench, and he retrieved a small spiral notebook with a pen lodged through the metal loops from his pants pocket. He flipped through the worn pages quickly until he reached a blank one toward the end and began scribbling furiously for several minutes. Satisfied, he stowed the notebook and turned to face me.

"That one I started yesterday and thankfully, no episodes so far. It took me a few weeks to realize what was happening. I would be out having drinks with some of our founders, when suddenly things would skip forward a few seconds. Almost as if someone had hit fast forward in my brain. Or I'd blink and be back in my apartment, brushing my teeth. At first I thought I was just drinking too much. God knows how much alcohol I've consumed in the service of my job. But then it started occurring at all hours of the day. Lost minutes here, lost minutes there. Finally, I couldn't take it anymore and told Jeff I needed some time off, that I was creeping toward burnout. He gave me a few weeks, and I flew back to New York at the end of March."

"Why didn't you reach out to me then?" I asked.

"I didn't think it had anything to do with you. It wasn't until I got an email from Jeff a few days after I landed I heard you had gotten fired and that's when I finally remembered how weird our dinner had been."

"Yeah, and thanks again for that."

"That wasn't my doing, Jen. But I know you had something to do with this," he said, gesturing to his head.

"Yes, you keep saying that. But all I see is a man who cracked under the pressure of his job, who invented a fantasy about a real-life video game after spending too much time flirting with every female engineer he came across."

"You know what, Jen? Fuck you. You think you're so sweet and innocent, but I know the truth, that deep down, you-"

Duncan's jaw suddenly went slack and his eyes stared off into space, just like at dinner that night. I waved my hand in front of his face cautiously, waiting for him to come to, a pit forming in my stomach. Finally, after another 30 seconds, the look of recognition reappeared in his visage, and he nearly fell backward off the bench.

"Jen, I, umm. One second."

He pulled out the notebook again and perused his notes from just a little while ago, and when he looked up at me again, his demeanor was noticeably calmer.

"How much did I lose this time?" he asked.

I paused for a moment to consider how to respond. Could I take advantage of the flaw in Duncan's notebook "system" and make him think that we had spent hours together and hashed out our differences? Or was this just a test, and in reality he had written the timestamp at the end of every entry and knew exactly how long he had been "out."

"What's the last thing you actually remember?" I said.

"I was on the train, one car away from you, earlier this morning. I hadn't initially planned on following you down to DC. It was too big a risk, straying that far from home. But I chickened out before your trip to Boston and concluded that if I didn't go after you now, you might never come back."

"I see. So you've lost almost the entire day. I can't imagine how that must feel."

"No, you can't," said Duncan. "But you can help me."

"How so?"

"You can cut the act, admit what you did, and help me find a cure."

I looked at the man Duncan had become, with his memory note-books and his memory blackouts, and I felt pity for him and guilt for what I had unintentionally done. But I didn't have the time or the mental space or the knowledge to help him. And I suspect Beatrice didn't either, if I could ever find her. She had been using the serum on her husband and her kid for who knows how long and had never mentioned anything like what Duncan was now experiencing. Something else had to be going on and I was determined to figure out what.

"I admit it," I said. "At our last dinner. I did something to your memory."

Duncan's eyes widened at my admission, and he quickly began writing down what I was saying in his notebook, convinced that any moment he would lose this knowledge forever.

"Why?"

"Because I wanted to. Because I thought you were cheating on me and I was right. Because I needed to know if our entire relationship had been a lie or only part of it. Because I deserved to know the truth."

I finished and let Duncan finish his live transcription, secretly hoping that this memory would give out and I could swipe the page he just wrote. But after a few more seconds, he stowed his notebook away, and I silently cursed my bad luck.

"I hope it was worth it," he said. "I hope it was worth destroying my life to find out that your long-distance boyfriend was sleeping around. Of course I was! I thought it was pretty obvious."

"Then why the hell did you ask me to move to Hong Kong? To mess with my head? To laugh when I said yes and then you could say you were only joking? And then your whole storming out of the hotel room after I got mad that you were giving me an ultimatum?"

"You want the truth?" he said, the temperature in his voice rising.

"I think I'm entitled to it. If you want my help."

"Fine," said Duncan. "But you're not going to like it. And if I tell you, you still have to help me. Deal?"

"I don't like a lot about you, so how much worse could it be?"

"That depends. Do you care I tried to get you to break up with me so that I could get equity in RPGLab?"

"Excuse me?"

"If I ended the relationship, Jeff wouldn't have staked me. He didn't want me dumping you right away, and you getting pissed at me and the fund and somehow sabotaging the investment."

"What???"

I couldn't believe what I was hearing. Was he really that maniacal that he had resorted to all these mind games just to get me to end things?

"So I took extra weeks in Hong Kong, I missed our daily calls on purpose, I-"

"You thought I needed help getting dressed to go to a party."

Duncan's head jerked up in surprise and I realized too late that I should have kept that secret to myself.

"What ... how ... how did you know that?"

I pursed my lips and paused for a few moments, as if I was about to read his thoughts again like I had at his boss's party so many moons ago.

"Whatever you think you've learned about alchemy, yes that's what it's called if you didn't know, I know more. Much more. But I'm sorry, I interrupted your little confession. Please continue."

"I will. But afterward you'll tell me how you did it."

"We'll see how I feel about you then."

And if you still remember this conversation, I said to myself.

"None of those things worked," he continued. "You seemed perfectly content with our arrangement, but after Jeff's party, I took some extra time away to work out an even better plan."

"The proposal," I said, the solution to the puzzle of Duncan's behavior last winter suddenly becoming apparent.

"Yep. I thought it was the perfect out. I knew there was no way you were going to say yes. But what woman could be mad at their boyfriend for wanting to marry her? So once you had some time to think things over, I figured it was as good as over. Little did I know who I was dealing with! I doubled down during New Year's and thankfully your loner instinct kicked in hard, so I was able to make you look like the bad guy. And then everything was all set for our rendezvous in Paris. But you fucked that up, too. Did that have anything to do with what's going on now with Lisa and Stacy? Or did you do that afterward?"

"What are you talking about?"

Duncan shook his head, but I remembered what the woman at the Night Market had said all too well. I just hadn't wanted to believe it the other day.

"Unbelievable. You don't even care, do you? They were your friends! And you made them forget you completely for whatever reason."

"I ... I didn't mean for it to happen," I stammered. "It was an accident. It was only supposed to erase what they remembered me doing to them at the Met."

"Oh, only that? Well, why didn't you say so? That makes it all better! You think I have it bad, but do you want to know what is happening to them?"

"I know what is happening."

"OK good. So what are you going to do about it?"

"I ... I don't know."

"You don't know? You knew this whole time and yet you're gallivanting up and down the East Coast doing nothing?"

"I found out literally three days ago! It's not like I've been calling them on the phone every night to shoot the shit. They. Don't. Know. Who. I. Am. I thought it was just best if I left them alone, for now. I'm trying to-"

"You're trying to what, save your own head while we all lose ours? That's fucking great, Jen. I wish you good luck in your Ques-"

As Duncan's mind hit reset again, I again contemplated stealing his notebook and redoing this entire conversation over in a less confrontational manner. Or just fleeing and hoping he wouldn't find me again. But running away from him and Lisa and Stacy had only brought their problems right to my doorstep, when they were the last things I needed. If I couldn't shake him, then I could at least use him to my advantage.

It took almost five minutes before Duncan came to again and when he did, it was with the same startled reaction as before.

"How much did I lose this time?" he asked.

"Oh, only about 10 seconds," I said, with a smile. "Don't worry, you got it all down in your notebook."

CHAPTER TWENTY-TWO

INKED BONDS

"A week has passed and the children returned to me, box in hand, and smiles on their faces. They placed it on the table in my expansive study, and Lorna opened the lid."

"I don't like it," said Ty in the Acela lounge a few hours later. Duncan had excused himself to go to the bathroom, so I finally had a minute to explain my new plan.

"What's not to like? He provides us with the ability to walk right up to D.C.'s front door and ask for help. No breaking and entering. No subterfuge."

"Yeah and you're assuming that what you need to fix Boytoy's memory is the same thing as nemosyne. So even if your plan succeeds, you'll still fail."

"That's where you're wrong," I said, tearing open the free bag of trail mix I had grabbed on the way in. "We're not asking for the nemosyne. Just some of the raw ingredients. You'll go look through the Guild library to find out what else we need and figure out where we can get it. Ugh, this is disgusting. Why did I try this?"

"Because you never think two steps ahead," said Ty. "Or really one. Even I know you shouldn't eat the free train lounge food. Your second wrong assumption of the afternoon is that the raw ingredients of nemosyne are also the same as what you need to cure Duncan. They're not!"

"And I never thought they were. But with the ingredients in hand, we'll be in a much stronger position to barter."

"With whom?"

"With the Van Asch Corporation."

Ty looked at me like a kid who just found out Santa Claus wasn't real.

"You can't be serious. That's who you think we're better off dealing with head-on than D.C.? My mom barely talks to them anymore. And for good reason. They've cornered the market on alkahest and a dozen other rare substances, not to mention the hoard of Dragon's Blood that they stole from Starkey's heirs stashed somewhere. I'm sure they have multiple Philosopher's Stones at this point."

"OK, OK. Don't try to barter with the immortal gold makers. Got it."

"Not gold, just the quasi-immortal part," said Ty, who had somehow fashioned herself a small cocktail even though all the booze in the lounge was being guarded by a stern-looking woman with a hairnet and horn-rimmed glasses.

"Why are you always drinking? I knew NYC private school kids were fast, but this is ridiculous."

"The better question is, why aren't you?"

"Because I tried drowning my problems with alcohol and still ended up right here. I need all my facilities intact to focus. So it's true, then, about the Philosopher's Stone? It grants immortality?"

Ty looked over my shoulder to see if Duncan was on his way back or if anyone seemed interested in our conversation.

"Shh," she said. "We're not at headquarters. Use a little discretion. And no, not immortality per se. But a good substitute. The Elixir of Life, once imbibed, will bring you back from the dead, but only once. After that, you need to drink another Elixir for the next time you get killed and so on."

"Oh," I said, one more shocking revelation of the power of alchemy threatening to melt my insides. "So what happens if your body is just too old to function? Will the Elixir keep you alive?"

"No, it will not. But it ensures that the individuals in charge of VAC stay so for a very long time. So, no, we are not going be negotiating with them. Got any other suggestions?"

"Yes," I said. "I think one of us needs to go find Duncan. It's been 20 minutes, and he still hasn't returned from the bathroom."

"He's all yours. I'll try to save you a seat at a four-top in the quiet car, but can't make any promises."

"Fine," I said, grabbing my duffel and darting to the men's room. A guy wearing an oversized pinstripe grey suit stared at me as I walked past him when he opened the door, and I quickly surveyed the gross interior to locate Duncan, finally finding him in the last stall, which thankfully he had left unlocked.

"Dunc," I said, slowly pushing the door in. "Are you OK?"

Duncan looked up at me, his eyes brimming with tears.

"No, Jen, I'm not," he said, his voice trembling. "The whole day, it's gone again."

"But you have your notebook," I said.

"That's all I have. A bookcase filled with notebooks of days I don't remember. Tomorrow I'll remember forgetting today, then the day after will be the same. I don't care what I lost. I just want it to stop."

Duncan burst into a fit of sobs, and I wished I had been strong enough to comfort him. But instead, I stood there, surveying the wreckage of a man I had once known.

"I'll help you," I said, hoping I meant it. "Don't worry. I'll help you."

"Look at you, you're like two peas in a pod," said Ty when I spotted her table at the very back of the train in the quiet car. Duncan was barely conscious when I had finally coaxed him out of the bathroom stall, and his only brain activity was the signals to move his legs. I slid his arm off my shoulder, and he slumped into the outer seat, which forced me to awkwardly climb over him. Ty snickered, and I shot her a dirty look.

"Shove it," I said. "His latest memory episode has been different from the ones I saw earlier. Who knows what he's going to remember when he comes out of this?"

"That's easy," she said. "He'll remember whatever you want him to remember."

"It's not," I said. "He's got a notebook detailing everything that happened to him today. What am I going to do…"

"…replace it with one you've written? Yes, exactly."

"Right, and I'm sure he won't notice the handwriting that's clearly not his!"

"Shh!" said a woman sitting in front of me,

"He won't after he reads what you write with this."

Ty placed a nearly empty vial of black ink, a little quill, and a folded piece of paper on the table.

"That's not what I think it is, is it?" I asked, picking up the vial, which was surprisingly heavy despite the fact that there couldn't have been more than a few dribbles of ink left.

"Depends what you think it is."

"Compulsion ink," I said, remembering the uncannily dark ink from the note from Beatrice. "But how … how did you get it?"

"I think you already know the answer."

The words of Frankie's note rose to the forefront of my mind.

"*Open the box and then die*," the note had said. And Frankie had complied without protest.

"This … this is what Doug used to kill Frankie. Which Polly must have given him in exchange for helping her heal her dad. Which she got from…"

"The woman you're trying to find, if I'm not mistaken," said Ty. "And technically it's not called Compulsion ink, although that's cute. Its real name is pellerium."

"I don't care," I said. "I'm not touching that stuff. Not now. Not ever. I've felt what it does. I've seen what it can do. So whatever you want me to do with it, you can forget it."

"Who said anything about you being involved?"

Duncan stirred to life suddenly, and I felt the snapback of Ty's foot on my ankle. Foolishly, I looked down to confirm what I already knew she did, and in that moment, Ty unfolded the piece of paper and pushed it across the table toward him.

"Duncan, no!" I said, holding back a scream in the near-silent car. But it was too late, as Duncan's eyes connected with the words on the paper.

"*Duncan, trust Jen Jacobs*," the note said.

What happened next was something I had experienced too many times. Duncan's eyes went glassy as the command rippled through his brain, but then, just as quickly, they returned to normal.

"What just … huh?" asked Duncan, who tried to look down at the note again, only for Ty to wrest it back. More than anything, I wanted to reach across the table and do violence to this girl who wielded power with such impunity.

"Ask Jen," said Ty, and Duncan turned to me like an obedient puppy, waiting for a command.

"You had another episode," I said. "But just before that, we were discussing a new way to deal with them."

"That's right," Ty chimed in. "No more memory diary for you. From now on, Jen's going to be your memory minder so you don't have to spend so much time with your face in that book."

Duncan scoffed.

"As if I'd ever agree to that. Then Jen can just make up whatever she wa-"

"Dunc, I think this plan is for the best."

The words fell out of my mouth before I knew what I was saying, and as they reached his ears, I saw his demeanor instantly change.

"Oh … OK. That makes sense. Even though I shouldn't, I trust you."

"See," said Ty. "You're a dynamic duo. Like Batman and Robin. Or Pyramus and Thisbe."

"Who?" asked Duncan.

"Never mind. In any event, Jen here thinks you should take a nap for the rest of the train ride."

Duncan looked over at me, and I nodded, at which point he leaned back and shut his eyes.

"You're a real conniving bitch, you know that?" I said after a few minutes.

"You should be thanking me. I got rid of your stalker problem, and in the process gifted you a personal servant. If it's all so bothersome, I'm sure you could get him to never bother you again, with the right prompting."

"No," I said, horrified by what she was suggesting. "I told him I would help him and I will."

"OK, great. Let me and my mom know how that goes. I'm sure it won't affect the actual task you're supposed to be accomplishing with all due haste before the next Guild meeting."

She had a point. Babysitting Duncan was a distraction that I couldn't afford at the moment, and even though he had somehow made substantial progress up the Questing ladder in two months, I doubted he would be of any assistance.

"What's going to happen at the meeting next month? And what is this inquest your mother asked for?"

"You'll triumphantly return the Compendium to my mother, everyone will marvel at your accomplishment, and the inquest will reveal nothing of any importance."

"Then why did Dalia request one?"

"To stall, to divert attention so that we may counter J.P.'s machinations appropriately."

"Well, have fun with that," I said. "Trying to bribe two Guild members is more than enough for me."

"Speaking of, what's the deal with D.C.?"

The First Seat of my table had said little at the meeting the other day and had barely reacted when Jade's glamour had deactivated. I took that as a good sign, but what did I know?

"His name, for one. D.C.'s family is one of the Guild's oldest. Goes back nearly to the founding, maybe even all the way. I haven't checked the records in a while. His father was a legend."

"A legend in what?"

"In crafting," said Ty.

"Very funny. Are we in a video game?"

"You are one of the fortunate ones who doesn't have to play the game. But, yes, D.C.'s skills bear some similarity to what you are thinking of."

In *Hero's Bane*, the game I worked on at my old company, crafters were a class of NPCs that, well, crafted new weapons, armor, or items if you brought them the right ingredients or raw materials. The deeper you ventured, the more fantastical things could be created from the spoils of your battles.

"I see, and what has he been crafting lately?"

"Something one of us might need if the vote of no confidence doesn't go according to plan. *Durandal*."

"You say that as if I should know what that is," I said, not wanting to hear the rest.

"The Rock Cleaver. Wayland's Folly. Roland's Bane," said Ty, and I shook my head again. "Your lack of basic alchemic history is super annoying, did I ever tell you that?"

"No. So enlighten me."

"I will. Tomorrow, after you meet with D.C. You'll get a full tour of the Guild's library, and boy are you in for a treat."

CHAPTER TWENTY-THREE

ROLAND'S BANE

*"I looked inside to find a shining red, jagged stone and nothing else.
'Well done,' I told them. 'Rita would be proud.'"*

D.C.'s mansion looked ominous, even in broad daylight. It was the size of three houses. New York City-sized houses, so not large by suburbs standards, but still large just the same. It made the walk-up I grew up in look like an alleyway dumpster. But that was in Homecrest and this was Carroll Gardens, which was a world away despite the short physical distance. Maybe if my line lasted long enough, I too would one day have an entire city block to pass along to my children.

The street was quiet at the mid-afternoon hour as Duncan and I walked past the manse for a third time, trying to figure out which door was the front door.

"This guy is something else," said Duncan. "He lives here by herself?"

"I hope so," I said. "Either that or he has a basement full of guests who overstayed their welcome. Regardless, this is only an introductory meeting. We go in, feel him out, don't over-commit, and then reassess with Ty this evening."

"Fine, but as soon as the swords come out, I'm gone."

I had filled Duncan in on some of the details of D.C. and why we needed his help. Which he had promptly forgotten so many times that I had contemplated making a set of index cards for him.

"It happened again," he said a moment later, and I launched back into the same speech yet again.

"I need to get this memory out of my head. You need to keep memories in your head. This will solve both our problems."

And then he always says…

"How so? It's just going to take the memories out of my head. And then what?"

And then I say…

"Yours is a problem looking for a longer term solution. But until I figure that out, this will let you keep all your memories intact and then, when you're better, you can retrieve them. You can stop taking notes and you can stop relying on me. Trust me, OK?"

Duncan nodded as Ty's command kicked in. When I had successfully hunted down the Compendium, my first order of business before giving it back would be to demand the antidote for that stupid ink.

After some more pacing, we decided to try the large arched door in the middle of the complex. As I banged the silver knocker three times, I half-expected a tiny slot to appear and to be berated by an angry doorkeeper, but instead, the door swung open of its own accord. We stepped inside with trepidation and into a small antechamber no bigger than the size of a phone booth, with no other way out.

The front door closed behind us suddenly and I found myself pressed together with Duncan in the dark, nearly cheek-to-cheek. In the past, this would have been the beginning of something else, but now I felt a combination of awkwardness, anger, and shame. Duncan tried to shift away from me, and I hoped that one of his episodes wouldn't trigger while we were trapped in this claustrophobic box.

"So far, your plan is working perfectly," he said after a minute of silence.

"Of course it is, we just need to wait for-"

The floor suddenly drop out from under me, and I screamed as we fell into more darkness. Well, more like slid. Because after a few seconds, we landed with a soft thud on what must have been a gym mat. I untangled myself from Duncan's limbs and stood up, only to be greeted by the sight of D.C. holding an extremely large metal mallet and wearing a thick smithing apron, a set of beaten leather gloves, and a pair of goggles perched on top of his messy hair. A foul odor emanated from his body, and I didn't want to guess the last time he had showered.

"Why did you come in that door?" he said, after recognizing me. "That's the trap door."

"Sorry," I said, pushing myself up and looking around. "It seemed like the obvious choice."

"And that's why it's a trap," he replied. "Normally there's a row of very sharp spears here, but fortunately for you, they're being sharpened."

"That is fortunate," I said.

"Who's the spare?" said D.C., pointing the mallet somewhat menacingly at Duncan. Despite its gargantuan size, he held it aloft in front of our faces like it was a dainty umbrella.

"This is my ex, Duncan," I said. "We're hoping you can help with a problem."

"Why would I want to do that? You've not exactly endeared yourself to any of us. That Seat has been empty from the very beginning and within a month of you taking it, look at all the chaos you've caused!"

"Sorry," I said. "It's not exactly been easy for me, either. It feels like I've been jumping from one collapsing pillar to another, trying to reach stable ground. If you'll just hear me out, I promise I won't waste your time."

"OK, OK, but I've got my hands full here in the back, so make it quick."

I craned my neck to see what was in the "back." We were in an empty basement, save for a glowing light and what looked to be a workbench about 100 feet away. From the smell that had wafted up to my nose and D.C.'s outfit, it appeared we were in some desolate blacksmith forge.

"Hands full with what? Looks like the crafting business has been slow as of late."

"That's cute," said D.C. "Tell me, why did that scofflaw annoyingly send you to my doorstep?"

"She said you were the one to go to if we needed something rare. But I see we were mistaken."

"Appearances can be deceiving," he said. "Let's take a walk. I need to get back to work."

We traversed the length of the room and arrived at what was indeed a small wooden bench next to a blazing forge, a wooden barrel, and a gleaming silver anvil. Something glowed brightly within the fire, and D.C. finally set down the mallet and picked up a pair of tongs that were balanced on the edge of the forge, which he used to withdraw the glowing object: the blade of a sword.

Placing the white-hot metal on the anvil, D.C. grabbed the mallet again and pounded it against the sword, sending sparks flying everywhere.

"What are you doing?" I yelled in between swings.

"What does it look like I'm doing?"

"Making pancakes," offered Duncan, and I repressed a snicker.

D.C. glared at us and went back to his work.

"He's funny. Why'd you dump the funny one?"

"Reforging *Durandal*," I said. "Seems like you're a way off."

"Do you know what my initials stand for?" D.C. asked abruptly.

"No," I replied. "Should I?"

"D'naeraeon of clan Crenshezbon," he said matter-of-factly.

"Can't see why you wouldn't want to go by that," said Duncan. I glared at him as if to say, "stop quipping with the guy with the enormous mallet that could knock your head off," and he took the hint.

"That is an … interesting name, but what does that have to do with the sword?"

"My clan dates back more than two thousand years, maybe longer. We were charged as the keepers of *Durandal*, some say, by the remnants of Troy."

"Wait, hold on," I said, Frankie's voice echoing in my head.

"I'm not the Guild's Keeper. Far from it."

Maybe it was a random choice of words, or maybe it was indeed Keeper with a capital K. Beatrice had claimed that she was the Keeper of the Medoblad in an unsuccessful bid to impress Dalia, but Frankie had proved that the title was more than a throwaway honorific.

"You mean Troy, as in the Trojan Horse, Achilles, Hector, that Troy?" asked Duncan.

"Yes, but clan lore, as I'm sure you can imagine, gets very muddled after a few hundred years."

D.C. brought the mallet down onto the metal with a loud bang that forced me backward, but he seemed unaffected. Given his frame, I wondered how he managed to lift the implement off the ground even an inch.

"Anyway, we carried out our charge successfully until my ancestor, also named D'naeraeon, was betrayed by his friend Roland, who stole the sword in the 8th century. But our failure not only doomed our line, but Roland as well."

"What do you mean?" I asked.

"*Durandal* is a remarkable Relic for two reasons. First, it is one of the sharpest blades in history. The human body is like butter before it. Needless to say, Roland killed a lot of people with it. Second, and perhaps more importantly, it is indestructible."

Another mallet blow and another spray of sparks erupted from the mythical metal.

"Not to state the obvious, but it looks pretty destructible right now," I said.

"Yes, well, that's what happens when you go around stealing swords that don't belong to you."

I shrugged my shoulders, not getting the reference, and D.C. shook his head.

"You know, you could have saved me some time and just gone to the Guild library first. One of the D'naeraeon's from the 18th century recorded this for posterity."

"It's my next stop, I promise, but since we're already here, can you indulge me?"

"Fine. But then you tell me why you're here and get going post haste."

"Deal," I said as D.C. shoved the metal unceremoniously back into the forge and stoked its fire with what appeared to be coal briquettes sitting in a burlap sack next to the anvil.

"Roland, for all his hubris, knew when he was beat and didn't want to let *Durandal* to fall into the hands of the Saracens, who were hot on his heels after the Battle of Roncevaux Pass. Trying to escape back across the mountains to France, he drew the sword and, with a single stroke, sliced through the Pyrenees, creating what is now known as Roland's Breach."

"Wait, he cut through the actual mountain?" asked Duncan. "You said the blade was sharp, but–"

"It can cut through *anything*," said D.C. quietly. "Marble. Stone. Iron. Diamonds, if anyone was dumb enough to make diamond armor. And any alchemic material. Except on that day, Roland's past caught up to him, and the blade shattered into a dozen pieces. My ancestor recovered half of them before he was forced to flee. It took eight hundred years to find the rest. We've been reforging the sword ever since."

D.C. plunged the metal into a water bath and an eruption of steam burst forth from the barrel, causing Duncan and me to cough uncontrollably. When it finally cleared, D.C. had already put the sword back into the fire and had removed the leather gloves.

"Wait a minute," I said. "You're telling me that your family..."

"Clan," corrected D.C.

"...clan, OK, has been trying to repair the sword since the 1500s?"

"That's right," he said, smirking at the disbelief on my face. "Did you really think Relics are so ordinary that it would require otherwise?"

"I ... I never thought about it like that. I always assumed that the important knowledge was lost centuries ago but never considered the effort to create a Relic in the first place."

"See, that's the problem with the lot of you," said D.C. "You think that alchemy was just magic that made everything easy. And now that it's mostly used and gone, all that's left to do is cling to the tiny scraps we still have or send idiot scavengers off by the thousands to somehow locate what centuries of alchemists haven't been able to find. But there is another way."

"And what is that?" I asked.

D.C. gestured to his set-up and tools.

"This is the way," said D.C. "We hammer away the sins of the past. We strengthen the bonds of our clan. We restore our legacy. And we forge a new future."

I glanced at Duncan, who seemed ready to launch into a tirade, but instead, his eyes fluttered and his memory fell into the black hole that I had created. When he came to, the fire was gone, and he looked at me for some purchase, something familiar.

"What's wrong with him?" asked D.C. "He looks lost."

"I'm what's wrong with him," I said. "I used too much letherium on him, and now his short-term memory is on the fritz."

"That's so nice that you care so deeply about him to waste a favor on that," said D.C.

"Waste a favor on what?" asked Duncan matter-of-factly. "And what's with the blacksmith get-up?"

"Wow, you weren't kidding," said D.C. "Where'd you even get enough letherium to do that?"

"What's letherium?" interjected Duncan.

"Duncan, can you go wait over there while I talk to D.C.?" I asked. He hesitated, and I added the word "please," which did the trick.

"It's a long story," I said to D.C. "But I promised him I would help undo the damage I did, even if he doesn't remember right now that I'm responsible. And until I figure out how to do that, Ty said you have one of the only stashes of nemosyne left on the East Coast."

"Not sure how she knows that, but it's true," said D.C. "And if that's what you're after, the answer is a firm no. Besides, I thought you wanted to plug the hole in his head, not empty it all the way."

"This is just a stop-gap," I said. "Ty needs time to figure out a more permanent solution."

"Still no," said the blacksmith.

"You haven't even heard what I'm offering."

The truth was that I had very little. He probably already had a Guild cloak. The vitality serum was on Jade's "track," not mine, but in any event, not very valuable to a guy who was content hammering away at a piece of metal for the rest of his life. The glamour stone was worth more than the ink, present circumstances aside. On the walk over here, I had resigned myself to giving it up if that's what it took to find Beatrice, taking the risk that it would reactivate as soon as I touched it again. But this conversation had reminded me I had more than that.

"I know what you've been searching for all this time, and I can give it to you."

D.C. cocked his eyebrows at me and even Duncan looked at me sideways.

"I'm listening."

"The secret to reforging *Durandal*."

The First Seat let out a laugh that echoed through the basement chamber.

"That's a good one. I told you the secret already: time. Nothing ventured, nothing gained. And what we're trying to gain is-"

"But that's exactly what I'm offering, my dear D'naeraeon. Time itself."

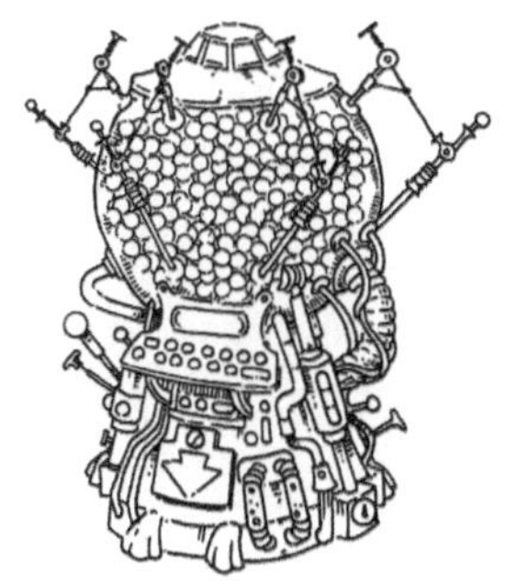

CHAPTER TWENTY-FOUR

MECHANICAL
KNOWLEDGE

"They drank in the adulation, something that has been severely lacking in their hardscrabble life to date. That is all about to change."

O f everything I had experienced so far in the last year, few things quite compared to the thrill of speeding down Manhattan's streets hopped up on a piece of Beatrice's speed buff. I had circled the lower part of the island with ease, my body and mind shifting into overdrive, trying to unlock the mysteries of Frankie's tattoo. And it had worked, although at a cost. The aftermath had temporarily turned my mind to mush, and I had nearly forgotten the revelations discovered during my run. I neglected to disclose that to D.C. as I explained what I was offering him in exchange for the memory ink.

"This all sounds too fantastical to be true, which is saying something," he said. "Such alchemy would not have gone unnoticed by us."

"That's where you're wrong," I said. "It was noticed. Ask Ty about it the next time you see her. I'm sure she'll tell you all about the woman she stalked for years as Gilbert, trying to find out her secrets. The woman she tried to kill."

"The Guild tries to kill lots of people. Sometimes successfully," said D.C. "Did you bring a sample of this 'buff' with you, or am I going to have to take your word for it?"

"I didn't."

"Then we're done. Show yourselves out. I need to get back to work."

"But-"

A sudden blast of steam filled my field of vision as D.C. plunged the white-hot metal into the water, and when it cleared, he had returned to his hammering. I looked at Duncan, who either seemed lost in thought or mesmerized by the clanging of metal on metal, and a bad idea percolated in my brain.

"Look, I need a little of the ink before I can get you the buff," I said, and was again ignored. "But what if I put up some collateral?"

"Tokens? No thanks. Got plenty."

"Not tokens," I said. "Something better: an apprentice."

This got his attention, and the hammering finally stopped.

"You're kidding, right?" asked D.C. "Your boyfriend looks like he's never done a day of hard labor in his life, let alone re-forged one of the most powerful Relics in-"

"So you'll teach him. And then you'll get a much needed break. Which is all the time I need to retrieve the buffs for you."

"I hate to interject your bartering," said Duncan, pulling me halfway across the basement with a yank of his arm, "but have you lost your damn mind?"

"No," I hissed. "But you have. And this will help you stay focused and grounded. It's just what the doctor ordered. Trust me."

Again I saw the whisper of the ink's command wash over Duncan's face, and he nodded.

"OK," called D.C., interrupting my guilt trip.

"OK, what?" I asked.

"Leave him here until you get back with the buffs, and I'll put him to work."

"So you'll give me some ink then?"

"Yes," he said. "Enough for six words, if you choose wisely. Take it or leave it."

I spent the subway trek from D.C.'s mansion to Guild headquarters with my arms awkwardly crossed tightly to my body, the vial with pure memory ink, albeit a very tiny amount, resting in the inner pocket of my jacket. But any joy from completing this task had been outweighed by the terrible power I had wielded to achieve it and the desperate bargain I had struck to inch one step closer to Beatrice.

What would happen if I found her, and she had no buffs, no Compendium? Or even if she did, why the hell would she want to part with either? As far as I knew, she hated me for hiding the gold token from her for so long, for letting her expose herself, for letting her take the fall while I soldiered on, a good little supplicant to the Guild. How many lives would I throw into turmoil because of my reckless desire to push forward, no matter what?

I grasped my locket, as if doing so would somehow make everything easier. But all it did was remind me of the woman who had given it to me, who was no longer here.

"Happy 11th birthday, Jenny Bean!" my mom had said that day.

I had opened the box and looked down at the stupid locket that had been my only present.

"Wow, it almost looks like real silver," I had replied, and my mom's smiling face had immediately changed to crestfallen. "Just like the silver purse I actually wanted. Thanks for nothing!"

My mom, for all her faults, had been gracious, and never brought up the locket again. When she died, putting it on was the least I could do, but I still hadn't forgiven myself and didn't think I could until I learned how the token that Rita had hidden in 1787 had ended up around my neck.

That could finally happen today, though, if Ty was to be believed. The streets outside Guild headquarters were packed with departing children from the nearby school and so I awkwardly donned my cloak, drawing stares and laughs along the way. A few rotations around the block and I found the space to disappear from the world. Returning to the unmarked entrance, I gingerly pushed it open and darted into the darkness. The now-familiar staircases greeted me, and this time I walked up two times and found myself standing before yet another foreboding door.

Its wood was intricately carved with spiraling symbols and a repeated motif of circles embedded in triangles that I stared at for way too long. Finally giving up on my ability to decipher whatever cryptic message was hidden within, I grasped one of the metal knockers that could have been a triplet to the ones on D.C.'s mansion and banged it.

The door opened slightly after a few seconds, and Ty poked her head out.

"You could have just come in," she said, looking annoyed. "Do you know how loud that thing sounds from inside?"

"Sorry," I said. "Force of habit, I guess."

"This isn't the *Wizard of Oz*, Jen. You're a full Guild member. You're allowed to be here."

I shrugged.

"It still doesn't seem that way. I saw how D.C. looked at me. As if I was a carpetbagger who parachuted into his Table. I mean, the guy and his family have been forging that stupid sword for centuries and I'm … it's like every day I have to prove myself all over again."

"That's a good thing," said Ty. "Our ranks need more of you, not less. Anyway, that's a discussion for another time. You're here for a reason. To even your odds."

"Yes," I said.

"Then let's get started."

She beckoned me inside and my mind flashed back to that day in Beatrice's apartment, entering her secret lab behind the bookcase, when I had first learned some hard truths about alchemy. Except unlike that room, this one looked like an ordinary, dusty library, similar to the one I had worked at for so many summers.

"Right this way, right this way," said Ty, walking past the first three rows to the middle of the collection. My tutor-of-the-day stopped at a set of shelves that were pressed together so tightly I could barely see the seam and I doubted any light could pass through, let alone an actual person.

"Doesn't your mom have enough money to afford a bigger room for her library?" I asked.

"It's not so simple," said Ty. "Most of the Guild families have their own private collections, their own caches. At some point, the sharing of knowledge went out of style, and so no one really cares about this place anymore. Which is a pity, as there's so much treasure here just waiting to be rediscovered."

Ty placed her palms on each of the shelf ends and then somehow passed through the wood as if she was Patrick Swayze in *Ghost*. I stood there, dumbfounded at yet another branch of alchemy I didn't even know about.

"Let's go, Jen!" Ty shouted from somewhere within. "It's an illusion. It won't kill you. Press your palms like I did and then walk through!"

"I don't have time for your illusions!" I yelled back. "Can't you people just make a normal room?"

"You know we can't!"

"Fine," I said and complied with the cryptic instruction. The wood felt warm to the touch and after a second of feeling like an absolute idiot, I walked into the shelves, expecting to break my nose into a bloody pulp. But I didn't and instead found myself in a cozy little antechamber. Weirdly glowing candles dotted the brick walls and in place of books and bookshelves, there was only a weird contraption that looked like a gumball machine straight out of a steampunk nightmare.

A large glass vat sat atop of the machine, with a combination of metal and clear tubes snaking out of it in every direction, some of which eventually ended a foot or two above the floor. Nestled at the center was an archaic console, with an old mechanical keyboard, a glowing green dot-matrix monitor, and a rusty bronze slot at the bottom.

"Where are we?" I asked. "That didn't feel like a vervorium portal."

"I told you, it was an illusion. Like a glamour, except an inanimate object. And much simpler from a creation standpoint, and you know, not actually banned."

"See, that's what I still don't get," I said. "You didn't know me from a hole in the wall, and you gave me the glamour like it was a common trinket. Surely there were easier ways to protect me from Doug."

The one thing I could say about Ty was that despite her age, she was extremely well versed in maintaining her stoic exterior, a trait I assumed she had inherited from her mother.

"Because it was what you needed," she replied. "Because I knew Doug was after you, that he knew what you looked like."

"Yeah, thanks for that," I said. "You have any more deranged trainees running around the city that I should know about?"

"Not at the moment," said Ty and my eyes widened. "Oh relax, will you? Doug was a convergence of circumstances, all of which then broke the wrong way. The only one I'm trying to mentor now is you."

"Fine," I said. "Never thought I would be studying under someone who isn't even old enough to drive."

Ty snickered, breaking character for once.

"You're a lot funnier than him, I'll give you that," she said. "So, you're probably wondering what this insane-looking machine is, right?"

"Yes, exactly."

"It's an atheneum. When the Guild moved headquarters in the 60s, it was decided, as both a practical and logistical matter, to convert the library's contents into electrum."

"I'm sorry, what?"

Rather than answer, Ty walked to the console and punched in a series of numbers and letters. The machine suddenly sprung to life, smoke emitting from various ill-fitting joints, weird sounds emanating from … somewhere, until finally a bell rang.

"Come and get it!" said Ty, who waved me over to the slot at the bottom. I lifted its metal cover to reveal a small silver bead.

"What is that?" I asked as Ty handed me something closer to a stale cocoa puff than a precious metal.

"I told you, it's electrum. Bottoms up!"

She jerked my palm up to my lips, forcing the little sphere into my mouth before I could stop her. After experiencing all manner of Beatrice's buffs, this newest piece of alchemy tasted sweet, like an ice cream sundae with salted caramel. But the saccharine sensation ended there, as my eyes roll back into my head and the next thing I knew, I was crouched in a bramble bush wearing in a long, calico dress, a shotgun in my hands and a compass dangling from a chain around my neck.

"Ready, Hector," I said in a chipper tone, like a schoolgirl trying to show off in front of the headmaster.

The weathered man nodded, and I aimed my gun toward the sky.

KNOW YOU ARE

"'Do you know what this is?' I asked them, holding up the red rock.
The girl nodded. 'It is a Philosopher's Stone.'"

"Pull," a man shouted gruffly behind me and a few seconds later, a gray pigeon flew into view about 10 yards ahead and above me. I raised my gun, sited the target, and fired. The poor bird fell to the earth, a puff of dust erupting in its wake.

"Pull," the man said again, and this time, it was two birds. I made short work of them once again and the batch after that and the one after that, too. I was handed a different rifle at some point, and we repeated the exercise. Then a third. Then a fourth. I felt like that upstart Annie Oakley must have when she bested her future husband after 25 shots. Before I could get too proud of myself, I felt a wet cloth being wrapped over my eyes and tied around my head.

"What in the…" I began to say in a mixture of my voice and someone else's, but the man suddenly spun me in a circle and then knocked my legs out from under me. The gun dropped from my hands as I fell, and I tasted blood in my mouth a moment after my face hit the dirt. The whole world was black, and I was reminded of the blindfold that had stolen my sight on my first walk to Guild headquarters. I wanted to scream, to escape from the nightmare, but my body had other ideas.

My hands reached out for the gun, and finding it, I pushed myself back to my feet. I waited for the call signaling the final round of birds, but all I heard was a deafening silence. After a few minutes, though, everything changed, and the symphony of the meadow started singing in my ears. It took a little bit to separate out the sound I was looking for, but I found it soon enough, and with my newly honed senses guiding my limbs, I aimed and fired.

The first bird met an untimely end and then the next and then the next. I would have continued on all day had the man not grabbed my shoulder and then unwrapped the dampening cloth from my eyes.

"Well done, Erica, well done," said the man, who had a worn face, a voluminous salt and pepper beard, and a pile of firearms sprawled around his feet.

"Thank you, Hector," I said, again with that combined voice. I desperately wanted to ask for a mirror to see whose body I was inhabiting, but found that I was only a passive visitor in whatever fantasy I had stumbled into.

"Now be a good lass and help me carry this arsenal back to the 'stead. Your husband already thinks it strange for you to be learning the skill from me. Let's not give him any other ideas."

"Certainly," I said, bending down to pick up one of the smaller rifles. Before I could make any further progress, the man called Hector, who was now visibly shaking, signaled for me to crouch down behind the bramble, and I complied. I closed my eyes, and again the auditory world revealed itself to me. The footsteps of the interloper were far away, but grew closer to our hiding spot as we huddled in silence. I waited patiently for the signal and when Hector tapped me on the shoulder three times, I rose from the ground in one smooth motion, opened my eyes, and fired.

I walked over to the man I had shot in the middle of the chest, the smell of powder wafting around my curly hair. He was clutching the dripping red wound close to his heart with one hand and I saw that in his other was a very large dagger. I stepped on his sternum with my left boot, and he screamed, the blade falling free from his fingers. Its handle was still warm when I picked it up and as I plunged it into his abdomen, I …

… was sopping wet in the Guild library, my body involuntarily shivering. I looked over at Ty, who was holding a metal bucket and grinning with that stupid trademark teenage smile.

"What. The. Actual. F-"

"Keep your voice down, Jen," she said. "We're in a library."

She handed me a blanket that had appeared from somewhere and it was like being curled up in front of a roaring fire on a cold winter's day. I was half-expecting a piping hot mug of cocoa, but the only thing Ty offered me was another silver bead.

"No, thank you," I said. "Not until you tell me what the hell just happened!"

"Congratulations!" she said. "You are now a proficient marksman … err, woman."

"What are you talking about? I swallowed that stupid bead you forced into my mouth, and the next thing I remember is you dumping that water on me."

"Yes, exactly."

"Can you just, for once, be straight with me? What did you do to me?"

Ty shook her head.

"Seeing is believing," she said. "I know a good range in Flatiron. Let's go."

I stared at the paper target, whose bullseye was now full of holes. My hands ached and my shoulder would probably be black-and-blue in the morning from the recoil. But the biggest pain was the cognitive dissonance in my head at my newly acquired shooting skills.

"See," said Ty as I exited the booth. "You're a natural."

"No, I'm not," I said. "I've never fired a gun before. And yet…"

"And yet, the electrum did its job."

"How?"

"You sure you want to know? What if I told that you by swallowing a jar of electrum that you could gain an immense assortment of skills without the tens of thousands of hours of practice? Wouldn't that be enough?"

I thought about how I felt a few moments ago in the booth. I had picked up the gun in a certain way, sited the target for a certain number of seconds, and pressed the trigger in with a certain cadence. All of these things I had never done before. But someone had.

"Whose memory was it?"

Ty cocked an eyebrow at my question and I knew I had the right of it.

"You never cease to surprise me, Ms. Jacobs. A woman named Erica, if I'm not mistaken. She went on to kill dozens in the Spanish-American War as the top member of the Lady Sharpshooters, an all-female brigade of … well, sharpshooters, that officially never existed."

"But, I don't remember anything," I said.

"Your muscles do, though. Such is the marvel that is electrum."

I closed my eyes and tried to think about my knowledge of sharp-shooting, of how to properly clean a rifle, of how to stab someone in the precise way such that they bled out the quickest, of how …

"Stop," said Ty. "Trying to remember what you forgot will lead to all sorts of headache. Electrum is different from nemosyne in several ways. First, the memories can be replicated over and over again. That bead you swallowed earlier? If I wanted to, I could make another copy and relive the same five years of Erica's life."

"Five years! You're telling me I was trapped in that memory for five years?"

"Yes, and look how proficient a killer you've become! But thankfully, the actual memories fade away upon reawakening. Which is why your brain hasn't turned to mush and why you don't want to wear a ridiculously long skirt right now."

Even though she told me not to, my mind started scrambling, trying to recall the details of this woman whose life I had lived. But it was like grasping at straws dipped in grease and then dunked in oil. Any sliver of detail that floated to the surface of my consciousness immediately slipped away into the ether.

"So I just have five years' worth of random skills from the woman now? And I'm going to find out I know kung fu the next time someone tries to attack me in a dark alleyway?

"No, of course not. That would be quite stupid and inefficient. And sorry, you don't know kung fu. Yet. But each electrum bead comes with this handy-dandy card of the skills contained inside."

"Show me," I said.

Ty handed me an index card with Courier text printed on the front.

```
Bead 5136:
Riflery.
Dagger and knife combat.
Crocheting.
Length: 1912 days.
Time: 37 minutes.
Time period: 1882-87.
```

I flipped over the card, expecting a longer explanation, but there was nothing else.

"Is this a joke?" I asked, slipping the card into my back pocket. "'Knife combat'? That's super helpful. How the heck am I supposed to fight with a knife if I can't remember a minute of my 1912 days spent reliving this Erica's person's life?"

"When the situation arises, you'll know," said Ty. "Also, if you feel like making me a scarf by next winter, I wouldn't say no."

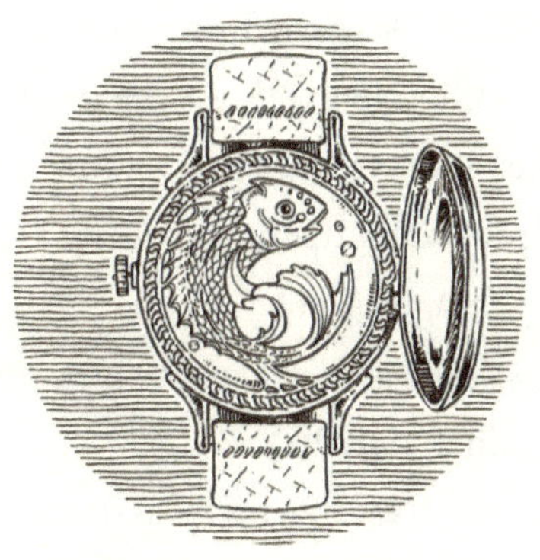

CHAPTER TWENTY-SIX

MILLENIAL EXTRACTION

"'Well met, Lorna van Asch,' I said to the newly minted heir. 'And you, Duff, tell me, what are the ingredients required to make the Stone?'"

"That was fast," said Hugo the next morning when we met him at a random pier downtown. "And I normally don't say that."

"Didn't we just have a talk about this?" asked Ty. "I'm in high school, remember?"

"Sure you are," said Hugo. "When was the last time you actually attended class for more than an hour?"

"Yesterday, for two hours," she said. "Lunch and study hall."

"Of course," said Hugo. "And fine, I'll try to keep it PG from now on. It's just weird, after spending so much time with Gilbert, that

I was talking to you the whole time."

"Yeah, sorry about that," said Ty. "And you should probably apologize to me also for like 60% of the things you said to me."

"Fair point," he said. "Now, let's see the goods."

I pulled out the vial that D.C. had given me, along with a quill that Ty had provided, and a little notepad, and Hugo nodded.

"Are you ready?" Hugo asked.

"I think so. I just need to visualize the memory and then write it down like it's happening, right?"

"In theory," he said. "Never actually used the stuff."

I gingerly pulled on the tight-fitted cork, careful not to let any of the precious ink splatter out, and then dipped the tip of the quill into the neck of the vial before removing it a few seconds later. Closing my eyes, I pictured that scene from Beatrice's downtown apartment, and the images resurfaced. She had handed an envelope to her trainee Kate and then had muttered to herself, "well, time to start over again,"

I opened my eyes, and those words were now on the page, the quill still resting against the wet ink. It didn't seem like anything particularly magic had happened, but then I lifted my writing hand up and everything changed.

My head suddenly titled back and my eyes were forced shut and I had returned to the memory. Except this time, it was as if a gale force wind was in the apartment with me, sucking those few seconds out of my brain. For some reason, my mind was hesitant to let go, but the nemosyne was too strong for me to bear, and it claimed its prize.

"What … what happened?" I asked as I came to on the ground and saw that there was now a third person hovering over my collapsed body.

"You really shouldn't have done that in public," said Lucca Josephie, my Second Seat, who was wearing a bright red vest, a beanie, and horn-rimmed glasses, with a blue messenger bag slung around her neck. "This is super weird, even by New York standards."

"My apologies," said Hugo. "I thought this would be a quiet spot for our work."

"Why is she … why are you here exactly?" I asked, grabbing Lucca's extended hand and pulling myself up.

"You successfully extracted the memory, congrats," she said, running her fingers over the sentence I had written. "But how did you think you were going to form it into something useful? With your mind?"

"I hadn't gotten that far, to be honest," I said, rubbing the back of my head and trying to replay the memory, but finding that it now stopped just short of that moment.

"That seems to be a theme of yours," Lucca said. "But don't worry, I am at your service."

"You are? So you're in Dalia's camp?"

"I suppose," she said. "If you're able to find what she's looking for."

"You want what's in the Compendium, too," I concluded.

"Correct. As well-stocked as our library is, there is a gaping hole no amount of electrum can ever fill as long as the Guild's oldest knowledge remains lost to us. Now come, my lab is nearby."

The four of us walked backed into the confines of the grid until we reached a pretentious-looking SoHo gallery filled with dozens of paintings, each with a two-letter abbreviation that on closer inspection turned out to be elements from the Periodic Table.

"This is it?" asked Ty. "I thought you were out in Bushwick."

"I was," said Lucca, nodding to the bored salesgirl lounging on the lone piece of furniture in the spartan space, who didn't return the gesture. "But my 'artwork' has seen a huge uptick in sales ever since a collector stumbled upon my Hg painting, so I upgraded my digs."

She led us to a spiral staircase that we carefully ascended upward 30 feet into an opening in the ceiling. At the top was a small landing and a hulking metal door with no knob. Lucca rummaged in her bag for a few seconds before pulling her now glove-adorned hand out and pressing it against the slab, causing a red glow to emanate from her palm. It spread the length of the door and then contracted, taking the entire metal slab with it.

"What just happened?" I asked, as Lucca presented a tiny version of the door to me to hold, which I turned over in my hands.

"Dynium!" she said, beckoning us through the now open threshold, behind which was a regular door with a knob. "A recent invention of mine. You can grow and shrink objects to your heart's content. I'll take that back, please."

Lucca took the little rectangle from me and, with one smooth motion, threw it towards the gap with her gloved hand. It enlarged mid-flight and slid roughly against the concrete floor the last few inches until it was again blocking the doorway.

She casually opened the regular door as if the last 30 seconds hadn't happened, behind which was a room that ran the length of the art studio below. Except instead of terrible looking paintings, the space was filled with networks of glass tubes, humming machinery, something that looked like a replica of Manhattan covered in colorful blinking dots, overstuffed cabinets, and tables upon tables cluttered with beakers, burners, and other scientific paraphernalia.

"This is quite a set-up," I said. "You may have Beatrice beat."

"What's she like?" asked Lucca, a glint of curiosity in her eye that could have been a platonic science girl crush or the beginnings of a new Tesla-Edison rivalry.

"She's … uhh … intense, driven. Probably mad at the Guild? I mean, Ty tried to kill her and-"

"I was testing her," the teenager interjected. "And she passed. Cost me a good enforcer, but I think it was worth it."

"Kind of a weird test," Lucca said. "You should have put her through an unofficial Gauntlet, tested her disciplines. We're not a Guild of murderers, *Gilbert*."

"Well," I said, "there was the whole crazy stalker-"

Ty drew her finger across her neck, and I quickly shifted course.

"-crazy stalker from her old job. He stressed out so much that she fled town, taking the Compendium and her bag of tricks with it. And so here we are."

"I'd like to meet her when this is all over," said Lucca, who had walked over to one of the cabinets and was busy fishing something out from inside, random things crashing to the floor as she did. "Ah, here it is!"

She held aloft a metal rod that could have passed for a magic wand if you weren't looking too closely and flicked her wrist. A blue flame erupted from the tip and then immediately extinguished itself a second later.

"Is that…"

"Hellfire, yes!" said Lucca cheerfully, and my mind rewinded back to the last laboratory I had been in and the unnatural smell of burnt, well, everything.

"What … why do you have a varutium starter?"

"What else is going to be hot enough to liquify the nemosyne? The paper, please."

I handed Lucca the ink-written page, and she stuffed it into a beaker, which she placed into a lab clamp, and I turned away as she re-ignited the starter. After a few seconds, she tapped me on the shoulder, and I looked back to see that the beaker now held a grayish sludge.

"This way!" Lucca exclaimed, donning thick purple gloves to carry the vessel over to yet another station, where she poured the contents into a pear-shaped piece of glass mounted on a metal arm.

"Separatory funnel," she said, before I could ask. "We'll separate out the paper residue and get that pure, pure memory! That reminds me, do you want it back?"

"Want what back?" I asked.

"Whatever moment you extracted from your head," said Lucca. "Because if not, this will probably go a lot quicker."

"Umm, I think I'm good. I never wanted her memories in the first place. If I had more ink, I would remove them all."

The truth was, I still didn't know how much of Beatrice's mind had seeped into mine during our fateful encounter at the Hampton's party all those months ago. It had only been after a sleepy subway ride that I had witnessed the entire showdown between Beatrice and Kate, and I was loath to explore what else I could now recall about her life.

"OK then! Hugo, how big is the opening?"

Hugo pulled the watch out from the inside pocket of his blazer and set it down on a relatively empty spot on the workbench. Its silver surface reflected all sorts of colors from around the lab like a kaleidoscope. He hit one of the side dials and the cover snapped open, revealing an intricate-looking clock face. Before I could take a closer look, Hugo moved his fingers to the dial at the top of the watch and began winding it, causing the face to slowly disappear somewhere within the inner recesses of the contraption. In its place was an etched illustration of a fish on a small disk.

"What is that?" I asked.

"Nothing," said Hugo, quickly popping the disk out of the watch and replacing it with a fishless one that had a circular groove in the center. Lucca peered at the timepiece and nodded to herself, before spinning the separator like a pinwheel for several minutes. We all awkwardly stood in silence as Lucca hummed an upbeat tune that sounded as if it could have been from an old Super Nintendo game.

Finally, a ding rang from somewhere within the chaos of the lab, and our host placed what look like an ice cube tray below the contraption and excitedly loosed the stopper.

A stream of pure silver trickled down out of the separator, just enough to fill one of the circular voids in the tray, which Lucca grabbed after a few seconds and then ran off. Catching up to her, I saw she had placed it into what could charitably be described as a mini carbonite freezer. Steam rose from the sunken chamber in the base while Lucca watched, a pair of purple goggles covering her eyes.

"Don't get too close," she said. "Not unless you like skin grafting."

I kept my distance and finally Lucca, now donning a different set of purple gloves (I was sensing a theme), reached down into the contraption to pull free the tray.

"Here you go. One tiny nemosyne bead!"

"Thanks," I said as Hugo offered me his wrist. I placed the memory inside the watch, and he pushed the cover shut.

"Now what?" I asked.

"Now you give me a second, please. I'm calibrating."

Hugo twisted and pulled the various dials and then closed his eyes, as if he was trying to commune with the timepiece. Finally, he opened his eyes again, a serene look on his face, which suddenly changed into giddiness.

"It's coming from inside the building!" he exclaimed.

"Are you fuc-"

"I am," he said with a smirk. "It's that way."

He pointed toward the west-facing side of the lab and then walked as far as he could, stopping just short of a crazy machine that was emitting blue smoke.

"Hmm, I'd say it's west by southwest. And from the strength of the signal, it's faaarrrr. Probably not Asia, but Hawaii is not out of the question. Best bet is for-"

I screamed. It was a loud, guttural cry that rang out through the lab. The confluence of the nesting doll quests, the flood of skills and memories into my brain and body, the promises and favors to repay, the people I had hurt, the fate of the Guild, it all came down on me at once like an anvil in D.C.'s forge. I crouched to my knees and attempted to shut it all out, but, as with everything else in my life, failed miserably.

"Hey," said Hugo, tapping me on the shoulder. I opened my eyes to see his outstretched hand, which I took, pulling myself up from the floor.

"Sorry, I…"

"It's OK, we've all been there."

Lucca nodded and even Ty gave the equivalent of an encouraging look.

"Anyway, what I was about to say was, your best bet is for me to fly you cross-country in my jet."

I stared at Hugo wide-eyed.

"You have a jet?"

"Yeah. I mean, who doesn't?"

"I … I don't even have a-"

"Sorry, not the right time for that joke," he said.

"It's OK. When can we leave?"

CHAPTER TWENTY-SEVEN

JOURNEY TO THE WEST

"Duff looked at me, his brow furrowed. 'The components of the Stone have been lost to time,' he replied. 'Says who?' I countered. 'The Sources, the Quartos, the sparse surviving remnants of the Chronicles, on this they all agree.'"

At around 15,000 feet, I opened my eyes again to see swirling clouds passing by. The cockpit was aglow with so many instruments that it made me anxious just thinking about what they all could do. In the pilot seat, Hugo was taking a nap, which wasn't helping. I had nearly walked off the runway after he had revealed that he was going to be piloting. But after first joking that it would be his 10th flight and that he had finally gotten the hang of things, he admitted he had been flying since before he could drive. That had assuaged my nerves until the moment he had throttled the accelerator, causing us to speed down the empty airstrip and into the sky.

Looking down at the nav console, I saw we were smack dab in the middle of Nebraska, as if we were on any other cross-country flight. But this was anything but. Hugo had spent the first hour with the navigation computer turned off and instead let his watch-adorned hand gently guide us. I had watched his fingers twitch in reaction to the unseen force within the tracking device as if an invisible string was tied to it, the other end wrapped around Beatrice.

I still couldn't believe that we were actually on our way to find her. She had been my alchemy north star for the past year and I had felt her absence these two months, bouncing from Guild member to Guild member in search of steady ground, not knowing who I could really trust. But had I ever really trusted Beatrice? After all, she had threatened to hunt me down on more than one occasion if I crossed her. Even though I had saved her life, I wasn't sure whether she was in my debt or whether I was one more attachment to get rid of.

"Got one!" Hugo mumbled in his sleep, and I wondered if he was dreaming about fishing. Why anyone would need a magic tracking watch to fish, I wasn't sure, but it seemed very personal to my guide, so I didn't push further. Every few minutes, he would seemingly wake from his stupor, hold his hand out in front of him, and then adjust our course before falling back asleep. As we continued our journey westward, I pondered what corner of the country we would find Beatrice in. Was she off in the backwoods, chopping logs to heat a wood-fired stove in a tiny cabin? Or had she become a drone in the hive of another big city? Maybe she was living on a farm, growing crops with prima materia fertilizer. Wherever she was, I hoped beyond hope that she still had the blank Compendium with her, or this entire side quest was going to crash and burn in spectacular fashion.

As if the plane was reading my mind, a red light suddenly started blinking on the cockpit controls.

"Hey Maverick, wake up!"

I poked Hugo in the ribs with my elbow, and he startled back to consciousness.

"What … did I win?" he asked.

"No," I said. "We're both about to lose if that red light means something bad."

"Oh that," Hugo said. "That's just the low fuel indicator."

"You're kidding, right?"

"Relax, we have hours left. Maybe not enough to go where we need, but enough to get us safely back on the ground. So let's see where that should be. Oooh, Aspen! My college girlfriend lives there. It's settled then."

"This mission isn't for you to get some action, which it seems like you have no trouble acquiring. We have to find Beatrice!" I pleaded.

"What are you in, ninth grade? I'm perfectly capable of wooing Charli and locating your friend at the same time. I need to readjust our heading anyway."

I relented and left Hugo to his sexting while I tried to focus on the task at hand. Once again, I found myself needing more from Beatrice than I could offer her. But it would have to be enough, and if anything, I had gotten good at extracting what was required before the final bill had to be paid.

We landed smoothly on a runway surrounded on all sides by green mountains, a gunmetal gray Mercedes S-class waiting for us at the bottom of the airstairs. Hugo beckoned me into the front passenger seat as he took the keys from a tall blonde wearing an incredibly exaggerated version of a pilot's uniform.

"We'll be back in the air in two hours, tops," he said, quickly throttling the car up to 88 mph before we hit a traffic light. "Ugh. This road is way too short. They should have built the airport farther from town."

"What am I supposed to do while you're off cavorting with your ex?"

"Go get a stiff drink. It seems like you need it," said Hugo. "Or catch up on your studies. Ty told me she gave you the library tour. You could probably make your way through several lifetimes of skills if you brought the right electrum along."

I nodded, not wanting to reveal that I had spent the previous night lost in the life of a 19th century Parisian baker and that I could speak fluent French if given the opportunity. That was in addition to the hand-to-hand combat primer I had ingested, reliving a 25-year-old American's sojourn at a Shaolin monk temple in the early 90s. Despite Ty's warning, I felt my mind drifting back to those forgotten experiences, wondering if they were nestled somewhere in my brain, just below the surface of my subconscious.

We quickly reached the main drag of the town and Hugo loudly pulled into a parking space in front of a trendy-looking coffee shop next to a particularly rundown dive bar.

"This is where I leave you," he said, stepping out of the car. "Meet back in 90. Wish me luck!"

"I will do no such thing," I called out, but he had already made it halfway down the block before I climbed out of the ridiculously uncomfortable passenger seat. Part of me wanted to just stay where I was and try to sneak in another electrum session. I had gone heavy on the languages in my stocking up before the trip, thinking it would be cool to suddenly know what everyone around me was saying. But putting myself into a near-comatose state in the middle of an unknown town seemed like a bad idea, and so I took Hugo's advice and headed into the bar.

I regretted my decision immediately as I spotted a familiar cowboy hat-wearing man trading jokes with the bartender. Before I could even think of retreating, J.P. Laurel turned around and locked eyes with me, almost as if he had sensed my presence. He gestured at the empty stool next to him with his cane, and I found myself slowly walking toward the man who had managed to upend the Guild.

"Why are you following me?" I asked, dispensing with any sort of pleasantries.

"Nice to see you, too. Ms. Jacobs, is it?" he replied. "And who says I'm following you?"

"Tequila, neat, please," I said to the bartender, who nodded and scurried away. "You're here now, and you were in DC on Tuesday when I was there. Can't be a coincidence."

"I find the topic of coincidences fairly interesting," said J.P., tapping his nullifier cane against the marble bar. "Is it a coincidence that not one but two of our members were utilizing glamours to hide who they were? Is it a coincidence that our beloved Chair sent not one but two holders of the Second Seat of the Pavonia Table on Guild errands that resulted in their deaths?"

"What ... what are you talking about? And Emma is very much alive."

"Yes, thankfully. The girl is very clever. Especially under pressure. The former could have been said about her father, but not the latter, unfortunately."

J.P. dipped his head slightly, the cowboy hat brim covering his eyes.

"I knew that Emma's dad had passed away, but she never-"

"It's not something that she openly talks about," said J.P. "And why would she? Do you know how it must have felt to be told your dad died on Guild business and to be forced to continue that business or lose the Seat? I still haven't gotten over it myself. It's one of the reasons I called for a vote."

"You're following Hugo, aren't you? Trying to win him over to your side," I said. "You believe I'm a lost cause, but you think he's in play."

"Oh, I never count my chickens before they're hatched, Ms. Jacobs," he said. "That goes for the both of you."

"You really like your agricultural metaphors. Do you even own any chickens?"

"Yes, several hundred thousand in fact," said J.P. "I don't know why my Second Seat is always focused on the animals no one thinks existed when we have such magnificent creatures at our disposal."

The bartender finally brought over my drink, along with a frosty mug of overflowing beer for J.P. and we awkwardly clinked glasses.

"I don't know when you planned on speaking with Hugo, as he's probably between some girl's sheets right now, but I'm here and I'm listening."

J.P. took a long, drawn out sip of his beer and when he put the glass down again, it was empty.

"Listening for who? I heard Dalia double-backed on her rejection and now you're a full-throated member. Congratulations."

"Somehow I don't think you mean that," I replied. "And like you said, I passed the Initiation. I earned my spot."

"Yes, and in the process, you nearly got my goddaughter killed," said J.P., his face red either from the drink or from anger.

"That … that wasn't me," I said, not knowing how else to respond, but realized my mistake too late.

"You're telling me it was … forget it. I was right about you from the very time I laid eyes on you. And in the end, y'all be finding out soon enough what I have planned for the Guild, so I might as well tell you, so you know what's coming."

"Which is what?" I said with a smirk. "A cattle stampede?"

"Now that's a good metaphor!" said J.P., slapping the counter, drawing stares from the other patrons. "But we're not quite there yet.

The stampede is the end result. I'm what spooks the first heifer."

"Dare I ask who the heifer is?"

"You already know," J.P. said as he brazenly reached behind the bar and activated one of the taps while the bartender was distracted. He then helped himself to a pile of napkins to mop up the overflowing head that had spilled everywhere.

"Sorry, this place is not known for its service. Anyway, where was I? Oh right, the heifer. It's of course Dalia. She is clinging to the past, trying to regain what was lost. Why she tasked this errand to you, after your performance in Boston, I haven't the slightest idea."

I tried to feign surprise, but gave up almost immediately.

"You didn't believe you were going to get half the Guild to help you without it getting back to me?" he asked, and I frowned. "If so, you're more naive than I thought."

"I don't particularly care what you think about me," I said. "I didn't choose any of this. It's Guild business. As you said, you do it or lose the Seat."

"What if there were another way?"

"I don't follow," I said. "Dalia is Chair. Even if you become Chair, it will be someone else we all have to listen to."

"See, that's where you're wrong. It wasn't always this way. My inquest committee is hard at work, uncovering all the ways that Dalia has forced the Guild into a rut of stagnation that it can't get out of. It's not just by putting her thumb on the scale by gaining an extra vote. There used to be collaboration, rigorous debate. I'm not saying it was the Agora, but it was nothing like we have now."

"Which is what exactly? Seems like the two Guild meetings I've been to so far have been par for the course."

"Worse than that, I'm afraid. It's been 11, well really 10, people all out for themselves. Half the time, we barely reach a quorum at the meetings. It's impossible to get anything done. It's as if Dalia is content waiting another decade before something comes of her Quest Board project."

I wanted to interject, to tell him that the project had succeeded in at least two respects, but thought better of it.

"So you want her out so you can what, hold a big press conference downtown and announce yourself as the most powerful alchemist in the city? Somehow, I don't think that's going to turn out the way you'd like."

"The world is not quite ready for a return to the old ways," said J.P. "Ever since Newton told all of Europe that he was seeking to create the Philosopher's Stone, we have been forced to hide in the shadows. Skulk around in secret with our cloaks. But there is only so much we can do on our own. We need to build, and to do that, we need a partner. An organization nearly equal to our own."

And who is that?" I asked, although I already knew the likely answer.

"The Van Asch Corporation. They have the means and the influence that we have let wither."

"From what I know of them," I said, "it sounds like they do not need to get in bed with us."

"That's where you're wrong, Ms. Jacobs," said J.P., pushing himself to his feet with the help of that awful cane. "The agreement has been signed, sealed, and delivered. A merger of two historic institutions. All that remains is for me to assume the Chair so that it can be ratified. So good luck to you, but it won't make a lick of a difference. The votes are already in and it's coming up roses for the new Van Asch Guild."

CHAPTER TWENTY-EIGHT

INTO THE WOODS

"I stared at the boy. He is sure, yet unsure of himself. 'But you have the fire of Newton within you, do you not?' I said. He considered my declaration for a moment and then nods. 'Then, what does Duff say?'"

"How long have you known?" I asked Hugo as we flew over the last of the mountain ranges on the way to our apparent destination of Fresno.

"A while now. For all of J.P.'s traits, being quiet is not one of them. He's been yapping about an alliance with Van Asch for what seems like forever."

"You didn't think to mention that to me?"

"I did, but decided it was better for you to hear it from the horse's mouth, as it were."

"Wait," I said, "so this whole stopover was a set-up? You knew he was going to be there?"

My indignation at being played began to rise, but before I could do anything, Hugo hit a bunch of buttons on the console and beckoned me to join him in the back of the plane.

"Don't you need to … you know … mind the seven thousand dials and gauges in here so we don't crash?"

"Nah," he said as he fixed himself a martini from the well-stocked bar before plopping himself down on one of the enormous leather chairs. "If something goes wrong, I'll have at least a minute to run back to the cockpit."

"How reassuring," I said. "Now, would you mind explaining why you told J.P. what we were doing?"

"As I explained to you the other day, I'm on no one's side but my own. You've come to the assumption that just because I'm helping you means I want to help Dalia. So let me correct that now."

"What are you talking about?" I asked.

"J.P. is correct about one thing. Things need to change. We're stagnant and it's not good."

"And you think this merger is the right idea? Ty shot me down pretty fast when I suggested getting help from the VAC."

"Honestly, I don't know," said Hugo. "And of course she did. Dalia has a sordid history with them. Same with her grandmother before that."

"You mean Thera DeWitt, who she named her fashion line after?"

Hugo nearly spit up the generous sip of his martini he had taken, before calming himself and checking our bearing with his watch.

"Signal's getting stronger," he said. "Shouldn't be too difficult to find her once we land. And if you believe that sappy tale, I have a gambling den under the Brooklyn Bridge to sell you."

"I don't understand," I said, recalling Dalia's keynote speech at the Met.

"Thera DeWitt was the Guild Chair before Dalia. Which I'm sure J.P. will be happy to point out. Between the two of them, they've been head of the Guild for the past 75 years."

"Did her home actually burn down?" I asked.

"Who?"

"Thera's. Dalia said her grandmother lost everything when her family's hundreds-year old house burnt down."

"Is that what she's telling the normals? No, I'm afraid that's another fanciful fable. Maybe it works on her investors, but we all know the truth."

"Which is what?"

"Thera's manse on Fifth Avenue is still standing strong. I think Dalia donated it to an all-girls' private school sometime back. Didn't want to pay the real estate taxes. As if it were even her money."

"Why lie about that?" From the limited time I had spent with Dalia, caring about what others thought about her seemed like something that would be far beneath her.

"Dalia is a mythmaker. And it works wonders on the right people. Who wants to support another spoiled Upper East Side denizen charging inflated prices for clothing you could get at any fast-fashion outlet? But if it's a bootstrapped, hard-working stepped-on-her-whole-life girl from the Lower East Side gutter, who worked her way up from nothing, well, that's something else. It's too bad for her she couldn't pull the same trick on us. She might find herself in a different position right now."

"Do you think she has the votes?"

I tried to recreate the tally that Ty and Dalia had come up with, but gave up after realizing I still had no clue how anyone really felt about the state of the Guild. Hugo evidently was having the same problem, as I watched his eyes twitch back and forth, presumably sorting everyone into columns.

"It's going to be close. Dalia was very astute in sending you to retrieve the Compendium. It may turn the tide in her favor, or worse, leave things in a draw."

"Ty told me if it's a tie, then draconian measures would be necessary."

"That's one way of putting it," said Hugo.

"What's the other way?"

"I'd rather not say," he replied. "You have enough pressure on you as it is. And don't let my feelings for Dalia get in the way of your quest. I hope you do succeed so that our vote isn't just a formality."

Before I could press further, the plane lurched downward, causing Hugo to spill the remaining portion of his drink all over the front of his shirt.

"This was brand new! Serves me right, I guess. Back to the cockpit, please."

We returned to the cockpit, and Hugo for the first time concentrated solely on flying the plane. The turbulence was like nothing I had ever experienced, almost as if someone on the ground was controlling the weather, trying to force us off course. But somehow we landed in one piece, and as soon as the wheels hit the ground, I ran to the back and threw up in the most spacious airplane bathroom I had ever seen.

"You couldn't have waited until we were on the runway?" Hugo asked, shaking his head in disbelief. "You know what they are going to charge me to clean that, especially here?"

"Sorry," I croaked. "Nice flying, though. I really thought we were going to—"

"Oh, that? I've flown through much worse."

Through the bravado, I saw the small beads of sweat that were still resident on his forehead and dropped the matter. We rented the nicest car left available, an old Acura RSX that Hugo fell in love with immediately, and soon we were cruising down Route 99 toward our (unknown) destination, past miles of green farmland.

"This place is super random," said Hugo, as we approached an interchange. "She ever mention anything about wanting to travel to middle-of-nowhere central California?"

"No," I said. "She preferred to keep things closer to the vest. One time I stepped over that line and she didn't talk to me for a month."

"What'd you do?"

"What I thought was the right thing. She knocked herself unconscious trying to punch through a vervorium portal, and I brought her home."

"Hmm," said Hugo, shaking his wrist back and forth. "She's east of here, maybe in the mountains."

We curved around the interchange loop like a street racer drifting through the Tokyo highlands before Hugo kicked the car into another gear once we hit the next highway.

"And did you say she tried to punch through a vervorium-backed door? Where? Why? How?"

I contemplated coming up with a fanciful tale about how we were searching for a long-lost cache of dodo beak powder, but instead offered a diluted and edited version of the truth.

"That's quite an adventure," said Hugo, after I finished explaining how I had dragged Beatrice out of the burning lighthouse, leaving out the part about Frankie. "So we have you to thank for getting back half of the Compendium, it seems."

"What's so important about it?" I asked. "Beatrice thought it was this tome of incredible knowledge, but you already have this crazy library with lifetimes of memories and skills. What does Dalia need a dusty old book for?"

"The library is great, don't get me wrong, but that represents a fraction of what was held by the Guild and its predecessor."

"What predecessor?" I asked.

"How well do you know your American history?"

"I thought I knew it well," I said. "Until I read Rita van Asch's diaries."

"How did you … you know what? I don't even want to know. If you read those diaries, you understand the Guild has been here since the beginning. But before that, it was something else, over in the Old World. It's those records, plus the early Guild exploration of the New World, that has been lost for several hundred years."

"I see. And you never wonder what Dalia would do with that knowledge?"

Once again, I returned to Frankie and her dying words.

"*For 200 years, my family has kept the cave and that box hidden from the Guild.*"

Someone had gone to great lengths to hide the Compendium, and I still had no idea why.

"That's a loaded question if I've ever heard one," said Hugo. "Did she put you up to it?"

"What? No! I just … I feel like I've been thrown into Mariana Trench with a two-ton weight strapped around my waist, with no choice but to sink to the bottom."

"And in that lovely metaphor, Dalia is the weight or the trench?"

"I don't even know," I said.

We drove down the highway in silence for another half an hour; me having exhausted my desire to pump my escort for information and Hugo having exhausted his desire to be interrogated. Towns passed us by with no end in sight, and I wondered if we were truly headed in the right direction.

"We're about to run out of road," said Hugo. "After that, it's mountains and forest. And I really didn't sign up for a trek across the Donner Pass."

"That's thousands of miles away!" I said.

"Good, no cannibalism for us then."

A bright green sign indicating we were entering Three Rivers appeared, and Hugo shook his wrist again.

"We're close!" he said, a chipper note in his voice. "If we end up finding her, I think this will go down as one of my most successful trackings. Cross-country location based on nothing but a memory. A quest worthy of recordation in the Guild library!"

"I'm glad you're pleased," I said. "Finding her was the easy part. Getting her to part with the Compendium will be the true challenge. And don't make a quip about-"

"I wasn't, I wasn't!" said Hugo, chuckling. "Looks like this is the place."

We turned off of the highway onto a barely present gravel road that wound its way up a hill. Several minutes later, we were parked next to a small, simple house that couldn't have been more than three rooms inside. The front door was surprisingly unlocked, and a quick walkthrough confirmed the abode was a far cry from her Madison Avenue palace. However, something was else was missing besides the fancy furnishings: the woman herself.

"She's not here," I said, after the fifth sweep through the first and only floor. The place appeared barely lived in. The kitchen sported a linoleum table that looked older than the house, the bedroom had a tiny cot supported on a metal frame, and the living room had a dumpy couch that would probably swallow me whole if I sat down on it.

"Tell me something I don't know," said Hugo. "It's weird, because … of course, why didn't I realize it sooner?"

Hugo glanced at his watch and then shook his head several times in exasperation.

"You gave me a memory, so the watch is tracking the memory of her. Who knows far behind we are?"

"Not that far, I think," I said and ran to the bathroom, where a tortoise-shell handled hair brush was resting on the edge of the cast iron white sink. I brought the treasure back out to Hugo, whose eyes widened.

"As meticulous as she kept this place, she wasn't meticulous enough," I said, pulling out a strand of jet-black hair from one of the brush bristles.

"I thought you said she was blonde?" Hugo asked. "As a rule, I'm not into-"

"Is that the only reason you came along on this trip? To try to hook up with her?"

"No," said Hugo, sheepishly. "I mean, not going to lie, the thought crossed my mind several … dozen times."

"Great," I said. "I'll make sure I only ask for your help in the future if it involves someone you can-"

"Point taken," he said. "I will keep things above the level until we're done. Now, let's get reoriented."

Hugo removed the memory bead from the watch and carefully placed the strand of hair inside the empty slot. He flicked the cover shut and did his whole "I'm becoming one with the watch" routine before opening his eyes and pointing at a random wall in the house.

"That way," he said.

"She's here?"

"No, that direction, but close. Come on."

We returned to the car, and I watched the unpretentious house retreat into the distance. It seemed completely out of character of Beatrice to have maintained such a threadbare existence. Could she have actually abandoned alchemy for a such a simple life out here in the middle of nowhere? Something didn't add up.

The watch led us up into the mountains and we soon reached a small booth guarding the entrance to Sequoia and Kings National Park. Hugo dutifully paid the entrance fee, and we continued onward, snaking around the winding road that meandered through the park. Finally, we pulled over at the head of the Sherman Tree Trail and continued on foot for close to an hour through the woods. Trees stretched up into the heavens, and I wondered what Beatrice had discovered about this place that had made her set up shop so close.

We rounded a bend and there, standing at the base of the largest tree I had ever seen, was Beatrice Taylor. Her long blonde locks were gone, replaced by a bob of black hair that matched a spandex workout ensemble that had seen better days. She had her palm pressed against the bark of the trunk, as if she was trying to commune with the giant sequoia.

Hugo stayed put as I approached her with extreme trepidation, unsure as to the welcome I would receive, but before I could say anything, Beatrice broke out of her trance and stared at me with those piercing green eyes.

"Jen," she said, a confused look on her face, "why are you back so soon?"

CHAPTER TWENTY-NINE

REUNION

Only three months had passed since the fake gold token had exploded in the Greenacre fountain, but in that small space of time it felt like I had undergone a metamorphosis of sorts, and from the looks of it, so had Beatrice.

"Umm, hello to you, too," I said, as she walked slowly toward Hugo and me. "What do you mean, 'why am I back so soon?' I've only just found you!"

"You haven't. You didn't," she said blankly. "You were here four days ago. We had a very frank conversation about my vitality serum, you slept outside my tent for several nights, which I thought was weird, and then when I woke up this morning, you were gone."

"Beatrice," I said. "None of that happened. I've been working with Hugo—he's a Guild member—all week to locate you. We just flew in from-"

The realization hit me like a ton of bricks, and as much as I didn't want to know the truth, I asked the question anyway.

"Which me was here?"

Beatrice cocked her head and stared at me, as if trying to pierce through a glamour that wasn't there.

"Jade, with the red hair. Except she said to not to call her that anymore. Said she had found a more suitable name."

"And you still thought it was me?" I asked.

"Yes," she said. "Who else would it have been?"

"Jen," interjected Hugo, "what did you do with the glamour necklace?"

"I put it in my office and closed the door behind it. You don't think … but no one else can get in there."

"That's correct," said Hugo. "But that doesn't mean that someone can't get out from the inside."

"Did you two come all the way out here to chat amongst yourselves?" asked Beatrice. "I thought you were looking for me. Here I am. What do you want?"

I looked at Hugo, who shrugged, so I tabled the troubling revelation about my office theft and got right to it.

"The Compendium," I said, my voice barely above a whisper.

"Ah," she said. "Well, then you came all the way out here for nothing. I don't know where it is. Now, if you don't mind, I need to get back to work."

Beatrice turned away from us and shifted her attention and her hand back to the giant tree. Hugo and I stood there in awkward silence, not knowing whether to interrupt her or whether to leave and come back later. There was something … off about my former mentor. It wasn't just her clothes or her hair. It was the cadence of her voice, like she wasn't all there. Had the stress of the explosion, Garrett's surprise divorce, and her flight cross-country finally cracked that hard exterior front she had always labored to maintain?

"What do you mean, you don't know where it is?"

She ignored me, her focus directed entirely at the tree. After a few minutes of silent reflection, something changed within her posture. She became more rigid, more still, her breathing slowing to a crawl. If I had smacked her on the head, I doubted she even would have registered the blow.

"This is who you thought was going to help you?" asked Hugo. "She's lost her damned mind, trying to talk to a tree."

"It wasn't like … she's clearly not herself. You weren't there that night."

"Neither is that version of her," he replied. "Are you planning on waiting here all day?"

"Maybe," I said. "I've got nowhere else to be."

"That makes one of us," said Hugo. "I'm needed elsewhere, so if you are going to-"

A guttural suddenly cry rang out, disturbing the peaceful forest like a lightning bolt crackling down from the sky. If there had been a flock of birds nearby, they all would abruptly taken flight. Hugo and I covered our ears to block it out, but it was useless. I crouched down in pain, as the sound overwhelmed me and when I finally forced my eyes back open after it had stopped, I saw the still-stoic Beatrice standing there, just as she was. Except something was different.

Her hand was glowing.

It was faint at first, a blue shimmer that could have been confused for the sun's rays reflecting through the canopy. But then it grew both in size and brightness, enveloping her palm as if she was charging up a fireball in a video game.

"What … what is she doing?" I asked Hugo, who looked as if he had just seen the ghost of a long-dead family member.

"You never mentioned this," he said gruffly.

"I don't know what 'this' is!" I hissed. "She never told … I never saw her do anything like that before."

The blue glow continued emanating from Beatrice's hand and spread up her arm and across her body. I was reminded of the purple power she had siphoned from her ring, enabling her to punch through solid stone, but it was absent from her fingers. Whatever this was, it was something new.

As was the green glow that had suddenly appeared on the portion of the tree that Beatrice was touching. She had noticed it too, as her stance had changed just slightly and her catatonic face now bore the makings of a snarl. The strength of the arboreal opposing force continued to grow, and so too did Beatrice's resolve. Sweat formed on her brow and I didn't know whether to shout words of encouragement or run as far away as I could.

The green and the blue kept pushing against each other until their combined output threatened to overwhelm my retinas. Even with my hand covering my eyes, I could still see the battle raging before me, like two samurai trading blows but unable to land the kill stroke. Not even the earth around us was immune, as I felt rippling tremors pushing against my feet.

Beatrice broke her silence and screamed, and I realized that the first shriek earlier hadn't been from her, but somehow, the tree, which now echoed its opponent.

Finally, a blinding flash erupted from the nexus of colors, which cascaded out into the forest, throwing Hugo and me onto our backs when it reached us. I tried to get to my feet, but found that the wind had been knocked out of me, and so I crouched on the ground for several minutes while I recovered.

I looked over to where Beatrice had stood moments ago, only to find an immense cloud of dust suspended in the air, blocking my view. The tree still towered above us, so whatever she had tried to do thankfully hadn't sent it crashing down. Hugo stumbled over to me and offered his hand, before a coughing fit doubled him over, and instead I helped pull him back upright. We stared at each other, not knowing what to say or what to do. Even with all I had witnessed since my initiation into the world of alchemy, this encounter had shaken me in a way I hadn't felt before, and I wondered if Hugo shared that sentiment.

A figure appeared within the dirt mass and a few seconds later, Beatrice herself emerged. Her face looked ashen and drained, as if she had poured her life essence into that blue glow. Blood dripped down from her nose and poured forth from her attacking hand. But the most visible sign of her encounter was the gray streak of hair that was now interlaced within the black strands. She hobbled toward us and I wasn't sure if she was going to make it the last several feet. Before I could reach her side to steady her, she stopped in her tracks and stared blankly ahead.

"I failed," she whispered.

And then she collapsed.

The woman who had attacked the largest known tree in the world lay asleep in her cot of a bed, a damp towel pressed against her forehead. She had been sleeping since we had dumped her onto the mattress last night, after carrying her along the trail back to the car and then another hour and a half of a silent ride "home." Looking around the spare house, Hugo had decided as soon as we had parked that a random Airbnb was a better option, and he had departed in silence and had not yet returned. To be honest, I wasn't sure if he was actually going to return.

He was shaken by what he had seen out in the forest, that much was certain. After Beatrice had fainted, Hugo rushed us away from the General Sherman Tree within seconds, as if it was about to uproot itself and attack. He had said little during the trek down the mountain, only mumblings of "unnatural" and "forbidden" here and there.

At half past 11, he finally returned, a tray of coffees in his hands.

"Here," he said, handing me one of the drinks. "Had to drive halfway back to Fresno to get these."

"I was a few minutes away from renting my own car," I said, sipping the lukewarm brown liquid and resisting the immediate urge to spit it out. "You sure you weren't just deciding whether to bolt altogether?"

Hugo checked his watch and grimaced.

"Of course not. Plus, the plane won't be ready until tonight at the earliest. Thanks again for that."

"Don't mention it," I said. "What are you tracking now?"

"None of your damn business," said Hugo, before turning away and staring out the window.

"Fine, sorry I said anything. Was just curious."

"Yeah, and I was just hoping not to cross paths with a thaumaturge this decade."

"A what?" I asked.

"He means me," said Beatrice, who stumbled into the living room and nearly fell over before I braced her over my shoulder and sat her down on the loveseat next to the couch I had slept on.

"I don't understand," I said.

"What else is new?" said Beatrice and Hugo almost at the same time.

"Oh, now you two are a comedy duo?" I said, shaking my head.

"A thaumaturge is an alchemist who relies on forbidden sources of prima materia," said Hugo.

"They didn't use to be forbidden," Beatrice replied, rubbing her temples and clearly still not recovered from her ordeal in the forest.

"Yes, that's correct," said Hugo. "So you're not totally ignorant about the world you are trying to upend."

"I'm not trying to upend anything," said Beatrice. "I was minding my own business when the Guild came after *me*. So excuse me for wanting to defend myself when you assholes try to kill me for a third time."

"Where did you get it?" Hugo asked.

"Do you really want to know?"

"Yes," he said. "I need to understand who I'm dealing with."

"So you can do what? Report me to the alchemy police? In any event, it's gone. Used up. Didn't think that tree would fight back. Should have known better."

"Yes, you should have," said Hugo. "The brazenness of attacking an Ancient and thinking you could waltz out of there with its power. I'll ask you again, where did you get that blue?"

"Where else?" Beatrice said with a chuckle that made her grab her ribs in pain. "From people."

CHAPTER THIRTY

A MEMORY
OF SCORN

*"'Then I am sure, Duff van Asch, that you will be a fine
standard bearer for Rita's legacy.'"*

"What have you done?"

I stared at Beatrice and once again, a memory from ages past bubbled up to the surface of my subconscious and popped into being.

"*Wouldn't that mean that there was magic in people too?*" I had asked Steve over grog all those months ago.

"*Hmm. Probably. But the amount that could be pulled from a person is not worth the price of admission.*"

"No one will miss them," said Beatrice with an empty smile.

"I can assure you of that."

"How many?" asked Hugo, his hands suddenly shaking.

"A dozen here. A dozen there. I don't keep an exact tally. It was getting harder and harder to track down suitable candidates without drawing attention to myself."

"I'll bet it was," said Hugo. "But there's a reason that the Treaty of Verdun banned the-"

"Do you know what happened two towns over last year? The mayor's brother was out drinking with his buddies and got into a scrape with the man dating his ex-wife. Punches were thrown. It should have been just another barroom brawl. Except the next night, the second guy comes back from a midnight grocery run to find a raging inferno where his house had been."

"I didn't think arson had been upgraded to a capital crime by the unmasked vigilante council," I said.

"Oh, it hasn't," said Beatrice. "And I wouldn't have bothered if the asshole had succeeded in sending a message like he planned. But as it turned out, the place wasn't empty. Because that morning, after hearing what had happened at the bar, his ex had fled to that very house, thinking she'd be safe there. Now, the charges didn't stick, and no one cared that three kids have to grow up without a mother. But I found out the truth and set things right."

A sharp pain erupted in the back of my head and my vision became spotty, and when I blinked my eyes open again, I was standing over a man strapped to a raised platform, a weird metal contraption impaled in his chest. There was a sock taped into his mouth and he was-

I blinked, and I was in the woods shoveling dirt into a freshly dug hole, sweat glistening on my brow, a smug look on my face. There were several burlap sacks in the pit I had created, and as I covered them up, I wondered whether the next time would-

I opened my eyes wide and was back in the drab living room, clutching my head and watching Beatrice do the same.

"Hmm, didn't think that link still existed," said Beatrice. "What a stupid experiment, in retrospect. Not sure what I was thinking there."

"Where … what happened to…?" I asked, confused about what I had accidentally pulled from Beatrice's memory.

The other two ignored me. Hugo's hands and face were now beet red, but Beatrice remained oddly calm, as if she was completely detached from reality.

"So you set things right by making his kids orphans instead, is that it?" Hugo asked. "And siphoning off the minuscule amount of prima materia inside of him as a reward for doing so?"

"Precisely," said Beatrice. "I'm not a monster. If I was, this whole experiment would be a lot easier."

"I'm done," said Hugo. "This … this is beyond the pale. I can't … you'll have to find that stupid book on your own."

Without another word, Hugo strode toward the rickety front door, pushed it open, and didn't look back as it slammed against the frame.

"He seems nice," said Beatrice.

"Where is the rest?" I asked, the scattered images of Beatrice's unspeakable acts still randomly playing in my head. "I only saw the before and the after."

"They're forgotten, but not gone," she said, again her voice nearly robotic.

"What does that mean? What happened to you? You're … it's like you're here, but not here."

"An excellent question," said Beatrice. "What happened was you tricked me into finding that gold token, which I dutifully threw into the fountain. Then all hell broke loose, and I did the only sensible thing: I ran. But before I could even pack a bag, I came home that night to divorce papers and my son's pleading eyes."

"And you decided that kidnapping was the answer?"

Beatrice pushed herself slowly to her feet and walked into the kitchen, and I followed. She rummaged through the refrigerator, which looked liked it had maybe hours to spare before it broke down forever, and pulled out a plain aluminum can. Opening it generated an uncanny hiss far different from the one that greeted you when drinking a soda, and she downed the contents in a single gulp.

"Not sure what you're talking about," she said, and I swear I saw a blueish sheen around the outside of her pupils that quickly vanished just as fast as her posture and poise seemed to improve. Whether it was her improved vitality serum, the blue prima materia she had stolen, or something much worse, I wasn't sure I wanted to know.

"You took … forget it, it doesn't matter."

"That's right, your betrayal doesn't matter. The Guild coming after me, it doesn't matter. What matters is my work here."

"They're not," I said. "Coming after you. Dalia, the Guild, they have bigger things to worry about than you at the moment. That's why I'm here."

"For a blank book?"

"I could lie to you and say yes, but I think you know it's not really blank," I said.

"Well, that's nice of you, Jen. Or Jade. Or whoever you say you are."

"What's that's supposed to mean?" I said. "You know who I am. What we've gone through."

"Ah, but that's the thing," said Beatrice. "I don't anymore. Come. Let me show you something."

She beckoned me into her tiny bedroom, and I watched as she fiddled with the wall before finally pulling one of the panels free and tossing it on the floor. I looked over her shoulder to see a small nook had been cut into the sheetrock, and resting inside was a mason jar. A mason jar filled with silver rings.

"What is this?" I asked. "Please don't tell me those are yours."

"Of course they are," said Beatrice, picking up the jar and shaking it. From what I could see, there must have been dozens and dozens inside. Were they singular moments that she had excised or had she gone deeper, removing entire years of her life? And how did she even have the knowledge and raw materials to accomplish such a task? But instead of those questions, the only thing I blurted out was a single word.

"Why?"

"That is the wrong question. The correct inquiry is why I didn't think of this sooner? What I'd managed in the past decade pales in comparison to what I've accomplished in the past three months. I guess, in a roundabout way, I should be thanking you, for setting me on this path."

"What path?" I asked. "The path that led you to become a cold-blooded psychopath? You sound barely human. How much of your past did you dump into this jar?"

"Not enough," she said. "Because you know what I felt when you showed up? Both times? Anger. And I can't afford to be angry."

"Well, if being angry prevented you from siphoning off whatever was in that tree, then I'm glad to have caused it!"

"You're starting to bore me," said Beatrice. "And I have so much work to do, now that I tapped out nearly all my power. So if it's the book you want, I'm afraid you'll just have to be on your way."

"Because where you hid it is one of those rings in there and you don't know which?"

"If only it were that simple," she said. "I knew this day would come, so I took precautions, although I didn't think you would be the one to show up here."

"I didn't have a choice!" I said, but my plea fell on deaf ears, as she walked out of the room, leaving me alone with her memories. I picked up the jar and resisted the urge to smash it against the floor, as if that would somehow force the memories back into her head.

I found Beatrice in the kitchen a few minutes later, standing over the stovetop, stirring what appeared to be hot water in a pot with a wooden spoon.

"You know, it's customary to add the ingredients first," I offered.

"I'm not cooking anything," said Beatrice. "It helps me think in my current state."

"As opposed to what other state?"

She turned around suddenly and stared directly into my eyes, and before I could react, I was falling into a deep abyss that thankfully ended a few seconds later. I looked around in a mild panic before realizing where I was.

"So you actually did it. I thought maybe there was a chance you were faking this whole thing," I said, turning a full circle to see that the expanse that had once held a galaxy's worth of bright memories was now dark. No, that wasn't the right word. It was empty.

"I've been here once before. Do you still remember?" I asked. "When we were in the lighthouse, when I needed to reach you. I forced my way in through our link and I found you. There."

I pointed off into the distance and was surprised to find the dim light of that awful memory present in the night sky of Beatrice's mind.

"Yes, it's still there," she said. Beatrice materialized a few paces away, looking the same as she did in the real world. Except the outline of her visage was fuzzy, and it blinked in and out like a TV trying to pick up a signal, a proper representation of the incomplete person I saw before me.

"Figured that would be the first thing you would want to forget."

"I thought so too," said Beatrice. "Was saving it for last. I would have been a clean slate, with nothing standing in my way except the limits of my ambition. But I realized something right as I was about to put pen to paper. I couldn't forget that little girl. Couldn't toss her away."

"Beatrice, I'm…"

"You're what? Sorry for what you did? For not telling me you had a gold token this whole time?"

"Don't you think that would have been the first thing I would have mentioned if I had known?" I said.

"So I'm supposed to believe that you spent years, even before you found out about the Quests, with the long-lost Guild token around your neck?"

Anger infected her voice, and Beatrice's figure became clearer, as if the remnants of her emotional core were trying to reboot her being. She realized it too and tried to steady herself, but that had the opposite effect.

"Yes, because it's the truth!" I pleaded.

"I only know one truth," said Beatrice. "That nothing will stand in my way again. Not the Guild, not you, not even the tallest fucking tree on this planet."

Lightning cracked across the black sky, illuminating Beatrice's empty inner world and causing me to shield my "eyes" from its unyielding brightness.

"What … is that?" asked Beatrice, and I realized she had not theatrically summoned the bolt to intimidate me.

"Dunno," I said with a chuckle, "but if I had to guess, it's something trying to stand in your way."

Beatrice pushed me out of her mind just as quickly as she had pulled me into it, and I collapsed backward onto the kitchen floor, my head pounding. The entire house was shaking, dishes were falling out of the cabinets, and the refrigerator door had come free from its hinges, revealing shelves full of unmarked aluminum cans. But I couldn't focus on yet another fridge stocked with mysterious alchemy, as there was the very real possibility that whatever or whoever was causing this chaos was intent on burying us alive in the rubble of the little shack. I ran toward the front door, only to nearly collide with a retreating Beatrice.

"This way!" she cried, directing me into her room. The jar was still in the nook where I had returned it and somehow in one piece. That wasn't the item she had sought to retrieve, however, as Beatrice was instead frantically searching through a chest of drawers next to her bed. After dumping piles of matching blue overalls onto the floor, she pulled free a familiar looking key and darted into the kitchen. I joined her there a few moments later to see that the key that had once been a mottled doorknob was already inserted into a lock on the back door, and when Beatrice yanked it open, I was face to face again with a vervorium portal.

"Follow me," she said and was about to step into the darkness when she saw the hesitation on my face.

"It could be Hugo. Let me go out and talk to him, before it's too late," I said, but she just shook her head and stepped through.

I considered my options, all of them terrible, and after making one more circuit through the house, decided the only choice was to follow Beatrice into the unknown yet again.

CHAPTER THIRTY-ONE

WHAT WAS
LEFT BEHIND

"The brother and sister eyed each other, as if they did not believe their good fortune. But they have earned it. Of this I am certain."

One day, when all the craziness died down (which I suspected would be never), I was going to hunt down whoever invented vervorium and punch them in the face. Because despite traversing through numerous portals with unknown destinations before, this time, both my mind and my body rebelled against me.

I floated through the ether without end, trying not to panic, trying not to think about the weight of everything that had been stacked on my shoulders, but the more I tried not to, the easier those thoughts passed through the flimsy mental barriers I had erected. Until it all became too much and I screamed a silent scream. And, of course, that was the trigger that unlocked the exit.

I swam up to the light that had appeared far above me and when I finally reached it, I found myself falling face forward onto a wooden floor at the top of a rickety set of stairs. Flickering bulbs were hung along the wall that lit the way down, but other than that, the space beyond was completely dark.

"You followed," called Beatrice from somewhere down below, her voice echoing.

"You sound surprised," I responded, timidly walking down the creaking steps before locating Beatrice sitting at a wooden desk a few feet from the bottom of the staircase, a banker's lamp casting a greenish glow on her and the book she was writing in.

"It's been six hours. I was pretty sure you threw your lot in with whoever had come to kill me."

"Six hours?" I said. "It's never taken that long before. How far away are we?"

I peered out at the expanse beyond the desk, but it was pitch black.

"Vervorium doesn't work that way," said Beatrice. "Your conviction, or lack thereof, determined the length of your traversal. For me, it was only six seconds. And to answer your question, we're hundreds of miles away, on the other side of the mountains."

"Great," I said. "Looks like I need a new ride home. What is this place, exactly? Another secret headquarters of yours?"

"Something like that," said Beatrice, who pulled a chain on the lamp down, causing dozens of tube lights overhead to spring to life, revealing a massive and mostly empty warehouse that stretched out for hundreds of feet. Nearby were metal shelves that were also, for the most, part barren, except for the ones nearest to Beatrice's desk. These contained glass jars, metal cans, and other small boxes, all neatly spaced and arranged methodically and carefully. It was the opposite of the unordered chaos of her previous headquarters and I suspected that this marked change in organization was the result of her personality erasure.

I waded into the array of shelves and found something familiar: the raised platform where Beatrice had drained the prima materia from her first victim. A blood-stained sheet was draped over it, hiding a lumpy figure underneath. I approached with trepidation, the horrid memory of the shackled man with the nefarious device gratuitously inserted into his body, and lifted the top of the covering to find … a collapsed cardboard box labeled "OLD" in bright red letters.

"Hoping to get a glimpse of my next sacrifice?" said Beatrice, who closed the small journal and stowed it in one of the desk's drawers when I returned to the front area.

"I don't understand. I knew your past, but what you've done now … it's unspeakable."

"Why?" she asked. "Because all life is precious? Or some other bullshit you were raised on? I don't believe it. Not anymore."

"How did you even get here? I could barely find a drop of nemosyne to pull one of your old memories out of my head to find you. The amount you must have acquired to render your past into that jar …"

"Yes, it's quite impressive," said Beatrice. "And funny enough, you provided the key."

"What do you mean?"

"Your use of the speed buff to decode the tattoo and then to solve your little work problem, it got me thinking. What if there was a way to unlock the mind-expanding power of that buff without the debilitating after-effects? And so I went to work."

"The vitality serum recipe," I said. "You improved it and then combined it with the speed buff."

Beatrice smiled, and it almost looked genuine, but I could tell that she was struggling with all her might to appear normal.

"Exactly. And that was only the beginning! Once I completed

my first successful human transmutation, anything was possible. But the after-effect of killing even that scumbag gave me nightmares. So I had to devise a solution."

"By ridding yourself of your memories? But why didn't you just remove the act itself? Why did you turn yourself into this?"

"You make it sound so simple," said Beatrice. "Like removing a puzzle piece and tossing it in the garbage. But it isn't, I can assure you. The act of taking a life, any life, cannot so easily be excised. Not as I was. So I became something better."

"You call this better?" I asked. "My ledger is nothing compared to yours, but I couldn't look at myself in the mirror if I just magicked away what happened to Frankie. What happened to Doug."

"This is exactly what I'm talking about," she said. "Those names mean nothing to me. They're faint ripples on the surface of a pond that will disappear just as quickly as they appeared."

"And yet," I said, "you did not choose the same fate for your memories of me."

"Yes. Despite how much I didn't want it to be the case, I concluded that I still needed you. I now see how wrong I was."

"Because you don't like how I'm holding you accountable for what you've done."

"No, not at all," said Beatrice. "I left you a trail of breadcrumbs to come join me. And instead, you let that woman find me."

"I did no such thing! She took control of me. For two weeks, she trapped me. That's when she must have figured out that-"

"Another set of excuses from you. How typical," she said. "And I really don't have time for this Socratic dialogue any longer. Show yourself out upstairs. Now."

I stared at Beatrice, whose eyes bore a glimmer of anger, anger I knew she resented having to express. But I was nothing if not stubborn, and so I held my ground.

"There is still the matter of the Compendium," I said.

"I told you already," said Beatrice. "I don't know where it is. Even if the jar and the memories survived, you won't be able to find the location in there. And I'm glad they're all gone. Now I won't be tempted any more."

"But they're not, I'm afraid."

I pulled out the mason jar from the inner pocket of my jacket that I had rescued in the last fleeting moments before stepping through the portal, and set it quietly on the wooden desk.

"I left that in the house for a reason!" she screamed, as I saw the carefully crafted wall around the remnants of her old self crumble. "How dare you take it!"

"Of course I took it!" I yelled. "It was the only chance I had to put you right. You claim to be this cold, calculating, objective woman, and yet you're blind to what you've become. What would have happened to you if we hadn't shown up during your battle with the Ancient? You would have died."

"Maybe," she said. "But maybe if you hadn't distracted me, I would have prevailed."

"Keep telling yourself that," I said. "You don't want to help me? You don't want to help yourself? I'll have to resort to other means."

I pulled out the other contents of my jacket, a small vial filled with blank ink, a pen, and a piece of paper, and set them on the desk next to the jar.

"What is that?" asked Beatrice.

"You don't remember this?"

Beatrice shook her head slowly from side-to-side.

"Unbelievable," I said. "You completed a Raid with the girl you killed, Kate. She found it underneath a mattress. You gave the bulk of it to the Requester, but kept some for yourself. This I know too well. Did you ever stop to think who you had given it to? You thought you were trying to get it before the Guild could, but in reality, you were working for them all along."

"Great, so I found some ink and killed someone. What does it do?"

"I'd rather not have to do this," I said. "So I'm going to give you one chance, to willingly undo what you've done to yourself. Before I force you to."

I drew the small quota of ink from the vial into the pen and wrote a single word at the top of the paper.

"*Beatrice,*" it said.

"You wrote my name," she said. "And nothing happened. That was your big plan?"

"No," I said. "It's what comes next that you're not going to like."

I set the pen tip back down onto the paper, and very carefully and very judiciously wrote one more word with the remaining ink that I had, in a fit of weakness, begged Ty to give to me.

"*Remember.*"

Before Beatrice realized what was happening, I held the paper in front of her eyes, which turned glassy as the pellerium began its work. But instead of robotically taking the rings out of the jar and putting the memories back into her head, as I had planned, all she did was sit in a stupor, until finally the life returned to her gaze.

"What ... what did you to do to me? There was a woman on the island with me. Leah. She led me to ... somewhere. It's too fuzzy. And then, there was ... another. A girl. A warrior. The true Keeper of the Medoblad. She was inside my head. But the rest of it, it's all gone. I can feel its absence now. Only shadows remain, taken by the two of them."

"What are you talking about?" I said, my lip quivering. "You told me you found the Medoblad in the stones of the altar at the Temple of Artemis!"

"I did … and I did," said Beatrice. "But that wasn't the truth. The woman, Leah, she took the real memory and layered over it with a fake one."

"So that's all that it did," I said, a pit forming in my stomach.

"No," said Beatrice. "There's more. A bench. Central Park. Your specter, Jade. She used that ink to get my attention. She wanted my help. I said I would give it to her. But she never showed. Until now."

"I don't understand," I said. "How could you have forgotten this much and still have so much left in your head?"

"This wasn't what you wanted," said Beatrice. "The ink, you were going to make me put everything in the jar back. And hope that my old self would help you?"

"Pretty much," I said. "But I only had enough for two words."

"You chose the wrong ones, then. If I had that ink-"

"You did though," I interrupted. "You kept some of it after the Raid. You used it on me. What did you do with the rest?"

"I don't remember," said Beatrice. "But I want to."

"Of course you don't," I said. "Wait a minute. What did you say?"

"Your dumb, stupid plan worked," she said. "You unlocked what I didn't even know I had forgotten, and I see now that there are other forces at work here that have already bested me. And made me look like a fool by thinking they could just wipe all traces of themselves from my head."

"Are you saying you…"

It took all my willpower not to break into a huge grin.

"Yes," said Beatrice. "Open the damn jar."

CHAPTER THIRTY-TWO

TOTAL RECALL

*"I picked up the Stone and weighed it in my hand. A fine simulacrum,
but it will not last very long. These two children need it more than I do, if they are
to survive into this new world I have initiated them into. So I bequeathed it to them
along with the rest of their spoils."*

The prior and current incarnations of Beatrice were nothing if not methodical. Despite the large number of rings in the jar, it only took a few hours for her to work her way through every single one. I couldn't imagine what it must have been like, to slowly remember bits and pieces of your life, all out of order, all without any context. But somehow she managed it, not even pausing to eat, only taking sips of her new-and-improved serum. A serum I realized Jade traveled across the country for.

"What did you tell the glamour, exactly?" I asked, the disparate parts finally coming together.

"Ugh, my honeymoon," said Beatrice, vigorously shaking her head back and forth as if she had drank something bitter. "Two pumps and done every night. Should have known then."

"TMI, TMI!" I yelled. "That's what you're focused on now? With everything that's happened?"

"I can only process what's in front of me," she said, dropping yet another ring onto a piece of paper and staring into the memories that soon appeared on the page.

"Jack-Jack," she muttered a few moments later. "He was so little, I had forgotten, even before."

Beatrice wiped a small tear from her eye and I pretended not to notice while she reached her hand into the jar again.

"And to answer your question, I told her more than I wish I had. Especially now that I know what she did to me."

"Great," I said. "Another angry magic being wandering free."

"That's my fault, is it?" asked Beatrice, snatching a handful of rings and dumping them on successive pieces of paper. "You're the one who took that necklace, you're the one who wore it around the city like a trendy piece of clothing, you're the one who seems to have fed her enough life-force or whatever metaphysical thing exists inside us to let her break free."

"I didn't have a choice!"

"You keep saying that," said Beatrice quietly. "But it's not true. You *always* have a choice. You had a choice when I offered you the contract. You had a choice when they offered you money beyond imagining to give up your gold token. Yet you convinced yourself that you are helpless. A pawn. A stone cast into a river's flow. But I don't buy it. I don't believe it."

"What would you have done, then?" I said. "You controlled me, made me put on that ring. I was just suppose to say no thanks?"

"I would have let you go," she said. "Found someone else."

"Sure you would have," I said. "Like you let Doug go. Like you let Kate go."

"I can change," said Beatrice. "By the time I met you I–"

"Yes, definitely," I said. "That's why you had to turn yourself into an emotionless robot."

"And that was a mistake. I understand that now," she said. "But what do you see when you look at yourself? A coward who's too afraid to challenge anyone?"

"You met Dalia," I said. "You know what the Guild is capable of. What am I supposed to do?"

"If I help you retrieve the Compendium, and you bring it back to them, do you honestly think that will be the end of it? That it will be all unicorns and rainbows the rest of the way?"

"I … I don't know. But I need to find out how my mom was connected to all of this. I need to keep going. I need to see this through."

"Then you're dumber than I thought," said Beatrice, turning the jar upside down and letting the last few rings drop with a thud onto the wooden desk. "And that's why I won't be helping you. There's a cot in the back corner over there. It's yours for the night, but tomorrow, I'm sending you on your way."

I tossed and turned in Beatrice's stupid, uncomfortable cot all night. How could I sleep with all that had happened over the past day? I had been trapped in an endless void, attacked by an apparently sentient tree, forced my ex-boyfriend into an indentured apprenticeship, and flown across the country to find out that my former mentor had become even more of a sociopath. And with all of that, the thing that was actually keeping me awake was Beatrice's words.

"You *always* have a choice."

But who was she to judge me, after all she had done? I had made a choice, sure, to pick that apple pie Quest that had delivered me into her waiting arms, and I had made a choice not to cower before her when she tried to force her way into my mind.

But then something had happened.

Maybe it was the command Beatrice had implanted in me. I had felt so helpless at how my body had rebelled against me. At how I couldn't even take off a tiny piece of jewelry from my finger. Then I had won her approval and let her control me in a different way. I had stood by while she forced my friends to trash the Met. Heck, I was the one who made them do it, with barely a protest.

And in the aftermath, instead of trying to help them, I had made them forget what I had done. Then I had doubled-down and done the same thing to Duncan. Did they deserve what I thought I was doing to them? Maybe Duncan did. But none of them had deserved their current fates. And that was something I had put to the side for too long.

I sat up from the cot to find Beatrice still hunched over her desk. I watched silently as she wrote copiously into a little notebook, her hand whirring down the lines of the page like a virtuoso, stroking her bow back and forth across the strings.

"What are you doing?" I asked quietly. "Is your mind…"

"No, it's normal. No buffs tonight. But having all of my memories again seems to have jumpstarted something inside me. I need to write it all down before I lose this spark."

"I see," I said. "Been thinking about what you said, and what I've done. I need to set things right. Need to mend what I've broken. Will you help me?"

"Probably not," said Beatrice. "I have to reassess the last few months with clear eyes. And that doesn't leave much time to-"

"The memory serum, it did something," I said. "To Stacy, to Lisa, and to Duncan. They're forgetting themselves. If I don't reverse it somehow, there will be nothing left of them soon but empty shells."

"And I suppose you're going to blame me for that, too?"

"No. You may have provided the means, but it was my decision. My choice. And it was a bad one. And I need to fix it."

It felt good to say those words out loud, even if they were just words. But words are the first step toward action. And I was tired of being paralyzed by my failure to take any.

"I will help you," said Beatrice, closing her notebook. "It was my serum and it was imperfect. But I think I've rectified my errors. Come."

She walked along the empty metal shelves, and I followed, wondering if it was going to be that easy. At the far back of the expansive warehouse basement was a sidewalk cellar door, like the kind you find on every New York City street. Beatrice pressed her palm at the seam where the two halves met and it glowed in response before vanishing. A set of cinder stairs lay underneath the barrier that was no longer there.

"Don't tell me you have an entire second basement hiding under this one?" I asked, worrying that the answer would be yes.

"No," said Beatrice, descending into the darkness. "Even if this place is pretty much impregnable, I needed a place to hide my most valuable research."

The vestibule that greeted us at the bottom of the bottom was a study in contrasts to the room we had just left. Bright white walls were covered with erratic streaks of paint that circled the entire space, as if Jackson Pollock had been reborn inside and was trying to paint his way out.

"What is this?" I asked.

"An earlier experiment," said Beatrice. "Keeping everything in my head while operating a higher plane of thought was proving too taxing, so I needed a way to get it all out. This was the result."

"It's kind of messy," I said.

"From a certain point of view," she replied. "I eventually found something better. But this is not why we're here. Stand beside me, please."

Beatrice motioned me toward the center of the small room and pressed her back against mine.

"Don't move, or the next few moments will be very unpleasant."

"Not moving," I said, as I heard the drawing of a blade free from a metal scabbard.

"Is that the Medoblad you just unsheathed? What … what are you doing?" I asked, resisting every urge to turn fully around and stop her from impaling me with its stone-turning edge.

"Unlocking my *secreta.*"

I craned my neck as far as I could and watched in horror as Beatrice scored the Medoblad across her left palm. She let the blood drip onto the pale white surface below for a few seconds and then clapped her hands together before slamming them both into the floor so loudly that I thought the walls would crumble. A flash of blinding blue light erupted from where the blood had fallen and my eyes were forced shut.

Even closed, I could see some sort of runes rising up all around us, an ancient and powerful language long forgotten by the world. The floating symbols affixed themselves to the walls and the gears of what sounded like a great metal machine began to turn and turn, until the room finally fell quiet and I opened my eyes to find myself standing in the middle of rings of concentric shelves chocked full of anything and everything.

"What the hell was that?" I asked, my body refusing to move even an inch. "What the hell is this?"

"I told you," said Beatrice quietly. "This is my *Secretum Secretorum,* my secret of secrets, and I am its key."

CHAPTER THIRTY-THREE

SECRETUM SECRETORUM

"'You now have a foundation,' I told them. 'Our world is anxious to see what you will build on it. But one final piece of advice, or perhaps it is a word of caution. Two van Asch branches sprout where one was planted. Those branches will bear fruit. Do not let that fruit poison the tree. Create something everlasting.'"

"Please tell me this isn't the decorative lobby before we have to walk into yet another hallway to get to yet another chamber before we finally reach where you keep whatever you don't want anyone living to find?" I said, as Beatrice studied her unblemished palm in the aftermath of her unlocking alchemy.

"As I told you, this is it," said Beatrice. "The last one. Nothing else left."

She bent down to pick up the fallen Medoblad, resheathed it, and tucked it in her jacket before stumbling and nearly falling over.

I steadied her and directed her over to the uncomfortable looking wooden chair that was sitting in between the first ring of shelves.

"You're not just talking about this room, are you? That was the last of the magic you had left inside you, wasn't it?"

Beatrice nodded slowly and tried to stand, but fell back down into the seat.

"Very perceptive. Wasn't sure I even had enough to unlock the *Secreta*. That would have been … unfortunate. As it was, that was a much more painful experience than before. I don't know if I'd want to do it again."

"Of course it was," I said. "You sliced your hand open!"

"No, not that," said Beatrice. "You know that side of the blade cannot really harm me. It was the blue essence itself. It felt dirty. Like …"

"Like you had slaughtered a dozen people and stolen their souls?"

"That's not what I did and you-"

"Don't try to sugarcoat it," I said. "For whatever choices I made, yours are far worse. You can't run from what you've done."

"You don't think I know that?" said Beatrice. "That's why I went after the Ancient. Even in my former state, I was reaching my breaking point. I needed another source, and that tree, its power is pure. Help me up, please."

I extended my arm, and she grabbed it, then linked hers with mine as we walked forward together. Seeing her up close, I finally noticed the toll that this West Coast excursion had taken on her. It wasn't just the huge gray streak from before, but little white strands speckled throughout her now-black hair. Her face bore the brunt of it too, and if I had met her for the first time today, I would peg her age about 10 years older than it actually was.

"What?" asked Beatrice, turning us into the third ring of shelves. "You're staring."

"Have you looked at yourself recently?"

"No, but I know what you're thinking. And despite how I may appear, the last five minutes and yesterday's encounter aside, I've never felt better."

"If you say so," I said, quietly.

We finally stopped in front of a shelf that was filled with jars of dead animals floating in yellow liquid, some misshapen tree branches, torn vellum, and a small set of vials arranged in a rack. Each had different colored tablets inside, a veritable alchemical pharmacy, I surmised.

"One of each of these will counter whatever ill effects your 'friends' are suffering," said Beatrice.

"That's it? How do you know? Wait, please don't tell me. It's already hard enough for me to forget how you built all of this," I said.

"Suit yourself," said Beatrice. "You'll just have to trust me when I say that it's all been thoroughly tested."

"Why did you do that?" I asked.

"Do you really think I came up with the memory rings as my first foray into forgetting? When I already had something I thought would do the trick?"

Beatrice unstoppered each of the vials and slowly collected three tablets from each, before offering me the palmful of what could have been knock-off Pez.

"It happened to you too," I said. "The mental unraveling. How much of yourself did you lose?"

"Too much," said Beatrice. "Fortunately, I diagnosed the problem fairly quickly and was able to reverse it. I can't promise the results will be the same for you. A lot more time has passed, and although the mind is more resilient than we know, there is a limit."

"Thank you," I said. "I hope it's enough, but if it's not, then I'll just have to live with it."

"We both will," she said.

"And umm," I said, "while you're doling out magical tablets, I may have promised some of your speed buffs in exchange for someone taking Duncan off my hands."

I partially explained my bargain with D.C. and his thankless reforging of *Durandal*, which made Beatrice's eyes light up.

"What other Relics are you aware of?" she asked abruptly.

"Does this mean you'll give me some?"

"Depends on your answer," said Beatrice.

"Fair enough," I said, trying to catalogue every mystical object I had seen. "There's the Medoblad, of course. The dagger *White Hilt*, which is the cause of Polly's dad's current predicament. Its wielder Emma might have a second one, a longsword, but what it does, I'm not sure. And then there's *Curtana*."

"You mean the sword that Dalia tried to impress us with? You think that's a Relic too?"

"Why wouldn't it be?" I said.

"Fine. Anything else?" asked Beatrice.

"Well," I said, wondering whether it was smart to reveal the last secret in my arsenal. But a display of good faith was needed if I was going to pry Beatrice's secrets from hers. "There is one more thing. Although I'm not sure if it technically is a Relic or something greater."

"Spill, Jen," she said.

"The Philosopher's Stone, the Elixir of Life, they're real."

Beatrice exhaled sharply before bracing herself against the shelf behind her.

"No, that's … it's a fiction made up by Newton," she said. "He threw away years of his life seeking it, almost destroyed his legacy. It's. Not. Real."

"I can assure you that it is," I said.

"You've seen it then?" said Beatrice, a manic look appearing on her face.

"No," I said. "The Guild doesn't have one. Dalia sent me to Boston to retrieve the key ingredient. She wants to create one. For what purpose, I don't know."

"And you want to hand Dalia her book of lost secrets, then? So she can live forever?"

"It doesn't work like that," I said. "The Elixir saves you from dying, but it won't keep you from death."

"That's very reassuring," said Beatrice. "I'll just wait 'til her body falls apart before sleeping soundly again."

"I told you back at the house, you're not on the Guild's radar," I said.

"Sure. But they happen to know that I have the Compendium and that you are supposed to get it back," said Beatrice. "And when you don't, someone else will come here looking for it. Either way, I'm screwed."

"Does that mean you're going to give it to me? Are you sure that the empty Compendium isn't lying on one of these shelves?" I asked before Beatrice shot me a dirty look. "What? Can't blame me for asking."

"Yes, I can," she said. "I wish we had just given her the stupid book that day."

"So does Dalia," I offered.

"Not helping," said Beatrice. "I'll give you the speed buff, but that's it. I figure by the time you get back to New York and announce your failure, I'll be long gone from here anyway."

"About that," I said. "You think I used the clues you left to find you. But I didn't. We found another way to track you. And Hugo still has it. If he stays on Dalia's side, he'll come after you, no matter where you run to."

I stepped away, waiting for Beatrice to lunge at me with the Medoblad, but she just crouched down on the floor and gripped the back of her black hair tightly as if she going to tear it out.

"I'm … I'm sorry," I said. "I thought I would get the book from you and then we would go our separate ways. I figured you would want the Guild off your case after all this time."

"It seems you've backed me into a corner. And there's only one way out," she said softly, before staring off into the distance. "You're going to kill me."

"What? No, I'm not. What are you even suggesting?"

"Yes," said Beatrice, who pushed herself up from the floor with a buoyant energy that scared me. "It's the only way. Of course, I won't actually be dead, but in your memories, there will be a struggle. You tried to be reasonable, but I attacked you. And you had no choice but to fight back with the only thing within your reach. The Medoblad. The blade will have to be 'destroyed,' too. Maybe that vial over there will shatter after it's over. Engulfing my statue and the blade. Yes, that will do. I can make up anything in the memory, as long it looks believable enough to whoever comes prying into your head."

"No," I said. "I'm not doing that."

"I didn't say you had a choice in the matter," said Beatrice. "Do you think you could stop me?"

"Depends on what we're fighting with," I said, the various skills I had imbibed from the Guild's library ping-ponging around in my brain, waiting to be released. "And even if you get the upper hand, me thinking you're dead still won't do anything to get your hair out of Hugo's tracker."

"Why would anyone go looking for a dead woman?" said Beatrice. "Especially if you bring back the Compendium."

"That's your trade?" I asked. "You'll give me the book in exchange for…"

I considered it for longer than I should have. It would solve a lot of my problems and end this stupid Quest. I would return the victor and allow Beatrice get on with whatever she wanted to make of her life. Except that second part would be a lie. A lie that would put yet another weight on my soul, another person dead at my hands. And it wasn't a lie I could let my naive self live with.

"I can't," I said.

"I figured," said Beatrice.

"So what now?" I asked, trying to ignore that I was surrounded by an arsenal of alchemy and a woman not afraid to use it to get what she wanted.

"I don't know," she said. "As much as this plan makes sense, and I know you won't believe what I'm about to say, I don't want to force you to go through with it."

"Why not? You've never shied away from forcing others to do anything before."

Beatrice sighed.

"Yes, you keep reminding me of my past after handing it back to me. Can we just move on?"

"How can I when it keeps resurfacing? Either we figure this out together or I'll hand you over to the Guild myself."

I skulked away with a flourish and left Beatrice to her thoughts, confident that in her current state, she couldn't chase after me. Her *Secrata* was impressive, for Beatrice Taylor standards of secret locations. I wasn't sure how she had accumulated so many books and vials and random artifacts in the months since I had helped relocate her possessions to her island. Had she been holding out on me this whole time? But then I too had leveled up my own skills and knowledge as well, thanks to the Guild's electrum. And suddenly I knew how I was going to pry the Compendium's location out of Beatrice.

I walked back over to her and sat down next to her to remove my right boot. Although I had left a sizable collection in my overnight bag that was hopefully still on Hugo's plane, I had purposefully secured one particular morsel of knowledge on my person. The thought had crossed my mind when I had made my library withdrawal that the electrum could be used to bargain with Beatrice.

"What are you doing?" she asked me, as I collected the oldest recorded memory in the Guild's library from in-between my big and pointer toes.

"Proposing a new trade," I said. "Do you trust me?"

I offered the electrum to Beatrice, and she looked at it like a cat eyeing a crispy treat.

"Yes, but only because I don't think you're clever enough to trick me into swallowing poison. What is this?"

"You have to eat it," I said and Beatrice shook her head vociferously.

"Oh no. I am not going down that road again. Even if I just re-membered it for the first time."

"What are you talking about? You know about electrum?" I asked.

"Electrum? Never heard of it. But orichalcum, I have a bad his-tory with, apparently."

"As much as I would love to hear that story," I said, "this is noth-ing like that."

I lied.

"How would you even know?" said Beatrice.

"Because anything that scares you would petrify me and I've already eaten a dozen of these. You'll be fine!"

"I will turn you to stone for several days if I'm not!" said Beatrice, who finally grabbed the bead from my palm and put it in her mouth.

After a few seconds of chewing, her eyes rolled into the back of her head like mine had and off she went into the memory ether. I took the intervening half hour to carefully secure the Medoblad somewhere out of her reach so that when she reemerged from the past, no stabbing would be forthcoming.

"You're a goddamn liar, Jen," she said upon waking. "But that was … extraordinary."

"*What did you learn?*" I said in Dutch.

"*A great deal,*" she replied. "*How much of this are you offering for the Compendium?*"

"Alles ervan," I said. "All of it."

CHAPTER THIRTY-FOUR

HOUSE OF HEALING

"The children departed with their treasures. And now I can take mine:
the gold token and the Chair of the Guild."

"I want to go inside," said Beatrice three days later at our old stomping grounds, Bleecker Street Grounds (pun intended). She was dressed like she had fallen in the dumpster behind an East Village thrift store and had shorn her black hair into a bob, but for some reason, had kept the gray streak in the front.

"Out of the question," I said. "Even if I sneak you in with my invisibility cloak," Beatrice's eyes lit up at the mention of it, "I'm sure there are a dozen other things inside that could detect you."

"No one seemed to notice the glamour waltzing out of the north tower," said Beatrice. I had explained the circumstances behind her apparent escape from my supposedly impenetrable office. "And I can't believe the Guild was hiding right there, just blocks from my apartment this whole time. They didn't need to do anything to keep an eye on me. I walked by that stupid fake castle multiple times a week!"

"It was fate, I guess," I said. "And what do you plan on doing if I get you inside? Stroll up to Dalia's office and punch her in the face?"

"No," said Beatrice. "Stab her in the gut with the Medoblad and then keep her statute in my den for the next 10 years."

"You don't have a den," I pointed out. "Just a warehouse in some godforsaken former mining town."

Beatrice rolled her eyes.

"Yes, thank you for reminding me I am yet again between places. By the way, did you tell anyone you were back in town? Hugo didn't come calling to take you home in his fancy jet?"

"I didn't," I said. "Figured he can come find me if he wants."

"So you still think it's a total coincidence that you two show up at my nice little bungalow and then the next day someone blows it up?"

"Not sure what I feel about coincidences anymore," I said. "But maybe you should be asking a different question. Do you think it's a total coincidence that you tried to drain the energy or life force or whatever from the largest tree in the country and then the next day someone tries to blow you up?"

"I had asked myself that question," said Beatrice. "And why I was so arrogant to think I could have succeeded in what I set out to do that morning."

She got up ostensibly to refill her giant mug of coffee, but I knew better. I wasn't sure whether I liked this "new" version of Beatrice, who seemed to be lacking some of the stone-cold resolve I had seen so many times. In its place was a much-needed sliver of vulnerability, but when push came to shove, which woman did I want in my corner?

Before I could wrestle with that quandary further, the front door chime sounded and in walked Duncan. He was clean-shaven, dressed in a non-stained shirt, and his appearance rekindled some of the same feelings I felt for him when I first spotted him back at RPGLab all those years ago.

"Hi Dunc," I said, waving him over to our table and he sat down in Beatrice's seat before she could return. "You seem…"

"Normal. You can say it," he said, with a half-smile. "After the first hour of hammering in the forge, D.C. couldn't stand to look at me, so he made me shave with a straight razor and brought me some new clothes."

"Lover boy, move," said Beatrice, who returned with an extra mug of piping hot coffee, and Duncan gave me a look before shuffling to the other seat.

"Um, OK. Who are you?" he asked.

"A friend," I said. "She's going to cure you. Remember? The reason I needed D.C.'s help in the first place?"

"Not really," said Duncan. "The last month has been kind of a blur, to be honest."

"A month?" I said. "Dunc, I've only been gone a week. Has it gotten that much worse?"

"No," he said. "It did the trick, like you said! Hammer all day, sleep all night on a cot at the other end of the forge. Or maybe the reverse. There's not a lot of natural light down in the basement. It's hard to tell sometimes. But the monotony meant I never forgot anything because every morning it was the same as the day before."

"You're welcome?" I said, not quite believing that my half-baked idea had actually worked. "But that's over, hopefully. Drink this."

I pushed the coffee in front of Duncan, whose pupils dilated slightly, and he starting chugging the whole thing.

"Not all of it," I said, and he immediately put the mug down and wiped the brown liquid from his chin.

"You neglected to mention this," said Beatrice out of the side of her mouth.

"What?" I asked.

"That he's, you know, enthralled."

"I didn't have a…" I stopped myself before Beatrice could bite my head off, and turned to face Duncan.

"Hey," I said to him, and he looked at me like a puppy waiting to be scratched under the ear. "You don't have to trust me anymore."

The solution was so simple I was annoyed at myself for not thinking of it earlier. For no sooner had the words left my lips did Duncan's eyes go blank for the last time, and when he came to again, it was as if a boulder had been shoved off of his back.

"What … what just happened?" he asked. "You did something else to me, didn't you?" There was an accusatory note in his voice that had been sorely missing since our train ride up to New York, and while I was happy to hear it, it would all be for naught if Beatrice's tablets failed to live up to their end of the bargain.

"Yes," I said. "We've been over this."

"Have we?"

I paused. Did he still remember what I had admitted? With all the lying and the compulsion, I wasn't sure. But for all I knew, he had hidden a recorder in his pocket and had tapes of everything, the diary a convenient cover to distract me. And did I want an unhinged Duncan out for revenge? Even if he was now cured, there was no telling how much the memory loss would haunt him going forward.

I shook my head back and forth like I had eaten a sour lemon. That was not the person I wanted to be, just trying to duck my problems and hoping they went away.

"Sorry, what were you saying? Do you not remember what I told you in DC?" I asked, acting naive.

"You know I don't," said Duncan. "I went down there to confront you and somehow you still haven't admitted anything, despite my best efforts."

"Yes, well, now it's time to come clean. I did this to you and I'm sorry. And if you drink the rest of that coffee, I promise it will stop and you'll be back to as normal as you can."

"I knew it," he said, banging his fist against the table and spilling some of the coffee. "I fucking knew it!"

"Hush, you stupid man child," said Beatrice. "And quit wasting that! Do you know much it's worth?"

"Sorry," he said. "It's just ... I've been waiting for her to admit what she did for so long. I can't believe she actually said it."

"Me neither," said Beatrice. "But drink up please before I decide to do something else to you."

Duncan nodded and gulped down the rest of his coffee without another word.

"For the record," I said. "I already admitted what I had done. It's not my fault you failed to write it down before you forgot it."

"You can pat yourself on the back for that moral victory then," said Duncan as he finished.

"Did it work?" I asked. "He doesn't seem any different."

"Of course it worked," said Beatrice, grabbing the empty mug from him and inspecting its lack of contents. "But he won't be convinced of it for a while."

"I'm convinced," said Duncan. "It's like ... a fog has been lifted. And ... I can see the way forward now."

"That's a stupid metaphor for someone with memory loss," said Beatrice. "Just ring Jen tomorrow and tell her you remember everything from today and we'll all call it square."

"It won't be," he said. "Not even close. And what about the other two?"

"They'll be here shortly," I said. "I'm trying to make good on what I did."

"I don't think you'll ever be able to do that," said Duncan. "Last time I spoke to them, they were hardly functioning. It's amazing that Lisa's husband actually went through with the wedding."

"That you somehow remember?" I said without thinking, and Beatrice glared at me.

"Umm, no," he said sheepishly. "It was in one of my notebooks."

"Oh. Sorry," I said. "Look, Didn't mean to-"

"Yes, we'll all deal with Jen's moral reckoning later," said Beatrice. "It will be a ticketed event. But for now, I need you to skedaddle so we can wrap up this mind-healing pop-up store before someone says something."

"No," said Duncan. "I want to watch, to make sure she goes through with it. To make sure it works."

"I'm afraid that's not possible," said Beatrice.

"And why not?" said Duncan, getting indignant. "This was all an act, wasn't it? You gave me some temporary fix to get me out of your hair and by tomorrow I'll-"

"Because you're annoying me. And Jen told me what you did to her. Despite what she ended up doing to you, I don't fault her for trying to get back at you, you boorish prick."

"Fuck you!" said Duncan. "You don't know what I've been through, you can't-"

"Actually, you're wrong," said Beatrice. "I know exactly what you've been through. And if you don't get the fuck out of my coffee shop right now, I'm going to add you as a decoration."

"What the hell does that mean?" he said, smirking. "You going to turn me to stone or something?"

I resisted the urge to laugh as Beatrice pulled out a Tupperware container.

"Hey, you're smarter than I thought," she said, opening the lid and pushing it across the table to Duncan. He and I both peered inside to see a small stone mouse.

"What is that?" I asked in faux shock.

"What it looks like: a mouse that I turned to stone. With my magic knife," said Beatrice. "If you come back tomorrow, I'll do a live demonstration for you."

"What. The. Hell," said Duncan. "You're fucking nuts. I'm done with this."

He pushed his chair back and nearly toppled over onto the ground before running out the door.

"Wait!" I yelled, to no avail. "You forgot the package for D.C. Ugh, fine. One more errand to take care of."

"Can I come along?" asked Beatrice.

"Maybe," I said. "And thanks, by the way."

"For what?"

"For sticking up for me."

"Don't mention it," she said. "It probably won't happen again, but I can't stand men like him."

"What was that about this being your coffee shop?" I asked.

"Oh, just a thought I had earlier. I always liked this place. Was thinking of buying the building. And buying out the owner of BSG too."

"That's … that's great?" I said. "But I didn't think you were going to stay here in the city. What with your ex and-"

"They're gone," said Beatrice. "Garrett took Jack-Jack and moved down to Florida to live at his parents' house for the winter. At least that's what I was able to find out a few months ago. Not sure where they are now. Maybe in Newport. I'm a year out from seeing him. And that's if I don't get into any trouble."

"I'm so sorry, B, I had no idea," I said.

"It's OK," she said. "It was my fault. Should have kept a more level head."

The front chime sounded again and in walked Lisa and Stacy, to whom level headed could not even charitably be used. For no sooner had the door closed did the two of them just stop and stare off into space, as if an invisible hand had shoved them through the precipice and then departed. I couldn't believe how much worse Lisa seemed than from when I had seen her only a week ago.

"Ladies!" shouted Beatrice enthusiastically. "Please join us." They complied and sat down at the two empty chairs at our table, where they continued their staring-into-space contest.

"Why are you so chipper?" I whispered to Beatrice, when it was clear that my erstwhile friends were not planning to engage any further unless prompted.

"Because," she said, "I'm excited to see how effective these tablets are. I prepared two different versions using two different methods, one incredibly more time consuming than the other. If both work the same, then this could be huge in terms of-"

"So you're using my friends as guinea pigs?" I hissed. "What if it just makes it even worse?"

"Not possible," said Beatrice. "The alchemy is rock solid. Plus, I already tested it on actual guinea pigs. And then some of the individuals I had used for my other … work. But of course I was unable to test the long-term effects, so-"

"Listen to yourself!" I said. "You sound like the other version of you. Just cure them and let's move on!"

"Normally I would agree with you Jen," called out a familiar voice behind us and I turned to see Lucca Josephie standing in the entrance-way to the coffee shop's hidden back bar wearing her trademark beanie. "But there's something to be said for advancing the cause of progress."

"Who is this?" asked Beatrice as the purple-haired alchemist came over to join our now-crowded table. "Who are you?"

"I'm Lucca," she said and reached out her hand to Beatrice awk-wardly, as if she was meeting a celebrity. "Second Seat of the Breuckelen Table. It's so nice to finally meet you!"

CHAPTER THIRTY-FIVE

BOINK

"I presented my token at the meeting today. Thanks to Rita's recruitment efforts over the years, no one questioned her directive naming me as her Seat's heir. And no one opposed me when I nominated myself to serve as the 7th Chair."

Beatrice did a double take between me and Lucca several times, before reaching inside of her jacket where I imagined something awful was stashed.

"You're a goddamn liar," she said to me, her voice rising. "What the hell were you thinking?"

"I'm not," I pleaded. "A liar. I didn't tell anyone we were even in the city!"

"Your friend is innocent," said Lucca. "At least of ratting you out. But you can't expect to come onto this island with a Relic and not have me find about it. Alchemy that strong, it calls out like a whale singing to its pod. You just need to know what to listen for. And my druithyl network is specifically attuned for Relic-class items."

"I should have known," said Beatrice. "Guess I was lucky you didn't track me down earlier."

"Believe me, I thought about it!" said the Guild's resident scientist, who placed a silver metal briefcase onto the table with a thud that made me jump. "I left you alone for a long time after you first brought whatever is in your jacket back to the city, but I couldn't hold back any longer."

"Great," said Beatrice. "What do you want?"

"To see you work. To see what makes you tick. And to run some tests on your handiwork. I've found that the progress of alchemy can only move forward with us all working together."

Beatrice looked at me to give her some sort of gauge as to Lucca's sincerity, and I shrugged. In the short time I had known her, she seemed to be the least psychotic member of the Guild, but who knew what she was really like behind closed doors?

"I work alone," said Beatrice. "You're welcome to test one of my tablets, but considering my past history with the Guild, you'd have to believe me to be an idiot to think I'd trust you."

"Of course! Trust is earned, not given. Let's get started on that."

Lucca unclasped the briefcase, and it unsealed with a hiss that gave off a cloud of purple steam. I peered inside and saw a series of glass beakers arranged from smallest to largest in one half and a series of pipettes filled with different colored liquids in the other half.

"What is all this?" asked Beatrice.

"It's my mini-lab!" said Lucca. "I figured you would never agree to come to my actual one, so I brought a piece of it to you. These beakers are specially treated to detect particular prima materia and any impurities that could be present."

"So you think my alchemy isn't sound, is that it?"

"No, not at all!" said Lucca. "But from our two silent guests here, it looks like you are about to do something rather drastic. You can proceed if you want and we'll do the test after, but might it be more prudent to do it in reverse? Just in case?"

"Doesn't matter one bit to me," said Beatrice, clearly annoyed with Lucca's implication about her alchemic prowess. "Jen, they're your friends. You decide."

"If it's all the same to you," I said, and I suspected it wasn't, "let's do the test first. I won't be able to forgive myself if we rush this."

"Fine," said Beatrice. "What do you need me to do?"

"First things first," said Lucca. "There are a few too many people here. I know most New Yorkers live in their own little bubble, but even that has its limits. And we're about to breach them. So if you don't mind, let me just…"

She withdrew a small remote control with a red button from underneath her hat and pressed it, causing the fire alarm to immediately start blaring.

"I thought you were going to create some sort of illusion or something, like in the Guild library!" I shouted over the piercing siren.

"Why would I do that?" asked Lucca, who smiled as the half-dozen other customers and the barista scrambled to leave the shop. She followed them out, but returned 30 seconds later. "There. I told the girl running the counter to come back in an hour after I fixed the alarm."

"And she believed you?" I said.

"I also gave her a fifty. Sometimes money trumps alchemy. Anyway, now that we have the place to ourselves, we can get started."

Lucca pressed the button again on her remote, and the bleating stopped. Throughout the commotion, Lisa and Stacy had sat perfectly still, like two victims of the Medoblad. Or more like robots, waiting to be commanded. That thought pulled at the back of my mind, but I couldn't quite identify why.

"May I have a set of the tablets please?"

Beatrice nodded, placing four of them on the table, and Lucca began removing some of the beakers from the case along with three pipettes full of black liquid. She deposited the contents in equal distributions among the glassware before withdrawing a loupe from the outer brim of her beanie and inspecting each of the tablets.

"Why four?" she asked.

"They work in tandem," said Beatrice. "One to metabolize any of the remaining memory loss serum left in the person's body. One to open the path to the subconscious. One to drag the forgotten self back to the surface. And finally, one to heal all the damage."

"That's … that's more robust than I was expecting," said Lucca. "And from what I overheard earlier, you tested this on yourself?"

"Yes," said Beatrice. "But as I told Jen, I fixed myself fairly quickly. It's been several months already for these girls, unfortunately."

"I see," said Lucca. "Well then, all the more reason we get this party started."

She picked up the tablets and dropped one into each beaker. They dissolved immediately, colored wisps of smoke pouring out of the tops like a homemade volcano. Except for the last one. That beaker shattered into two dozen pieces, covering the table.

"Huh," said my Second Seat. "That was weird. You said you made the same tablet with a different method?"

Beatrice nodded silently, perhaps happy that neither of us had yelled out "told ya so," and held out her palm to offer the second version. Lucca quickly prepared another beaker/pipette pairing and put the replacement tablet inside. This time, the beaker erupted into flames, and after a few seconds, only a puddle of translucent goo remained.

"That's … not good," said Lucca. "There is something off about these tablets. Which one was it?"

"The remembering one," said Beatrice.

"Ah. Then it's a good thing you didn't actually have them eat it. They'd probably both be dead already," said Lucca.

"I took three of these!" said Beatrice.

"Yes, well. That's also curious. Are sure you're still alive?" asked Lucca.

"You're nuts," said Beatrice. "I know what I'm doing. They would have been fine. I'm fine. Duncan is fine too."

"There's no need to be defensive," said Lucca. "The truth passes no judgment."

"So what do you suggest we do, then?" I asked. "Lisa and Stacy are scarcely functioning. It's a miracle they even made it here today. Can we just give them three so they don't get any worse?"

"Hmm," said Lucca. "You two, what day is it?"

Lisa and Stacy slowly stirred to life, like a wind-up doll who had its key turned, and then both of them eked out a barely audible whisper.

"Today."

"Yeah, no," said Lucca. "Three of the four will turn them into empty shells with a bit more lucidity. Any new experiences will imprint strongly and prevent their old selves from resurfacing. It will be like trying to recover a backup onto a hard drive that's been through a fresh install."

"FUCK!" I yelled, startling everyone, even Lisa and Stacy, who looked around searching for the source of the disturbance but couldn't find it.

"Jen, calm down," said Beatrice. "Even though I'm not convinced that the tablet won't work-"

"It won't," interjected Lucca.

"-I will put my pride aside for the moment and find a solution with your friend here."

"You consider me a friend?" Lucca said to me, a puppy dog look in her eyes.

"I … what?" I stammered.

"I'm just kidding," she said. "Also not sure I want to be your friend, considering what happened to your last two. And your boyfriend. You seem to go through people rather quickly. But I hope you can at least trust me. If you all will kindly accompany me to my lab, we can get to work."

I signaled for Lisa and Stacy to follow us out of BSG, but they ignored me as if I was invisible. Beatrice stepped in and directed them instead, and we were soon on our way to Lucca's loft, an unexpected fellowship of five.

"Do you trust her, Jen?" asked Beatrice, once we were out of earshot. "Because I swear if I end up a trophy in Dalia's office, you're the first person I'm coming for after I escape."

"As of right now, yes," I said. "But if my judgment is off, I'll promise I'll try to visit you once a week."

It took a lot to impress Beatrice, but fortunately, Lucca's lab was up to the challenge. After a bit of schoolgirl awe, the two alchemists got to work, deconstructing the faulty tablets and formulating a plan on how to fix them. As I sat next to Lisa and Stacy, I felt like a piece of aimless driftwood, being tossed around by forces more powerful than me. And maybe I deserved to be cast aside, while others fixed the problems caused by my search for easy solutions.

I waved my hands in front of the two women, but their reactions remained the same. It was hard to tell if they were even aware of their surroundings, or whether they were already completely devoid on the inside, just bodies without minds, like …

"What do you know about glamours?" I asked as I ran over to Lucca, the pieces of the puzzle finally snapping into their awful place.

"I know their creation is banned, but if you wanted to, how would you do it?"

Lucca's demeanor shifted in an instant, and instead of the buoyant, jovial woman I was used to, a different one surfaced, one who looked like she had also done the unspeakable acts that Beatrice had accomplished in the last few months.

"Why … why are you asking that question?"

"Ty already told me the true nature of a glamour, but like, I assume it's not something that you willingly volunteer for," I said.

"No it is not," said Lucca. "At one point, there was a network of alchemists across Europe who would scour hospitals looking for braindead patients and then make off with the bodies. Those glamours … did not work out very well for their creators, and eventually the effort collapsed. And thankfully with it, the precise knowledge was lost for generations."

"I don't know if I agree with you," I said.

"What do you mean?" asked Lucca.

"It's just a hunch," I said. "And I'm not sure you're the person I need to be telling. But look at my friends. They're almost like those braindead patients."

"I'm not following," said Lucca. "And I don't like where this is headed."

"Neither do I," I said. "But what if there was someone else out there today who rediscovered the knowledge, and devised a means to create a new generation of glamours, one that could be sold to the highest bidders? Or maybe something far worse."

"What are you talking about?" asked Beatrice, peering out from behind the maze of heated glassware.

"She was right there in front of us," I said. "Eva, Polly's glamour. I know who created her."

CHAPTER THIRTY-SIX

RESTORED SELVES

"The Guild and the country are at a crossroads. There are thousands of miles of land to explore, and we must be the ones to discover its secrets first."

I n the end, the solution was elegant but time-consuming. As D.C. had told me, you couldn't rush things. And the problem about warping your mind, as Beatrice had done, was that you were eventually going to miss something. But thanks to Lucca's fastidiousness, the pair had corrected the slight imperfection in the tablet's recipe that had led to its catastrophic failure, even if it meant we were one week closer to the Guild meeting with still no Compendium to show for my efforts.

I spent that time stewing over my latest revelation in the lab day and night without the means or help to do anything about it. Neither Beatrice nor Lucca seemed interested in going toe-to-toe with someone capable of creating new glamours, even he had been reduced to a rapidly aged old man. And there was no telling how Polly would react if we told her that the Eva skin she wore about the city like a costume was an actual person.

"You were lucky," said Lucca. "The memory loss you inflicted on your own mind was not as severe, so the tablet's odious effects weren't able to trigger."

"Thanks?" said Beatrice. I hadn't told Lucca about the sequel to her original foray in memory erasure or any of her other misadventures out west. Not after how Hugo had reacted. But she would find out soon enough, and I wanted Beatrice far away from here when she did.

"It's time," said Lucca, and Beatrice handed her the other three tablets, which she put together with the new fourth one in a mortar. A pestle appeared and much grinding transpired, at the end of which a multi-colored powder was produced. This was placed equally into two glasses of tepid water, which Lucca stirred with metal straws. She motioned Lisa and Stacy to her side and handed one to each of them. They looked at the concoction for a moment before they both sucked down the entire contents in less than five seconds.

"Huh, wasn't expecting that," said Lucca. "Don't think it tastes very good."

"Now what?" I asked. "They don't seem to be getting better."

"Give it a second," she said.

I did as instructed and sure enough, Lisa and Stacy's blinking increased rapidly, their arms started to twitch, and they began to stomp their legs to a rhythm only they could hear. Then they started swaying back and forth and that was when something clicked in Lucca's head and she ran off into the back of the lab. She returned a minute later with a small blue square which she threw across the room just as Lisa and Stacy fell backwards onto the concrete floor. But they didn't. Instead, the blue square expanded into a full-size blue gym mat that slid to a halt behind the falling women, who landed with a plop. I hurried over to them and was met not with stares of indifference, but with knowing looks.

"JJ?" said Stacy as she sat up. "What … just happened? Where am I?"

"Why does it feel like someone drove a metal spike through my head?" asked Lisa, who spritely got to her feet and immediately began gawking at all of Lucca's lab equipment.

"You know who I am?" I said, my heart pounding in my chest.

"Of course we do," said Stacy with a slight scowl. "You're our slightly less cooler friend who went AWOL on us right before Lisa's big day because you were insanely jealous."

"Why weren't you at the wedding?" Lisa demanded. "And why haven't you returned any of our calls for the last three months? Who does that?"

I gave Beatrice a "what should I do?" look, but she just shrugged her shoulders. Fortunately, Lucca came to the rescue.

"If you're about to do what I think you're going to do, then bring them in slowly. Pretend they're toddlers trying to learn about the world."

I nodded.

"You two should sit down," I said.

"That went better than expected," said Beatrice several hours later in my cramped studio apartment.

"Lisa tried to strangle me!" I said, collapsing onto the worn-out sofa that the previous tenant had left here. "Before having a nervous breakdown. And who knows what Stacy would have done if Lucca hadn't stepped in with her flaming glove?"

"As I said. If that were me, I would have at least managed to stab you in the abdomen or something."

"Then I sure am lucky!" I said. After the attempted violence, Lucca had calmed both of them down and offered to introduce them to one of the lower-level clans in the city if they wanted to continue learning about alchemy. They nodded sullenly and Lucca handed them leftover pamphlets from the early days of the Quest Board, when the Guild had expected a slightly higher advancement rate than what had eventually been achieved.

I had snagged one too, and was astounded at the level of detail contained inside. From a brief listing of old Night Market locations, to the best sources for local prima materia flora and fauna, to animals likely to have useful concentrations of the same, and even a glossary of some of the more potent substances, it was something I wished someone had given me at the start of my Questing journey.

"You are lucky," said Beatrice. "You cleaned up most of your loose ends, your conscious is clear, kind of, and now you can get back to stealing that library of insane memories and skills that you promised me."

"Oh, right," I said. "Not sure that's the best idea now. It's going to look not-at-all suspicious when I pump that machine for every last bead of electrum right after Lucca discovering that you're here in the city."

"Then I guess you really don't want the Compendium back," said Beatrice, who walked into the small barely-a-room kitchen but returned later with a huff. "Why is your fridge filled with nothing but off-brand bottled water? And you have absolutely no alcohol."

"I've spent two waking minutes in the past three months here," I said. "It's been one thing after another ad infinitum."

"Then let's go somewhere when I can get a drink," said Beatrice.

"It's 11 a.m.!"

"Did you just spend a week bent over a labtop trying to fix other people's problems? Didn't think so."

"Fine," I said. "I know a place that might do the trick."

We trekked off to Firebird, and I was surprised that it was open at this hour. And even more surprised to see Svetlana tending bar. And even further surprised when she said, "Emma's friend. You're back."

"Why the hell would you take me to the one bar where they actually know who you are?" scowled Beatrice.

"Because before I was wearing the glamour!" I said. "And now I'm not. I'm not, right?"

"You're not," said Svetlana. "But I still saw through you that night."

"Am I the only one in Manhattan without a warehouse full of druithyl?" I said.

"I didn't need that to pierce through your glamour. Which I hope you got rid of, by the way. They're horrific."

"I did, inadvertently," I said. "But if you didn't have druithyl, then how did you do it? And why didn't you rat me out to Emma?"

"Figured you had a good reason for using one," said Svetlana, who slid two drinks our way even though we hadn't ordered anything. "And I'm a bartender. I'm around people all the time. You looked uncomfortable from the moment you sat down. Like you were wearing an ill-fitted costume. It's not hard to spot if you know what you're looking for."

"You haven't seen, umm, me, recently, have you? Or any other glamours?"

"Can't say that I have," she said. "But I'll be on the lookout."

"What is this?" asked Beatrice, who drank the whole glass before Svetlana could respond.

"It *was* a Rush Hour," said the bartender. "Bourbon, tangerine, and maple syrup. A cocktail of my own concoction."

"Another," said Beatrice.

"Coming right up," said Svetlana, who walked away to give us a modicum of privacy.

"Now that Ms. Busy Body is here, we may as well go back to your apartment," said Beatrice.

"*No need*," I said, pushing my thoughts into Beatrice's head, like we had in the past.

"*I can barely hear you*," she replied. "*You really want to go down this path again? I think we both regret it.*"

"*What's done is done*," I said. "*We should take advantage of our advantages.*"

"*That was louder*," said Beatrice. "*And not sure if I agree. But at least this chick makes a mean drink. So we can stay put for now.*"

"*Good*," I said. "*Because I'd rather we be in public for what I'm about to tell you.*"

"What?" said Beatrice out loud.

"*We're not going to be able to sneak into the Guild. Not now*," I continued. "*So we need a new paradigm. A way to solve all our lingering issues.*"

"*You're not suggesting what I think you are, are you?*" asked Beatrice.

"*Yes*," I said. "*I am. We go right to the source of everything. To Dalia. You trade the Compendium for a fresh start. And maybe she'll be in a charitable mood and just hand you the key to the library.*"

"Absolutely not," said Beatrice, pushing me out of her mind with a violent shove that made my own head burn. Svetlana conveniently returned with a new round of drinks, all the while pretending that Beatrice was not talking to herself.

"Why not?" I asked.

"It would have made more sense a few weeks ago, but right now? When I'm at my weakest? Might as well just hogtie me over a spitfire and invite her to dinner."

"That's quite the image," I said. "But I don't think it will go down like that." I took a sip of my still-full first drink and recoiled at its bitterness. "I thought you said this was sweet!"

"I didn't. I match the drink to what the person needs," said Svetlana.

"So I need to be bitter?" I said.

"No," said Svetlana. "It's more of a wake-up. Supposed to help you remember the bitterness in your life."

"Why would I want to do that?" I said. "We came here to get away from our problems. Not be reminded of them!"

"I don't agree," she said. "You could have gone to any of the dozen establishments within a few blocks of here. Yet you chose my bar. Why?"

"Yes, why Jen?" asked Beatrice, who began sipping her second drink.

"You were hoping to run into her here, weren't you?" asked Svetlana. "Something happened between the two of you."

"That's putting it mildly," I said.

"Sorry to hear that," she said. "But I haven't seen her recently. You'll have to find her some other way to apologize."

"What … are you in my head?" I asked.

"If only. That would make my job a lot simpler," said Svetlana. "I think if you both finish your drinks, though, you'll figure out what you need to do."

I took another sip of the drink, which went down slightly easier the second time, and let the flavor wash over me.

I was back in the Board Room. Emma was there, and I was happy to see her alive. But then I saw her hand, saw her demeanor, heard her ordeal, and realized what my carelessness with the glamour had done.

I took another sip, and was in the Met bathroom, giving the note to Stacy, watching her act against her will, then doing the same to Lisa a few moments later, and then abandoning them to their fates, so eager to run off with Beatrice. And even though I had "fixed" the damage afterward, absolution would not be as simple as ingesting a magic drink.

I blinked and saw Svetlana smiling at me.

"How was that?" she asked.

"What did you put in here?" I asked, fighting back sobs. "The memories, they were so vivid, what I felt, it was like I was reliving it the first time. That wasn't just my own doing."

"Trade secret," said Svetlana.

"So you're drugging us?" asked Beatrice.

"That's an ugly word. I prefer inebriated therapy."

"This has been super fun," said Beatrice. "But I'll be going now."

"You didn't finish your second drink," said Svetlana.

"Doesn't look like something I want to do," replied Beatrice, "after seeing what it did to her."

"Indulge me," said the bartender. "Cards on the table. I put Hohenium in your drinks. It's my calling card. Thought your friend here knew that. You drank the first one so fast that it didn't have time to kick in. If you don't like the experience, feel free to splash the remaining contents in my face in a theatrical way."

"Fine," said Beatrice. "How is this supposed to work?"

"Take a long sip and swallow. And then let go."

Beatrice complied, and I waited to see what sort of reaction Svetlana's alchemy would generate. I watched as her pupils shifted back and forth rapidly, as if she were asleep. But she still managed to take seven more sips before opening her eyes a few moments later.

"Thank you," she whispered, turning to the side to wipe the newly formed tears from her cheeks.

"Happy to help," said Svetlana with a smile.

"I want him back," said Beatrice to me.

"Who?" I asked.

"Jack-Jack. And she will help me."

"You don't mean…"

"Yes, Dalia. Your plan may get us both killed or worse, but I'm done running. Set the meeting. Let's make a deal."

THINGS THAT WERE LOST

"I obtained the only copy of the diaries of Lewis. We will use these to plot our own expedition to the West. Unlike Rita's trip to New Orleans, for this one, we must not leave anything to chance."

It took longer than expected to arrange a meeting with Dalia de Wyck.

I thought she'd jump at the chance to finally get back the Compendium that the Guild had been missing for so long, but evidently I was wrong, as Ty informed me via text that her mother was currently sunbathing in the south of France until the end of the month. She said we could meet her there, but couldn't guarantee we would get through the lobby of her eight-star hotel. So we waited like patient school girls waiting for the headmistress to enter the classroom until she blessed us with her presence in that same boring Midtown conference room that we had first met her earlier this year.

"Ladies," said Dalia, whose noticeably darker skin evidenced the truth of Ty's story. She wore a shimmering white spandex workout outfit embroidered in gold with the familiar Thera DeWitt tree featured and several rings that appeared to have the same sigil. Our own outfits and complexion paled figuratively and literally in comparison.

I couldn't help but notice that Dalia's brow was dripping with sweat, and I wondered if she had run here from uptown, or had just finished a workout and was graciously fitting us in to her busy schedule. Who would be crazy enough to train the head of a secret magical guild?

"It is good to see you. Both of you."

"I highly doubt that," said Beatrice.

"And why is that?" asked Dalia. "Is it because you think so low of this new look you've assembled for yourself? I rather quite like it. It's edgy."

"Enough of the faux politeness. Your newest member tracked me down and somehow convinced me to treat with you. I have your blank book. What-"

"No, you don't," interrupted Dalia. "You don't even know where it is."

"Of course I do," said Beatrice, while at the same time whispering in my head, *"You didn't tell her, did you?"*

"No!" I said. *"Why would I?"*

"Do you think I built a successful fashion line from nothing on the side while running the Guild day-to-day without being able to cut through bullshit?" asked Dalia, who walked over to the drink cart and poured herself a glass of what appeared to be the same brown liquid we had drank at our first meeting, before returning to the head of the table. If she could detect our mental chatter, she showed no outward signs, but I didn't want to chance it.

"Hypothetically, let's suppose you're right, and I didn't know where it was," said Beatrice.

"Of course, hypothetically," said Dalia.

"And hypothetically, let's suppose I could easily find out, if it was worth my while."

"And what is that?" asked Dalia.

"I imagine the Compendium's value to you is approaching priceless. If that's true, then I would imagine that what you'd be willing to trade for it is quite a lot," said Beatrice.

"I can imagine far better than you," said Dalia. "But enough dancing around the edges. You plainly want something specific. Name it and let's be done with this."

"Fine," said Beatrice. "I want four things."

We had discussed three, so now I was curious.

"One, full access to the Guild library for an indefinite amount of time. Two, full immunity from the Guild for any past and future transgressions. Three, your assistance in securing full custody of my son, and..."

Beatrice paused to gauge Dalia's reaction to her list of demands, but the chair's stone-cold demeanor didn't falter.

"Yes?"

"...a copy of 12 pages from the restored Compendium."

I stared at Beatrice quizzically, wondering why she hadn't mentioned this before. Did she still not fully trust me?

"Your terms are acceptable," said Dalia.

"They are?" I stupidly blurted out, but Beatrice ignored me, perhaps also in shock that Dalia had agreed so readily.

"Yes, with two slight modifications. One, I choose the pages of the Compendium that you will receive."

"Fine," said Beatrice, without skipping a beat.

"And two," said Dalia, "I'm coming with you to retrieve it."

Beatrice finally blinked.

"Absolutely not," she said.

"Why not?"

"Because I erased the location of the book from my memory. And retrieving it is something I need to do alone," said Beatrice.

"That's unfortunate," said Dalia. "My terms are non-negotiable."

"Then you won't be getting your book back."

"Suit yourself," said Dalia, taking a sip of her drink. "But when you walk out that door, know that all bets are off."

"What is that supposed to mean?" asked Beatrice.

"It means," said the Guild Chairwoman, clenching the edge of the table with her ring-adorned fingers, "that I will retrieve the Compendium from you, one way or another. You choose the way."

It may have been a trick of the setting sun shining into the room, but I could swear that the trees in her rings began to glow ever so slightly before she pushed herself up and walked to the back door.

"Wait," said Beatrice, and Dalia turned around to consider her.

"I accept your terms."

Dalia's stoic features finally relented into a grin, and she returned to the bar cart to grab two more glasses and the decanter of the magic brown whiskey, which she poured for each of us.

"To new beginnings," she said, holding her glass up. We raised ours in response, but I could see the hesitancy in Beatrice's face, as if she was already regretting this deal. The whiskey tasted just like last time, the explosion of contradictory flavors and textures hitting a different note than Svetlana's spiked concoction.

"Now what?" asked Beatrice.

"Let's go," said Dalia.

"Right now?" I said.

"Yes," she said. "The Guild meeting is nearly upon us and I want the fully restored Compendium in my hands ahead of time so I can rally the last few votes."

"Fine," said Beatrice. "As I said, I have no idea where we will eventually need to go, but the first leg should be relatively short."

She unclasped the necklace that I hadn't noticed before from around her neck and set it on the table. At the end of its chain was a silver key with a large green stone inset in its base.

"Wait," I said, the significance of the jewelry become immediately apparent, "you had the memory of the Compendium's location with you this whole time?"

"I never told you I didn't," she responded, glowering at me for saying too much. "And so what if I did? Do you think that makes you entitled to it because we didn't have to go on a worldwide quest to find it?"

"No," I said, sufficiently chided, "but-"

"It's not the hiding place that was the burden. It's what this is."

"Just looks like a trinket to me," said Dalia, and I almost grabbed Beatrice's hand to stop her from doing something stupid.

"It is not," said Beatrice. "It is the push gift I was forced to buy for myself after Jack-Jack was born after my idiot husband couldn't be bothered to get me one. Or be home for even a few days before running back to the office so he could get fucked by his boss."

"So?" said Dalia. "Your husband is terrible. News flash, lots of men are terrible. That doesn't mean you deserve a prize. If it did, the entire Guild headquarters would be filled with mine."

"This isn't helpful," I said. "You don't have to-"

"She started it! She started all of it!"

Beatrice smashed her half-full glass onto the floor, sending shards of crystal everywhere, but not the whiskey, which pooled into neat little beads, like brown marbles. If Dalia was fazed by Beatrice's tantrum, she buried her reaction deep within her, because instead of erupting into an equal fit of rage, she calmly walked to the corner of the room, pushed forward into the wall, and withdrew a broom and dustpan from the hidden closet. After a few aggressive sweeps, the floor was clean, and we were all back at the table as if nothing had happened.

"What do you need to unmake that?" asked Dalia.

"Just this," said Beatrice, who retrieved a piece of parchment out from under the back of her Lycra workout shirt and placed it next to the necklace. The little key began to wiggle back and forth as if being pulled by an invisible magnet, and a few moments later, it zipped toward the middle of the paper before melting in a pool of silver. The liquid metal spread out over the page until it was covered with several lines worth of cursive handwriting.

Beatrice picked up the vellum, causing the now-orphan green stone to tumble onto the table. She began muttering the written words to herself under her breath, perhaps hoping that it would be enough to stave off reliving the forgotten memory. Except her plan didn't work, and her eyes blinked out as if the rest of her had been transported to a journey to a far-off place. And when she finally came to, there was no sense of relief on her face, no jubilation at having the last piece of herself back in her head. Instead, she grabbed the emerald jewel and walked over to the window to stare down at the honking cars below.

"Well?" I asked. "Where do we need to go?"

"Fort Totten, in Queens. You ever been?" Beatrice directed her question at Dalia.

"Can't say that I have," she said.

"Oh, then you're in for a treat. It's an abandoned Civil War fort built on the real Willets Point, not the repurposed one they came up with later for that junkyard craphole and its matching baseball team."

"Excellent," said Dalia. "Then I won't have to cancel my dinner reservation tonight at Masa."

"I don't know about that," said Beatrice. "Not sure you are going to be in the mood for it after we're done."

"What?" I said. "What aren't you telling us?"

"I need to show you," she replied. "But not until we get there."

"What fun," said Dalia, stowing the whiskey back on the cart. "I can't wait to hear the bad news in the middle of nowhere."

"At this time of day, it will take us hours to get all the way out there," I said, pulling up the fort on my phone. "Can't we just go tom-"

"Do I look like the type of person who is going to suffer through bumper-to-bumper traffic in the back of an Escalade with the two of you? The answer is no. Now, let's go. I don't want to keep Frederic waiting."

"Who the hell is Frederic?" asked Beatrice.

"My pilot," said Dalia. "He's already warming up the chopper at 34th Street. Onward and upward, ladies."

CHAPTER THIRTY-EIGHT

STAR'S END

"I debated with myself for many days about whether I must go with the expedition. There is a part of me that still remembers what happened the last time I was caught unaware, and I hate to admit it, but I am afraid of it happening again."

The less said about my first (and hopefully last) helicopter ride, the better. After chasing Dalia down to the heliport, we soon found ourselves airborne and with a glass of champagne in hand to boot. And even though I was now no stranger to small aircraft travel, soaring over the city low enough to count the individual cars backed up on the LIE was an altogether different experience. But when we finally reached the northern edge of the borough, a new problem popped into my head.

"Where are we going to land?" I yelled over the whirring blades. "There doesn't seem to be any helipad nearby."

"Don't worry," replied Dalia. "Frederic has done this many times.

He's very good at using available space. If only my bill to reinstate rooftop helicopter pads in Manhattan would go through the City Council, he'd be having the time of his life."

We flew slowly toward the fort—and a little too close to the Throgs Neck Bridge for my liking— until we were perched over an enormous expanse of green that my map told me was several soccer fields. Which was all that our pilot needed, for five minutes later, we were scrambling away from the helicopter's blades while Dalia greeted the rush of EMS cadets from the nearby training academy with a flourish and a stack of paperwork apparently giving her the right to land her aircraft wherever she chose.

We trekked onward, until we passed by a castle-looking red brick building, which Dalia scoffed at.

"Gothic revival, a terrible style," she said.

"Like the Guild's headquarters is any better," said Beatrice. "It looks ridiculous next to all the Madison Avenue brownstones."

Dalia shot me a glare, but I tried to brush it off like I didn't care, except my stomach was busy turning itself in two. Beatrice may have negotiated herself amnesty with the Guild, but that didn't mean that I was in the clear.

"Our building is perfectly suitable," said Dalia. "If you don't like it, you don't have to come inside."

"I thought we agreed to no more bickering?" I interjected. "We're out in the hinterlands of New York City. Let's just get to it."

"Fine by me," said Dalia. "Although I am quite enjoying the greenery out here. And the smell of the river is not as nauseating as I had expected."

"Glad you're having a wonderful afternoon," said Beatrice. "Now, this next part is a little tricky. Let me do the talking."

A small visitor's center loomed at the end of the path and Beatrice jogged ahead and scurried inside. By the time we reached the front, she was back outside, her cheeks flush.

"We're good," she said.

"What happened in there?" I asked. "You didn't…"

"… kill the park attendant? Let him cop a feel? Remind him of the command I had given him? Take your pick."

"Got it," I said. "I'll mind my own business."

"Yes, you will," she said. "Now, let's go."

She pointed to a series of bay doors built into the hillside behind the visitor's center, and we followed her around a half-completed fence toward the structure.

"What is this?" I asked. "It looks like a stable for very short horses."

"Storage bays for the fort's cannons," said Beatrice. "General Lee designed this place to protect against anyone sailing through the Long Island Sound."

"The head of the Confederate Army?" I asked. "Why was he designing a fort in New York City?"

"He was good friends with Joseph Totten. They were in the Army Corps of Engineers together and-"

"Are you actually a tour guide here or are you going to show us where the Compendium is?" Dalia scoffed.

"Fine. I thought it was interesting history," said Beatrice.

"Some history is," said Dalia. "This is just boring."

"Suit yourself," Beatrice replied. "The tunnel is up through here."

We walked past more bay doors until reaching an arched opening that extended down into the hillside. Beatrice hurried us along, and we walked in silence through the near darkness, as the lightbulbs flickered on and off overhead. Random graffiti and words adorned the sides of the tunnel and I wondered who had bothered to come all the way out here to tag such moving sentiments as "Remember the

Maine." Finally we reached the end and emerged onto a wind-swept promenade lined with stone arches.

"Now this is something worth taking in," said Dalia, who ran her hand over the granite with approval. Inside the arches were small windows that looked out to the water, and in one of them the back of an old cannon blocked all light from coming in.

"This place is eerie," said. "What made you come all the way out here to begin with?"

"It seemed fitting, I guess," said Beatrice. "It's weird. Even though I remember why I chose it, in my head, it still feels like I'm watching a movie when I think about it."

"Yes, well, that's the danger of that particular branch of memory storage," said Dalia. "The entropy involved never results in a perfect refitting. Now, behind what cranny did you stash the Compendium?"

"It's not that simple," said Beatrice. "Follow me."

She directed us up a nearby stairway, and we walked to the second level of the fort, which looked like a crumbled Roman ruin. At the far end was a pair of red-rusted doors that were set against the hillside. A little padlock barred our entry, but before Beatrice could try to pick it, Dalia had withdrawn a morsel of golden thread from the embroidery on her shirt, tied it around the shackle, and pulled. The metal dissolved like a stick of butter, causing the lock's body to fall to the ground with a thud.

Dalia beckoned us to open the doors, which, lacking handles, was slightly difficult. Beatrice and I each grasped one of the slots set toward the bottom and pulled, the resulting metal-on-stone scraping noise besting cat claws on a chalkboard for the most excruciating sound I had ever heard. When we were finished, we were greeted with yet another barrier: a chain-link gate. This thankfully swung open without alchemy to reveal a small dark arched chamber inside. More importantly, it was completely empty.

"There is nothing here," said Dalia. "You have several seconds to explain yourself, or I will most likely rip one of those blocks from its foundation, tie it to your ankles and toss you into the river."

"I didn't realize you were that strong," said Beatrice. "But if you would calm down for just a minute, I'll show you where I hid the book. And then you can carry out your drowning."

"What are you talking about?" asked Dalia, as Beatrice walked to the back of the chamber toward a little red door set in the corner of the back wall. She crouched down and inserted the green stone from what had been her key necklace into one of the gaps in the wood, and the door somehow disappeared and the rest of the back wall with it. In its place was the real back wall, with a metal slab that ran from floor to ceiling, outfitted with a familiar brown doorknob.

"Where does that door lead?" I asked.

"Open it," said Dalia. "Now."

Beatrice complied, grasping the vervorium knob we had liberated from the Met and turning it to the right, before dragging the door slowly backwards. Inside was the black nothingness we were so familiar with.

"Where is the matching knob?" asked Dalia. "How far did you travel to hide the book from me?"

"Nowhere," said Beatrice. "That's the point. I knew that even if I journeyed to Antarctica and hid the tome in a filing cabinet in Orcadas Base, that you'd still be able to track it down. And I knew if I destroyed it, I'd lose my leverage. So I devised a third option." She pointed to the other side of the slab and that's when I saw it: another brown mottled knob.

"I don't understand," I said. "The portal just leads back to itself? So where's the book?"

"In there," said Beatrice. "In the nothingness. Perhaps if you walked through this singularity, you'd pull yourself back out. Eventually. But a book…"

"It's gone then," I said. "We came all the way out here so you could show us how clever you are? Well, mission fucking accomplished!"

"I didn't know!" said Beatrice. "And did it look like I was happy to find out?"

"No. But why? Why is this any better than just burning the damn thing?"

"This wasn't your original plan," said Dalia. "You did want to hide it far, far away, like you said. And you came here to establish the first portal. And then you were going to figure out a place that no one would ever want to find. Isn't that right?"

"Yes," said Beatrice, dryly. "How did-"

"But once you attached that first knob, the enormity of everything overwhelmed you, didn't it? Then, when you held the second one in your hand, you saw a way out. You created this anomaly and tossed the book inside. And you didn't care if the thing ever came back out."

Beatrice crouched down on the ground and began to sob into her hands, utterly destroyed by Dalia's simple deconstruction.

"It's true. All of it," she said after a minute. "I just wanted it to be over. And then right after, when the enormity of what I had done hit me, I hated myself for being so weak."

"And that's why you pulled the memory from your mind. And everything else," I said.

"Get up," scoffed Dalia, as if she was chiding a tantruming toddler.

"Why? Because it's more honorable to kill me on my feet?"

"No. Because this is not becoming of an alchemist of your standing. And I need your help."

"With what?" asked Beatrice, who slowly sprung up to face her would-be nemesis.

"With retrieving my property."

Dalia pulled up the back of her shirt to reveal a black square of fabric taped just below the clasps of her sports bra. She pulled it off with a yank, sending the small objects that had been pressed between it and her skin falling to the stone floor.

"Those are…" said Beatrice.

"Yes, the Compendium," said Dalia. "The rings of knowledge pulled from its pages. It's what you found in the cave. And it's what will help us pull the book out of your never-ending circle."

She bent down to pick up the scattered treasure and then handed each of us ten rings.

"What are we supposed to do with these?" asked Beatrice.

"Do you make it a habit of asking stupid questions? They're rings. You put them on your fingers."

We both complied, slipping one silver circle onto each of our fingers, while Dalia was busy fussing with the rings on her own fingers.

"What are you doing?" I asked.

"Getting ready," she said, as she detached the tree sigils and threw them to the ground, revealing her own panoply of matching Compendium rings. "Now, this is going to be slightly uncomfortable, but do as I say, and you'll probably make it out with most of your hair unsinged."

Dalia walked over to the portal and extended her palms, before nodding to herself.

"Now what?" asked Beatrice. "Are we going to hold hands and make a wish?"

"Not exactly," said Dalia. "Put your hands as close to the door as you can without falling through."

Again, I did as I was told, but Beatrice held back, still not entirely trusting Dalia or her motives. I brought my hands up to the darkness, and when my fingers reached the edge of the precipice, I felt a minuscule tug pull them forward.

"I felt something," I said. "Is it…"

"Yes, the Compendium," said Dalia. "The rings are tethered to the book, even in there. We'll pull it out. Together."

I nodded and Beatrice looked at me like I was crazy, before bringing her own hands to the edge to confirm for herself.

"There are hundreds of pages in there," she said. "And we've only got 30 rings. I barely feel the auragen link. It won't work."

"If I wanted your opinion, I would have asked for it," said Dalia. "You're the one who tossed the Compendium away like a ratty phonebook. Now step aside and watch your better fix your mistake."

She strode up to the portal and stuck her hands straight out in front of her, before curling her fingers downward and pulling on the invisible auragen strings.

"Jen, on my left. Beatrice, on my right."

We complied and took our places next to her, mimicking her stance.

"Pull!" shouted Dalia.

I balled my fingers and tried to imagine myself yanking a tractor stuck in the mud. But instead, it felt like we were trying to reel in a kite miles up in the sky. I looked over at Dalia, whose eyes were now closed, and saw her muttering under her breath. Were they words of encouragement or some sort of magic spell? As far as I was aware, there was no such thing in alchemy, but my reservoir of knowledge was so shallow that maybe I had missed something.

"Back up two steps and keep pulling!"

We did, until we found ourselves at the front of the chamber 20 minutes later, sweaty and tired, but with no book to show for it.

"Stop," said Dalia. "We need to try a different tactic."

I unclenched my hands and felt the book, however far away it was, drift off even further into the abyss. Beatrice had done the same before collapsing onto the ground. Dalia, meanwhile, began fiddling with the embroidery on her shirt, and a minute later, had not only completely removed the rest of the golden thread, but had also fashioned the end into a loop. Which she was in the process of slipping around her waist.

"What … what are you doing?" I asked.

"What does it look like I'm doing? Getting my book back."

"You're joking, right?" said Beatrice. "You can't go in there. You won't come out."

"I don't joke. And I'm coming back out. The rings, please."

Neither of us were in any position to stop Dalia, so we quickly pulled the silver off of our fingers and gave them to her. A minute later and her fingers were three deep in rings and she had tied the other end of the thread to the metal gate. What had formerly been a magnificent tree was now unwound into a surprisingly long reel of string, sufficient perhaps for a 20-foot dive into the East River, but would it be enough for the paradoxical void Beatrice had created?

"When I tug three times, that's your signal to pull me back out. Understand?"

"Yes, ma'am," said Beatrice, who started raising her hand up to salute, before I yanked it down.

"And whatever you do," said Dalia, getting into a runner's stance, "do not let that thread break, or so help me when I emerge from that portal in a hundred years, I will hunt down your descendants and toss them inside."

With what, she pushed herself up and sprinted off into the darkness.

CHAPTER THIRTY-NINE

SILVER GLASS

"I have decided to remain behind. A duchess is not meant for such travel. I will have to wait until the western lands are tamed in my next lifetime before seeing them with my own eyes. I eagerly await the first missives from our expedition leader and hope that the journey will be a fruitful one for the Guild."

The golden thread uncoiled and uncoiled until it became taut at the gate. I stared at Beatrice and she returned a matching bewildered look.

"She is certifiable."

"I would say so," I said. "But you didn't really give her another option."

Beatrice's face broke into an uncontrolled grin, like Lucifer finally revealing himself to the naive mortal he was pretending to help.

"Exactly," she said, pulling out the Medoblad from the sleeve of her shirt.

"What ... you can't cut that! You heard what she said!"

"I most certainly did," said Beatrice. "And that's why once I cut her loose, I'm going to destroy both knobs and that will be the end of Ms. Dalia de Wyck. Simple as that."

"No, it's not," I said. "And what about the deal you struck? That was all a ruse, too?"

"Yes, one of my own making. I only realized it after I put the memory back. That this was my plan all along. It was quite brilliant, if I do say so myself. Thank you for playing your part."

Before I could do anything, Beatrice brought the Medoblad down onto the golden thread in one fell swoop. But rather than the blade slicing right through it, that portion of the rope instead became gray and brittle, and we both considered this unexpected turn of events.

"Huh," said Beatrice. "Guess it's made of sterner stuff. Well, another swing should do-"

The thread suddenly cracked apart, sending the loose end tumbling toward the void. Without thinking, I sprinted and dove to catch it, my stomach hitting the stone floor with a hard thud.

"What are you doing?" asked Beatrice indignantly. "This isn't just my chance to be rid of her. It's your chance too!"

"I can't," I said. "I need to-"

"-see things through? So sorry, Jen, but Dalia isn't going to be able to tell you why your dead mom hung that locket around your neck."

"Don't you talk about-"

"What about what you said before?" she said. "I thought you were done letting others make your choices."

"I am. It would be so easy to let go of the rope. But as hard as it is for you to imagine, there are worse things out there than Dalia. And so that's why I am choosing to do this."

I grabbed the remaining thread and tried to attach it to the knob, but Beatrice pointed the dagger at me. As much as I didn't want to believe that she would turn me to stone, I couldn't take that chance.

"You think I'm going to let you pull her out?" said Beatrice with a laugh, as I inched toward to the doorway, my hands fumbling behind my back.

"No," I said, as I quickly pulled the rope through my belt loops before attaching the new snare I had tied to one of the knobs. "But I think you'll pull me out."

I turned and faced the doorway, ignoring Beatrice's screaming in the background, and walked through.

I opened my eyes and was surrounded by pure white all around me, including under my feet, which were firmly planted on the "ground." Where was the dark void of the vervorium portal I was so used to? Where was the empty expanse? I looked down and saw that the rope was still slotted through my belt loops, except that the end that led back to Fort Totten was shorn. But the other was somehow still tense.

I followed it forward and as I did, I saw the brightness fracture as if there were a thousand crystal facets surrounding me. I reached my hand out to touch one, but felt nothing but air. The gold thread continued onward and so did I; however, as long and as far as I think I walked, I had no idea if had really traveled anywhere.

"Dalia!" I screamed, expecting my voice to echo outward like a whale calling out to its pod. But instead, the sound reverberated off of the crystals that weren't there, stinging my eardrums. I pulled the rope, hoping that she would stumble forward, as if she had been a few paces in front of me this whole time, but all that did was burn my hands. Finally, I gave up and turned around to walk back to where I entered this hellhole.

And there she was, sitting a few feet ahead, the Compendium nestled in her lap and the other end of the rope tied to her waist.

"What are you doing here?" she asked, as she slowly pushed herself up.

"The rope," I said. "It broke. I think it couldn't withstand being caught between both sides of the portal. So I grabbed it before it disappeared through the door and came in to find you."

"I see," said Dalia. "Well, that's nice, but all you've done is trap yourself in here with me. Maybe your friend will grow tired of waiting for us to return and remove the doorknobs so we can end our misery."

"She won't," I said. "She'll stay until we get back out."

"And how do you suppose we will manage that?" asked Dalia, who began walking in a circle for no apparent reason. "Do you think I was sitting here because it was fun?"

"No. I just assumed that you were waiting for us to come get you, maybe. This place makes no sense."

"It makes perfect sense," she said. "How did you find me?"

"Umm," I said. "I tried walking toward the end of the rope. But then I only found you after I-"

"-turned around," said Dalia. "It's the same way I found the Compendium." She flipped open the book, and I saw that some of its pages now contained writing.

"You put back the rings?" I asked.

"Yes," she said. "I hoped that something within these pages would help me get out of here. But alas, I chose poorly which ones to bring."

She shut the book again, sending a rustling gust of wind that went nowhere.

"Can I ... can I look at it?"

"Sure," said Dalia. "Maybe you, who barely knows anything about alchemy, will be able to find something in there that I haven't."

I took the book without reply and began flipping through it to find the page about the dodo bird, only to remember that we had ripped it out in our foolish attempt to convince Dalia that we hadn't found the entire Compendium. But to make up for that missing piece, there were now 30 others. Most appeared to be written in another languages and in other alphabets. Some had diagrams, some had drawings, a few had full-color paintings, and some even had musical compositions.

"This … wasn't what I thought it would be," I said, reaching the end of the restored pages. I handed the book back to Dalia, who placed it on the ground between us.

"It's magnificent," she said without a hint of irony. "You were expecting more dry encyclopedic entries like the one you gave me before? That knowledge we already have. These and the rest, they're the foundations of the work that we had been doing over the centuries. Until it was stolen from us."

"You lied to me," I said, before realizing what I'd let out of the bag.

"How so?" asked Dalia.

"You told me that Frankie was the Guild's keeper," I said, putting my cards on the table. "But she wasn't, was she?"

Dalia sighed.

"No, she was not. She and her family were the ones who stole the Compendium from us in the first place. As I'm sure she told you, before the poor girl was forced to cough up the key."

"She died because of that!" I said. "She died because … because of me."

It was the last stain on my ledger and it was one that I would never be able to remove. And with that realization, I broke down fully and began sobbing into the white abyss.

"Get up," said Dalia finally. "This is not becoming of a Guild member."

She extended her hand, and I took it, pulling myself up and nearly tripping over the Compendium and almost falling face first into the open page. I looked down Which happened to be one of the paintings, of a dragon eating its tail.

I carefully picked up the book and handed it to Dalia.

"Look," I said.

"How grotesque," she said.

"That's not the point. Does it not remind you of our current situation?"

"The ouroboros," said Dalia, her eyes betraying just for a second that she knew more than she let on. "One of the oldest symbols in alchemy. Its meanings are many, but what it stands for above all else is the eternal cycle."

"What do you mean?" I asked.

"*Hic est Draco caudam suam devorans*," she said, reading the Latin caption under the painting. "This is the Dragon which devours his tail."

"An endless loop?"

"No," said Dalia. "Rebirth. Rejuvenation. The defeat of death. The Dragon's blood that you stole from the museum, that we need to get back from Emma, it was the only ingredient of the Philosopher's Stone that we still knew about. Now that the Compendium will be restored, we can find the others."

"To what end?" I asked. "We fashion ourselves as gods? Unchanging and unyielding? You know that's why J.P. is moving against you, right? He thinks the Guild has stagnated for too long. And if you are really trying to get the Stone, to preserve yourself, I'm beginning to think he's right. Maybe we are better off siding with VAC."

Dalia laughed.

"That's his big plan? To join with those red-headed stepchildren of one of the greatest leaders our Guild has ever known? Ha! I didn't even need you to get the Compendium back, if that was all he is proposing."

"From how he was talking, it sounded like he thought he had everything already locked up." I said.

"All this has happened before and all this will happen again," said Dalia, closing the Compendium. "I am more than confident that things will go my way once the votes are cast. Once we figure out how to get out of here."

"I think I have a solution," I said. "You talk of cycles, but I see a loop. A portal only connected to itself. And we only found what we were looking for by going in circles. How does one break free from such a thing? Not by anchoring yourself to the past, not by being pushed by the tide of history, but by letting it go."

I held up the rope that joined us and that presumably still led back to the knob at the fort.

"I'm sorry if I don't have utter faith in your junior college philosophy bullshit," said Dalia. "But if you break that, we'll never be able to find the entrance."

"You're wrong," I said. "We're stuck in a circle. But the thing about circles is that they have no end. You'll never get out unless you choose to."

I extended my hand to her, and she reluctantly began untying the loop around her waist.

"If this doesn't work…" said Dalia, handing me the golden thread.

"…then I hope you won't waste any time killing me." I said.

I pulled out the portion tied through my belt loops until I was holding the uncoiled rope that led back to nowhere.

"Take my hand," I said, and she intertwined her ringless fingers with mine.

"Now what?" she asked.

"Now," I said, dropping the rope, "we go home."

I closed my eyes as the floor dissolved under my feet and smiled as I felt my body fall into the abyss.

TRIA PRIMA

The Greeks called it the Ariostlian Principles. The Jabirians called it the Balance. The enlightened would-be alchemists of the Renaissance called it the Tria Prima. But to me and my brothers and sisters, it was merely the Three. We marveled at our discoveries as we ran rampant over our lessers for centuries. But although we liked to think of ourselves as something greater, in the end, we were still only human. And that meant one thing: conflict.

It has been a fruitful hundred years since I freed Ariella from her indentured matrimony. Even though I was happy to let her go while she was in her prime, she refused, relishing the double life I provided her. But all good things must come to an end, and as I stood at her unmarked grave, wrapped around my new host, I felt a mixture of sorrow and fear. Sorrow at the loss of my partner and friend, and fear for what the future held.

Such thoughts dog my steps in the coming weeks, but again, I am, or was, only human, and so they fade into the background as I begin my new life in this new century. And with the tumult and conflict of a scope that I had not seen in ages, they further retreat into the deep recesses of my subconscious, until one day I find myself frantically searching for someone to carry me on through the century after.

Rare is the person I would trust with my life and my failure to secure such an individual first, before all else leads to decades of fumbling and reactionary thinking. But then happenstance grants me a reprieve, and I seemingly find the perfect host who will let me do my bidding uninterrupted. And that kismet almost proves to be my downfall. For there is no such thing as perfect and for someone such as myself who should know better, it is all the more troubling and all the more foolish that I could have not seen this coming.

He summons me, and despite knowing that the meeting was an obvious trap, I go anyway, bolstered by a false sense of confidence and burning with an anger that matched the inferno that had claimed the home that Ariella and I had built together. He laughs at me, coldly, beneath the castle tower and beneath the glamour of my lover, and deflects my weakened attacks, my power drained by that stupid girl. Yet another small mistake that has cascaded into a boulder beyond my control.

But before I can launch the finishing blow I know won't finish him, I am betrayed by the one person I foolishly ignored. And although my own hubris has crescendoed to an unacceptable level, my opponents suffer from an even higher quotient. So that is how I find myself awake again and around the neck of a young woman staring at me in a hotel mirror.

She calls herself Jade, like the color of my stone, and I watch her like a disinterested observer, waiting for my true jailer to show their face once more. For it is not out of kindness that I have been granted my freedom, but for some ulterior motive I cannot yet discern. And I am rewarded for my patience, as Jade leads me right to him. Both of him. If I could, I would cry at what has been done to him. But I can't. Not yet.

Jade is a curious host, so unsure of herself, and so desperate to prove her mettle that she gives up her own identity and takes mine. Still, there is something familiar about her, but I cannot quite determine what it is. I let her use me as a costume as I have done for so many others, as she jumps through the Guild's hoops, but she soon finds herself at her wit's end and I am forced to intercede, only slightly. Then he appears yet again as if to taunt me, but I can't let him know I am awake.

And so I watch. I watch as Jade is fed to the wolves by my former host, given an impossible task, either so she can fail and be disposed of, or so she can become another useful tool to be manipulated. I watch as Jade endears herself to the girl named Emma, and I watch as she unwittingly makes the girl's secrets pour forth. I watch as the two delve deeper into the secret of the dragon, and I watch as they find what was stolen from me—a portrait, *my* portrait—that I had painted with the blood long-thought lost. I watch as the flames around the painting erupt and that's when I feel Jade's will begin to falter and I briefly take control again to remind her I am waiting just below the surface should the need arise. I watch as Emma's hand is trapped within the burning painting, and I watch as the two come up with a desperate plan to save the mission.

Until I can watch no more.

I shift Jade's arm slightly to the right, speak the words that someone said to me long ago when they thought they had killed me, and smile as everything goes to hell. Somehow, Jade escapes, but thankfully without the portrait. She claws her way back to her hotel and buries my stone in her suitcase. As if that will protect her from me. For she has made the same mistake that so many others have: she has treated me as a tool and not as an ally. And so when she removes the stone from her body, my body does not go with it. It is a discovery I made long ago, and it is useful in situations such as this. This is a distressing revelation for Jade, and I take full advantage. She screams into her pillow, a cry made in desperation, a cry seeking comfort from some deity from above.

But there is no one there to hear her except me.

And I am not there to soothe her, or to tell her that everything will be all right, or to ease her burdens.

Well, that last one is not entirely true.

I push through the thinned boundary between us and grab full control of Jade's body, lifting it off of the hotel bed, and retrieving the real jade from her suitcase. I walk her into the bathroom, gently place the necklace over her head, and tuck my stone into the confines of the garish looking sweater she is wearing. I feel the unity between glamour and stone re-solidify and my mouth curls into a smile.

"That's better," I say, before appearing before the real Jade inside her head. She is scared and confused at what is happening, and rather than giving her an explanation, I seize her by the shoulders and slam her down into the deep recesses of her subconscious, where she will stay for a fortnight, if she's lucky.

I walk back over to her suitcase, zip it closed, and roll it out into the hallway and into the elevator. I stare at myself in the mirror at the rear and marvel at my restored freedom of movement and my radiant smile, but quickly remind myself that this time is fleeting.

I exit the hotel and walk into a waiting cab. I tell the driver to take me to Terminal E and then rifle through Jade's bag to find the rewards credit card and forged passport with my picture inside. What a clever girl my host is. We reach the airport half an hour later, and

I stride up to Departures board, scan it quickly, and then stroll to the nearest ticket counter.

"Where are you headed, Ms...."

"...Peters. Jade Peters," I say. "And I would like a ticket to..."

So much of the Old Ways have been lost to the blistering sands of time. Other knowledge remains in plain sight, but castigated by so-called serious scholars, who believe the Principles, the Balance, the Tria Prima are just fanciful narratives that belong in a children's bedtime story. The remaining Chronicles, however, have not been lost, only hidden by those who think they are clever. They lock it behind secret doors nestled in forgotten libraries or bury it in the ground in godforsaken places. That is their critical error, though. Because I know those places too. And for all my faults, I am far more clever than they will ever be. And now I will get the chance to prove it.

"...Florence."

It is time to get to work.

CHAPTER FORTY

A FRESH START

*"It has not been an easy two score. The Laurel expedition faltered and many
members were lost. If I had been there, would things have gone differently?
This question plagues my sleep of late."*
– LADY MELANIE FITZJAMES, DUCHESS OF MONTAGU
NEW YORK, NEW YORK, MARCH 1, 1855

"**S**he kept her promise," said Beatrice, as I walked with her down the steps of the family court building on Lafayette Street. "Unbelievable."

Gone were her VillagePunk clothing and black locks, and in their place was a very Upper East Side-y ensemble complete with pearls and a blazer, and a blonde hair dye job that camouflaged her still-remaining gray streak. I wondered if that gray would ever go away or if the tree had somehow marked her with it as a reminder.

"I think she wants to keep an eye on you," I said. "With full custody of Jack-Jack, no more gallivanting across the country or the world in search of ancient sources of prima materia."

We had deliberately not spoken about what Beatrice had done at Fort Totten since Dalia and I had emerged from her roundabout portal last week. Despite our successful return, my anger had not entirely subsided over her double-cross. I had even considered wiping the memory from my head so I couldn't betray it in a moment of weakness, but decided that such tampering would only do more harm than good. Still, I wondered if Dalia suspected the truth.

"That's fine," said Beatrice. "I want to keep an eye on all of you as well. To figure out who tried to kill me. And if her monitoring me means I get to digest the entire contents of the Guild's library, then I'll make that trade."

"You're not moving into your old place, are you?" I asked.

"Which one?" she said, with a laugh.

"On Madison."

"Oh, no, definitely not," said Beatrice. "The doormen would never let me back in the building. Besides, I need a little distance from the lot of you."

"That's for sure," I said, as we approached Bleecker Street Grounds. The old name of the cafe had been scraped off the front window and replaced with a stylized "BSG," alongside a sign that said "Under new management."

Svetlana perked her head up from behind the La Marzocco espresso machine as the door chime sounded.

"Morning, ladies," she said, pushing two small handleless cups our way as we approached the bar. "How'd it go?"

The cafe was mostly empty, save for a few normal looking people with their heads buried in their laptops. I wondered how long it would take for the prior clientele to realize that this establishment was not what it used to be.

"Let's just say that I am now back in the mothering business," said Beatrice, who was about to chug her shot before she threw her new barista and store manager a look. "Did you put anything in here?"

"Yes," said Svetlana. "Espresso, using that shipment of Ethiopian beans that you somehow managed to acquire in a week."

Satisfied that she wasn't about to experience another round of memory resurfacing, Beatrice chugged the shot and I followed suit.

"Delicious," she said. "Another. I have a long day of work upstairs."

"Yes, ma'am," said Svetlana, who dosed out a portafilter worth of beans and tamped it down in one fluid motion before inserting it into the machine.

"What are you doing up there?" I asked, as we walked through the rear of the shop to a spiral staircase that was a bit too narrow for my liking.

"I had done some preliminary demo for what I thought would be Jack-Jack's room," said Beatrice. "But now that I know that I have him back, I can really get started."

"I'm happy for you," I said. "I just hope that Garrett doesn't come after you. Again."

"He won't," she said, as we reached the second floor landing, which was lined on both sides with a set of three doors. "Unless he wants a certain folder of compromising pictures and stock trades sent out into the world. That was a nice icing on the cake from your boss. Come, there's one more floor to go."

"She's not my boss," I said, my legs aching as I walked up the next flight. "After everything, I don't even know if she still wants me in the Guild."

When we had returned to Frederic's landing spot, instead of the waiting chopper, there was a garish Bentley. The ride back to Manhattan had been slow and quiet, with Dalia spending most of it pouring over the restored pages of the Compendium. At one point, Beatrice had asked to take a look, but Dalia had refused.

"You can review your excerpts once the book is complete," she had said, and those were the last words she spoke to either of us in the car or since.

We reached the top floor, and my eyes were immediately drawn to a familiar-looking knob fastened to the only door on this level.

"That doesn't lead to where I think it does?" I asked.

"Of course it does," said Beatrice. "Why would I give up such a prime space just because I am back in New York?"

"I can give you a lot of reasons," I said. "Not the least of which is that your son will try to open that one foreboding door in like five seconds, and then what?"

"That's why it's locked," said Beatrice.

"Great, so he'll either have nightmares about the scary locked door for years or tell his friends about his mom's secret room and you'll have a gaggle of boys trying to break in."

"Why don't you let me worry about the parenting, yeah?" said Beatrice, withdrawing a key fastened to the chain around her neck. "And you worry about the secret magical organization in the midst of an upheaval. Be right back."

She inserted the key into the knob, turned it, and disappeared into the darkness beyond, leaving me alone to reflect on tonight's Guild meeting. It had been radio silence not just from Dalia, but from everyone else as well. I took that as a sign that both sides thought my vote was irrelevant, as Ty had said after my initiation. I didn't know whether to feel useless, as if all my efforts these past two months had not amounted to anything, or relieved at being ignored by people more powerful than I could ever hope to be. And I certainly didn't know what to make of Beatrice. As much as I wanted to trust her and rely on her and dare say call her a friend, there would always be that image of her devilish self surfacing and upending all that I had work toward. Deep down, I knew that it was only a matter of when, not if, it would happen again.

Before I could sink into more internal reflection, Beatrice returned from her warehouse holding a small envelope.

"What's that?" I asked.

"More buffs for Lucca to study," she said. "She stopped by here the other day. As did D.C. I guess Dalia told her that I was no longer persona non grata within the Guild. It feels…"

"…freeing?" I ventured.

"Maybe," said Beatrice. "I'm not dumb enough to think the past has been completely swept away. Especially because your new boyfriend Hugo probably still has a very negative opinion of me."

"He is not my boyfriend!" I said. "And he's gross. I'm pretty sure he was mad at me for giving up the glamour only because he enjoyed looking at Jade more than me."

"If you say so," said Beatrice. She locked the door, and I followed her back down to the second level, where she grabbed a buzzsaw out of one of the rooms.

"Since when are you a contractor?"

"Since that insane machine in the Guild library spit out the first electrum I asked for," said Beatrice. "It took all my willpower this morning to not skip the hearing and binge early 20th century martial arts. Still, I'm not entirely convinced this will work. It just feels … off."

"I thought the same," I said. "Until I saw the hits on the bullseye."

"Yes, well. Shooting at a target at a gun range is one thing. What about something less manufactured?"

"I don't know," I said. "I hope not to find out."

"Good luck with that," said Beatrice. "And with tonight's festivities. As much as I thought I wanted to join the Guild, can't say I envy you at this particular moment."

"I'm just hoping not to be hit with an alchemic nullifier or tied up this time around," I said with a nervous laugh.

"I could go to the library tonight, during the meeting," she offered. "If you need back-up."

"Thanks," I said. "That's … nice of you. But truth be told, that would make things worse. For both of us."

"I think you're right," said Beatrice, who fired up the saw and began cutting 2x4s with aplomb. I covered my ears and tried to shout something over the noise, but gave up after a few tries and waved my goodbye before heading downstairs.

Svetlana had a latte waiting for me in a newly restyled BSG mug, with matching letters formed in the milk. I eyed it suspiciously, and she chuckled.

"I'm not going to spike your drink without telling you every time you see me," she said. "Just that first time. And also now."

"What will happen to me after I drink this?" I asked, picking up the cup and taking in the aroma.

"You'll be extra caffeinated," said Svetlana. "And then the weight of your troubles will feel as if they have been lifted."

"That seems … oddly specific."

"It's my specialty," she said.

"Why are you working here?" I asked, sipping the not-too-hot, not-too-cold latte.

"I'm not," she said. "I'm co-owner, master barista, head mixologist, and chef de cuisine. Where else was I going to get that opportunity?"

"Beatrice made you co-owner? You just met her two weeks ago!"

"She didn't make me anything," said Svetlana. "I put up a good amount of the capital for this place. Years of scrounging tips from the right patrons coupled with some shrewd investments in the right prima materia suppliers meant I have a lot of money and tokens lying around. Your friend may be many things, but she's not stupid. And neither am I."

"On that we agree," I said, drinking the rest of the concoction and closing my eyes. "Nothing's happening."

"Why would I give you something that will calm your nerves when you're sitting here comfortably under my watchful eye?"

"Good point," I said. "I guess I'll be seeing you soon?"

"I hope so," said Svetlana with a grin. "And if things go well for you, tell your Guild friends about our new establishment. Reputation is everything in this business, and scoring some high-profile clientele early on will do wonders for our cash flow."

"No promises," I said. "But if the entire organization isn't thrown into chaos after tonight, I'll see what I can do."

"Thank you, Jenny," said Svetlana, and I bristled.

"My name is Jen," I said. "Jenny Bean was a little girl who disappeared a long time ago."

"Are you sure?" she asked.

"I'm not sure about a lot of things anymore," I said, "but of that, I am certain."

CHAPTER FORTY-ONE

INQUISITION

"Meanwhile, Rita's two heirs have flourished. They took my advice and formed their own company, the Van Asch Trading Company, and have been quite successful with their new mail-order catalog. Through several shell companies of my own that have been in existence for generations, I at least own a piece of their success."

My office was empty save for the old wooden furniture that had been dumped into the room upon the Guild's move to its current headquarters. And that meant that Beatrice had been telling the truth, because the only thing I had added was now gone: the green glamour stone and its necklace. I didn't want to believe that Jade had self-actualized and exited under her own power. No, there had to be a trick, a back door, another key that Gilbert—no, not Gilbert, Ty—hadn't told me about.

I walked over to the spartan looking wooden chair and sat down. To my surprise, despite the lack of any cushioning, it felt like I was sitting in a comfy leather chaise in front of a roaring fire. So much so that all I wanted to do was close my eyes and fall asleep until someone came to wake me. Which, given the provenance of this room, would be never. Instead, I mentally traveled around the Guild's Tables trying to guess how the votes would land, but quickly stopped when I realized I knew nothing about the politics of the organization beyond the members I had spent time with over the past month. And even then, I could see each voting for either side.

I gave up on pontificating and journeyed back to the south tower, passing the gauntlet of tapestries again, before the one of the purported witch burning caught my eye. The three individuals surrounding the accused were faceless, but from their clothing, I surmised two were women and one was a man. They were posed as if they were praying to a deity, rather than committing unspeakable violence, and I was about to turn away and continue to the end of the tunnel when I noticed something I hadn't seen before. Each wore a full-length cloak, much like our Guild cloaks, and holding the cloaks together just below the neck was a small brooch that was embossed with a spiral-looking symbol.

I walked closer to the tapestry and my mouth dropped when I saw that the shape on each brooch was of a serpent eating its tail. Running my fingers over the threads, I confirmed that the ouroboros was really there and not just a trick of my memory. Its faint golden red color seemed out of place with the rest of the tableau and I searched for other hidden details I may have missed the first time, but came up lacking.

Still puzzled, I left the tunnel and walked up the two flights of stairs to the Board Room. Opening the doors, I immediately felt my body tense up, triggered by the memories of my prior visits to this place. Thankfully, the focus would not be on me, but that gave me cold comfort for what was to come.

The chairs were still mostly empty, with the disheveled looking Third Seat of the New Amsterdam table digging his hands into a pot of what I hoped contained only dirt and J.P.'s Second Seat Balthasar reapplying a large a bandage around his forearm. Lucca was in her Seat next to mine and to the left, the woman whose name I always forgot was sitting upright wearing a dazzling dress and matching earrings to boot.

I saw down in my Seat and took a deep breath, trying to forget everything that had happened since the last meeting and trying to forget what was about to happen. As the minutes ticked by, the Seats slowly filled and I tried to make small talk with Lucca, but even her usually chipper demeanor was tempered.

The silence was interrupted by the sound of the doors swinging open and knocking against the wood-paneled walls. I turned around to see J.P. high-stepping in with his stupid cane and his stupid cowboy hat and his stupid cowboy boots. He looked like a man who had won Best Pig at the State Fair, if that was even a thing. Or, more accurately, he looked like a man who was convinced that he was going to be the next Chairman of the Guild.

Behind him was Emma, who, similar to Lucca, was lacking any of her usual spunk. My eyes darted down to her right hand, which was now gray and weathered, as if it had aged 50 years more than the rest of her. She caught me staring, and I quickly averted my gaze until I noticed the final person trailing J.P. into the room.

Hugo.

He strode right by me without a second glance and took his Seat next to Emma, leaving only Dalia and Gilbert's Seats empty at the head of the Table. As if on queue, the back door of the room opened, and in walked the Chair and her daughter. Dalia wore a look that matched J.P.'s, but Ty's was the opposite, and she looked like a miserable teenager who had been dragged into the principal's office to be lectured at for some transgression. But before the former Gilbert could actually sit, J.P. banged his cane on the table.

"Stop," he said. "That's not your Seat, girl."

Dalia's demeanor shifted in an instant.

"Call my daughter 'girl' again and you won't have any hands to pull that stupid walking stick out of your-"

"My apologies, Madam Chair, I only meant that Seat belongs to 'Gilbert' and seeing as how he's not here, she cannot take it."

"I hold the gold token, you twit," said Ty, slamming the metal coin on the table, "so, yes, this is my Seat, whether you like it or not."

"We'll see," said J.P.

Dalia ignored the comment and turned to Ty, who pulled Gilbert's gavel out of the inside of her jean jacket.

"Roll call," she said before looking around the room. "OK, we're all here. Never mind. This 434th meeting of the Worshipful Company of Alchemists shall come to order. We have, umm, two outstanding items from the last meeting."

"Indeed," said J.P. "I'm sure you know most of this, Ms. Anzio, but my sub-committee has completed its Inquest report. Care to hear it?"

He grinned like a Cheshire cat and I thought for a moment that Ty was about to throw the gavel at him, but she merely nodded.

"Very well," he said, setting a spiral-bound booklet on the table and opening it to the front. "Our research is extensive, if anyone would like to read the full write-up after, but I'll stick to the highlights. The prior holder of the Second Seat of the New Amsterdam Table died without issue seven years ago. Or so we all thought. For after many months of searching, an heir was found in the Swiss Alps. That heir was Gilbert, who quietly took the Seat and didn't say much until very recently. I used to wonder why that was. Our august body can be intimidating, sure, but everyone eventually finds their sea legs, as it were. But now I know the truth. That beneath that cold exterior was a child. Dalia's child. And she has used her extra vote on countless occasions to steer the direction of the Guild on a course of her own making."

He shut the document with a flourish and sat back down, evidently very proud of his little speech. I looked around the room for some indication of how this information was playing with everyone else, but the assembled group seemed barely fazed by J.P.'s bluster.

"Is that it?" asked Dalia. "I was expecting something more hard-hitting. Did you not consider giving me a call? I would have told you some really juicy stuff."

"You think this is a joke?" said J.P. "You think we are only here because you haven't figured out a clean way to take our Seats?"

"It certainly would make these meetings go faster."

"Enough," said J.P. "That's enough."

"I agree," said Emma, who winced as she pushed herself up from her own Seat. "I wanted to know the truth, and all you've given me is the obvious. I wanted to know why, damn it!"

"Emmy, it's not that-"

Emma pounded her injured fist onto the table and I honestly thought it was going to shatter into a dozen pieces. The room fell silent, and everyone's eyes shifted between Dalia, J.P., and Emma, but no one had the courage to break the impasse. Finally, Ty cleared her throat, drawing a look from her mother, but she shook it off.

"It's my fault," she said. "I wanted to be on the Guild, ever since I was little. I knew I would one day take my mother's Seat, sure, but that eventuality felt so distant. And then Ayla died, and it seemed like kismet. Things were in a precarious position for us and holding a Gauntlet for the empty Seat would have only destabilized our standing. So it was decided to keep the Seat in reserve until a more opportune time."

"What do you mean, keep it in 'reserve,'" asked Emma. "And who decided?"

"Ah, yes," said Dalia, with a smirk. "I wondered when this little detail was going to emerge. I'm sure it's buried at the end of that dumb report, but a decision of this magnitude could not be done in secret. Why, that would delegitimize our whole organization! And so I called a meeting of the Firsts. Hugo's uncle, Charles. D.C.'s father, D.C. And of course, our esteemed colleague, Mr. J.P. Laurel."

Emma's eyes turned in an instant toward her own "uncle," whose face had turned beet red.

"You KNEW?"

"Now, Emmy," he said, "it's not that simple. We were-"

"-presented with the proposition of giving the Seat, temporarily, to one of the glamours in our possession," said Dalia. "And it was unanimously decided that this was the most prudent course."

A wave of murmurs swept across the room and I had to believe that this latest wrinkle might turn the tide against J.P.'s vote.

"Yes, unanimous," said J.P. "Or rather, we were cowed into agreeing with the Chair. But I knew, deep down, that this subterfuge would only come back to hurt us in the end. And no, I didn't know who was beneath the glamour until recently."

"That doesn't make it better!" said Emma. "You set this whole thing in motion, already knowing that there was no Gilbert. All for your own gain."

"No, Emmy, for everyone's!" said J.P. "Charles and D.C. were hesitant to go along with it too, but they're not here, so this knowledge fell to me and me alone. Believe me, I didn't want to do this. I wanted to give Dalia the benefit of the doubt, but when you returned from Boston and I saw your hand, I-"

"So this was all for me, was it? Well, maybe you should have said something BEFORE I nearly burned to death!"

Emma stormed out of the room like a toddler having a tantrum, and I resisted the urge to laugh at how this whole plan had blown up in J.P.'s smug face. After a few more moments of awkward silence, Dalia took the gavel from Ty and banged it on the table.

"I call the question of the Inquest," she said.

"Seconded," said Lucca.

"All those in favor of ending debate over the Inquest," said Ty.

A chorus of Ayes swept across the room with all but J.P. and Hugo voting in the affirmative.

"The question carries," said Ty. "We will now vote on the Inquest motion. All those in favor of continuing the Inquest."

The vote was a reverse of the previous one and a dejected J.P. slumped down in his chair, but only for a second.

"I move to take up from the table the vote on Chairman of the Guild," he said.

"Seconded," said Hugo.

"All those in favor," said Ty.

Surprisingly, the vote was unanimous in favor. I suspected Dalia didn't want this to drag out any further, and given the disastrous results of the Inquest and her own trump card, she felt the vote was even more in her favor.

"The motion carries. We will now debate the question of who will be the Chairman of the Guild. Mr. Laurel, the floor is yours."

"Thank you," he said, stopping for a moment to allow Emma to waltz back in and retake her Seat. "There's not much more that needs saying from me. We've seen how, under Dalia's leadership, our esteemed organization has become more irrelevant with each passing year. We are too slow, too set in our ways, to adapt to the world that is changing around us. And so, when I take the Chair, we will be reinvigorated by a merger with the Van Asch Corporation.”

Only D.C. had any sort of reaction to this news, and it was barely a chortle, but I immediately gathered that J.P. had probably rightfully concluded that the clan who had spent hundreds of years hammering away in a forge was not likely to throw its vote behind such an upheaval.

“I’ve told you all how this will benefit us, but you ought to hear it straight from the horse’s mouth, as it were.”

“Mr. Laurel, if you think for a second that I’m going to let those charlatans waltz right into my Board Room, then you have another thing coming,” said Dalia.

“Oh, I wouldn’t dream of it, Madam Chair! Even so, they’d like to all speak to you, and so the three of us have arranged an alternative method.”

I glanced around the room quickly to see if there was some video conferencing set-up that I had missed, but as I suspected, the only hangings on the wall were the odd assortment of banners and medieval looking metal shields. Before I could point out this deficiency, J.P. reached into his inner jacket pocket and retrieved two silver beads and a flask, which he put neatly on the table in front of him.

“You didn’t,” said Ty, shaking her head.

J.P. smiled and placed both pieces of silver into his mouth, which he chewed for a few seconds and washed down with a sip of something so strong that I could smell it from my Seat. His body immediately tensed up, his eyes began to blink rapidly, and he instinctively grabbed the front of the table. When he came to a moment later, his face had contorted into such an expression that it was as if someone had put on a loosely fitting J.P. mask onto his head.

“Hello, everyone,” said the woman’s voice that emerged out of J.P.’s mouth. His features suddenly shifted again and then a man spoke as well.

"We're so honored and humbled to be before this esteemed organization today."

"What's going on?" asked Balthasar. "Who are those people talking?"

"It's modified electrum," said Lucca. "An auditory memory, or in this case, two of them working together. As to who they are…"

"They're Lorna and Xander van Asch," said Dalia with a snarl. "Sibling chairs of the Van Asch Corporation."

CHAPTER FORTY-TWO

ROBERT'S RULES

"Each has married, but one better than the other. Lorna recently gave birth to twins, a boy and a girl. She was back at work within a week. I asked her whether she and Duff were twins, but she could not remember."

The room broke out into a raucous explosion of noise, which J.P. halted with a tap of his cane on the table, just before Lorna's voice emerged again.

"We're so sorry that we couldn't be there in the flesh, but we thought this would be the next best way for you to hear our pitch."

Lorna's words had a hint of some undecipherable accent, as if she wanted us to think she was both a normal person and a member of some bourgeois Swiss family that had lived up in a secluded mountain village for the last 500 years. And although it was hard to tell, it seemed like she was my contemporary.

"Our two organizations have long been in a cold war with each other," said Xander. Unlike his sister, he sounded as if he had been schooled at one of the Upper East Side's tony private schools and then never left. He too had a voice that was closer to 30 years old than 50, and I wondered how J.P. felt about turning the Guild over to a pair of kids. "We've worked together in the past, out of necessity. Our grandmother and uncle were big believers in intertwining and intermingling, but you know well the tensions have been brewing recently because of our recent price increases."

"Our mom always liked to say that 'it's just business, it's not personal,'" said Lorna. "But that's easier said than done. That was one of the reasons we convinced her to retire early. The company needed new leadership, new blood, fresh ideas, and she was happy to step aside and let us rise to the occasion."

"And when J.P. first approached us in a smoky backroom at the Standard, we were all ears," said Xander. "When we realized what our two storied organizations could do united under one banner, we immediately called a vote of our own Board, which unanimously agreed to the merger. Think about it: with our resources and reach, and your legacy and acumen, there is nothing we cannot accomplish."

"We know change is hard," said Lorna. "We know you might be worried about what your children will think when you tell them that their Seats now only have half as much pull. But once the dust has settled, and you can see what our new organization is capable of, I believe you'll be able to sleep soundly knowing your future is secure."

"Obviously we can't take questions personally, but J.P. is happy to fill in for us in that respect," said Xander "We look forward to a new beginning."

The tension finally left J.P.'s body, and he turned to the side to hack up the two electrum beads like they were cat hairballs.

"As Lorna and Xander said, I am here to answer any questions you may have," said J.P., smiling as if he already orchestrated the coup he had plotted.

"I have one," said D.C. "Are you out of your damned mind? You'd sell us to those snakes? Do you remember what happened at the last Conference? We were lucky they left us with anything in the Guild treasury!"

It was the most animated I had ever seen the master crafter, and I didn't have to guess where his vote was going to lie.

"I can assure you, I am not. Out of my mind that is," said J.P. "Once you see VAC's balance sheet, its stores, its network, its manpower, you'll come around."

"I have to hand it to you and the incest twins," said Ty. "That was even more meaningless than I expected."

"An immature joke, how appropriate," said J.P. "I liked it better when you were hiding behind that facade of a man. Now, does anyone have an actual question before I cede the floor?"

"How will it work?" asked the Third Seat of the Orange Table, the man who called himself Kildare. "You said it was a merger, but it sounds like a complete takeover. What will be left of our Seats in the combined organization?"

"Thank you, this is something I had wanted to raise," said J.P. "Our Tables will be folded into four Seats on the new Board. VAC will have four. And then Ms. and Mr. van Asch will hold the position of Chair to break any ties."

"So eight of us will be out on the street?" said Lucca. "Sounds like a win-win-win."

"No, of course not," said J.P. "Our four Seats will be subject to a new set of bylaws, and the vote of each new Seat will be determined by the former First, Second, and Third Seats of that particular Table.

We'll all still have a say. We'll all still have something to hand down to our heirs."

"Speaking from experience, I don't know that I agree with your math," said the woman with the shimmering earrings next to Emma.

"Our own bylaws won't protect us from the machinations of VAC," said D.C. "You've diluted our ancestral Seats and left us with a piece of paper for a shield. Nicely done."

"It's more than that," said J.P. "And I should have mentioned this sooner. Everyone will get a renewable line of credit and a yearly stipend that can be used to purchase prima materia from VAC's impressive inventory. When you see what they have access to, I think your concerns that we're getting played will fade."

"OK, phew," said Ty. "I was worried there wasn't going to be a bribe, but there it is."

"Shush, child," said Dalia. "I have one final question."

"Yes, Madam Chair?" said J.P. with an impish grin.

"What did VAC promise you to orchestra all of this?"

"I'm hurt at the implication," said J.P., "that I would be doing this for anything more than my desire to see our organization evolve to meet the needs of the times we are currently living in."

"I see," said Dalia. "How noble of you. Well, if there are no more questions, I think it is time for Mr. Laurel to yield the floor."

The room went silent and J.P. nodded.

"I yield my time back to the Chair," he said, "and I thank you for your consideration and for your vote."

Dalia didn't waste a breath in exchanging parliamentary pleasantries and instead withdrew the Compendium from under the New Amsterdam Table and dropped it onto its surface with a thud.

"This," she said, standing up to try to command the room, "is the Guild's Compendium. Its pages long-thought lost. Its contents long-thought scattered. And without those two, its knowledge would never again benefit our members. But tonight, never is over. For I have restored our heritage and with it, restored the promise of our future."

Someone's foot scraped against the rough surface of the wooden floor, but other than that, no one made a sound. I watched as Dalia's triumphant disposition began to bend until it reached a breaking point and she sat down with what could only be deemed a whimper. If my fate wasn't so tied to hers, I would have laughed at her complete failure.

After an excruciating half minute of silence, Kildare broke the tension with a question.

"May I see the book?" he asked, and Dalia nodded. The older man walked deliberately to the front of the room and began flipping through the Compendium's pages one by one. He paused periodically to run his fingers over the text or the drawings, and sometimes mumbled to himself. One section in particular caught his eye, and we all spent what seemed like half an hour watching his eyes scan every single line.

"Magnificent," he said, closing the back of the book and ambling back to his seat.

"Care to share anything else?" asked Hugo, who had a "what the hell did I just sit through" look on his face.

"Yes," said Kildare. "I will need to study the Compendium in much more detail to see what secrets have been returned to us. But my early analysis suggests this should be a cause for celebration. Well done, Madam Chair."

"Thank you, Kildare. I look forward to seeing what else you can uncover. If anyone else would like an opportunity to read the Compendium, I am happy to make a motion to table this vote so you all have a chance to-"

"No," said J.P. "No more stalling. No more games. The vote will happen tonight. I call the question of the Chair."

"Seconded," said the woman with the earrings.

"All those in favor?" asked the Texan.

This vote was closer than the Inquest vote, but still managed to pass, with only Dalia, Ty, and Kildare voting no.

"The question is called," said Ty. "We will now vote on whether to select a new Chair. Seat by Seat, Table by Table. As is protocol, the candidates for Chair will not have a formal vote. We will nevertheless start with the Chair's Table, and I guess that means I am first, so, umm, nay."

"Aye," said the disheveled gardener.

"Next, the Pavonia Table," said Ty.

"Aye," said Hugo.

"Abstain," said Emma curtly.

"Aye," said the woman with the earrings.

"We'll come back to you shortly, Emma," said Ty. "The Breuckelen Table?"

"Nay," said D.C.

"Nay," said Lucca.

"Nay," I said.

"A clean sweep," said J.P. with a chuckle. "That leaves my Table."

"Aye," said Balt.

"Nay," said Kildare, which made J.P. do a double take, as the vote was now 4-5 against him. I glanced over at Dalia, whose mouth had formed into a tiny grin, and everything clicked. She knew it would come down to the would-be monk, and I didn't have a doubt in my mind that this whole Compendium Quest was merely to secure his vote to her side. But still, that meant that-

"Emma," said J.P. "We return to you now, my dear."

"So you do," she said, drumming the fingers of her weathered hand against the Table. "Once more, you come seeking the Patel Seat, trying to save your skin. And today, you shall have our aid, but it will be for the last time. Aye."

Ty banged the gavel down on the table.

"It is a tie," she said. "Unless one of our candidates would like to concede, we'll move on to the tie-breaking procedure."

Ty looked quickly at her mom and J.P., and seeing that neither was willing to give up, quickly ran to the rear door and exited the room, only to return half a minute later completely out of breath and carrying a small red book, which she opened from the back.

"In the event of a tie," she read, "the challenger shall suggest the breaking method. If the incumbent agrees, then the incumbent shall have first preference. If the incumbent disagrees, a 2/3rds majority will be necessary to confirm the method and the challenger shall have first preference."

"What fun," said J.P. "I choose Trial by Relic. Do you agree, Madam Chair?"

Dalia looked at the man who would unseat her and then glanced around the room, stopping to meet each of our eyes, before nodding.

"Your method is acceptable. And I choose Ms. Patel as your champion."

The word "champion" snapped my focus back to what was happening. Champion implied a contest, a challenge, or something worse. If Dalia was choosing Emma, then that implied that she thought she was a poor choice for whatever reason.

"A fine selection," said J.P., "despite her current condition. I am happy to have her fight for me. As for you, I choose the Third Seat of the Breuckelen Table."

All heads quickly turned to me, and it took me a second to realize what had just happened.

"The match is set," said Ty. "Our champions will present their Relics in two weeks' time at the Armory. To the victor goes the Chair."

CHAPTER FORTY-THREE

LITTLE FISH

"The two complement each other well, but with any family business, there will eventually be tensions. Hopefully not for a few generations, though. In any event, I have secured favorable pricing for their goods for the next several decades."

"What the fuck just happened?" I yelled across the room to Dalia and Ty after everyone had cleared out.

"You were named as Dalia's champion," said Ty. "You'll present your Relic of choice at the Park Avenue Armory in two weeks and you and Emma will fight it out to see who will be crowned victor. And to the victor's champion goes the Chair."

"That much I gathered!" I said. "Never in my wildest dreams did I think this meeting was going to end with a 'fight to the death' royale with me at the center of it."

"I told you several times that a tie would make things more complicated," she said. "And it's not a royale. A royale implies more than one combatant per side."

"But you never mentioned this! Had I known that was even among the remotest of possibilities, I could have … I would-"

"You would have proceeded exactly as you already have," said Dalia, quietly. "Because that is who you are."

"I … you don't know a damn thing about me," I said. "All you know is that all I have left in my life is the Guild and you've taken full advantage of that, over and over again."

"You seem to forget that it was Mr. Laurel who chose you as my champion, not me," said Dalia.

"True, but it was you who agreed to Trial by Relic in the first place. Who did you imagine he was going to pick? Ty?"

"It crossed my mind," she said. "Her small-weapons combat is not one of her strong suits."

"Hey, I resent that!" said Ty. "But yeah, seeing what Emma did to those schoolgirls, she probably would do me over pretty quickly."

"And I'm going to do better?" I asked. "It seems like I'm getting set up as the sacrificial lamb!"

"An apt comparison," said Dalia. "But there is the new matter of Emma's injury. It worsens by the day."

I decided I had had enough half-shouting and walked up to the front Table.

"She could beat me easily with one hand on a bad day," I said, sitting in J.P.'s Seat.

"Also accurate," said Ty. "But you need to go more than skin deep. She's doing worse than you think."

"How reassuring," I said. "Well, maybe I'll stab her quickly with the Medoblad before she can slice open my stomach."

"Who said you could use that?" asked Dalia.

"Ty said I had to present my Relic of choice. As that's the only one I can borrow, it will have to be that."

"See, uh, that's the thing," said Ty. "It's not, you know, technically yours? It's Ms. Stallard's."

"So?"

"So," said Dalia, "she would be free to use it herself were she the named Champion. But you, you will have to find your own."

"Wait a minute," I said. "So not only do I need to fight Emma, who has not one, but two Relics at her disposable—one of which by the way rapidly ages you if you get sliced with it—but I also have to go get my own legendary weapon in a week? Are you kidding me right now?"

"No jokes here," said Dalia. "You'd better get searching, I think."

I stared at her in disbelief, wishing I had a shotgun in my hands so I could put my new shooting skills to the test.

"Sorry, that *was* a joke," said the Chair with a smile. "Hard to fathom, but I'm not a robot."

"What my mother was so unartfully trying to tell you," said Ty, "is that we know where you can get a Relic of your very own."

"Yes," said Dalia. "In fact, you are familiar with it already. During our first meeting, I believe I mentioned it."

"You did," I said. "*Curtana, the Sword of Mercy*. But that's the Guild's Relic. Not mine."

"Well," said Dalia, "not quite. *Curtana* was the property of our predecessor organization and it took many years to arrange for title to be relinquished to us. A party was sent to Glastonbury Tor to fetch the Relic and bring it to New York. They were supposed to have set sail on the *HMS Foxhound*, but the ship never arrived in the New World."

"So even Dalia de Wyck, fashion maven, Guild Chair, and terrifying specter, is full of shit!" I said with a laugh as I banged the Table. "That does make me feel a tiny bit better. And let me guess, it's up to little ol' me to somehow fetch your lost sword from the bottom of the Atlantic, right?"

"You're halfway there," said Ty. "Once you retrieve *Curtana*, by the law of the sea and by the laws of the Guild, it's yours. And fortunately for you, the ship didn't even sink in the ocean!"

"Then where, pray tell, is it?" I asked.

"The history books will tell you that there was no record of the *Foxhound's* last voyage. That it must have been sold for scrap. That is because we removed all traces of what really happened. That the ship was done in by the waters of the Hell Gate," said Dalia. "It's in the East River."

My hands fumbled with the regulator as I struggled in the darkness. The ankle weights tipped me to my side as I lost balance, causing the air cylinders on my back to hit the bottom with a soundless thud. They taunted me with their oxygen that was just out of reach, and I tried to slow my breathing and let my muscle memory work through the last steps, but the disorientation, the cold, and the complete lack of vision overwhelmed me. I let out a wordless curse, detached the weights, and surfaced.

"That was terrible," said Ty, who was waiting for me at the edge of the frigid pool. I removed my polyprene blindfold as I began to shiver uncontrollably.

"F-f-f-uck you!" I said, trying to push myself up from the water but failing, thanks to the now-heavy canisters still strapped to me.

"Just being honest," she said, offering her hand and then a preter-naturally warm towel. "If you can't get your equipment right in this controlled environment, you'll never survive the Hell Gate."

I undid the Velcro straps on my shoulders and the metal cylinders hit the pool deck with an unceremonious thud. It was three in the morning and we had purloined the only Olympic size pool in Manhattan for an overnight training session through a combination of subterfuge, bribery, and breaking-and-entering. Despite the ease with which we had obtained access, I knew that our time was short and the sense of urgency made my heart beat loudly in my chest.

Ty offered me another bead of electrum and I swallowed it eagerly like a dog who had just performed a trick. The memories of an excursion in the South Pacific waters consumed my mind and when I regained consciousness a few minutes later, I read the corresponding card quickly to see what new experiences I had acquired.

"Somehow, I don't think scuba diving in Tahiti is going to be applicable here," I said.

"It's the only other deep-water dive we have in the library," said Ty. "Better than nothing."

"You know what would be better than nothing?" I said. "A robot submarine so it could go down to the bottom of the dirtiest and coldest waterway on the East Coast instead of me!"

"We're already getting one of those for you," said Ty. "But you'll still have to do the actual dive. It will just be tagging along as support."

"Or I could yield the fight immediately and then enjoy my new line of credit from VAC," I said.

"Yeah, not how that's going to go," said Ty. "Everyone will be fat and happy for the first year, and then, one by one, there'll be a rash of resignation, disappearances, or maybe just straight-up murder."

"That's not the pitch I heard," I said as I tossed the canisters back into the pool so I could fetch them again, all in the name of "training."

"You weren't listening very well, then" said Ty. "These people, they're ruthless. They'd bulldoze our headquarters because they want to and then donate the land to some woke non-profit, or maybe an orphanage, just to rub it in our faces."

"Fantastic," I said. "Even more pressure on me."

Ty pushed herself up from the side of the pool as if she was leaving, only to instead knock me over the side with her knees.

"Hey!" I said, the chill of the frigid water hitting me like a punch in the guy. "What the hell did you do that for?"

"Pressure makes diamonds, Jen," said Ty, smiling. "Go get the weights and then dive again. I'll be timing you!"

"And I'll be murdering you!" I muttered under my breath as I quickly climbed out of the pool and dove headfirst back in. I grabbed the weights at the bottom and resurfaced. Reapplying the blindfold, I hit the little button attached to the top of my dry suit, which triggered the chime on the scuba equipment 10 feet below me, and returned to the water. This time, thanks to the extra memory, my fingers didn't fail me, and I successfully equipped myself in the dark.

As I drew my first breath, a part of me started to believe that I could actually pull this off. But my optimism died as soon as I hit the surface and saw Dalia standing next to Ty, in black high heels and a bright red dress, with a bag that cost more than my life hanging from her arm, as if she had just returned from a gala.

"Status?" she said to Ty, who shook her head.

"She finally completed one beginner circuit," said the teenager. "And only after ingesting the last memory."

"Unacceptable," said Dalia, and I couldn't tell if she was lecturing me or Ty. "We have another day or two, at best, for this preliminary task. And then there is the matter of her actually wielding *Curtana* properly so that she doesn't get impaled in 30 seconds."

"I can hear you," I said as I climbed out of the pool. "And this is doing wonders to my confidence, by the way. You try learning to scuba dive in five hours!"

"My bad. Did I hurt your feelings? Is your ego bruised? I'm sorry if I don't give a fuck," said Dalia. "Everything and everyone is on the line. You, me, the Guild. I don't think you get that. Failure is not an option."

"Then help me!" I yelled. "You're the schemer, the planner, and yet for all of your foresight, all you could scrounge up was a tie."

"And whose fault is that?" asked Dalia. "Last month, before I went to Europe, I had six votes. I leave you alone with Hugo for three minutes and suddenly the Woo Seat, which had been a trusted ally for generations, goes right to Laurel. What happened?"

"Give me something more than swimming lessons and I'll tell you," I said.

"Fine," said Dalia, taking out a small leather-bound notebook and pen from her bag. She scribbled for a few seconds, tore the page out, and handed it to me.

"Izzy 'the Spark' Weston," I read. "Essex Street Market, Stall 20A. Who is that? One of Phineas's stock boys?"

"Not quite," said Ty. "He's a trafficker, but of information, not goods. We have it on good authority that he knows where to get a copy of the plans for the *Foxhound*. You will need that to help you navigate the ship quickly once you reach the wreck."

"Fine," I said. "Yet another person to charm. Hopefully, he is more pleasant than Phineas."

I stuffed the page into my duffel bag that was resting near the edge of the water and began to walk to the locker room to get dressed, only to find my path blocked by Dalia.

"Who says you're done here?" she asked. "Back in the pool. There are still many more hours before sunrise. And I don't have anywhere to be until lunchtime."

I stared at her blankly, my teeth involuntarily chattering and the remaining cold water dripping down my thighs.

"You're serious? Fine. As you wish, Ms. de Wyck," I said as I gave an exaggerated curtsy before jumping into the pool backward.

She ignored me and instead began writing something down on a new page in her notebook, which she ripped out and handed to her daughter.

"This is an interesting list," said Ty. "And a long one. And it doesn't even include what we need *after* she gets *Curtana*. Are you sure she's up for it?"

"Come here," said the Chair, and I swam over to the edge of the water. Dalia somehow bent down, heels notwithstanding, until we were nearly eye-to-eye.

"For the two weeks, your life, body, and mind are mine. You will do what I say, be where I tell you to be, and ingest a thousand years' worth of memories if that is what it is going to take to get that Relic back. Are we clear?"

I paused before answering, trying to assert what little power I had. "Crystal," I said.

"Good," she said, withdrawing a silver electrum from her bag, which she threw into the center of the pool. "That was from my private library, an account of the recovery of the *Antikythera* shipwreck in Greece. You have 30 seconds to eat it or I'm turning the temperature down another five degrees."

CHAPTER FORTY-FOUR

FOUND THINGS

"A letter arrived from England. The century-long negotiation has been completed, thanks to Lord Theo's yeoman-like work. Soon we will reclaim one of our lost treasures. If only it could be useful to us now."

Every limb in my body felt like it was going to detach as I lowered myself onto the bar stool in front of the shiny espresso machine the next afternoon at BSG. Svetlana handed me a warm cup of cocoa spiked with vitality serum, and I downed it as if I was competing in an Oktoberfest beer chugging contest.

"You look like you're on a mission," she said, taking back the empty mug. "And not from a heavenly deity."

"Correct on both accounts," I said, closing my eyes as the serum's effects washed over me. I stood up slowly and shook my arms and legs to find all the soreness and stiffness gone. Thanks to Dalia's spot-on embodying of Sergeant Hartman and some additional well-selected electrum beads, I foolishly believed I could probably make it through the first week of Navy diving training with flying colors. Whether that would be enough to survive the 100-foot depth of the Hell Gate's waters, I had no idea.

"I hate to drink and run, but I have an appointment with a random stranger."

"Sounds about right," said Svetlana. "Let me know how it goes."

I waved goodbye and hurried out the door. Fortunately, Essex Street Market was only a short walk from BSG and I soon reached the gleaming building on Delancey and Essex. Despite it being midday and midweek, the market's aisles were packed with a flurry of people lined up at the various vendor stalls. I navigated through the crowds, searching in vain for stall 20A, but after three laps, came up empty, and finally decided to rest at the counter at Shopsin's, which somehow had a single stool open. After downing an Oreo brown sugar pancake and marveling that it only cost $8, I worked up the courage to ask the waiter where stall 20A was, only to be looked at like I was crazy.

"That's across the street," he said.

"OK, thanks. So toward the front or-"

"In the old market. It's closed."

He shuffled away to serve one of the other customers, leaving me to ponder how to break into an abandoned building. Thankfully, it was super easy, barely an inconvenience, as the second door I tried pushed open without a fight, and I was soon walking through a very different market. Empty shelves, deserted fixtures, and random debris littered the place. Where in the new market the glass cases were bursting with fresh produce, meat, and fish, here they were barren and cold. And yet, despite the void that had been left by the migration, I felt that this space was still very much alive in a way that the shiny development would never be.

I heard a soft meowing in the distance that repeated over and over again, and walked on to discover its source. Sure enough, it was coming from exactly the place I was looking for, Stall 20A, which had seen better days. In its past life, it had been a fruit and vegetable stand. Or maybe a craft beer shop? Or possibly a Japanese deli. It was impossible to tell, as remnants of all three were scattered across the small enclosure.

And standing in front, at attention like a sentry, was a single black cat. It looked at me with its green eyes and purred before rubbing against my ankle and then circling several times. Then, with one final meow and a too-long-for-a-cat stare, it retreated back into the abandoned stall.

"Hello?" I called. "I'm here to see Izzy?"

"You don't sound so sure of yourself," called a voice. "If you are, say it with conviction."

"Sorry," I said. "I am here to see Izzy Weston. I need his help."

"That much I know," said the voice again. The guard cat reappeared, this time perched on top of an empty display refrigerator. At least, I think it was the same cat. Because another cat suddenly scurried between my legs from behind and then ran off as quickly toward the voice. A moment later, its source appeared. He had unruly curly black hair and the same piercing green eyes as the cats and he was wearing a slightly tattered brown trench coat that fell the length of his body.

"Are you Izzy?" I asked.

"Depends who's asking," he said. "Ghost thinks you're trustworthy enough, else I wouldn't even have come out, but Mystic isn't so sure. So, can you shed a little more light on the purpose of your visit here?"

"My name is Jen Jacobs," I said. "I'm a member of the Guild. I was told you could help me find something."

"Which Guild?" asked the man.

"Umm, the Worshipful Company of Alchemists," I said.

"Hmmm, never heard of that one. Plenty of Guilds where I came from, not all of them good. But not all of them bad, either. A Guild's only a reflection of the people who decide to stand against the bulwark of its past, you know?"

"Not really," I said.

"Well, you seem good enough. And Ghost has a better nose than Mystic, anyway. That's why I keep him around while the others are out gathering."

"Gathering what?" I asked.

"Food, information, whether the mail will be on time."

"You get mail here?"

Izzy laughed.

"No, not for me. I find that the delivery of the mail is a good barometer. When it's early or on time, that means everything is A-OK. When it's late, it means something bad is going to happen."

"I see," I said. "Do you get many visitors down here? Seems like you don't want to be found."

"Oh, absolutely I don't," said Izzy, who somehow produced a can of tuna and had opened it for Ghost to eat. "I'm still in hiding. Still on the run. Although I haven't run much lately."

"Who are you hiding from? Maybe we can help you."

"Can't say, won't say," he said.

I decided not to press the subject.

"I'm looking for the plans for an old ship. The *HMS Foxhound.* Have you heard of it?"

"I haven't," said Izzy. "But that doesn't mean I don't know where the plans are. Just give me a second to gather my thoughts. Ship plans that are old and made of paper. Paper comes from trees. Trees grow in the ground. The ground is made of dirt. Yes, yes, yes, that all makes sense."

"It does?" I asked. "Well, I'm glad it did to at least one of us."

Ghost meowed three times.

"Two of us," said Izzy. "Ghost was just saying that he ran through a plant nursery on Rivington the other day and on the wall, there was a giant framed plan of a ship. It seemed odd to him, but this neighborhood is a bit eccentric. Anyway, that should be the ship you are looking for."

"Are you sure?" I asked.

"Quite sure. Ghost has an excellent memory."

"Thank you, Ghost," I said as I bent down to give the cat a playful scratch on the head, which he leaned into. "I've been on too many adventures lately and was worried this was going to require another cross-country excursion."

"I'd like to have one of those when I can stop running and hiding," said Izzy, a sad note in his voice.

"I'd like that for you," I said. "And thank you as well. I appreciate the help. If you need anything in return, just name it."

"That's a kind offer," he said. "But the cats are all I need."

"I'm glad you found them, then," I said.

"Don't be silly, young lady," said Izzy with a smile. "The cats found me."

"Not sure why you had to go back and steal the actual plans," I said to Ty. "The picture I took was fine for our purposes."

"They won't realize what they're missing," said Ty, who had unrolled the purloined parchment onto a card table in the middle of the deck. "Besides, do you want to get all the way down there and not know where to go because your dumb phone camera didn't have enough megapixels?"

"Point taken," I said. "But tomorrow you're swapping them back."

We were anchored just off of the Hell Gate Bridge in the East River. It was 5 a.m. but between the choppy water, the summer breeze, and my anxiety, I was shivering. Beatrice had provided the marine craft, reluctantly, and had barely let her eyes off of the teenager since we left the dock.

"You're a noble bright," said Ty. "It's admirable. Sometimes. Anyway, according to these, the captain's cabin was toward the rear of the ship. That's the first place you should check. Then, if it's not there, you'll punch your way through the floor to the Board Room. If it's not there either, then you'll resurface and we'll reevaluate."

"This is nuts, did I mention that?" said Beatrice, shaking her head. "You're going to let her do this, *Gilbert*? And you, Jen, I still can't believe you agreed to any of this!"

"As crazy as it sounds," I said, "I can do this. My body remembers. All I need to do is make my mind follow."

"Easier said than done," said Beatrice. "Especially when you're a hundred feet down in the dark."

"We don't need your negativity," said Ty. "Just your helmsman skills and your alchemy. And besides, we have our little mechanical friend here to help guide the way."

She tapped a rather expensive looking underwater drone with her foot before unceremoniously tossing it into the water.

"Still not sure why the robot can't just get the Relic," said Beatrice. "It's got a claw. It can pick up the sword. Or we could hire, you know, an experienced diver to go down and retrieve it?"

"Yes, that would be a good alternative," said Ty, "if we didn't want Jen to be the rightful owner of *Curtana*. I guess she could always challenge our hypothetical diver friend to a fight to the death over ownership, so maybe instead you could go get those tanks you promised?"

Beatrice wisely decided not to pick a further fight with her former arch-nemesis/now-teenager and rolled two canisters toward me.

"The red button on the hose releases strength, the blue one speed, and the green vitality," she said as she hooked the tanks onto my back next to the air. "Use them sparingly. I know you practiced punching through boards earlier this week in the shallow end, but the pressure will be much greater down at the wreck. It won't be as simple."

"Speaking of, here," said Ty, handing me a tablet that looked like an oversize Tylenol.

"What is this?" I asked.

"Your deepest dive has been 30 feet. You would pass out in five seconds if you tried to get all the way down to the *Foxhound* without training another month. This fixes that. At least for the next 90 minutes. And it also spares you the hassle of half a dozen safety stops down to the bottom."

"Fantastic," I said, swallowing the pill. "Alchemy saves the day. What happens if it takes longer than that?"

"It won't," said Ty. "Because you'll run out of air before then. Remember, efficiency is the name of the game. Your goal is 10 minutes down, 10 minutes to find *Curtana*, 10 minutes to surface. So nothing to worry about."

"It sounds so easy when you put it that way," I said as I fastened the last sets of snaps on my alchemic wet suit, which Dalia had reluctantly fashioned in the span of 24 hours.

I walked and sat on the edge of the boat. Beatrice handed me the full-face scuba mask, which I gingerly pulled over my head, while she finished attaching the intricate tank get-up to my air supply.

"Come in, Red. Come in," said a voice in the mask's speaker.

"Red here, over," I said. "And why am I Red again?"

"Because everyone else in the Guild thought you had red hair," said Ty. "So the name stuck."

"Great," I said.

I turned around and Beatrice give me a thumbs up, which I returned.

"Clock is ticking," barked Ty in my ear. "Time to get in the water! The drone will be right behind you."

"Getting in the water," I said.

I bent my knees, took a deep breath, and plunged into the abyss.

CHAPTER FORTY-FIVE

ROLLING IN
THE DEEP

"Disaster has struck. It seems to be a theme for this era or perhaps someone's joke. The Foxhound has been sunk by the Hellgate, sending our Relic to the bottom of the river along with a bevy of other valuables Lord Theo had secured. And despite our abilities, we have no means of retrieving the cargo from the depths in this age."

A surge of muscle memory flooded into my body as I snaked my way down the wreck reel that Beatrice had set the other day. Although I couldn't remember the details of the bead Dalia had fed me after my insane training all-nighter, all of my limbs did, and it was as if I had been exploring sunken ships in the Caribbean and the Mediterranean for the better part of my life. Except here in the muck of the East River, all I could see was the line leading me down to the bottom. To where the Hell Gate had claimed its last victim.

The little diving drone circle around me as I descended, providing extra light and a bit of comfort that I wasn't entirely alone. And of course, recording for posterity my potential horrible death-by-inexperienced-scuba. I tried not to think about the most likely outcome and instead just kept spiraling down.

At 50 feet, the temperature reading on the gauge on my wrist began to dip. Still, it was a far cry from the freezing swimming pool I had trained in, and I suspected Dalia had put me through the paces so that the actual dive would feel like a walk in the park. Or, more appropriately, a swim in a gentle pond.

"All good, Red?" crackled a voice in my ear.

"All good, over," I said back at Ty.

"Good to hear. Air supply looking stable. See you at the bottom, over."

"Fun times," I said, but received no response.

The further down I dove, the more aware I was of how many more breaths were needed to fill my lungs. With barely anything to look at to distract me, it was like a tiny pebble in my head that kept gathering speed and strength as it rolled downhill. Thankfully, Beatrice interceded before I had a full-on freakout.

"Your heart rate is elevated a bit," she said, interrupting the silence. "I'll talk you the rest of the way there."

"Copy," I said, not wanting to waste extra breath with a longer response.

"You're doing great," she replied. "Honestly, I didn't think you had this in you. The Jen I met that first day at BSG certainly wouldn't have made it this far. But something inside of you has awakened. It's taken you to heights and depths, across the country on a whim, and into and out of anomalous voids that shouldn't exist. So just keep pulling yourself down, inch by inch, foot by foot. And go find that stupid sword."

I did as she said, trying not to get emotional, as those were the nicest things Beatrice had ever said to me. Maybe later she would say it was all just a motivational tactic get me to the finish, but for the moment, I wanted to believe that she truly meant it. In any event, it did the trick, and I soon found myself reaching the bottom of the reel a minute ahead of schedule.

"Landed, over," I said, and I turned my head slowly to survey the wrecked *Foxhound*. The reel had brought the drone and me to the stern of the ship, which was almost covered in yellow blooms of coral. Yet the vessel still seemed mostly intact, which was surprising, given the 150+ interceding years and the toxic cesspool that was the East River. I nodded to the drone's camera, set my feet against the line, and pushed myself forward.

"Stay clear of the coral. It's sharp, over," said Ty.

"Copy, over," I said.

The little robot whirred alongside me as I swam over the top deck, a small comfort in a place where comforts were glaringly absent. One of the masts was still in once piece and upright, a fact we had marveled at during the drone's first reconnaissance trip. I reached it and, ignoring Ty's advice, ran the rear of my gloved hand across the base, which, unlike the rest of the ship, was covered in a deep blue coral.

"Ow," I said, pulling back to see that the polyp had made a sharp incision in the fabric.

"I told you, over," said Ty, but I ignored her. Thankfully, the cut had not made it down to my skin, but now I had to contend with the added annoyance of the tepid water flowing into the glove.

"Lose it, over," said Beatrice. "The water temperature is not that bad. You'll be fine."

"Copy," I said, pulling the damaged glove free and adding it to the wooden graveyard below.

"No more stops," Beatrice continued. "You gave back your extra time with this dalliance, over."

"Understood, over," I said. Fortunately, the aft cabin was not much farther and with a few more kicks, I had reached it. The drone caught up a minute later, slowed by the cable tethering it to the surface. It moved forward purposefully with its grabber claw outstretched and tapped the knobless door, which was also remarkably still in one piece and free of coral.

"Does it look solid to you?" asked Beatrice. "Hard to tell from the video, over."

"Yes," I said.

"Try pushing it in," she said.

"Copy."

I swam forward and pushed the door with my gloved hand, but nothing happened. A second push had a similar lack of success, and pushing with both hands didn't do the trick either.

"Activating strength, over," I said. I tapped the red button and took several deep breaths. A moment later, I felt the buff's power flowing through my body, and I cautiously approached the wooden barrier again. Forming my gloved hand into a fist, I tried to smash through the door, but was defeated by the water's resistance.

"You need speed, too," said Beatrice. "Otherwise, it will be like slowly hitting a punching bag with a 100-pound weight. But only a little. And then after you break through, hit the blue immediately so your body can recover, over."

I hit the green button as instructed, inhaled once, and waited for the world to slow around me. Except that 100 feet down in the muck with only the wooden door to look at it, I couldn't even tell if it was working, until Beatrice tried to talk to me again and all I heard was gibberish.

I ignored her, pulled my arm back one more time, and punched.

And instead of the door smashing apart, I was knocked backward, as if there was an equal and opposite force behind it waiting for me.

"Shit," I said, as I frantically pushed the blue button and inhaled.

"… unexpected," said Ty, as the world returned to normal speed.

"Shit is right," said Beatrice. "It must be hardened with alchemy."

"That much I gathered," I said. I glanced at my watch to see how much air I had left, and immediately realized what a mistake that was.

"Calm, Jen, calm," said Beatrice. "You have plenty of time still. We'll figure this out."

The drone's propeller kicked up and began inspecting the surrounding area. I swam out of the way to let it work, lest I get tangled in its cable. After a minute of exploring, its claw moved forward and grabbed something on the deck just outside the door.

"What are you doing up there?" I asked.

"Finding you your way in," said Ty. "Look what our little friend discovered."

I swam to the drone and looked at its now-outstretched "hand." In it was a familiar looking token. It was not gold, like mine, for it had been on the bottom of the river for too long, but it still bore the Alerion sigil.

I stared at the token and then stared at the door, and sure enough, there was a circular-shaped slot in the center, the same as the one in my Guild office.

"How … what-" I said.

"No time for questions," said Ty. "Just open it."

I nodded and grabbed the token from the drone, swam all the way up to the slot, and placed the circular key inside.

Nothing happened.

"Huh, over," said Ty. "Maybe it broke after-"

The door started retracting into the side of the cabin and when a large enough gap had appeared, I kicked myself through, until I was in a small chamber that extended only a foot beyond the door. I quickly scanned the far wall and found another sliding door, but with no second token to unlock it, I feared there would be no way to enter the cabin.

"What is this room, over?" I said.

"Dunno," said Ty. "This isn't in the plans. It just shows one large chamber."

"Maybe you need to close the outer door, over," said Beatrice.

"Copy," I said. "I guess this is where I leave you."

"Good luck, Jen, over," said Beatrice.

I pushed the door with my naked hand and watched the drone disappear as it slid closed.

Again, nothing happened. But then something completely unexpected did. The grinding of metal on metal sounded all around me and I looked up to see the water level slowly dropping.

"The water is draining," I said. "Holy shit!"

"No way!" said Ty. "It's getting pumped out somehow."

The small chamber continued to drain until I was forced to swim to the bottom, and when the water lowered to just below my knees, I set my feet onto the ground and stood. Finally, when the last of it was gone, I heard a loud hiss and the second door slid open.

"I'm walking—not swimming—into the captain's cabin, over," I said.

"A rudimentary airlock!" said Beatrice. "Unbelievable!"

"It must have been designed as a failsafe," said Ty. "To preserve whatever was in here if the ship was lost."

I entered the inner chamber to find something I was not expecting at 100 feet below the surface: a room filled only with air.

"The cabin seems to be watertight, over," I said. "Maybe I can-"

"Do not take your mask off," said Beatrice. "That air has been sitting there for over a hundred years. There's no oxygen left, over."

"How do you know that?" quipped Ty in my other ear.

"My past life as a chemical engineer," said Beatrice. "Haven't you ever heard of Henry's Law?"

"Yeah!" said Ty. "I mean, no. Must have skipped that day last semester."

"It's like how oxygen gets into your blood," said Beatrice. "And carbon dioxide comes out. All the oxygen escaped a long time ago. You take your mask off, Jen, and you'll get a heaping breath of CO2."

"OK, understood. Not taking my mask off, Professor, over."

The room was pitch-black, save for my headlamp, and I turned slowly in a semicircle to see what other secrets were hiding down here. To my left was a small bookcase, and for a moment, I grew excited at the prospect of recovering another set of alchemic records, but sadly, it was completely empty. The right side yielded a painting of the *Foxhound* in its former glory. I walked toward it and ran my bare fingers along the canvas, hoping to maybe find a cache of Dragon's blood hidden within, but the surface felt dull and flat, almost as if someone had screen printed the picture on.

I followed the wall with my light to the back of the room, where I was greeted with an eerie sight: a carbon copy of the desk from my Guild office. I relayed my discovery to my support team, but was met only with skepticism.

"Don't think they're the same," said Ty. "My mom always said she wished that Grandma Thera had spent more than 10 minutes furnishing headquarters."

"If you say so," I said. "But why does it feel like there's something you're not telling me?"

"What do you mean, over," said Ty.

"This wasn't just some transport-for-hire," I said. "This was a bona-fide Guild member."

"An interesting theory," said Ty. "But for a later time. You need to keep moving. No telling how long that magic airlock is going to hold up, especially after all these years."

"Fine, over."

The desk's top two drawers were completely empty, but as I was closing the third one, I heard a rattling noise, as if something was rolling around inside. I inspected it again, but felt and saw nothing. That was, until I ran my bare hand one final time along the bottom and finally found what I was looking for: a small indentation that would have gone unnoticed if I hadn't torn my glove in the first place. I pushed down on it and the front popped up to reveal the source of the noise: a large-ish silver bead.

I picked it up, expecting it to be just another piece of electrum, but it was noticeably heavier, with intricate lines circumscribing its surface, and it felt ice cold.

"I think…"

I stopped myself before I finished uttering the thought. Something still didn't feel right and this hidden trinket was perhaps at the center of it. So I tucked it away in one of the wetsuit's many pockets for further study outside the purview of certain companions at the surface.

"…that I need to keep searching the room, over."

"Agreed," said Ty.

I peered awkwardly under the desk, trying to avoid tipping over, but found the space underneath completely empty. The same was true of the rest of the cabin, and I felt my pulse begin to quicken as the futility of this entire ordeal crystallized inside my head.

"There's nothing here!" I said. "Where's *Curtana*?"

"Are you sure?" asked Ty. "It has to be down there. Keep looking, over."

"I've looked," I said. "Another five minutes isn't going to change anything except the amount of air I have left."

"But you haven't," said Beatrice. "Walk along that wall again. Does it go straight from back to front?"

I quickly traversed the edge of the room and reported back that it did.

"The plans show an inset space," said Ty.

"The painting," said Beatrice.

"What about it?" I asked.

"Take it down."

"Fine, over."

I walked over to the painting and tried to remove it from whatever hanging mechanism had kept it there for over a century, but found it surprisingly stuck to the wall.

"Too heavy," I said. "Won't come off, over."

"Then it's a good thing you're hauling those extra tanks on your back," said Ty.

"Copy," I said, hitting the red button again and inhaling a larger dose of strength than before. I counted to five, grabbed an end of the painting with each hand, and pulled.

I don't know if it was the increased strength hit or the lack of resistance thanks to the lack of water, but the next thing I knew, I was on the ground, the painting on top of me, and staring up at an alcove in the cabin wall, inside of which was a long wooden box with an ornate handle and hinges on its side.

I struggled to get back to my feet, but found that the blowback from the strength buff made every movement seem like I was trapped in hardening concrete. Somehow, I forced my hand forward a few inches, pushed the blue vitality button with one final burst of energy, and gulped the next breath of air as if it was my last.

"What happened, over?" said Beatrice.

"Pulled too hard," I said as I got to my feet. "But I think I found it, over!"

"Well done, well done!" said Ty. "Now let's blow this thing and go home!"

I walked to the wall, grabbed the handle on the box with my bare hand, and removed it from its hiding place. Which is right before I noticed a trickle of water seeping down the back of the alcove.

"Umm," I said. "I think we have a problem, ove-"

The East River smashed through the cabin's wall like a boxer landing a body blow, knocking me off balance. Before I could regain my footing, the ceiling of the cabin gave way as well, sending wood and water crashing down on top of me, and the last thing I remembered before blacking out was the frantic voices from the surface screaming in my ears.

CHAPTER FORTY-SIX

SURFACE

"An unmarked carton arrived today at my manse, and inside was a well-polished skull and one gemstone. Where the other two are, only my tormentor knows. I shed a single tear for my loss because there is no time for any more."

The waters were blue and warm and colorful coral dotted the sunken wreck. Although my surroundings were pleasant, my predicament was not, as what was supposed to have been a routine survey dive had gone south when a piece of the *Antikythera*'s mast had come loose and pinned me to the deck. I struggled for a few minutes, trying to pull myself out, but the wood had landed precariously close to the hose connecting my mask to the air tank, and I feared that one wrong move would leave me free but trapped a hundred and fifty feet underwater with no oxygen.

I closed my eyes and steadied my breathing, remembering what the master diver had taught me those many years ago.

"Panic and fear are the enemy," he had said. "You can banish them to the dark recesses of your mind if only you will it."

"Easier said than done," I muttered.

I opened my eyes and surveyed my surroundings. My left leg was trapped at the ankle, but the rest of my body was free. I used my hands to sweep the coral-filled deck, wincing at the pain, until my fingers felt something starkly different than the sea life that had claimed the ship for the past 2000 years: a circular piece of metal.

I stretched to reach it and with my free foot and my hand, I was able to drag it toward me. It wasn't just a metal trinket, but an intricate wheel that could have been a gear in an ancient machine. I apologized in advance to the antiquity societies that would probably trade my life for the metal as I used it as a wedge to-

"Red," said a voice in my ear that I didn't recognize. "You need to wake up!"

What a silly call sign. My hair was clearly blond and besides, I didn't remember hiring a teenage girl as a tender. What was going on at that surface that-

"Jen," said a different voice. "Please. You're babbling nonsense about some Greek food you ate last night."

Something was definitely wrong. Maybe my tank had sprung a leak, and I was hallucinating after breathing too much carbon dioxide. I tried to center myself again with slow, deep breaths, but the nagging women in my ear would not relent. I ignored them and returned to the task of freeing my leg when I happened to glance at myself in the signal mirror on my wrist and found that the face reflected back at me was not my own.

"What ... what is going on?" I said, in a voice I didn't recognize.

"You're trapped," said the girl.

"I know that," I said. "But who are you and why do I look and sound like a 25-year-old?"

"Because," said the older woman, "you are. Something happened down there and somehow you slipped into the *Antikythera* memory that Dalia gave you. You're reliving it instead of it feeding your subconscious."

"You're nuts," I said. "I'm getting out of here and away from the two of you and whatever you put in my tank."

"Find your center," said the girl. "Remember who you were. Remember who you are. Remember who you're going to be."

"Nonsense, it's all nonsense," I said. "I'm shutting off my comm now. Good day to you both!"

"I'm sorry, but you're only a remnant," said the second woman, and I paused. It couldn't be true. I couldn't just be a memory. I was real. A daredevil who had braved the deep all over … wait, why couldn't I remember my last dive?

"I don't know what's happening to me," I said. "Help me. Please."

"We will," said the girl, "but you have to trust us."

"If you can't find your own path out," said the woman called Beatrice, "then I'll create one for you."

"OK," I said. "But how?"

"You just need to surface," she replied. "It's like any other dive, yeah? Come back to the surface. Come back to yourself."

"I can't," I said. "My foot is trapped … I'm trapped … and I…"

"Start with your foot then," said Beatrice, "and then the rest will follow. Can you do that?"

"Yes," I said, grabbing the gear again. I pushed the metal down and the mast gave way slightly. Another burst of effort resulted in another shift, but it still wasn't enough, and I collapsed backward onto the cold deck, the stark reality of my situation becoming clearer by the second.

"Again," said the girl.

"Can't get sufficient purchase to move it," I said.

"Don't care," she replied.

"Well, that's nice of you," I said. "Fine."

My third attempt failed as well and this time, for good measure, the gear broke in two.

"Thanks, you dumb kid. Now I'm completely fucked," I said.

"Not yet," said Beatrice. "I want you to push the three buttons on the dongle connected to the hose and then breathe in."

"That will cut off my air entirely!" I said.

"It won't. Please. Trust me."

I tried to pull my leg free one last time, only to wince at the wood pressing down even harder into my ankle, and then slowly brought my hand up to the hose.

"OK," I said. "Here goes nothing."

I pushed down on the buttons, took three deep breaths, and then watched as the world dissolved around me.

I was still underwater, still trapped under a piece of wood, but I was no longer at the bottom of the Aegean Sea and I was no longer someone else.

"Red here, over," I said, but all I heard in response was muffled static in my ear. I took in my surroundings and found my ankle stuck under a section of the cabin's wall, a piece of the painting's frame wedged underneath. I moved my leg, and, buoyed by a combination of all three buffs, I kicked the wood away like it was a twig, and then pushed myself upward.

I rotated my headlamp in a circle to try to find *Curtana's* box, but found that the airlocked room was no more, as the crush of the intruding water into the cabin had reduced it to a shattered wreckage, like the rest of the ship. Before I could start flinging away the centuries-old timber, a slow beeping sound pervaded my ears, which, had I been at normal speed, would have been a glaring alarm. But it was loud enough for me to grab the air tank's pressure gauge, which for some reason showed I only had a few minutes left of oxygen.

"Shit!" I yelled, but again, the time displacement caused by the speed buff left little hope that the duo up above heard more than a chirp. I swam forward, hoping that the robot would be waiting just outside the room, only to find a wall blocking my path. I looked up, finally realizing that the pressurized blast had not only destroyed the cabin, but had blown a hole in the floor down to the Board Room. Which is where I evidently now found myself.

Sufficiently reoriented, I combed the room with my light, and eventually located *Curtana's* box next to one half of the ship painting. I swam over to it in an instant, but the *Foxhound* continued to mock me, as it was empty. My anger reaching a boiling point, I put my palms together, pulled my arms back, and then propelled the water forward, unleashing a guttural cry into my facemask.

The resulting wave swept through the room like a giant fireball, creating a maelstrom of wood and coral in its wake. It was then that I saw it, a shining beacon in the dark chamber, twirling in the current I had unleashed. I pressed my flippered feet against the floor and launched myself up, catching the sword just below its blade.

My headlamp decided at that moment to burn out, but it didn't matter, because I had a new north star. I extended my newly claimed Relic out in front of me and followed its light back up to the surface.

"This isn't a sword," I said, placing a large brown case down onto the Guild's Board Room table that evening.

"Was there a cello in there when you bought it?" asked Ty with a snicker.

I undid the clasps and opened the lid, its hinges protesting wildly, to reveal a long wooden pole with a sharp blade fastened at the end. Removing the Relic carefully so as not to accidentally stab someone, I hoisted it into the air, my two hands gripping it tightly, before placing the bottom on the ground. Its height nearly dwarfed mine, and I pictured myself in the Armory, wielding it against Emma's twin blades, but all I could imagine was the Guild onlookers collapsing into fits of laughter as I clumsily tried to defend myself.

"I never said it was," said Dalia.

"Yes, you did," I said. "You sent me to get *Curtana, the Sword of Mercy.* It's in the name!"

"That is true, but names can be deceiving."

"What am I supposed to do with this thing?" I said, placing the "sword" back inside the case.

"May I?" asked Dalia, as she ran her hands down the length of the staff.

"You don't need my permission," I said.

"Yes, in fact, I do," she said. "This Relic, by the laws of the sea, of the Guild, and probably the Commonwealth, now belongs to you. It is only polite to ask a Relic's owner before one picks it up."

"Permission granted, then."

"Ty, go get me one of our more useless books over there," said Dalia.

She pointed to the bookcase at the back of the room and Ty scurried over, returning shortly with a rather large tome that sported a frayed black leather cover. The Guild chair, at least for a few more days, lifted *Curtana* into the air deftly as if it was a feather, before settling into a two-handed stance, her high-heeled feet shoulder width apart.

"Pull!"

Ty tossed the book, with some effort, upward and as it reached its zenith, Dalia rotated her body backward and then brought the Relic down in one swooping motion to slice the whole thing in half. As the pages rained down around us, Dalia twirled the staff in a horizontal circle, dicing the loose vellum into pieces, before setting *Curtana* down into its case.

"That," she said, "is what you do with this 'thing.' Now get back to work."

She left the room through the rear with a flourish, the door slamming behind her for good measure.

"Your mom knows that I nearly died just this morning at the bottom of the East River, right?"

"Ugh, again she leaves me to clean up her mess," said Ty, ignoring me to bend down and pick up the remains of the book, muttering under her breath as she did. "Sorry, what were you saying?"

"I got trapped in the memory from that electrum she gave me! And got trapped under the weight of the destroyed cabin! If Beatrice hadn't force-fed me that super serum she brought, I probably would have died from decompression sickness."

"Yes, well, you didn't," said Ty. "So, in my mom's eyes, the mission was a complete success. I mean, also? Seeing you explode out of the water like some kind of mega dolphin holding *Curtana* aloft? It was worth the price of admission."

"I don't remember any of that!" I said. "But I'm so glad I could entertain you."

I felt my heart racing and took a deep breath to slow my anger.

"Umm, you didn't happen to snap a picture?"

Ty laughed.

"No, but you'll have to take our word that you were a sight. Now, I could use some help picking up the re-"

"Why is this a Relic?" I said, grabbing my new partner with one hand. Despite the length of the pole and the thick metal blade at the top, it felt about as light as the old broom that had been left in the coat closet in my apartment.

"You'll have to ask King Henry," said Ty.

"Not helpful," I said, trying to mimic Dalia's twirling strike without stabbing myself or Ty. Instead, I tripped and knocked the large case off of the table and onto the same foot that had been trapped on the ship. My eyes widened as the Mediterranean waters swirled around me and scuba gear began appearing on my body. I blinked, and the room was completely gone, replaced by the underwater nightmare that I was intimately familiar with.

"What's happening?" I yelled into the scuba mask that was now secured to my face. I closed my eyes again and steadied my breathing, remembering what the master diver had taught me those many years ago.

"Panic and fear are the enemy," he had said. "You can banish them to the dark recesses of-" A sharp pain reverberated across my cheek, and suddenly I was on the floor of the Board Room, the Relic's case pushed to the side, and Ty standing over me.

"I was afraid of this," she said, extending her hand to help me up, which I took.

"I fell," I said. "Back into the memory. I thought the electrum only inserted the memories into my subconscious."

"I did, it does," she said. "But you broke the barrier when you were down there. And it seems like it's seeping through whenever you get close enough to what happened."

"So now I'm going to believe I'm underwater every time my foot gets trapped under something?" I asked. *Curtana* was splayed across the floor next to the table and I picked it up and returned it back into its case, afraid that if I fell again, I would lose myself.

"No," said Ty. "Because I came prepared." She fished into her jean jacket pocket and placed a gold bead on the table.

"What. Is. That." I said. "Never mind, I don't want to know. No more beads, no more memories."

"It's not a memory," said Ty. "The opposite, in fact. It will draw out the diving memories, like poison from a wound. You won't be a master diver anymore, but I doubt you'll mind."

"And then what?" I asked. "I don't know how to fight with a sword. And certainly don't know how to fight with whatever this stupid thing is."

I smacked *Curtana*'s pole, which just made my hand hurt.

"I believe it's called a glaive," said Ty. "And as to your earlier question regarding what's so special about your new Relic, we're still combing through the restored Compendium, but the only relevant part we've found so far is one cryptic line."

"And what does it say?" I asked.

"*Curtana* is mercy."

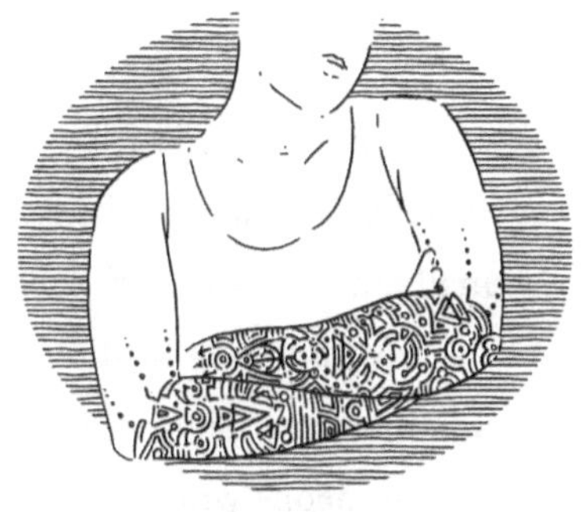

CHAPTER FORTY-SEVEN

TRAINING DAY

"What remains to be seen is whether this is the same adversary that plagued Rita at the end of her life or whether the fragile truce with the East has been broken. I do not know which I prefer."

"**Y**ou're holding back," said Beatrice, who thrust forward with the Medoblad, as I struggled to parry the small dagger with the much larger pole arm. "Your opponent won't."

"You try fighting with this thing!" I said. I tried to swat Beatrice's wrist aside with the body of the staff, but every memory of what her blade had done came pouring back in all at once, and instead I stepped to the side, as I had been doing all morning.

"Gladly," she said. "I'm already imagining how quickly I could slice off someone's arm."

"That's not how I want to fight," I said, assuming my spread-foot stance again and waiting for Beatrice to come at me. This time she didn't, and I was forced to make the first move. I rocked back and forth on the balls of my feet before deciding to try a horizontal swipe. But thanks to my momentary hesitation, Beatrice was already ready for the attack, and blocked the pole with her padded forearms, before countering with a quick stab that pierced me right in the gut.

I looked down at my side, but thankfully, I was not turning to stone. Instead, only a small amount of blood had seeped out of me, thanks to the nature of the Medoblad's healing end, which caused the wound it made to close up immediately. Of course, it had a much greater effect when used on someone who was already stone, but this ability allowed us to better emulate an actual fight.

Beatrice set her Relic down on the small table she had brought down to BSG's basement, which she had cleared out for our training exercises, and grabbed one of the silver beads that were laid out on its surface.

"Here," she said, handing me a piece of electrum that Ty had given me earlier in the day, but I nearly shoved her away.

"No," I said. "No more of those."

"OK then," said Beatrice. "Your key to victory then will be your sheer force of will. It's not as if Emma is an accomplished street fighter. I'm sure you'll do fine."

I tossed *Curtana* aside, and it slid unceremoniously across the cement floor, before kicking over the training dummy nearby for good measure and letting out a primal scream.

"Oh, are we about to have another Jen pity party?" said Beatrice, smirking. "Save it for someone else. Whatever happened to you down at the wreck is over. You need to move past it and focus on what's next."

"So I don't have a choice, then?" I said. "I thought you were all about choices now. I don't want any more memories in my head. That's my choice."

"Then have fun with your 30-second duel," she said, as she set the dummy back upright. "Why go through all the trouble of retrieving your own Relic if you won't learn how to use it?"

"I do," I said, "just not like this."

"Well, if you're not going to eat this one, let me show you what you're missing."

She ate the electrum bead, and her face blanked out as the memories flowed into her head. Just as quickly, she returned to herself and I nodded as she bent down to retrieve *Curtana* from the ground. She marveled at the Relic's airy quality and took a few practice swings before assuming the stance I had been using for the last hour. But rather than attacking with clumsy downward swipes, Beatrice spun *Curtana* in a circle like a baton, slicing through the dummy in a flurry, before bringing it around in one smooth swing to cut the head clean off.

"Holy crap," I said.

"See?" said Beatrice, smiling. She withdrew a handkerchief from her pocket, wiped the dust from *Curtana's* blade, and then placed both down on the table.

"I do," I said. "But … you weren't down there, trapped in someone else's past. I don't know if I fall into that abyss again, I'll be able to surface."

"Actually, I do know how it feels," said Beatrice.

"What do you mean?"

"It's how I got this," she said, holding up the Medoblad. "The former Keeper's memories. They were stored, preserved, in a bead of orichalcum. The principles probably operate similarly to electrum, but-"

"I need to show you something," I said. I pulled out the bead from the *Foxhound's* cabin and laid it flat on my palm.

"Did you try to eat that?" she asked, taking it from my hand and putting it against her ear.

"Maybe last week I would have, but now…"

"Good," she said. "Because if you had, it would have made your diving debacle feel like a picnic."

"Why is that?"

"Because that also happens to be a bead of orichalcum," said Beatrice.

"What's so different about this that made you so afraid?"

She licked the bead and grimaced before putting the whole thing in her mouth and swallowing. Unlike the electrum she imbibed earlier, this flavor kept her wide awake. But when her body started to move again, it was as if someone had attached strings to her limbs and was controlling her like a puppet.

She walked around the room, as if she was searching for something, and I had to step out of her way several times, as she seemingly had no idea I was even there. Finally, as she was about to pick up *Curtana*, I grabbed her wrist and her eyes snapped to attention. Only the person looking at me wasn't Beatrice.

"*We must smite the egg with fire before it hatches*," she said, with a strange accent.

Then she reached around me to grab the handkerchief on the table, and wretched into it.

"That … was unpleasant," she said, withdrawing the somehow still clean orichalcum from inside the cloth's folds.

"What just happened?" I asked. "It's like you were possessed."

"I was," she said. "I thought I was in a strange library, books stacked to the ceiling. But, *Curtana*, it was there too, along with someone else, and when I grabbed the Relic, I told them-"

I repeated the cryptic line, but even with the added context, it still made no sense to me.

"I wish you had let me stay in there a bit longer," she said. "To see what was about to happen."

"If I did that, you probably would have stabbed me," I said.

"No, I wouldn't have," said Beatrice. "Ordinarily, using orichalcum is like being subsumed into the recollections in the bead. But fortunately, I stumbled onto the key to staying myself quite by accident. The focus buff provides a counter to the weight of the orichalcum's stored memories."

"I didn't see you eat one just now though," I said.

"That's my secret, Jen," said Beatrice, tossing aside the padding to reveal an intricate network of jade green symbols tattooed on her forearm. "I'm always focused."

The next week was a complete blur. Training followed by more training followed by hours-long sessions where Beatrice would apply her buff ink to my arms in differing combinations.

She started small at first, tattooing only enough for a few uses, as I soon learned that like all alchemy, there was a finiteness to how long the ink would last before it was consumed. Even activating a three-second burst took many hours of focus and concentration. It was as if I was communicating with a new part of my body that my brain didn't know how to speak to.

That was not the only obstacle to hurdle, though. I still refused to use any of the electrum, but it was getting harder and harder to maintain the front, as one of the nights (I can't remember which), I arrived back at my apartment to find a briefcase full of the silver stuff on my bed with a note from Dalia that said "Return this to me empty."

That is not to say I didn't try to learn to master *Curtana*. There were other methods of learning that Beatrice had developed, as I discovered the next morning when she placed an old scroll in front of me and admitted that she had spiked my coffee with a focus buff. She unfurled it and my mind tore through the fighting stances and diagrams and movesets and theories like it was a sponge. When I came to who knows how long later, a new training dummy was a few feet away from me and *Curtana*'s case was open, a beckoning siren perched on a bluff in the sea.

I picked up its handle and the images I had digested flashed through my head. The muscle memory was lacking, but I surprised myself when I landed a flawless series of jabs that I finished off with a one-handed swing that knocked my stuffed opponent to the ground. My confidence increased with every moveset I executed, and by the end of the day Saturday, I had managed to knock the Medoblad out of Beatrice's hand through a combination of strength, speed, and a roundhouse kick she was not expecting.

"When did you learn that?" she asked, as I helped her up from the floor.

"Dunno," I said, looking at my forearms to find all traces of ink gone. "Must have been an insert stuck in *Talhoffer's Techniques*. Should we go again?"

"Negative," said Beatrice.

"Why not? It's only 11 p.m."

"Because you're delirious," she said.

"Am not!" I said, but Beatrice just rolled her eyes.

"I have a seven-year-old who is going to come barging into my room in a few hours demanding to know how the espresso machine works for the umpteenth time. And I still need to apply a fresh set of ink to your arms. You've gotten better at controlling the duration, but you need to be able to activate a light touch, so that you can last the whole fight."

"All the more reason we should practice again once I'm re-inked. I-"

Beatrice shook her head.

"I'm calling it. You've done all you can. Plus, I finally made headway on your glamour side project. If I'm going to have any chance of finishing before your fight, you need to let me rest a bit. Especially now that our betters have summoned us."

She grabbed her phone and handed it to me.

The group text from Ty was brief:

"Mooney House, 12:30 p.m."

And so, after a delightful brunch prepared by Svetlana, who also somehow knew how to cook the perfect omelette, the two of us found ourselves on the doorstep of the Guild's downtown annex. We approached the old manse with trepidation, as this had been where Ty had confined Doug while she molded him into the Gilbert she had hoped he would become. The front entrance bore the same lock as my office and the *Foxhound*'s cabin, and so it opened easily after I slid my gold token into the nook. I looked over at Beatrice as I pushed open the creaky door and wondered if she ever wished that our tokens had been reversed, that this was her burden to shoulder, instead of mine.

Ty was waiting inside in the kitchen, perched on top of a white marble counter that was wildly out of place compared to the rest of the room. She hopped down and walked silently toward a particularly old looking wooden door, which barely managed to open. Behind it was a set of stairs that I thought I was going to fall through that led down into absolute darkness.

At the bottom, Ty stomped on the bottom step twice, and the chamber beyond flickered to life thanks to tiny glowing orbs inset in the walls.

"This place," said the teen, "is the oldest surviving row house in the city. The Guild bought it from Mooney on his deathbed and has used it ever since."

"I am truly honored that you invited us to this hallowed ground," said Beatrice

Ty ignored her, and we walked onward into the basement, which was devoid of anything except the wooden beams holding up the structure above. And at the back of the room stood Dalia in a gleaming white dress.

"Why are we here?" I asked.

"To remind you what is at stake tomorrow," she said, rapping her knuckle against one of the beams. "The foundation of the Guild is still strong, but you need to fill the crack that has appeared. Are you ready to do that?"

"I hope so," I said.

"Hope is not enough," said Dalia. "The hopes of the many have been snuffed out time and again by the power of the few. We have labored for centuries as the bulwark against the exhaustion of the remaining magic in the world. We've gone up against things worse than those awful children who seek my Chair, but if they were to get that vial of Dragon's blood, there's no telling what they could do before we would be able to stop them."

"The way Ty tells it," I said, "they've already cornered the market on Philosopher's Stones. How much harm could one more do?"

Dalia glared at Ty, who shrugged her shoulders.

"A great deal," said Dalia. "Alchemy is more than just a list of ingredients. It takes skill, finesse, creativity, things that the Van Asch Corporation has sacrificed in the name of efficiency and scale. So yes, they may have multiple 'Stones,' but they have likely wasted Starkey's legacy crafting mediocre little gems that won't last more than one use."

"Not to mention," said Ty, "that the Compendium includes the true recipe for the Stone."

"There's a reason I didn't mention that," said Dalia, "especially given our present company."

"She deserves to know," replied Ty. "They both do. Jen has put herself on the line over and over for the Guild, for you. And Ms. Stallard, despite her past transgressions, has been a valuable asset."

"This is so heart-warming," said Beatrice. "It's like we're all having a moment."

Despite the snark, I had to marvel at the way things had seemingly turned. Despite our differences, despite the enmity, we had all united behind our common goal of making sure J.P. would never take the Chair's Seat.

"Indeed," said Dalia. "Ms. Jacobs, please lend your blonde friend your cloak. She should be in attendance during the Trial tomorrow."

I nodded, and Dalia turned to walk away, only to pivot on her heels suddenly and throw something at me.

But I was ready for her.

I closed my eyes and felt the speed buff's tattooed symbol on my skin, and my right arm vibrated in response. I opened my eyes again, and the world had slowed to a crawl. A silver dagger hung in mid-air a few inches from my face, as if it was suspended on a string. My fingers danced against the cold steel and for a just a second, I considered what I could do with this blade. But the moment passed, and instead, I grasped the dagger's handle, took another breath, and returned time to its normal pace.

Dalia's mouth broke into a small smile as I dropped the weapon onto the stone floor.

"I expected nothing less from my Champion. Until tomorrow."

CHAPTER FORTY-EIGHT

BEST LAID PLANS

"Lorna came to visit me today. She has grown into herself well and would be a force to be reckoned with in any era. Thankfully, I still have her favor, and the partnership between our organizations has been mutually beneficial. Although I do not wish to divulge the entire matter, it is clear I will need the help of the VATC if I am to restore that which was taken from me."

I couldn't sleep. My stomach growled and my entire body ached, but I kept myself steady by sipping Beatrice's vitality serum as the hours ticked by. By 3 a.m., I had given up any hope of slumber, and so I grabbed *Curtana*'s case and departed my tiny apartment.

As I walked out of Cobble Hill and slowly made my way to the Brooklyn Bridge, I couldn't help but think about how different things seemed from that first walk uptown in my invisibility cloak only a month ago. I marveled at what I had accomplished, how I had surmounted everything that the Guild had thrown at me. It wasn't that

I had become cocky, but for the first time in a long time, I finally felt like I was standing on solid ground, that I had earned my Seat in the Guild, and after all of this was over, I was going to get some answers about my mom and how she came to possess the long-lost gold token.

Even in New York City, a single woman walking the streets this late carrying what could be mistaken for a large guitar would be enough to draw attention, but the power inked on my arms gave me a newfound confidence that I hadn't had the last time I was summoned, when I was content to hide behind the cloak's alchemy. I threaded my way across the Bridge, through joggers, bikers, and bar patrons stumbling home from their Sunday night drinking, and headed uptown.

The gears of the city turned as I walked, the reverie of the weekend fading, soon to be replaced by the throngs of worker drones. By Thursday evening, things would shift again, as the pent-up energy from hours spent sitting at desks and staring at computers needed release, and the cycle would repeat, like clockwork. It amazed me that so many millions gave themselves to this cycle, never knowing the secrets that were threaded around them like an invisible spiderweb. I reminded myself that this delicate balance was on the precipice of being forever upended if I lost the duel.

Despite the onset of Monday morning, the Lower East Side still believed itself immune, with the sidewalks so crowded that several times I had to detour into the road to navigate *Curtana*'s case through the raucous throngs. I contemplated stopping for a drink at one of the emptier bars to loosen up a bit, but was immediately sidetracked when I caught a glimpse of bright red hair walking toward Houston Street. I followed behind as quickly and surreptitiously as I could, my heart beginning to beat just a tad faster, until I reached the thoroughfare. Sure enough, not 10 feet away, ambling along without a care in the world, was Jade, in the flesh.

I felt a different sort of energy radiate out from the center of my body as I walked closer. It was not the adrenaline that had been fueling me the last several days, but something else, something uncanny, almost as if I was being drawn toward my former avatar. But whatever I may have been experiencing seemed to have no effect on Jade, and instead, she continued onward to the very packed pancake spot a few blocks up and entered. I did the same, nearly knocking over everyone cramped in the inner vestibule trying to get through, and when I did, I found her staring ahead, absentmindedly, like a normal customer waiting for a table.

I grabbed her by the shoulder and spun her around, only to find a very confused and very not-Jade redhead glaring at me.

"What the hell?" she said.

"I … umm … thought you were…"

The woman stormed away, probably to get a manager, and I turned quickly to leave, only to see Jade standing just on the other side of the front window.

Her eyes met mine, and a knowing smile formed on her face. The weird feeling in my chest suddenly boiled over and spread to the rest of my body, but before I could do anything, Jade gave me a two-finger salute and walked off.

That's when I did something incredibly stupid: I activated one of the speed tattoos.

Thanks to the hours of practice, the lilac runes on my arm lit up immediately, and I exited the restaurant with ease (but not before grabbing a pancake off of a waitress's tray). Outside, the entire city had slowed to a standstill. Everyone except Jade, who was aimlessly strolling a block ahead of me. I pulled *Curtana* free from its case on the sidewalk, and sprinted after her, my Relic extended outward like I was a charging crusader, but no matter how close I got, she was always just out of reach.

And when I reached the East River promenade, Jade was somehow already behind me, walking the other direction back into the grid. I burned through more speed as the static world became a blur until finally I made it within an arm's length of her.

I lunged *Curtana* toward her, but she deftly turned to the side and pushed the Relic's staff down with one hand, and I would have toppled to the ground had Jade not steadied me with her other.

"Nice try," she whispered in my ear and that's when everything started up again and I collapsed onto the pavement. I stared at my forearms to find one last lilac strand remaining and the enormity of my mistake finally sunk in.

Things went from bad to worst, as I burst into BSG 15 minutes later and startled Svetlana, who was busy dispensing half a dozen espresso shots at once for some reason.

"Where's Beatrice?" I asked, before stumbling into a chair and tossing the re-encased *Curtana* to the ground unceremoniously.

"Dunno," Svetlana said. "Last time I saw her, she was with you, working on your arms. Then she went upstairs and hasn't come back down yet. Maybe she's-"

I ran past her, up to the second and then third floor, and was about to travel through the portal when I stopped myself from turning that brown knob. In my current mental state, there would be no telling how long it would take to traverse to the other side, and so I retreated solemnly down to the cafe.

"I'm so screwed," I said, rubbing my arm, as if that would bring the ink back.

Svetlana looked me up and down, before retreating under the bar for a few seconds, from which she withdrew a dusty bottle with a faded label I couldn't read and half-filled with a dark substance.

"One of my first concoctions," she said. "Needs to age several years to let its effects be more pronounced. Drink it right before you go in."

She poured the brown thick liquid into a paper espresso cup and pushed it toward me.

"It looks gross," I said, bringing the cup up to my nose before attaching a small lid.

"Tastes even worse. Just chug it in one sip and you'll be fine."

"What is it?" I asked.

"Liquid courage."

I stood before a cascading series of fire escapes that led up to the top of the Park Avenue Armory's front tower, holding the encased *Curtana* with one hand and my still full cup of Svetlana's so-called courage in the other. In the intervening hours, my frantic texts to Beatrice had all gone unanswered and so I tried to prepare myself mentally for a quick battle in which Emma hopefully wouldn't slice me in the stomach like she had done to Steve.

"Are you ready?" said a voice behind me and I turned around to see Ty dressed in a long flowing scarlet gown.

"Ready enough," I said. "Why are you wearing that?"

"Mom said to dress the part," said Ty. "Not sure what part she was talking about, but it didn't feel like something to press her on. Shall we?"

She walked to the ladder of the first fire escape and pulled it down easily with her hand before starting her ascent. I looked at my full hands and decided that now was as good a time as any for a drink and so I gulped down the brown liquid in one quick sip. Just as Svetlana had said, it tasted absolutely putrid, as if she boiled a gym sock in grape juice and then poured in some hot sauce and let it sit on a sunny windowsill for days. But after the initial shock wore off, I found myself staring up at the stairs like I could scale them in a single bound. And that whatever madness lay beyond was nothing I couldn't handle. So I charged upward, overtaking Ty, and reached the window that would be our entrance into the Armory.

As I climbed through to the other side, I felt the drink's effects begin to waiver just slightly, but before my confidence could crumble, I was steadied by the sight of the assembled Guild members who were in my corner.

"This isn't where we're fighting, is it?" I asked, peering around the mahogany-lined reception room. Its walls were dotted with historic portraits of important looking military men and its intricate woodwork could probably no longer be recreated by any living carpenter.

"No," said Ty. "I believe my mother made other arrangements."

"Ah, there you are," said Dalia, who broke off from her group and walked over to us. She was decked out in an equally formal and equally long dress as her daughter, with a small clutch in one hand and a drink in the other, as if she was attending a charity gala.

"Can't help feeling I'm a bit underdressed," I said. Unlike the cocktail attire everyone else was wearing, I was sporting a pair of spandex workout pants, sneakers, and a tank top, with my hair up in a high ponytail.

"Yes, well, we'd rather you win than look stylish, I suppose."

"You have such a way with words," I said, gripping the handle of *Curtana*'s case for a dose of confidence. Dalia bade me join her allies, who all nodded at me.

"Your friend's assistance was … helpful," said D.C., breaking the awkward silence.

"Good, I'm glad," I said. "Will it help you finish sooner?"

"Not sure," he said. "I've only used it for the mundane so far. Couldn't forgive myself if I rushed things and broke the blade."

"I see."

"Good luck," he said, and walked away.

"Wow," said Lucca, nudging me with her elbow. "You must be pumped up after that conversation."

"He's … something," I said. "I know I said this already a dozen times, but thank you for your help."

"You don't need to thank me," she said. "The work is its own reward. I'm just sorry I couldn't lend a hand with your other project. Some things I can't-"

"It's OK," I said. "I understand."

"I think you can win without it, though," she said with a half-smile.

I nodded and stepped back from the group, not wanting to engage in any more unhelpful small talk. On the other side of the room, J.P. was holding court, dressed in a white three piece-suit with a black cowboy hat, with a Lycra-clad Emma standing next to him. From the looks of her, she didn't seem too thrilled to have been chosen as a Champion either. A new tote bag hung around her shoulder and inside, no doubt, were her two Relics: *White Hilt* and whatever that giant sword was called. I had hoped that some obscure rule would prevent her from wielding both in our duel, but Ty had helpfully informed me that while one Relic was required to participate, there was no limit to how many a Champion could use.

I looked around for any sign of Beatrice hiding underneath my cloak—some mysterious noise, a person banging their ankle on an unseen obstacle—but came up with nothing. I contemplated reaching out to her with my mind, but didn't want the certainty of her absence to weigh further on my psyche. And so, as the impressive-looking grandfather clock chimed nine times, I was glad that the fight was actually going to begin after so much build-up.

"Shall we?" asked Dalia, and our group meandered over to the stairs that presumably led down to the lower level.

"Wait a minute," I said. "Don't tell me we're fighting in-"

"Yes," said Ty. "The main drill hall."

She pushed open a set of double doors and I stepped into the expanse beyond. The room ran unobstructed for the entire length of the city block, with a ceiling that soared probably a hundred feet into the air, huge metal arches holding up the roof. It was the kind of place you didn't think existed in New York City, outside of a sports arena.

"How did you arrange this?" I asked as we entered the giant space.

"Easy," said Dalia. "I booked a private event for Thera DeWitt and then forgot to invite anyone else."

"Then why did we have to come through the fire escape?"

"We didn't," she said. "Who told you that you-"

I turned around to glare at Ty, who suppressed a laugh.

"Please don't do anything more to torment our Champion until after this is over," said Dalia, who walked off in a huff.

"What?" said Ty. "I thought it would be a good warm-up for you!"

"You pull any other pranks? Did you steal *Curtana* and replace it with a broom when I wasn't looking?"

"No, just the one," she said. "Come on, the crowd is waiting!"

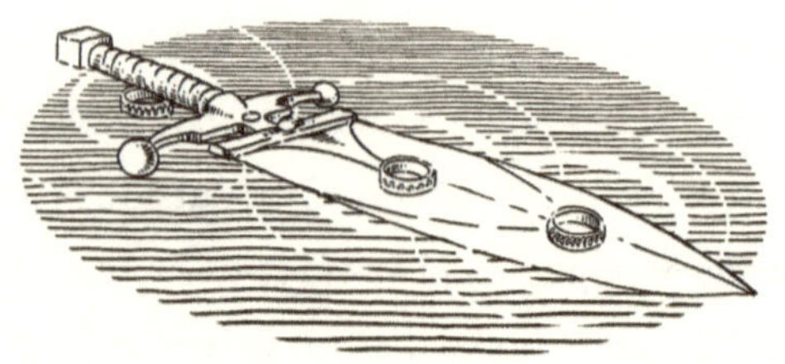

CHAPTER FORTY-NINE

DUEL RELICS

"James Laurel presented his late uncle's token at our latest meeting and demanded the First Seat of the Orange Table. The boy has borne much hardship, having also lost his father on the ill-fated western expedition. More remarkably, he personally retrieved the gold coin and brought back many personal effects of the other members lost. James is the kind of stock we desperately need in our ranks, but I worry he will carry an animus that will not easily be extinguished."

My footsteps echoed on the parquet floor as I approached the four sets of risers that had been assembled in a square at the other end of the hall. It was as if we were all here for a pickup basketball game and not a magical battle royale. I entered the enclosure to find a large circular mat had been laid down in the middle. It all looked so … casual that, for a moment, I forgot what we were doing here.

Dalia and Ty wandered over to the nearest riser and sat down in the front row. They were soon joined by the third member of their

Table, who had managed to clean up at least some of the dirt from his clothing and body for the occasion. The rest of us shuffled over to where our respective Tables were usually seated and we all stared at each other in silence until J.P. knocked his cane against the wooden bench and stood.

"I move to begin the Trial," he said.

"Seconded," said Dalia.

"The motion carries," said Ty. "Will our champions please step forward and present their Relics?"

I opened up my case to pull out *Curtana*, drawing a chorus of whispers from the other members. Emma, meanwhile, reached both hands into her bag and pulled out her two weapons with a flourish. We both walked into the circle and I tried my hardest not to look at Emma, but failed miserably. Her left hand held the giant sword and her right was adorned with the familiar auragen rings. With it, she gripped the horrible dagger that had prematurely aged Steve, although I wasn't sure how, as her fingers looked like they might crack into a thousand pieces.

"You first," she said to me.

"*Curtana, the Sword of Mercy*," I shouted and several Guild members gasped. I didn't know whether to hold it aloft like *Excalibur* or do a short demonstration of my martial prowess, so instead I just stood there, waiting for someone to tell me I was disqualified.

"Young lady," said Kildare. "Wherever did you get that magnificent weapon? My own records indicate it has been missing for some time."

"It's, umm, a long story," I said.

"But yet, a story we must hear," said J.P. "Who's to say you and your patron didn't just fashion a replica? That would violate the clear rules of-"

"Oh shove it," said Emma. "I know it's real. You don't need druithyl to see that."

"Trust, but verify," said J.P. "I will not lose this trial because you-"

"Now you're the one fighting?" said Emma. "By all means, take my place."

"That's not what-"

"Enough," said Dalia. "This squabbling is beneath all of us. If you would like to challenge the provenance of Ms. Jacobs's Relic, then say so."

"I … it's fine," said J.P. "If it's not the real deal, this battle will be over even sooner."

"We shall see, won't we?" said Dalia. "Now, Ms. Patel, if you please."

Emma nodded and held up her Relics.

"The *Dyrnwyn, White Hilt*!" she yelled, as if she was leading a war party. "And, *Solais, the Sword of Light*!"

She knocked both blades together above her head, releasing a blinding flash of light that enveloped the mini-arena for a moment. When the proverbial dust had settled, the sullen Emma was gone and in her place was a woman who looked determined to run me through with one or both Relics.

"Excellent," said Dalia. "Now, before we begin, we will set the terms of the-"

"Point of order, Madam Chair," said J.P., tapping his cane yet again, before sidling down the stairs to the parquet floor. "I believe your Champion is making use of an illegal substance, and I move for an immediate disqualification."

Dalia considered the latest wrinkle and glanced around the room to see if J.P.'s interruption had gained purchase before responding with a gruff sigh.

"What now?"

"Ms. Jacobs's arms," he said. "They are covered in-"

"-tattoos, yes I know. Anyone can see that," said Dalia.

"And anyone can see that these are no ordinary tattoos. They are imbued with-"

"-mind and body-enhancing properties, yes, we know," said Emma, of all people. "Don't care. I'll still beat her."

"No matter how confident you are, my dear, there is protocol and precedent that must be followed," said J.P. "And that forbids outside enhancement, so unless Ms. Jacobs can remove them in the next five minutes, I'm afraid the match will be forfeit."

I slammed *Curtana* into the ground, and all eyes suddenly focused on me.

"I'm ready to fight," I said. "Emma's ready to fight. The only one who doesn't want this match to start is you, it seems. If you'd like to come down here and fight me, by all means, but I've had enough of your bullshit."

I turned my back to him and walked toward the Breuckelen side of the ring as a cavalcade of whispers spread throughout the makeshift arena. Finally, just as I was about to sit down next to D.C. and Lucca, I heard that familiar tapping sound.

"I withdraw my objection," said J.P.

I smiled and tried to savor the minor battle I had won, but the moment was fleeting.

"Excellent," said Dalia. "Now, as I was saying, we shall set the terms of the match. In addition to the Chair, I will claim, for the Guild, the vial of Dragon's blood that Ms. Patel still hopefully has in her possession, should Jen prevail."

"That's it?" asked J.P. "I was expecting a bigger ask. But your mistake. Should Emma prevail and I take the Chair, I will demand the forfeiture of the Second Seat of the New Amsterdam Table."

"You want my Seat?" asked Ty. "You'll have to come and take it from my-"

"Agreed," said Dalia.

"You're joking, right?" said Ty. "You're going to let him kick me to the curb like a stray-"

"Hush, child," said Dalia. "They're my terms to set. Now that that's settled, we can finally begin."

Ty glared at her mother in disbelief, but received no acknowledgement in return.

"Fine. Champions, to their marks," she said.

I returned to my spot next to Emma, and we assumed our opening stances.

"Allez!"

I shifted my weight back and forth on the balls of my feet, waiting for my opponent to make the first move. But instead of attacking, Emma calmly sat down on her knees and perched her Relics on her lap. She then closed her eyes, taking deep breaths as if she was meditating at a yoga class and not in a battle for honor and glory. It was completely unnerving, and I didn't know whether to lunge at her or adopt a similar pose.

I considered using the entirety of my final speed rune. It would only last three seconds of real-time, but it would be enough to knock her out and end this before it could even start. But a tiny sliver of doubt stopped me. Perhaps J.P.'s objection had all been a show, accusing me of cheating when it was Emma who had a speed buff tucked away in her cheek. With that, she could easily dodge all of my attacks and my one trump card would be gone.

So I hesitated, and in that moment, Emma pounced. She launched herself up from the ground in a somersault, and came at me with both weapons extended outward, like a human spear. But I was ready. Just as I had practiced, I sped things up for an instant, allowing me to parry her blades away with a flurry of horizontal swipes. She retreated, and then lunged at me a second time in a circular rotation led by her sword. I sped up time once more, deflecting her sword and then her dagger one after the other as Emma twirled her body back and forth, and again she relented.

But when she came at me for a third time, I made my opening move.

I planted *Curtana* in the ground like a flagpole and used it to swing my body upward, kicking Emma square in the chest with a burst of strength that sent her staggering backward.

The victory was short-lived, however, as Emma spit a mouthful of blood onto the mat and then threw *White Hilt* at me. I knocked it away with ease, but at the expense of another microsecond of speed, and she snatched the dagger from the ground with her auragen tether.

"Impressive," she said. "Even with those tattoos, I didn't expect you to last this long."

"I'm just getting started," I said.

"So am I," she said and without taking a breath, flicked *White Hilt* at me in a sidearm motion. This time I ducked, barely dodging the spinning blade, but when I stood back up, Emma was already inches away from me and I felt something hit me hard in the gut. I looked down, expecting to see the sword stuck in my stomach, but instead, it was only its hilt.

"What…" I said, trying to stay upright, but the pain was almost too much to bear and I braced myself on *Curtana* to avoid falling over. And that's when I saw her left hand begin to wobble back and forth, which could only mean one thing.

With no idea how close the dagger was to impaling me from behind, I did the only thing I could do in the moment: I cross-checked Emma with *Curtana*, driving us both to the ground.

"Almost had you," she said with a wink, as she pushed me off of her and I quickly retreated.

Now it was my turn to go on the offensive. With barely any green left on my arm, I switched to my back-up plan, the focus-strength combo. A list of moves flashed through my mind and I selected one as if I was playing a video game, only I was the character being controlled.

I let out a cry and launched a barrage of horizontal strikes at Emma's head. But each time the blade was about to make contact, she either dodged to the side or deflected it with one of her own. She blocked everything I threw at her, even escaping unscathed as I executed the twirling strike that Beatrice had first shown me. My frustration grew with each failed attack, until finally I charged her straight on, like a pole vaulter running toward the take-off point. But Emma was ready, and she sidestepped me with ease, before jabbing me with the butt of *Solais* in the back, sending me flailing to the ground.

"Pathetic," she said. "Like you copied everything right out of a book into your head. No creativity, no improvisation. Do you want to try again, or will you just concede?"

"No," I said, pushing myself up. "I'm going to win."

"In what reality?" said Emma. "I can do this all day. And you'll be out of your magic ink well before I even break a sweat."

I charged her once more, but she easily blocked *Curtana* with the blade of *Solais*, releasing another flash of light and sending reverberations through my Relic up my arms. I tried a low swipe at her legs, but thanks to the *Sword of Light*, I could hardly see. Emma easily jumped over my clumsy attack and returned a counter at me, which I barely avoided, before tripping and falling backward on my ass.

"Don't worry," she said. "After this is all over, there won't be any hard feelings. Kicking the crap out of you in front of everyone will be a sweet revenge for what you did to me in Boston."

I knew she was trying to bait me, but I didn't care. And although

I could have kept holding on to that last bit of speed, I needed to send a message.

The green rune on my right arm glowed, and I let it all go. The Guild, the expectations, the consequences, everything. Emma stood as still as a statue two yards in front of me. Maybe she had noticed what I was doing, but it wouldn't matter, because her Relics would be useless against me. As I got close and saw the current state of her hand, it became clear how much she was holding back the pain, and I marveled that she fought with such prowess despite it.

I brought *Curtana*'s blade down to Emma's ankle to score a light gash, one that would hopefully slow her down. But the sharp metal refused to cut her and instead it was as if I was using a plastic knife. I tried again on the other ankle, but achieved the same result.

"What the hell?" I shouted to no one. "This is your mercy, you stupid sword that's not a sword? I need to win!"

Another move flashed before my eyes at that moment and I nodded, bringing *Curtana*'s pole behind Emma's neck, trapping her head in a makeshift vise. I leaned into her body and for some reason whispered "I'm sorry" and then pulled the Relic forward. As Emma tumbled slowly to the ground, the last of my speed ink evaporated, and I watched as time resumed its normal course and she hit the mat at full speed with a crunch. The force of the impact caused *Solais* to slide out of her left hand, but when I looked at her right, I saw that it was empty.

And that's when I felt it, a pain unlike anything I had ever experienced in my life, like something was siphoning out the energy in my body, little by little. I stared down at my stomach in horror to find that in that fraction of a second, Emma had stabbed me with *White Hilt*.

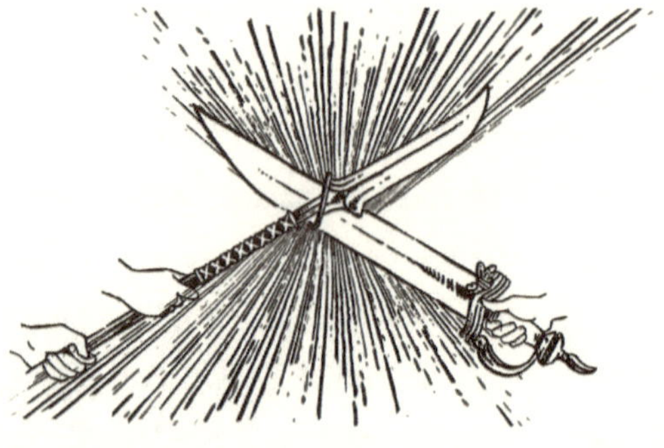

CHAPTER FIFTY

FULL CIRCLE

"Mercy is a mysterious concept. It can come in many forms. It can be found in many places. I have both sought it and given it. But after receiving the latest missive from Europe, the word no longer has any meaning for me."

"I'm sorry, too," said Emma, as she pushed herself up from the ground. She extended her charred hand, slowly wrenching *White Hilt* free from my stomach with her rings, and I let out a primal scream that rang out through the cavernous hall before collapsing onto my knees.

In those few seconds of agony, I saw the last few months of effort flash before my eyes. My journey to California and back, my reunion with Beatrice, my trip to the void, my scuba and weapons training, my dive into the deep, it was all for naught. I had failed because I had been careless and stupid and overconfident, and I was going to wind up a withered old crone to boot.

I reached my hand under my shirt, trying to find the probably-green glowing wound, but all my fingers felt was smooth skin.

"*Don't let her know,*" said a voice in my head and, before I could turn around in shock, the voice continued. "*I'm not here, so don't look for me.*"

"*OK,*" I said in my head, not believing that it was actually Beatrice. Perhaps the mental weight of everything had finally snapped the barrier I had erected in my mind and I was now imagining things. Maybe this whole thing was a delusion, and I was really still trapped at the bottom of the East River.

"*If you're not here, then how did you know?*"

"*I felt it,*" she said. "*Like the burning of a thousand suns. Nearly toppled over. For a moment, it was as if I was you. But then the pain suddenly subsided.*"

"*Are you still–*"

"*No,*" said Beatrice. "*Thankfully. But I regret even more this special bond we have. Now get up. You have a trial to win.*"

I complied and grabbed *Curtana* as I slowly got back to my feet, pretending to be in complete anguish. Wincing, I held the Relic aloft with my right hand, and with my left, I beckoned Emma forward, like I had seen in so many old kung fu movies.

"What?" said Emma. "You're still going to try to fight?"

"Why wouldn't I?" I said with a chuckle. "Was that supposed to hurt? I barely felt it."

"Shut. Up."

She tossed *White Hilt* at me end-over-end, but with the power of the focus ink, I studied its movements, predicted its path, and knocked it to the side with ease. The dagger flew back into Emma's hand and she tried again, but this time, I stepped forward and caught it. My opponent's anger began to build, as she yanked *White Hilt* from my grip so hard that she almost took one of my fingers with it. I steadied myself for another attack, but instead, in one raw burst of fury, she turned around and threw the Relic into an empty section of the Pavonia riser, shattering the wood where it made impact, and then hissed at Hugo and the earring-adorned woman when they went to retrieve it.

"I'm over here," I said, waving at Emma with a mocking smile.

In response, she moved both of her hands onto *Solais's* magnificent hilt, raised it above her head, and charged at me, screaming all the way. I parried her at the last second, almost losing my balance, but before I could take a breath, she brought the blade down to my feet, and I used *Curtana* to vault backwards. We danced around the ring, but without my speed, I could only play defense against Emma's superior skills. Even though she had the upper hand, there was a creeping desperation in her successive attacks, and eventually, she resorted to hammering *Solais* against *Curtana*'s pole so hard that I thought she was going to slice it in two.

"Just."

Slash.

"Give."

Swipe.

"Up."

Lunge.

"No," I said, barely blocking all three.

"Fine," said Emma, who delivered a sharp kick to my stomach that finally sent me to the ground.

"You're done," said Emma, standing over me with *Solais* at my throat. "Not sure how you shrugged off *White Hilt*, but you've got nothing left. You stand alone, your borrowed talent expired, bereft of friends or any means of defeating me."

"Not alone," someone yelled out from the audience and we both turned to see a blonde girl appear behind Ty, dressed in a black skirt and knee-high black boots. But it wasn't Beatrice. It was…

"Callie?" cried Emma. "Is that … how are you-"

"Callie is nothing but a faint echo," said the girl, holding up a glittering green-stoned necklace from around her neck. "And she belongs to me!"

"I'LL KILL YOU!" screamed Emma, abandoning her finishing pose and charging toward the edge of the ring. But before she could reach "Callie," I extended *Curtana* and knocked her feet out from under her mid-stride. Emma turned around, a burning fire in her eyes, but it was just enough of a pause for Dalia to intervene.

"There will be no killing," she said. "This isn't a fight to the death. Also, murder wasn't covered by the Armory's waiver. Your opponent is over there, Ms. Patel. You can deal with any extracurriculars once this match is done."

Emma glared at Dalia with the fury of a lion denied its prey and turned slowly back toward me.

"*You've got your distraction,*" said Beatrice, and I looked at "Callie," who had sat down quietly in her seat. "*Don't waste it.*"

Emma and I resumed our sparring, but she had clearly lost a step, as her mental energy was split between defeating me and puzzling over the sudden reappearance of the girl who had been her friend. Some would have called it a dirty trick and were it not for my own earlier stupidity, I probably wouldn't have needed it all.

But thankfully, I had taken Jade's words to heart. I made sure, no matter what, that I had a way to win. And that is why I had tasked Beatrice with hunting down Polly and retrieving the glamour she had called "Eva." Even weeks later, it still made me sick to my stomach to think about what Steve had done, how he had preyed on Emma and her friends, how he had crossed the pale into forbidden alchemy, and worst of all, how he had offered up the results to his own daughter. Remedying that wrong, however, would have to wait just a bit longer.

"She's not dead," I said, as I twirled around and knocked Emma in the side of her gut with *Curtana*. "For the glamour stone to work, it needs-"

"Don't you dare fucking say her name," said Emma. She tried to charge forward with *Solais*, but pulled back at the last second, the pain in her right hand too great to support the sword. It felt bad to take advantage, but I did anyway, tripping her again as she retreated.

"It's too much," I said. "You need to stop. Before your hand becomes-"

Emma spit in my face before sweeping *Solais* at my feet, in a clumsy repeat move I saw coming, even without the focus ink. I wiped the projectile attack from my cheek and launched a counter before Emma could get to her feet, stabbing at her midsection in successive alternating thrusts that tore up the bottom of her shirt. But no matter hard I sliced, the sword once again refused to draw blood.

Even in her depleted state, Emma came quickly to the same conclusion, that whatever secret magic *Curtana* possessed, its blade couldn't hurt her. She smiled and pushed herself up with her good hand, before discarding *Solais* on the ground.

"What are you doing?" I asked as I assumed a defensive stance.

"Don't need it to beat you," she said. "Not with your dull edge."

Emma tore through the middle of her shirt with her bare hands and tossed it aside, revealing a tank top underneath bearing a weird graphic of a two-headed elephant. I seized my advantage and launched a barrage at my weaponless opponent, which she effortlessly either dodged or blocked with one hand. I used my remaining strength ink to make every hit take a toll, but the resulting decrease in speed made it even easier for Emma to avoid my attacks.

My options fading, I activated the last of my focus ink and yet still, my thoughts drifted from path to path. I could keep fighting this uphill battle and eventually Emma would wear me down and I would have to give up. I could retreat into a defensive shell and hope that Emma would wear herself down. Or I could figure out *Curtana*'s secret, but all I had was one cryptic note in a hundreds-year-old book. Compared to the pieces I had assembled to unlock the Medoblad's puzzle, this was like being handed a single breadcrumb.

"*Help!*" I cried to Beatrice. "*I'm running out of options.*"

"*There's one thing you can do,*" she replied. "*But not sure your weird moral code of ethics will allow you to do it.*"

"*What?*"

"*You've been avoiding her weak hand for some reason. But why? No mercy.*"

I shook my head.

"*You're right,*" I said. "*I won't do it. I'm holding the Sword of Mercy, I have to-*"

"*Good luck then,*" said Beatrice. "*Let me know when you come to your senses.*"

She was right. It was absolutely illogical to not press the one advantage I had. But a small part of me resisted. How could I use that to win when it was my fault in the first place that her hand looked like a prop from a zombie movie?

My full attention turned back to the fight just in time for me to see Emma's fist coming straight toward my chin. With my forearms clean once again and *Curtana* down at my side, the only thing I could do was brace for the impact. The blow sent me staggering backwards onto the ground, and I saw stars forming in my peripheral vision. Sensing my moment of weakness, Emma went for the finishing move. She extended her bad hand out in front of her, and I came to the horrible realization that *White Hilt*'s return path from the Breuckelen section passed directly through me.

However, unlike in the alley, the dagger did not easily fly back into Emma's grasp. Her fingers trembled, and she let out a desperate scream as she tried to pull the auragen tether, but it was clear that even with her steeled determination, she just couldn't muster the strength to finish the job. Putting her out of her misery would almost be a mercy at this point, I thought, the amount of pain she was in.

The realization hit me like a ton of bricks, and a cold sweat broke out on my brow. It was so simple, so elegant. Of course there had been nothing else in the Compendium about my Relic. Perhaps it had been used hundreds of years ago in such a manner for soldiers on the battlefield, or perhaps it had been used to deliver the final killing blow in lieu of a more painful death. Whatever the reasons for its creation, its legacy, whether horrific or benevolent, was now in my hands.

The wood behind me finally splintered and with only a few seconds to act, I still hesitated, as a part of me pushed back against the enormity of the choice I needed to make. But that's when the small remaining sliver of Svetlana's courage surfaced from deep within me.

Too many times I had watched myself give in to forces that I thought were outside of my control, to people that I thought had absolute power over me.

No more.

And so, I grabbed *Curtana* with no hesitation, and with one sure stroke, cut Emma's hand clean off.

CHAPTER FIFTY-ONE

DARKNESS TO LIGHT

"Compared to his sister, Duff is still soft-spoken, thoughtful, and perhaps a bit naive. His wife and Lorna also stand on opposite sides of the mirror. His children take after their parents and this means that an internecine conflagration will be inevitable. I must prepare contingencies."

The cavernous room fell silent as *White Hilt* dropped harmlessly on the mat only a few inches behind me. Perhaps everyone was still in a daze from watching the fight, but for whatever reason, no one moved an inch, so in that vacuum, I took charge.

I caught Emma's slacken body before it could hit the ground and then pressed *Curtana*'s blade against her wound.

She let out a blood-curdling scream as I saw the Relic pulse red with heat, and I almost screamed too from the adrenaline, from the fight being over, from what I had done. Somehow Beatrice was already at my side, applying some sort of bandage to Emma's wrist after I had removed *Curtana.*

"If anyone has a semblance of alchemy healing expertise, now would be a good time to get the fuck down here!" she barked at the silent crowd and after a moment, the New Amsterdam Third Seat stood up and trotted over to us.

"Hybridized gotu kola for the wound and resin from the oldest Boswellia sacra tree in Africa for the pain," he said, extending his palm to reveal a large leaf and a clump of a milky substance. We quickly wrapped the leaf around Emma's wrist and then forced the resin into her mouth, and half conscious, she instinctively began to chew.

"We've all heard the tales of the lost Relic, of the Blade That Was Betrayed, but truly never believed that the day would come when it would–"

"Save the grand speech for when someone isn't about to die from sepsis," said Beatrice, "and go get an ambulance."

The Third Seat stared in disbelief at Beatrice, but eventually nodded and motioned to Balthasar, who dashed out of the drill hall.

The remains of Emma's hand had somehow turned into a pile of black dust, her rings scattered in the middle of it, and *White Hilt* beside them. I wrapped them all in her torn-up t-shirt and placed the fabric package next to her, as if that would provide her any measure of comfort in her current state.

Within minutes, a pair of paramedics burst into the drill hall, ignoring our weird assembly, the giant sword, *Curtana*, everything really. They picked up Emma in one fell swoop, strapped her to a gurney, and wheeled her out as quickly as they had entered. As soon as she was gone, the strange energy in the room dissipated, and everyone began yelling at each other, before Dalia took off one of her earrings and threw into the air several feet above her head, at which point it exploded in a blinding flash of blue light.

"Enough," she said. "The Trial is over. And now we must pick up the pieces of what we all have wrought. I move for a full inquest into J.P.'s relationship with the Van Asch Corporation."

The Texan, still stunned at Emma's defeat and his plans going up in smoke, stood slack jawed as Lucca seconded and the motion carried unanimously with two abstentions.

"The next order of business," said Dalia, "is the dispensation of the spoils. Now, Ms. Patel is not in any state to relinquish the vial of Dragon's blood, but when she is, we hope there will be no unpleasantries. Finally, as a show of good faith, Ty and I have decided that she will resign her Seat-"

"What-" said the bewildered teen.

"-effective immediately."

Ty stared wide-eyed at her mother, her body tense from hearing for the first time that she was being forced out of the Guild. But her moment of agita passed quickly, and rather than making an enormous scene, she nodded and stood to address the rest of us.

"Yes," she said. "This was only meant to be a temporary arrangement. And its course has run."

"It has," said Dalia. "Now, with the conclusion of this summer diversion, we have work that needs doing. The Second Seat of the New Amsterdam Table must be filled and preparations will need to get underway soon so that the Gauntlet can begin in the fall and then-"

The world suddenly lost focus, and I blinked several times to right myself, but the blurriness would not relent. I looked down at my arms to find that I was shaking uncontrollably, and the last thing I remember before passing out was Dalia matter-of-factly yelling, "Call them back."

————

All was peaceful, all was calm.

I was in a meadow.

No, a field.

It was a soccer field.

I was playing in a game in Prospect Park. I was 12, and the score was tied. I dribbled up the middle, defenders trying to swarm me like ants after a piece of food. I deked and weaved my way through them and passed to my winger, who drew the attention away as I continued my journey upfield. The cross came a bit high, but I was ready. Timing my jump perfectly, I connected my forehead to the ball and sent it through the diving keeper's outstretched hands. My teammates mobbed me and when the whistle blew a minute later, we all let out a big whoop. I looked over to the sidelines, to where my mom had been standing only a few minutes prior, but there was only an empty space.

She hadn't come home that night or the next morning, and by the time I saw her again later in the week, the exhilaration of the goal had dissipated. I think she apologized at some point, but this had been the period where we hadn't really been talking much after she had given me her locket for my birthday. The locket that I had hated. The locket that had changed everything. The locket that-

I lurched awake and the immediacy of the present pushed aside the distant past. Every part of me was screaming at my brain, trying to convince it they were the thing that hurt the most. Looking around, I discovered that attached to my body were an innumerable number of IVs, tubes, and devices I had never seen before, which were, in turn, all connected to a dozen blinking screens and monitors. But instead of the rest of the expected trappings, like a nurses' shift whiteboard, or a bulky CRT TV, my bed had been placed against the brick wall of a long windowless hallway. And next to me, in an equally hooked-up state, was Emma.

"Am in two-thirds of a hospital room?" I asked.

"Something like that," said Emma, who only looked to be in slightly better shape than me. "It's about time you woke up. Been right boring here by myself for the last two weeks."

"I've been out for two weeks?" I asked. "How is that possible?"

I tried to sit up from my reclined position, but my muscles were not having it, and I slumped back down as the equipment next to me started beeping uncontrollably.

"From what I gathered while you were out, sounds like you went through quite the ordeal getting ready for our fight. And during it, as well. Not sure how you shook off *White Hilt* so easily, but I guess I shouldna underestimated you. You're full of surprises."

Emma laughed before being overcome by a coughing fit that sent her own monitors into a tizzy.

"What's the point of all of this?" I said. "Is someone going to come running in if we flatline?"

"Eventually," she said. "There's a nurse at 8 a.m. and one at 8 p.m., but they won't tell me anything. Not where we are. Not when we can leave."

"Fantastic," I said. "Listen, Emma, I-"

"S'allright," she said. "It's done. It's over."

"I wouldn't be so sure," I said. "These past three months, all I've done is convince myself that if I just do this one more thing, complete this one more task, then everything will be smooth sailing, that I'll feel like I'll belong. That I'll finally get what I wanted. But that was only a hopeful delusion. I see that now. Because it's never going to stop."

"What do you want?" asked Emma, who pushed herself up slowly with her left hand.

"The truth," I said. "About..."

I looked down at my chest to find my locket gone. Panic set in, and I began frantically searching the inner folders of my hospital gown, but came up empty.

"Your locket," said Emma. "Dalia took it with her for safekeeping. Along with all of our Relics, my rings, my bag. I'm sure it's all waiting for us with bows on back at the Guild."

"It better be," I said.

"What's so special about it?"

"Nothing," I said. "And everything. It was my mom's. She gave it to me. I was ungrateful, hated her for it, she died, and then it turned out that the Guild's twelfth gold token had been hidden inside the whole time."

"And you feel like a git for pushing her away before she could tell you why she had it, yeah?" asked Emma.

"Exactly."

"I feel the same," she said, turning over on her side and facing me, like we were camped out on the floor at a sleepover. "My dad, he threw everything he had at finding the stupid Dragon's blood. It consumed him. Drove away my mom, who went back to England. Drove me away. I should have gone with her but fell in with the Vultures instead. Look where that's gotten me."

She held up her bandaged arm and gave me a weak smile.

"There's got to be a way," I said, "to give you a new hand. Between the mental firepower within the Guild, Beatrice, and the Compendium, I'm sure, somehow, that we can fix everything I did."

"Of that I'm certain," said a familiar voice. A black-hooded figure suddenly appeared in front of our beds and undid the gold clasp holding the invisibility cloak together. It fell to the floor, revealing the blonde girl I had known as Eva, but who I now knew was always Callie, the lost Black Vulture.

"You!" said Emma, the fire from our fight returning in an instant.

"Why are you still tormenting me with her?"

"It's not what you think," said the girl. "It's a necessary step if we want to get your friend back."

She pulled out a necklace that was tucked in her sweater and squeezed the shimmering jewel attached to it, and Callie fell away, much like the cloak, leaving Beatrice in her place.

"You have five seconds," said Emma, "before I climb out of this bed and strangle you with my one good arm."

"Don't be angry with her," I said. "This was all my idea."

"Explain yourself," she said. "Or the same goes for you."

"The last piece clicked for me, when I saw what was happening to my friends," I said. "Their memories were fading, and they were turning into empty shells. And then I realized. The drugs sold to the Black Vultures, the taking of Callie, Polly obtaining a glamour, despite them being banned for hundreds of years. Steve had somehow rediscovered the secret to creating them."

"So you had your friend 'rescue' Callie so she could distract me during the fight?"

"Yes," I said. "And no. I want to help bring her back. Because she's still alive in there."

"How do you know that?"

"Before I tell you, do you promise not to try to kill me?" I asked.

Emma looked at me like I was crazy.

"I guess I don't have a choice," she said. "But maybe your friend here should stand between us, just in case."

"I'm not attacking a hospital patient," said Beatrice. "Unless it's absolutely necessary."

"So helpful," I said, rolling my eyes. "Back in Boston, when we were in the lab, when the fire ... in that moment, the glamour I was wearing, she took over. She threw the vial at the fire. Whoever she was, she's still alive. And that means…"

"Callie is too," said Emma quietly.

"Yes," said Beatrice. "The Compendium has an intricate page on the creation of glamours, but it's nearly indecipherable. From what I can tell, though, is that the glamour requires the underlying essence of the individual, just a bit, to remain, once the body is transmuted into the stone. What Jen did essentially, by wearing her stone for so long, was feed the glamour so that it could reassert control. And that's what I'm doing for your friend."

"Why?" asked Emma. "Why are you helping me? Why do either of you care?"

"Because we're both done being helpless, done being pulled by puppet strings," I said. "And we want to make certain that no one else is."

"A noble goal, to be sure," said Emma. "But I've been around long enough to know that it's never that easy. The ones on high, they won't give up their positions so easily."

"I know," I said. "But we have to try."

CHAPTER FIFTY-TWO

ANSWER TOGETHER

– Lady Melanie Fitzjames, Duchess of Montagu
Boston, Massachusetts, May 1, 1865

"Those are my conditions," I said, a few days later, sitting somewhat nervously in my Seat. Beatrice was standing awkwardly behind me, and the mother-daughter duo was in their usual Seats across from us.

"I see," said Dalia, who, for once, was not dressed to the nines, and instead was wearing a hooded sweatshirt and sweatpants, but still managed to look absolutely spectacular. "You know, normally, it is better negotiating practice to specify your demands *before* you already do all of things you are promising."

"And normally," I said, "you are not within a finger's snap of losing your Chair. But yet here we are … umm … were."

"Again, your timing is off. But I recognize the effort you have displayed in service of the Guild these past three months, and I am gracious and thankful for it. So I will agree to your terms. You will have what you need to restore Emma's hand. Lucca will aid you with this. And we have asked Kildare to help study the Compendium and our library for more information about *Curtana*, so that you may better wield it in the future."

The blade had been waiting for me in my apartment when I had come home from the "hospital," polished and buffed, so that all evidence of the duel was long gone. Of the two things Dalia had taken from me, I was surprised that it was the Relic had been easily returned.

"And, finally," said Dalia, "as to the matter of your locket, I'm afraid we are at somewhat of a loss."

"You lost it?" I asked.

"No," said Ty. "We took it upon ourselves to study it, to analyze it, to figure out how this simple trinket ended up holding the long-lost gold token. Yes, we know that's where your token was hiding. And what we found is that it's anything but ordinary."

"What do you mean?"

"At first blush, it appears to be made of silver, an item you could purchase at the kiosk at the mall," said Dalia. "But it is not. From what we can tell, given our limited amount of time, is that it is a rare alchemic alloy. Which one, we're not sure. But what we do know is that it is most likely hundreds of years old, and that it was most likely crafted, in part, with molten lava from the fires of Vesuvius."

"Why are you at a loss, then?" I asked. "Sounds like you figured it out."

"Because," said Dalia, "although the volcano is still active today, the metal in your locket…"

"…is from the eruption that destroyed Pompeii," said Ty.

"OK," I said. "So someone dug out some solid volcanic leftover from the ruins of Pompeii to make it? Not seeing why this is such a big deal."

"No," said Ty. "You're not getting it. Whoever made your locket was *at* Vesuvius on the day the volcano erupted. While everyone died a horrific death, they scooped up the lava while it was still hot, and from that, they crafted it."

"I … see," I said. "So you want to know why my mom had a 2000-year-old locket made by someone who appears to be a sociopath? I have no idea, why don't you ask her? Oh, that's right. She's dead."

"I'm sorry," said Dalia. "We didn't realize."

"Yeah. Umm, so, this is awkward," said Ty. "But did she leave any notes or a diary or something?"

"No," I said. "I mean, I don't know. She died a few months before I went to college. And … I was so glad to get out of that apartment, I didn't exactly care about whatever crap my mom left in her desk. I assumed our landlord eventually sold it. But again, why do you care?"

"The gold token for the Third Seat of the Breuckelen Table was lost to the Guild over 200 years ago," said Dalia. "It was stolen from Rita van Asch, our sixth chair. She was headed to Europe, to deliver it to the heir of the prior holder, when her ship was boarded, the token taken, by the same people that stole the Compendium. We would like to know what transpired during the in-between, just as I'm sure you would like to know why your mom had it."

"Another errand you want me to run?" I said. "Haven't I done enough for you? When do I get to chart my own course?"

"It is not a demand," said Dalia. "But a mere request. One that I thought aligned with your interests. We will be busy with organizing the Gauntlet, so whether you would like to pursue this after that is over is up to you."

"Fine," I said. "But what, I'm just supposed to walk around the Pompeii ruins looking for a long-lost scroll or a 2000-year-old metallurgist perfectly preserved in the solid lava stone?"

"Our ranks are at your disposal," said Dalia. "We have one of the finest blacksmiths in the world. One of the foremost scholars of ancient texts, and a world-class tracker-"

"-who probably won't ever speak to me again." I interjected.

"So loose his lips, then," said the Chair. "Or drop my name. Whatever you need to do. I want our members to get along and work together. If there's anything you've shown us since joining our ranks, is that when we collaborate, we become more than the sum of our parts. When we go off to our little corners and shut out the world, we stagnate. I will not have that."

"A sentiment I fully agree with," said Beatrice.

"Ms. Stallard, why are you here?" asked Dalia, glaring at her. "Come to throw your name into the Gauntlet hat?"

"Pass," said Beatrice. "I mean, I would obviously win, but I highly doubt you want me in the Seat next to you. Besides, too many meetings. I have a business to run."

"Don't be so sure," said Ty. "What's the saying? Keep your friends close..."

"And that's my cue to head back to the library! It's been a pleasure, ladies."

Beatrice slowly backed away from the Table before nearly sprinting out the door, leaving me alone once again with the two women

I perhaps feared the most.

"Was there something else, Ms. Jacobs?" asked Dalia.

"Yes," I said. "What will you do with the Dragon's blood? Are you really going to create a Philosopher's Stone?"

"That," said Dalia, "is above your pay grade."

"Is it?" I asked. "I'm the one who got the vial back for you. I think I deserve to know what you're planning."

The mother-daughter duo exchanged a look before both nodding.

"One day, we will," said Dalia. "Dragon's blood is the major key to the Stone, but it will take time to search out the other ingredients and work out the intricacies from the pages of the Compendium, as Ty said. And months of study before I feel confident enough to try. Until then, we will use a tiny sliver to help with Emma's hand. It will be an excellent test of the sample's purity."

"And then once you actually make the Stone?" I asked. "You prolong your own life, rule over the Guild for another 80 years?"

"No," said Dalia. "I can't think that far ahead. This little takeover attempt by J.P., it was just a shot across the bow. The VAC is coming for all of us. And we need to be ready. We need to be able to protect ourselves. One Gauntlet is bad enough, and I will not see our ranks depleted."

"So that means…" I said.

"The Elixir of Life," said Dalia. "I will perfect it. We may all die in the months to come, but they will not have our deaths."

"She's lying," I said to Beatrice, after we were many blocks clear from headquarters.

"About what?"

"Maybe everything?" I said. "At least about the gold token."

"How do you know?" she asked.

"I saw what happened, remember? Rita hid the token in the bank downtown. For a rainy day. This whole pirate tale is bullshit."

"So what if it is? Does that change anything? It sounds like she's actually going to help you," said Beatrice.

"If she's lying about this, then maybe she's lying about my locket, too. And this Pompeii story is just a ruse to get me to do what they want."

"Jen," said Beatrice, grabbing my arm. "Enough. I know these past few months have been brutal, but you can't keep waiting for someone to screw you over. You've proven you can handle anything that's thrown at you. And if this ends up being a complete and total scam, you'll find a way to deal with it too."

"Thanks," I said, trying not to tear up. "You're right."

"Of course I am," said Beatrice, smiling. "Now, who's up for a girls' weekend upstate? I booked us rooms at this amazing mansion-turned-spa and Svetlana agreed to babysit Jack-Jack so-"

The color suddenly drained from Beatrice's cheeks, and I turned around to see what could have caused it, only to come face-to-face with Jade, standing nonchalantly across the street.

"Ladies," said the redhead. "Fancy running into the two of you here."

"I don't understand," I said. "How did you get out of my office?"

"You want answers? You'll have to catch me first," she said with an impish grin.

"This isn't a game!" I said, but she was gone. I looked over at Beatrice, but she was gone too. Without any ink left on my arms, there was no way I would ever find-

Wait.

Something round was in my pocket that hadn't been there a moment ago.

I quickly reached my hand inside, withdrew a lilac-shaded candy,

and seconds later, I was a speeding blur once more.

"*Where is she headed?*" I asked in my head, as I weaved my way through the standstill traffic on Fifth Avenue, hoping that the message would get through to Beatrice, even in our sped-up states.

"*Outside Grand Central,*" said Beatrice. "*I'm … we're already here. Upper level.*"

I blazed down the streets, my heart pounding, until I reached the Park Avenue Viaduct that traversed the Terminal. Another second passed, and I rounded the bend on the south side to find Beatrice and Jade, who were staring at each other in the middle of a dozen frozen cars.

"Ah, here's our third," said Jade. "No Relic this time?"

"I left it at home," I said. "You're welcome to come with me to get it."

"I've been to your apartment," she said. "Been you in your apartment. And I don't care to go back."

"What do you want?" I asked. "And what did you to do to me those two missing weeks?"

"Now, now," said Jade. "You haven't caught me yet so-"

A faint purple glow rippled through Beatrice, and even though we were already moving at incredible speed, somehow she blinked herself behind Jade before the latter could react and drew the Medoblad against her throat.

"My friend asked you a question," she said.

"Actually, it was two questions," said Jade. "But fair enough. You got me. I'll talk. At least until you come back down to earth."

"*Drop the blade,*" I said.

"*OK, but I'm not chasing after her again if she splits,*" said Beatrice.

"*She won't.*"

Beatrice withdrew the Relic and stepped away, but Jade thankfully remained in place.

"Thank you," she said. "No reason this can't be civil."

"I think we're way past that," I said. "You used me!"

"As if you didn't do the same to me," said Jade. "Wearing me around the city like a masquerade costume. Adopting me as an entire separate persona. Heck, you even got the new 'you' a passport. It's quite rude. Well, not that last part. That came in handy."

"You almost killed me, and I thought you had killed Emma! Why?"

"That was my painting," she said. "And you, your friend, the ones who had infiltrated the museum, you had no right to it."

"What do you mean, it was your painting?" I asked. "That painting is from the Renaissance."

"I know," said Jade. "And I was the one who made it. I slew the dragon and took its blood. And, knowing that others sought the fruits of my labors and that I would need those fruits one day, I painted myself facing down those who thought themselves my betters."

"But the box we found … it was too small to fit-"

"That's what's got you hung up? The painting's canvas is made of chrysomallos. It was hidden inside, where no one could retrieve it. Not even those thieves."

"Not true," I said. "They had unlocked the box, they were moving it out of the museum."

Jade smiled.

"That's so cute," she said. "Do you think it was a coincidence that the painting, after being lost for so long, was conveniently sitting there, out in the open, almost as if someone had left it there for you to find?"

"What … what are you talking about?" I asked.

"I'm sure you must have noticed," said Jade, "your particularly restless nights up in Boston. Did you not put two and two together after my sojourn?"

"So, the empty box, the fire in the lab, that was you? But, I saw the emails. The museum was trying to-"

"You'll find my words can be very persuasive," said Jade. "If they need to be. The staff did as they were told, although, of course, they remember none of it. And with the lab completely decimated, there was nothing left for them to discover, anyway."

My head started spinning, as I began to question everything that had happened to me up in Boston and all the weeks before, when I had been trapped under the glamour.

"Well done, by the way," said Jade. "I'll admit, I was a bit conflicted. That painting had a special meaning to me. I poured so much of myself into it, it's like it held a piece of me, but at the end of the day, I'm glad it was destroyed."

I felt my lips move to rebut her erroneous presumption, but forced myself to stop. Even though she had been able to track our mission in Boston, to take control of my sleeping body, to know exactly the right moment to intervene, somehow she was blind to the fact that Emma had extracted the Dragon's blood from the portrait wherever she had escaped to. And given the lengths that Jade had gone to secure its supposed incineration, this was a secret that she must never be allowed to learn.

"Why didn't you try to save it?" I asked. "If you're as old as you say, and you've waited this long to get the painting back, it would have been super easy to just take it, in that moment."

"You're forgetting a few things, Jen. There was the matter of the raging hellfire. Even I am not sure whether my stone would have survived its heat. And if I had somehow reclaimed the portrait, I didn't have the means at the time to safeguard it. You were a pliable host, but it wasn't until I had that particularly productive meeting in the forest with your friend that I was able to recover my complete freedom. And because, when you have lived as long as I have, you understand the importance of redundancies."

"There is another painting," I said, all the pieces finally clicking together. "And you took my body to go make sure its hiding place was secure."

"Clever girl," said Jade. "So now you know. And now I can be on my way."

"You haven't told us anything," I said. "Just a bunch of bragging about how smart you are. And that doesn't rectify what you did to both of us."

"You tried to control me," said Beatrice. "I remember our meeting now. In Central Park. I had to obey. And it was the same the second time. I didn't want to tell you my formula, but you-"

"Don't talk to me about control or being used. Do you know what I am? What they did to me? I was one of the most powerful women in the world. I had command of alchemy beyond your comprehension. But in the end, all I wanted was to be left alone. And they wouldn't let me. So now they will pay."

"Who?" I asked.

"You will know them soon enough, said Jade. "And when you meet them, I want you to give them a message. Tell them…"

She paused and her body began to glow with a green shimmer.

"…Kora Sotero is coming for them."

The glow expanded into a blinding flash, forcing me to shield my eyes. And when I opened them again, Jade—no—Kora was gone.

"That was…" I said.

"…unexpected," said Beatrice. "I hope not to run into her for a long while. What now?"

"I don't know," I said. "I feel like after all Kora just told us, I need to take my own advice, to stop being led around by others."

"But…"

"But even though it's what Dalia wants me to do, it seems like everything is telling me to uncover the truth about my locket, about my mom."

"So you're Italy bound, then? After the Gauntlet?" asked Beatrice.

"It would seem so," I said. "But there are so many unanswered questions. And one I haven't trusted to anyone, except you."

I pulled up my shirt to the spot where Emma had stabbed me with *White Hilt*. Weeks after the fight, where there should have been a green glowing scar, was … nothing at all.

"How am I still alive?"

EPILOGUE

RECALLED TO LIFE

ooney House was long past its prime, but it still had its uses. It was old compared to most of the buildings in the city, compared to most of the buildings in the New World in fact, but not so old when considered with all the Houses across the sea. Its bricks were specifically selected from the bountiful quarries that the Guild had surveyed and this contributed to its long-standing nature and to other peculiarities that would only emerge once one spent enough time in its confines.

Ty's late protégé Doug could probably have spoken to that, but the boy had become an unruly weed and had perished for it. It was for the best, Dalia had decided. There were too many wheels within wheels as it was, and she did not need the additional distraction of a rogue initiate almost starting a war with their enemy. Well, one of their enemies. The Guild, and Dalia, had a bad habit of collecting new ones as the decades ticked off.

It remained to be seen whether the VAC had joined that camp or whether it had been a mere folly championed by the worthless spare Xander, who styled himself as co-Chair. She was surprised that Lorna had gone along with it as the Lady-in-Waiting of the august institution once her mother ceded control to her on her 40th birthday. Dalia had known several Lornas and none would have let things come to a head as they had. Perhaps the bloodline had gone stale as of late.

Dalia reached the House at half past midnight and walked around to the back entrance. She placed her token, the original token, into the small door and it opened silently. Ducking her head, she descended into the basement through the darkness, her footsteps landing true despite the lack of light. Upon reaching the bottom, she saw the glow peek under the door from beyond, and she nodded to herself. She had expected resistance from her daughter when she had announced what she had intended to do, now that she finally had possession of the pure Dragon's blood, but in this, the two were in agreement.

The door opened on its own accord and Dalia stepped through the threshold to see what Ty's handiwork had wrought. Candles lit the room in a foreboding manner and on every surface, her daughter had drawn the magnificent runes with great care and detail. In the middle of the floor was a circle inside a square inside a triangle, where the final pieces were yet to be placed.

"Well done, daughter," said Dalia and Ty, who was listening to some Gods-awful music on her phone, removed the white ear buds and smiled.

"Thank you, mother," she said. "It has been a long time, but my hands still remembered the contours of the Great Circle."

"I would expect nothing less from you," said Dalia.

Ty took in the compliment with modesty and bent down to run her fingers along the edges of the chalk lines.

"I am in agreement, that we must do this, but I wonder if we are acting in desperation, necessity, or strength."

"I think all three," said Dalia. "His loyalty, his skills, and his tenacity have been sorely missed."

"I agree," said Ty. "Although the third of that list you perhaps long for the most. But we have new tools at our disposal at present, do we not? Ms. Stallard has finally been domesticated and Ms. Jacobs has developed into a surprisingly reliable woman of many talents."

"That may be, but a poker player would not be satisfied with two-pair when a full house was obtainable," said Dalia. "Now is not the time to be overconfident in our abilities, with snakes in our midst. We must win back the five who voted against me, one way or another."

"You could just kill all of them," offered Ty. "You always loved recruiting new members, I seem to recall."

"Those days are behind me," said Dalia. "And someone is already doing that work, of this I am sure. Charles, Akash, Laila. Their deaths were not accidents. I intend to find out who was responsible and when I do, I will rip off their toes one by one."

"Mother!" said Ty. "Please … you should let me do it."

"Perhaps," said Dalia. "Look, about your Seat…"

"I accept your apology," said Ty. "It was the right thing to do. And besides, he may very well win the Gauntlet, anyway."

"I have not decided if I will allow him to enter," said Dalia. "He might be better off remaining in the shadows. We can use him in other ways to keep the members in line."

"That is probably the prudent course," said Ty. "One more question, before we begin the ritual. Are you not worried about his baser characteristic surfacing again? You had tamed him for a time, but you know what an undertaking that was. Will it hold?"

"I have made sure of it," said Dalia, who withdrew the three gems from her pocketbook. "In my spare moments, over the decades, I have fine-tuned him to my liking. He will not remember what he had done to displease me and his essence has been pruned so that he will not try to again."

"I see," said Ty. "Do you think that was wise? What if he discovers the truth? There could be repercussions beyond your imagining."

Dalia normally valued her daughter's counsel, as she provided the necessary counterweight to her and helped her refine her stratagems and her thinking on so many occasions. But on this, she would not hear dissent.

Instead, she placed each of the gems on one vertex of the triangle. And for the inner circle, she withdrew the two last items in her bag, the skull that had been sitting on the shelf in her Guild office for too many years to count and the newly acquired vial of Dragon's blood. The skull she situated in the absolute center of the assemblage and the red pigment, she sprinkled along the edges of the triangle, on top of all three gems, and finally, on the eye sockets. Ordinarily, the amount of blood necessary for the ritual would be substantially more and would have made creating a new Stone nearly impossible, but thankfully, she had developed a work around.

"The knife, please," Dalia said to her daughter, who produced a shining silver blade from inside her jean jacket and handed it to her. She weighed the implement in her hand, and, satisfied with its craftsmanship and balance, kneeled down next to the Great Circle and scored the edge against her index finger. Blood dripped from the wound onto the white chalk, turning the spot red instantly. The crimson spread quickly through the rest of the runes, and, before wrapping her finger in the bandage that Ty had also brought her, Dalia smeared the final drops onto both of her palms.

"Are you ready?" asked Ty.

"Yes," said Dalia. "It is time."

She bent down on her knees at the top of the Great Circle, and Ty assumed the same pose at the bottom. Taking in the scene before her, Dalia could not believe that she had succeeded, in this age or at all. She closed her eyes, took a deep breath, and pressed her hands against the Circle.

A gentle breeze brushed across her cheek, which, of course, was an odd thing to feel down in the musty basement. Dalia opened her eyes to see the runes had begun to glow, but it was soft and faint and looked as if it would go out in a few seconds. This she would not have.

"We offer the Tria Prima and the Blood of the Dragon to the Great Circle, which has no end, which does not end!"

Her voice echoed through the basement, like a singer belting out an opera before the throne, and the light of the circle erupted into a blazing spectacle. She felt herself trembling against its might, and were she a lesser woman, it would have engulfed her entirely.

But she was not such a woman. No, she was a Valkyrie, she was an Amazon, she was the fire. And she would take back what was stolen from her.

"We speak now the ancient words of restoration, of rejuvenation, of reconstitution, to break down the barrier between life and death!"

She nodded to Ty, and the two opened their mouths together in song.

"Fac ex mare & fumina circulum, inde quadrangulum, hinc triangulum, fac circulum & habebis lap. Philosophorum!"

The triangle and the square and the circle all rose up and spun wildly and furiously, throwing off bits of lightning as they did.

"Regem lupus uorauit, & uite crematus reddidit!"

The three gems then began to glow, each sending bolts of color up into the spinning shapes.

"Hic est Draco caudam suam devorans!"

Finally, the Dragon's blood ignited into a crimson fire. It crackled against the other energies, but it was above them, it was above all.

"Sapientie humane fructus Lignum uite est!"

A thunderous blast ripped through the room and knocked Dalia backward onto the stone floor. Her brow was covered with sweat, her ears were ringing and her heart was racing, but she was alive.

And someone else was, as well.

For in the center of the Great Circle, where before there had only been the constituent parts, knelt a fully formed man, a purplish aura surrounding his body. Dalia pushed herself up, took up the regal walk of ages past, and extended her hand outward.

"Rise again, Lord Theo," she said.

"Lady Melanie?" the naked man asked, grasping her wrist with his fingers. She pulled him to his feet before studying the rest of him and smiling at his chiseled physique. Even two hundred years of dissociation had done nothing to weaken his features. As eager as she was to drink in more of him, she motioned for Ty to fetch the set of clothes from the corner.

"I have not been called that for many decades," said Dalia, as she helped the man put on the unfamiliar modern outfit. "So much has happened since you were taken from us. But there will be time enough to fill the blanks. For now, tell me, do you remember that day, on the hill?"

She stroked his cheek, and the man looked at her and then at Ty, before the memory resurfaced from within him.

"Yes," he said. "They had brought us to the center of the way stones, to laugh and to ridicule. They set pyres around us, as if we were an attraction to be enjoyed by those who were passing by. But the two of us, we persevered. One night, a great storm cloud appeared overhead and an instant later unleashed its wrath down upon us. Together, we lifted our bound hands to meet it."

Dalia pulled the man who had been Lord Theo into an embrace and let everything melt away. She felt his energy push against hers, like the crackling of the lightning they had captured so long ago. It was a reminder of an age long gone, one that would not be seen again. She wished she could stay in this moment forever and let the rest of the world-

"Ahem," said Ty.

Dalia pulled back from the man, slightly embarrassed that she had lost herself so easily, and her former lover stepped back.

"Sorry," she said. "It has been a long time."

"I'm sure it has," said Ty. "Let us finish and then I will take my leave."

"Yes," said Dalia, turning to face the man. "You have slept for over 150 years. The woman you knew as Lady Melanie is dead and gone. In her place now stands Dalia de Wyck, 13th chair of the Worshipful Company of Alchemists."

"A pleasure to meet you, Ms. de Wyck," said the man.

"And you again, Lord Theo Beauclerk. But today, you are reborn."

She bent down to wipe the remaining residue from the Great Circle onto her fingers and rubbed it against his cheeks.

"Welcome to the 21st century, Enzo Russell."

"Thank you, my lady," said Enzo. "What work needs doing?"

"A great deal," said Ty. "The nascent entity you knew as the Van Asch Trading Company, it has spread its tentacles far and wide, and in doing so, has forgotten its heritage. And our sister Alerion Guild, formed at the dawn of this country. They clothe themselves in the sigils of an order long dead, but they are alive and well, and we have only just undone their greatest attack on us. The homunculus rebels are still on the run. They are greatly diminished, but formidable just the same."

"Finally, our rival in the East," said Dalia. "You know firsthand their treachery, and I have spent many decades trying to gain back what was taken. You included."

"I see," said Enzo. "Then it seems my resurrection could not have come at a more pressing hour. Tell me, does that snake still draw breath?"

"Who, my father?" asked Ty. "Yes, the Hammer of the East is alive and well. But he has not been seen outside of his mountain estate for many years."

"There will be plenty of time to deal with my husband," said Dalia, taking Enzo's hand. "Tonight is about our new beginning." She whispered something in his ear that only he could hear, and he smiled. "Wait for me upstairs, would you?"

Enzo nodded and exited the basement through the front. When his footsteps had gone silent, Ty hopped down from her perch on the retaining wall and ambled over to Dalia.

"Mother, I haven't seen you this way in so long. You're like a blushing schoolgirl, it's so … cute!"

"Don't tease me, Ty," said Dalia. "Not tonight."

"Fine, fine. Go on, then," said her daughter. "I will clean up here, as usual."

"Thank you."

Dalia bent down to pick up the charred remains of the three stones and placed them back in her bag, before strolling toward the exit with a stride in her step.

"Will you go through with it?" Ty asked, as Dalia reached the bottom stair. "I didn't think it was something you would ever consider doing again. Not after what happened the first time."

Dalia considered the question for just a moment, but her path had been set on this course for so long, and there was no deviating now. After all it had taken to get here.

"Yes," she said. "I will become a mother twice over, despite the consequences. So much depends on it. Because you and that child, you will change everything."

FORTUNA

Guild of Magic: Fortuna takes place during the events of Guild of Tokens.

It assumes a familiarity with the poker variant No Limit Texas Hold'em. If you fall into that camp, flip the page.

If you have limited familiarity with poker, NL Texas Hold'em or otherwise, or have never seen the movie *Rounders*, below is a short primer.

Players are dealt two cards face down at the beginning of the game. These are called **the hole cards**.

A round of betting ensues and when it is finished, one card is dealt face down in the middle of the table, followed by three cards face up.

These three cards are community cards (i.e. any player may form a 5-card poker hand with them and their hole cards) and are called **the flop**.

After the flop is dealt, another round of betting occurs. At the conclusion, one card is dealt face down and then a fourth card is dealt face up. This card is called **the turn**. Players may form a 5-card poker hand with any combination of the four community cards and their two hole cards.

Once more, a round of betting takes place. Another card is dealt face down and then the fifth and final community card is dealt face up. This card is called **the river**. Players may form a 5-card poker hand with any combination of the five community cards and their two hole cards.

At this point in the game, depending on the players' hands and betting, there may be only a few players left. Once the last round of betting occurs, the hands are revealed and the best hand wins.

One other term to note is **the nuts**, which means a player's hand is the best hand possible given the community cards in play. This may or may not change as additional cards are dealt.

PRE-FLOP

"Order up for Who-go!"

"Jeez, Dom, I come in here almost every day for lunch. For the last time, it's Hugo! H-U-G-O!"

"Oh, sorry Mr. Yugo. I'll remember tomorrow."

Hugo Clouser, first seat of the Worshipful Company of Alchemists' Pavonia Table, ignored the second mispronunciation of his two-syllable name in as many minutes and grabbed the plastic-coated paper bag from the takeout counter. Outside on a nearby bench, he dug into the sizzling hot galbi dolsot bibimbap with abandon, ignoring the stares of passersby. Although his mom's family would be aghast at eating this dish in such a manner, in the food consumption department, Hugo took more after his dad.

Besides, the hour was growing late and he didn't have time for endless rounds of pickled vegetables, as there were things he needed to accomplish before tonight's game.

He glanced at his watch, a gift from his uncle, the previous occupant of his seat, upon his retirement from the Guild. It was likely hundreds of years old, no doubt crafted by the finest watchmakers in all of Bavaria or some other no-longer existent country. Hugo could appreciate the craftsmanship, but to him, the value was in the legacy it represented.

The hands struck 12 and 1, and when Hugo looked up again, the old man had appeared on the other end of the bench.

"Why do you always do that?" he asked. "Just come up and say hello like a normal, functional person."

"We both know," said the old man, "that I am neither of those things."

"I suppose that's true," said Hugo. "But it is nice to see you outside of whatever hole-in-the-wall you are operating out of these days. Is it still the stall in Essex Street Market next to that loud guy who makes the crazy pancakes?"

"No," said the old man. "He and I had a falling out, so I left a few months ago. Also they're moving all the vendors to some glittering new market soon and I can't abide by that."

"Fair enough. So where are you now then?"

"Here," replied the man.

Hugo rolled his eyes.

"Yes, I see that. I mean where are you operating the Night Market out of now?"

"Oh," said the man. "That's not what you asked. I moved out of Manhattan, got a nice set-up inside of Hunts' Point."

"The fruit market? Why on earth would you go all the way up there?"

"For exactly that reason. Being 'all the way up there,' I get many fewer visitors. Honestly, I can't believe we ever had stalls in the Greenmarket. The amount of-"

"Yes, I got it. You hate everyone trying to buy things from you. Good business to be in then. Do you have what I asked for, Phineas?"

The man called Phineas nodded and withdrew a small package wrapped in brown paper and twine from the inner pocket of his tattered coat.

"Excellent," said Hugo. "Will they work?"

"That depends," said Phineas.

"Depends on what?"

"On your luck," the man replied.

"I came to you so I wouldn't have to leave my fate to chance," said Hugo.

"There are no absolutes," said Phineas. "Not in alchemy and not in life. A lesson you should internalize if you are going to succeed in both."

"Yeah, yeah, yeah," said Hugo, rolling his eyes.

"Now, there is the matter of payment."

"Indeed. Here you are, as promised."

Hugo set out three stacks of silver tokens on the bench, equal in height. He worked his fingers to subdivide and combine the stacks several times, a habit he had honed over many evenings spent in smoked-filled backrooms, basement apartments, and other seedy places you might find an underground poker room.

Phineas eyed the tokens before shaking his head back and forth. "And the rest?"

"This is what we agreed on," said Hugo, suppressing the urge to dump the remaining bibimbap on top of the old man's head.

"What we agreed on in the abstract and the bargain to be made now are two separate things," replied Phineas, before picking up the package and waving it in the air. "Do you want these or not?"

Hugo considered the old man. He had not had many dealings with the Night Market proprietor before, but after each such occasion, he had sworn to never seek him out again. And each subsequent time, he had forgotten that vow, only to find himself yet again on the receiving end of a deal turned sour. And now apparently this time wasn't going to be any different.

"What else do you want?" he asked, trying to feel out how much this was going to cost him.

"Your watch," said Phineas blankly.

Hugo took a deep breath and tried to slow his quickening pulse.

"My uncle's watch? You're kidding, right? This watch has been in my family for generations. Every member of the Yoo family who has held my seat has worn it. It's my obligation to hold it for the next gener-"

Phineas got up from the bench and walked away, and Hugo cursed himself for going on too long, before trotting after him. He caught up with the old man on the corner and undid the watch's clasp.

"Here," said Hugo, looking desperate. "Take it. But if I come back to you in a week to buy it back, you'd better still have it."

The man let a tiny smile form on his mouth before squelching it.

"Deal," said Phineas, whose previously empty fingers now held the brown package again.

"Stop doing that," said Hugo, who took the prize from the old man and regrettably handed him the watch. "It's unnerving."

Hugo gently undid the top of the wrapping to reveal the word "Bee" on the top of a small cardboard box. He placed it inside his jacket where the tokens had been, and started to say something, but when he looked up again, the old man was gone.

"Every time."

THE FLOP

"I feel like Buckner walking back into Shea, but what choice do I have?"

The thing about underground poker dens was that there were only so many variations on the theme before you had seen them all. There were the smoky back rooms frequented by mafiosos, the games played at upscale hotel rooms, the ones played at some celebrity's Malibu manse with sunlight pouring in through wall-to-wall windows that overlooked the Pacific Ocean. Then there was tonight's game.

Hugo exited the cab at the South Street Seaport and made the short stroll over to the pedestrian walkway that spanned the length of the Brooklyn Bridge. It was still light out and he surmised that it would be light out as well when the game finished. Sure, he could have been dropped off closer to the entrance, but Hugo needed a few moments to collect his thoughts and calm his nerves before the festivities began.

The box of cards rested in the inner left front pocket of his blue blazer. His fingerwork had always been solid, but tonight would require another level, and only time would tell if it would be enough. But Hugo pushed any doubts aside and glanced at his watch to see if he was running late, only to be greeted by his empty wrist. He frowned and quickened his pace across the bridge, and the walkway eventually dumped him out next to a park and the federal courthouse. Hugo chuckled at the lawlessness occurring only yards away, but at the same time, he wouldn't be shocked if some of the judges were also patronizing the front parlor tonight.

After doubling back toward the bridge, he at last reached the purported entrance. The underpass was quiet, thankfully, and Hugo walked past a row of stone arches to a set of rusted loading bay doors. He selected the second door and rapped his knuckle against the metal ribs of the door and waited. After a few seconds, the door lifted slightly and out popped a weird looking mirror on a stick.

"Hello?" said Hugo, bending down to peer at the glass.

"Password," croaked a squeaky voice from inside.

"High society," Hugo replied.

The mirror shot back under the door, which closed with a thud. A clicking sound that wasn't a clicking sound then resonated somewhere inside the stone, and moments later, the bricks filling the stone arch to Hugo's left began to separate. When they were finished, a small passageway, barely more than a foot wide, appeared, and he squeezed himself through into the darkness.

A string of lights attached to the ceiling flicked on and Hugo found himself face to face with a lanky boy on the edge of puberty.

"Who are you?"

"Name's Andrew," said the boy with an indecipherable accent. "Andrew Kaynine."

"Canine? Your last name is 'dog'?"

The boy smacked his forehead.

"It's Scottish. Was Kennan when my great-great grandfather walked down the gangplank, but then got mangled to its current state by some inspector on Ellis Island and we were all too lazy to change it."

"I see. Why couldn't I go through the regular door by the way?" asked Hugo.

"S'broken," said the boy. "Stupid modern tech. Completely unreliable. My brother Ziggy is supposed to fix it next week though. What are you here for? Krabs? Biribi? Veintiuna?"

Hugo nodded.

"All of it," he said, patting his right front pocket.

"Good luck," said the boy, pointing to the top of a spiral staircase that descended into the floor. "Make yer way down to the lower level and they'll sort you out."

"Thanks," said Hugo.

The stairway was narrow and lacked a railing, and by the time he reached the bottom, Hugo was already dreading the return trip. But thankfully, a pretty brunette with bright red lipstick was there to greet him with a smile and a revealing red-patterned dress, and that made him forget his anxiety for at least a few seconds.

"Welcome to the Den," said the woman from behind a wooden partners' desk. "I am the Hostess."

"Hi," said Hugo, trying not to feel like a schoolboy with a crush. "So we're doing one of those things? No real names? Just everything gets appended with a 'The'?"

The Hostess opened her mouth and Hugo did a double-take as the woman's words came at him as a simultaneous barrage of languages, some of which he understood and some of which he did not.

"Mianhae," said Hugo, instinctively retreating to his second language. "*I didn't quite catch that.*"

"*I said,*" the woman uttered in Korean, "*my name is none of your business. Your name is, however.*"

"Fine," he said. "Hugo Clouser. First seat, Pavonia Table, the Guild. My uncle frequented your establishment many times."

"Thank you, Mr. Clouser. That wasn't so hard was it?" said the Hostess with a wry grin. "Now if you wouldn't mind, my associate here will check you in."

The Hostess stepped aside to reveal an equally stunning blonde, whose shimmering green eyes matched the color of the green-stoned necklace that hung around her neck.

"Do you happen to have a name?" asked Hugo.

"Yes," said the woman in a coarse voice. "It's Eva."

Hugo extended his right hand toward her in a friendly manner and in one swift motion, Eva grabbed his wrist and slammed it onto the surface of the desk. She quickly maneuvered behind him, took hold of his left hand, and pushed his body down onto the desk with hers.

"This will only hurt for a second," she whispered in his ear, and Hugo felt a jolt of something that wasn't quite electricity suddenly flow from Eva's bracelet-adorned hand into his wrist, up his arms, across his torso, and then out the other wrist into the woman's other bracelet-adorned hand.

"He's clean," said Eva to the Hostess, who nodded, at which point the blonde withdrew her clammy and preternaturally strong hands from his.

"May I ask," said Hugo, gingerly getting back to his feet, "what that was all about?"

"Just a precaution," said the Hostess. "My patrons expect their games to be free of any alchemy-related hijinks and cheats. I'm sure you understand."

"Of course. I'm here for a clean game, just like everyone else."

He exchanged a half-hearted a smile with the woman and wondered why she insisted on the ruse. Were people really that stupid?

"Now that the formalities are out of the way, how much are you in for tonight?"

Hugo started to pull out a handful of paper bills that reflected his balance at several area token banks, but the Hostess quickly shooed away his offering.

"This is a gentleman's game, Mr. Clouser," she said. "We assume you're all good for your debts."

"If you say so," he said. "I'll take three stacks then."

If there was one thing that needed to be changed about the underground alchemy world, it was the monetary policy. Simply put, the powers that be, of which he was a member, had foolishly created too few denominations of tokens and had also created the fiction that there were a pile of gold tokens sitting out there for people to discover some day. Not so. In fact, there were only 12 gold tokens, each representing a seat on the Guild's board. But to sell one for untold wealth would mean giving up said seat, and he didn't know anyone in recent memory who was stupid or desperate enough to have done so, save for one person.

So that made silver the de facto currency for old blood such as his family, and that had led to rampant inflation in recent years and a return to bartering treasure and even Relics. It was all very messy, as had been demonstrated by his transaction with Phineas, and he had half a mind to suggest that the Guild form a steering committee to discuss implementing a platinum token. But first things first.

"Excellent," said the Hostess, who whispered something to no one in particular. "Head downstairs and my banker will take care of you."

She motioned for him to descend yet another railless stairway and he complied, walking faster than he would have liked so as to impress the woman. Which is why he nearly collided with the brunette in high heels who was standing perilously close to the railless edge of the mezzanine balcony overlooking the Den's main hall. The woman turned around and Hugo's mouth dropped open.

"What in the-" said Hugo, before stopping himself.

"Hello," said an exact copy of the Hostess, wearing a turquoise dress and an equally shiny set of earrings.

"Yes, we look alike, my sister and I," said the woman.

"That's an understatement. Let me guess, you are-"

"The Banker, correct, Mr. Clouser. Here are your chips. Good luck tonight."

The Banker handed him a stack of chips of various colors and bid him toward the third railless stairway that finally led into the heart of the action.

The expansive cavern that housed the Den was in its previous life used as a wine cellar for the gilded rich and after walking around for a few minutes, Hugo could see why. Despite the mobs of people clustered around the various gaming tables, the place was downright frigid. He walked over to the bar and ordered an Irish coffee from yet another copy of the brunette, who called herself the Bartender, to warm himself up.

"Can I ask you a question?" he said to the woman, who had mani-fested a cloth from somewhere and was busy polishing the expansive marble counter that ran the length of the bar.

"Absolutely," she said, her earrings sparkling through the dim light of the cavern. "But can't promise I'll answer it."

"How many of you are there?"

The doppelgänger paused her cleaning and stared at him blankly for a moment, before a small smile appeared on her lips.

"There's only me," she said.

"Right, but, who ... you know what? Never mind. Thanks for the drink."

Hugo scurried away from the Bartender and nearly collided with a tall, stern looking man with salt and pepper hair wearing a white blazer.

"Sorry, I…"

"Watch yourself and your drink, Clouser," said the man, who Hugo now recognized. "You wouldn't want to have to pay for my dry cleaning bill, now would you?

"J.P., always a pleasure," said Hugo. "Care to join me at the biribi table for a spell? Winner caters the next Guild meeting."

"As delightful as it would be to empty your wallet, I've had my fill for the night," replied the First Seat of the Orange Table, who walked off toward the stairway.

"That guy," muttered Hugo to himself before beginning a circuit of the lower stakes tables as a warm-up. The thing about the games found in places like the Den was that they were just familiar enough for you to pick up after a few rounds but just different enough that all your previous experience and tactics weren't worth anything in the long run. This was something he had learned the hard way, but tonight, he would reap the fruit of what he had sown over these past few months in other establishments scattered around the city.

Hugo sat himself down at a nearly empty veintiuna table in the corner, where he could play on autopilot while his mind worked through the strategy for later in the evening, when a fourth copy of the woman inserted herself behind the other side of the table.

"I was hoping to avoid you," he said, shaking his head.

"What a rude thing to say, Mr. Clouser," said the woman no doubt called the Dealer. "My sister was right about you."

"In what way?"

The woman's stoic face held firm for a few more seconds as she shuffled the cards with impeccable speed before it melted into a mask of warmth that Hugo knew better that to trust.

"Shall we begin?"

THE TURN

"Listen, here's the thing. If you can't spot the sucker in your first half-hour at the table, then you are the sucker."

Veintiuna may have been the game where those who styled themselves gamblers went to make (and lose) their fortunes, but the bona-fide sharks were always found at the poker tables. It was the one game in the Den where the Hostess hadn't felt the need to revert to some extravagant or long-forgotten variant. Across the eras and the worlds within the worlds, the game unearthed the best and worst within its players. And tonight, Hugo was going to need both sides of that coin if he was going to pull off the job of the decade.

He had spotted them about half an hour into his session with the Dealer, and they had, in turn, pretended not to have seen him. The feeling was most likely mutual, but Hugo didn't have all night to play this dance. And so, he had rotated among the outer poker tables for a spell before finally sitting down at the lone no-limit hold 'em table, his stacks taller at the moment than the spire atop the tower downtown.

And like moths to a flame, soon the dapperly dressed couple sat down to his left. The man had slicked back jet black hair with a matching pocket square and a cigarette sticking to the bottom of his lips. The woman was many years his senior, although she didn't look it thanks to the alchemic enhancement she had no doubt purchased at one of the many such spas hidden in the Swiss alps. Her hair gleamed in the dark cavern, as if it was threaded with the Golden Fleece, and her lips shimmered a shade of red that Hugo hadn't ever seen before.

"You look ridiculous, Martin," said Hugo, as he checked pre-flop with the woman dealing. "What happened to your monocle, though? Didn't get it back from the glazier in time?"

"Clouser, I thought this sort of place was beneath you and your gilded lot," said Martin, tossing several chips into the pot, which caused the rest of the players, save one, to fold.

"Honey, where are your manners?" said the older blonde, who checked her paramour's raise, bringing the action around again. "Hugo, you know we both greatly admire how you and the Guild have handled things recently."

"Thank you, Dr. Petra, I appreciate it."

"It's Lester now. Martin and I tied the knot last winter in the Maldives."

Hugo of course knew all of this, but continued his aloof act for a little while longer.

"Well, congratulations are in order, then! Drinks all around for the happy couple!"

"That's not necessary," said Martin. "But we appreciate the gesture."

"Suit yourself, I'll just drink for all three of us."

Hugo flagged one of the waitresses down and whispered his order in her ear. The woman returned a few minutes later with a martini glass filled so high to the brim that it sloshed as she handed it to him. He took a quick sip and then pulled the olive toothpick out.

"Natalia, you were never one to turn down a gin-soaked olive. What say you?"

"Oh, thank you, Hugo, you were always such a gentleman," said his former paramour, who happily accepted the offering, much to her husband's chagrin.

To call his prior history with Natalia Petra a fling would be an understatement. The two had crossed paths multiple times at multiple galas before anything had happened, as each had preferred to dabble with partners more their own age (and Hugo even younger). But one night after a particularly boisterous event held in the abandoned tunnels of Fort Totten, the blonde had enthusiastically accepted a ride home on the back of Hugo's 1199, and the two would have made out down the entire length of the FDR if it wouldn't have led to their quick and fiery deaths.

Instead, they had waited until they reached Natalia's penthouse overlooking Washington Square Park, a place he had spent a good portion of the summer of 2009. Hugo wasn't sure how much longer their affair would have continued if he had not discovered the truth about her, but if anything, he was good at compartmentalizing. And tonight, he would have to do it again.

Hugo turned his attention back to the hand, ignoring Martin's grimace at the long delay between bets. He gave his cards a glance again. Ace-nine. Not bad, but nothing to write home about. That was, until the flop hit.

Ace, nine, eight.

Two pair for Hugo, a flush draw for someone else.

He continued to slow play; after all, it was only the first hand with the couple at the table and there was much to learn.

Another nine on the turn and Hugo found himself sitting with the nuts. But still, no one bit, and the three players limped into the river, where the flush draw hit. One more check and he smiled as Martin pushed three stacks forward. Natalia quickly bowed out and Hugo found himself in an odd quandary. There was something off about his stroke of good fortune, but it would make little sense for his opponent to come out swinging right from the opening bell. Even he had more good sense than that. And from what he remembered of Natalia's hands, they were rather clunky. Not the sort that one would ever confuse for a mechanic.

Still, it was worth losing a bit of his money to find out for sure, and so, Hugo slid three stacks followed by another three stacks into the center.

"Raise," he said, feeling the dread of uncertainty build in his stomach as his opponent looked at him and then at his cards and then at his wife, who gave him a weak smile. At that, Martin's hands moved not toward his chips but to his hand, which he tossed into the center of the table.

"Fold. Well played."

Hugo stared at the pot for a second, not registering what had just happened.

"Should have paid me off," muttered Hugo under his breath as he pulled his winnings toward his existing stacks. Did his old lover have such a good handle on him that she read whatever small ticks his face was throwing off? Or was his paranoia already getting to him?

He pushed such concerns to the side and took the deck from Natalia, who flashed him yet another smile. There was no trace of any bumps, indentations, or other marks, but Hugo worked the cards through his hands several times more than necessary just the same. He looked down at his hole cards after dealing and found an Ace-five unsuited staring back at him. But the flop rewarded him yet again with an Ace-five-three and a sense of deja vu rippled through him like a stiff drink.

"Check to you, Dorogáya," said Martin, smiling across the table to Natalia, who returned the gesture in kind.

"Spasibo, lyubimyy," she replied.

"I hate to interject into this touching moment," said Hugo, "but if you want to see the next card, stop speaking sputnik!"

"Sorry, Hugo," said Natalia. "We just got back from Sochi and the language just stuck."

"That's so nice, I'm sure you had a lovely time, but are you going to bet?"

"Yes," she said. "50 silver."

"Call," said Hugo.

"Too rich for my blood, love," said Martin, who tossed his cards into the center, along with everyone else.

The turn yielded another three and again, Natalia led off with a strong bet, this time 100 silver. If this had been a normal game, Hugo would have folded in an instant, not wanting to go toe-to-toe against a probable straight or full house. But there was a lot more riding on this game than a bunch of tokens, and so, he called the bet again and turned over the river card.

A five, completing yet another full house.

"Check," said Natalia and Hugo considered the possibility for the second time that he was being played. But normally such antics occurred when you weren't the person dealing the cards.

"150," said Hugo, pushing three stacks into the center. It was a lot of money to lose on a hunch, more than he had made the entire night so far. The price would be worth it, however, if he could glean even a hint as to what these two were up to.

Natalia flashed him that same damn smile and as her hands moved toward her chips, Hugo held his breath. Instead, she tossed her cards away like a used cigarette and gave him a small golf clap.

"Once again, you've bested me," she said as Hugo began counting his chips and he glanced at her sideways. Was it, though? Or were they both feeding him money and his ego? Several drinks and olives later, and nothing had changed. The cards kept coming in Hugo's favor and he alternatively took huge sums off of both halves of the seemingly happy couple. After one particularly big hand, which had emptied Martin's stash completely, he thought the night's activities were going to finally end, and without him having gotten the chance to do what he had come here to do. But that's when things finally took a turn.

"Mr. Clouser," said Martin, his voice grating, "I'm afraid you've wiped me nearly clean. But perhaps I can convince you to wager something other than these trifling tokens?"

"Doubtful," said Hugo. "Unless you're offering a night with your wife?"

He thought the barb would have yielded a visceral reaction from the man, but instead, he put his latest cigarette out in the ashtray and cooly lit another.

"You watch too many movies," interjected Natalia. "You had your chance, and I've moved on."

"Can't blame a guy for asking. So, if not her, what is it, then?"

Martin reached his hand slowly into the inner pocket of his jacket, withdrew it, and placed something on the table with a thud. As he unfurled his fingers, Hugo pretended to nearly spit out his gin mid-sip at what he saw.

A gold token. But not just "a" gold token, "the" gold token.

"Where … where did you get that?"

Martin smiled.

"I think you know. That's why you're here tonight, isn't it? To help your friend with his sizable debt?"

"Maybe."

"Well, let me tell you what you would have found out eventually. Your money and his money are no good. I've already spent a sizable fortune of several types of treasure to get this one. And I'm not looking to make a return on my investment."

"Then, what do you want?"

Martin glanced at Natalia, who returned a sheepish grin.

"What good is a Guild seat for myself when I need two?"

"You're out of your mind," said Hugo. "Do you know how long this seat has been in my family?"

"Oh, I'd say only a little longer than this token belonged to its former owner's clan, and yet, I took it just the same."

Martin grinned, his cigarette sticking to his bottom lip, and Hugo resisted the urge to punch him in the face.

"So, you just want to go heads up, one hand?"

"Not exactly," said Natalia. "That's not really fair to my hubby. If you want that token back, you'll have to beat both of us. We each re-stake and play until there's one left standing. Madam Banker!"

Natalia waved her hand in the air like an eager co-ed trying to get the attention of the gray-haired professor and a few moments later, the Banker, or one of her sisters, because who could tell the difference, walked slowly toward the table.

"Dr. Lester, what can I help you with this evening?"

The Banker's eyes shifted to the gold token on the table and for a split-second, Hugo saw her pupils dilate slightly before returning to normal.

"We have a special game we'd like to play and we need a little more coin, if you wouldn't mind."

"That depends," said the Banker. "How much are you three talking?"

"3,000 silver each," said Martin. "I'm sure you know my wife and I are good for it. What about you, Clouser?"

"Same."

In reality, Hugo's financial affairs were somewhat lacking at the moment, due to a downturn in the Relic trade and several recent Raids that had failed to pan out. That, and the temporary loss of his watch had left him with barely enough to walk into the Den and not get laughed out the front door. But in the end, if things went his way, it wouldn't matter in the slightest.

"Good," said the Banker, who was suddenly holding three glittering stacks of chips in each hand. "One more thing. A game with the stakes this high will require a chaperone. Can't have any shenanigans, it's bad for business, you know? But don't worry, you're in very capable hands with my sister."

Hugo turned around to see the Dealer taking a seat on the other side of the table, a fresh deck in her hands that she quickly shuffled and re-shuffled with inhuman speed.

"Let's play some fuckin' cards," said Martin, slapping Hugo on the back like they were old chums.

"Martin, please. There's no need for such vulgarity," said Natalia.

"My apologies, my love. Just very excited to finally get you the token you deserve."

"Over my dead body," muttered Hugo.

"That's the idea," he thought he heard Martin say. But the man's lips hadn't moved and Hugo took it as a sign that his nerves were finally getting to him. He shook it off and glimpsed his first set of hole cards: 7-2 unsuited.

It was going to be a long night.

THE RIVER

At 1 a.m., Hugo nodded off for a moment and suddenly found himself on the back of his old motorcycle, Natalia's arms wrapped around his waist. It was a good memory, preferable to the reality awaiting him when he opened his eyes again. After several hours of dull stakes, Hugo had hit a bad run and found himself at 50% of his stake. The easy wins of the first few hours had evaporated, and Martin and Natalia had alternated taking his money with relative ease.

It wasn't obvious. Good cheating never was. But Hugo was not in the right mental state to quite figure out how they were doing whatever it was they were doing. So he shifted his tactics until he could execute the endgame he had planned. He played a blitz of bluffs, but the duo saw through each one. He played tight, only going in for a top-12 hand. That fared a little better, but too often than not, the bad beats would find him. A couple of hands he played completely blind, but the odds at the moment were still firmly against him. At the current rate, he would be down to his last big blind well before the sun came up.

And so, a rattling was in order.

"Something is bothering me," Hugo finally announced around 3 a.m as the Dealer prepared to distribute a new hand.

"Yes, I imagine losing your family's inheritance would bother a person," said Martin, snickering while fondling his mile-high stack of chips.

"You already have a gold token," said Hugo.

"I can see why that would bother you. It must stick in your craw that I will soon be taking your friend's place at your Table."

In reality, Hugo had no friends amongst the Guild's other members, just fleeting allies. Friendship among thieves, scions of alchemic dynasties, and other blue-bloods got you nowhere. Or worse, dead. No, he was here for purely selfish reasons. A favor owed from Dalia was worth almost his entire net worth and he was going to be damned if he would let another member claim it. That and he had a reputation to maintain as the Guild's foremost tracker. It had taken him several weeks to track down the lost token's whereabouts and still another fortnight to know, with certainty, that the token would be here tonight.

"No, that's not it. You know, or will soon find out, that presenting a token will not guarantee you entry into the Guild. The Chairman certainly will not grant you that much control over Guild affairs by allowing Natalia to join as well."

"A mere procedural hurdle to be overcome. And if not, my wife will have a puppet to do her bidding."

"Maybe. But you also know that the tokens pass from generation to generation."

"Yes, of course," said Martin, sneering as he lit another cigarette. "That's why it's so hard to get one. What's your point?"

"So your spawn growing in Natalia's belly is already guaranteed your token. Congrats, by the way. Hope it's a girl."

"How did you … what gave it away?" asked Natalia sheepishly, whose urge to rub her ever-so slightly swollen belly evaporated now that the secret was out in the open.

"Let's just say I'm very observant, especially when it comes to the female form," said Hugo with a cocky grin.

"Clouser, that's enough," said Martin, who looked ready to flip over the table if taunted just a bit further. "That's my wife you're talking about."

"Before that, she was something else."

Hugo saw the punch coming, but it didn't matter. He let Martin's fist connect with his nose and collapsed onto the suede surface of the table, which was now a complete mess. Chips were everywhere, but the deck somehow had remained pristinely stacked a few inches from his right hand.

The Dealer had run off to no doubt fetch her sisters, and Hugo was glad he wore one of his older dress shirts tonight as he felt the wetness starting to gush out of both nostrils. Eva, the Dealer, and one other doppelgänger arrived moments later, but he waved them off, mopping up the excess blood dripping down his face with one of the Yoo family handkerchiefs.

"I thought this was a gentleman's game!" said Hugo, tucking the still pristine cloth back in his suit pocket. He watched the Dealer pick up the deck from the table and turn it over several times in her hand, before setting it back down, and his lip curled into a tiny grin.

"You called my wife a whore!" screamed Martin, which nearly prompted Eva to restrain him.

"I most certainly did not," said Hugo. "But since you brought it up, there was something I was wondering. Who is my token really for? The bastard you're siring on the side, or the one Natalia knows is inside of her?"

It was a risk, he knew. The man was quick to anger and even with the added security mere feet away, it wouldn't matter much.

"Now I've heard everything!" laughed Martin, who glanced at his wife for reassurance. But it was not forthcoming.

"Hmm, looks like you haven't," said Hugo. "Natalia, I'm just a little offended that you didn't come to me."

The woman turned beet red and Hugo thought he had maybe gone a little too far. But then he remembered who he was dealing with and it made him feel slightly better.

"Mr. Clouser," said the Hostess, or at least that's who he thought she was, "one more remark and I'm going to end the game now. You three have caused enough of a disruption for one night."

"My apologies. I was just making friendly banter. I'll keep my mouth shut."

Hugo sat back down at the table and surveyed his two opponents, who were locked in death stares with each other. Martin lit another cigarette, exhaling the first puff in Hugo's direction, and Natalia, without warning, grabbed Hugo's half-finished drink and downed the rest of it.

It was then that the world started spinning. Hugo glanced at the empty glasses, but their number was well below his usual tolerance. He closed his eyes for a few moments, trying to steady his mind and body, only to find himself staring directly at ... himself. His eyes shot open, and the outer-body experience ended, only to return when he closed them again. This second time, he noticed *where* he was observing himself from: Natalia's seat. The image was fuzzy, but he could make out her hands at the bottom of his field of vision, and then, as her head turned, he found himself looking straight at … himself.

The cognitive dissonance must have been too much to handle, because the next thing he knew, he was back in his own head. Hugo glanced at Natalia, who seemed oblivious to what had just happened. And Martin too seemed more concerned with trying to murder his wife with his thoughts than to figure out that Hugo had just broken through their cheating method.

It was an elegant if complicated workaround of the Hostess's security measures, but Hugo cursed himself for not realizing it sooner. The smoke from Martin's cigarettes when inhaled by Natalia, who had eaten the gin-soaked olive that he had stupidly offered her, activated the nagalate, opening the pathway into his head, not to hear his thoughts, but to borrow his eyes. It explained his earlier apparent successes, baiting him into a false sense of confidence. And it explained his terrible run just now. A normal player would have chalked it up to simply a string of bad beats, but Hugo knew that when there was so much on the line, most people would not leave their fates up to chance. He wondered whether it was just a waitress with a sizable debt or one of the sisters who had been in on the scheme, but that was a puzzle to work out for another time.

"Umm, are you all ready to resume?" asked the Dealer, holding the reassembled deck in her hand.

Hugo looked at his minuscule stack, but for the first time all night, he felt completely in control of the situation.

"I'm ready if the two lovebirds are," he quipped.

Both nodded silently and out the cards came.

Hugo peeled up his hole cards and was greeted with an Ace-3 suited. Not great, but not terrible, given the circumstances.

But then he felt it, like a pinprick in the back of his mind.

Why he hadn't earlier bothered him a great deal. Maybe it was the combination of drinks, lack of sleep, nerves, and a dozen other things. But now that he did, he kicked himself for being so stupid. He glanced over at Natalia, whose own eyes were fluttering open and shut. Their cadence matched the twitch he now felt inside his head, his erstwhile lover forcing her way into his head, into his vision, looking at the cards he was dealt.

He ignored her prying eyes for a moment, threw in a couple of chips, and watched the flop come out.

Ace-3-3. A full house for Hugo, but maybe a better one for his opponents if they somehow were dealt pocket-aces. It was the perfect set-up to get him to foolishly bet away all of his money, and so, he was left with two choices, neither of them good. He watched Natalia, looking for any sign that she was signaling to Martin what cards Hugo had. But either his earlier antics had destroyed the trust between the two of them, or they had been using celestonite to undetectably pass their thoughts all night. Whichever it was, Hugo did not feel like losing his token on this particular hand. And so, he tried to limp into the river, seeking to tease out how rigged the game was.

His opponents were having none of it, both folding against his weak bet.

Hugo tried a different tact on his next hand, which was absolute garbage. He postured that he was on the flush draw delivered by the flop, but was quickly called by Martin. Paying his way to the river revealed that his opponent indeed had the goods, and Hugo tossed his cards into the center face down.

Another hour went by of more of the same. Good hands were quickly snuffed out by immediate folds and every bluff was matched and bested. Hugo ran the math and it did not bode well for him, even if he was able to get lucky and win a backdoor hand every now and again.

"It's nearly 5 a.m.," said the Dealer. "You all maybe just want to call it?"

"Absolutely not," said Martin. "We play until it's over."

"Well, Mr. Lester, that's a nice sentiment, but seeing as how you three are the only patrons left, I'd like to go home at some point before this evening's session. So here's what we're going to do: the blinds are quadrupled and no folding until the river. You don't like it, go to the base of the Manhattan Bridge for all I care."

"No complaints here," said Hugo.

"Fine," said Martin, lighting up another cigarette.

"And no more smoking," quipped the Dealer. "Your wife is pregnant!"

Hugo stifled a laugh and resisted the urge to add his commentary on top. The new rules would certainly speed things along, but he needed more than that to pull out a victory here. And thanks to his quick finger work earlier, when the cards came out for the next hand, he finally saw it: the ever-so slightly shimmering border around each of the face cards he had been dealt. He played the hand aggressive and was paid off on the river when he hit two-pair. The Dealer's new rules had blunted much of his opponents' edge, but he was still at a severe disadvantage during each showdown.

But that was finally about to change.

THE SHOWDOWN

Hugo's uncle liked to fish. Despite his obscene wealth, his favorite hobby was waking up at 4 a.m., ambling down to Pier 11 with a wooden rod, a plastic soup container filled with worms, and his watch. While the other fishermen struggled with their graphite poles and fancy self-winding wheels, Charles Yoo somehow managed to outcatch them all, day after day, week after week. Hugo spent many summer mornings sitting with his uncle and trying to figure out how it was that the old man did it. Was it his patience? His finesse? His mindfulness? But Charles would never say and their many conversations had never even broached the subject.

During one of his last mornings with his uncle before he left for college, Hugo finally worked up the nerve to ask his uncle for his secret.

"What a ridiculous question, nephew," Charles said. "You know it's the watch. It's always been the watch. And this, it was never about catching the most or the biggest fish."

"What are you talking about?" asked Hugo. The watch he knew had been passed along the male line for generations, and given that Charles had no children, Hugo was in line to receive it. "It's just a watch. I mean, it's very impressive, what with it lasting so long, but it just tells time."

"It does not," said Charles, withdrawing what had once been a pocket watch, its silver band beaming in the early morning light. "It tracks time."

"Right, whatever. Same thing."

"They are not. Look."

Charles opened the watch and Hugo saw that in the middle was a small clock within its center panel. His uncle began winding the little dial at the top and the clock rotated up and out of view. In its place was a striped bass.

"I don't understand. It's a fishing watch?"

"No, nephew. Take it," said Charles, offering the heirloom in his outstretched hand.

Hugo obliged and gingerly picked it up.

"Push the dial back in."

He did so and the world seemed to slow around him. Hugo's eyes darted to the water and it was as if the schools of fish were singing a song just to him. His uncle smiled and handed him the rod and Hugo cast it into the water. He felt the line go taut a few moments later, and when he reeled it back in, at the end was the largest fish Hugo had ever caught.

"The watch, it tracks … things?"

"Yes, nephew. Things, people, emotions. I keep a few options set within the internal slots, but you should see what we have all crafted over the years. It's a veritable library of treasure. When it's your turn to take the seat, you'll see."

But that day never came. Instead, Hugo returned home for spring break that first year, only for his mother to share the news that his uncle had died in a massive fire at his estate, and with it, the Yoo workshop and he presumed, the collection of tracking disks. He remembered running to his room and instead of a final missive from his uncle, finding only a tattered envelope on his bed with the watch inside.

"The bet is to you, Mr. Clouser," said the Dealer, and Hugo emerged from his stupor to find a fresh set of hole cards in front of him. Thanks to the Dealer's rule changes, he had managed to edge slightly ahead of his two rivals, and he almost pulled out the watch that wasn't there to check the time, but he knew that this was the moment he had been waiting for.

Ace-7 offsuit greeted him when Hugo peeled up the edge of his cards and he felt the familiar tickle of Natalia poking into his head. Look all you want, he wanted to say, but instead he silently called the blinds.

The flop yielded the Jack of diamonds, a 7, and a three, giving Hugo a weak pair. He called the other bets silently, and was rewarded with the King of diamonds on the turn.

"10,000," he said, pushing about a quarter of his chips into the center. In a normal game, such a bet would have obviously signaled he was on a flush draw, but Natalia knew that he wasn't. Whether Martin did was another question. He watched the couple weigh the strength of their own hands, and tried to keep a stoic exterior. A bluff of a different sort.

His ex was the first to push her chips in and then the cigarette smoking doofus followed. No one was in a talking mood, and so the Dealer flipped over the final card of the hand, the ace of diamonds.

A strong two pair in normal circumstances, but this was far from normal. Dozens of scenarios ran through Hugo's head, but to hope for one in particular would be like Schrodinger's cat. Instead, he needed to focus on a different game first.

"10,000," Hugo said, as he pushed in most of his remaining chips.

"You're on a draw, Hugo dear?" asked Natalia, almost gleefully. "Go away, this one's not worth it." She raised his bet to 20,000 and Martin, again in silence, called.

Hugo looked at the bets, the cards, and his hand, sitting face down in front of him. His fate, the fate of his family, and maybe the fate of the entire Guild, rested with what he was about to do. All the posturing in the world wouldn't help him if even the slightest tick of his face gave him away.

"I. Bet. It. All."

He quietly pushed his remaining chips into the center, the stacks falling over and covering the five face up cards. However much she tried to hide it, Natalia couldn't suppress the entirety of her grin and Hugo breathed a short sigh of relief when she too brought the entirety of her chips into the pot to match his. That left Martin, who was deep in thought, no doubt wrestling with his own uncertainties, and no matter what happened at the end of the hand, Hugo would at least have the satisfaction of delivering that sliver of doubt into the man's mind as to his progeny.

"I call," said Martin, the trio's combined winnings now arrayed like a gleaming full moon in the center of the table.

"Mr. Clouser," said the Dealer. "If you would?"

"No," said Martin. "Ladies first."

"That's not how the order goes," the woman replied.

"Still. I insist."

The Dealer started to protest again, but Natalia shooed her away.

"It's OK. It's OK. Doesn't matter to me."

The blonde turned over her hole cards to reveal a pair of kings.

"Three kings," she said. "And you, my husband?"

Martin flipped over his cards and grunted.

"Three sevens," said the Dealer. "Mr. Clouser?"

Hugo placed his fingers on the edges of his hole cards. Without his watch, he felt completely blind, lost in a dark forest without a way out. It was like that moment back on the dock, when his uncle had revealed that it had been no inner magic behind his preternatural fishing ability. Just another skill borrowed from something or someone else. There was nothing special about his uncle, only the luck of his birth, the luck that Hugo possessed and now traded away. He remembered opening up the envelope from his uncle, and rather than feeling sad at the manner that the watch had passed to him, he only felt anger that his family's legacy was bound up in that stupid object.

But then another memory suddenly surfaced. Something his mother had said to him after he had wanted to throw the watch in the garbage and never think about it again.

"Give love its rightful time."

He hadn't asked her what she meant and had almost forgotten her words, which had provided no comfort to him in that moment. But that was the point, he now realized. The watch was more than a magic totem. It was a legacy, a promise from one generation to the next. And rather than traveling around the world in search of the fantastical, his uncle had spent his time with Hugo out on the pier, just fishing and talking, trying to slowly guide the next member of the family, and keeping the watch ready for the rightful time. And in his arrogance, he had perhaps squandered it forever.

"It's time," said the Dealer. "Either show or fold."

Hugo closed his eyes, took a deep breath, and flipped over his cards.

The ten of diamonds and the queen of diamonds greeted him warmly and he nearly choked.

"Royal … flush," Hugo said slowly and Natalia froze, before pushing the stacks of chips aside to uncover the rest of the hand.

"That's … you couldn't have. You tricked me!" she snarled.

"I don't know what you're talking about," said Hugo. "All I see is a well-played hand and a misbegotten wager. Martin, the token please."

The man was almost happy to part with it, as if a burden had suddenly been lifted and he wondered whether any of this had been Martin's idea or if he too had been played. But that hadn't stopped Natalia from making one last futile attempt to undo the result of the game by trying to stab him with a hairpin no doubt laced with something sinister. Thankfully the blonde named Eva had intervened, grabbing Natalia by the wrists from behind and sending her convulsing to the floor.

"That was quite a night," said the woman who sat down next to him at the bar 20 minutes later, whom he presumed was the Hostess. She handed him Phineas's deck of cards, all packed neatly back into the box.

"Thank you," said Hugo.

"Don't ever come back to my club again," she replied curtly, and walked away.

EPILOGUE

"I will … and I will."

The old man was waiting on the same bench when Hugo arrived at 1 p.m., just a few hours after his epic victory, and he was glad that another mysterious appearance wasn't in the cards.

"You have my watch?" asked Hugo, setting the deck of cards down between them.

"Of course," said Phineas. "You said to give you a week and yet it seems you didn't even need that long."

"No," said Hugo. "Thankfully luck was on my side."

"Luck, ha! As if that had anything to do with it."

"Whatever you say."

He was in no mood for the cryptic musings of the shopkeeper, especially when the matter of his watch was still not settled.

"How did they try to cheat you?" the man asked.

"Why should I give you any ideas?" Hugo replied. "The important thing is I bested them."

"…by cheating."

"What were they going to do? Call me for cheating better than them?"

"I suppose not. If all the cards are accounted for, then the watch is yours once more."

The man picked up the deck, shook it a few times next to his right ear, and apparently satisfied, retrieved the silver watch from his jacket pocket and set it down on the bench.

"That's it?" asked Hugo. "No tricks? No hard bargain?"

"What kind of person do you take me for, Mr. Clouser? A deal is a deal. And besides, you have a lot on your mind, I'm sure. What with the matter of who to give your new token to."

Hugo froze.

"Don't know what you're talking about."

"Please. Your acting might have worked at the poker table, but not with me. I'm impressed, though, with your plan, however foolish it might be. Do let me know if you need help finding a buyer. I know everything for sale in this city."

With that, the old man pushed himself up from the bench and ambled across the street. A speeding car passed between the two of them and by the time it had cleared the intersection, Phineas was nowhere to be found.

"Figures," said Hugo, grabbing the watch and sliding it back onto his wrist. He wound the dial and watched as the clock face rotated out of view and the empty slot crept into view.

Except it wasn't empty, because resting inside was something Hugo hadn't seen in a long time.

His uncle's striped bass.

GALLERY

EMMA

GUILD OF MAGIC MOVIE POSTER

SHOP THE
NIGHT MA
FOR ALL YOUR

KET
EMICAL NEEDS!

YOUR LUCK AT
E DEN

Clan
Spike & Devil
NEEDS YOUR
ALCHEMY SKILLS!

GUILD HQ

OFFICE OF THE CHAIR

Currently held by Dalia de Wyck. That may or may not be the skull of her mortal enemy on the shelf. Or her former lover. Who may be the same person.

LIBRARY

Appearances can be deceiving and not all knowledge is contained in books.

BOARD ROOM

4 Tables representing the 4 original Guild settlements. 3 chairs per Table. And unlike some, this council is not quiet.

FOYER

It's a foyer. Definitely not hiding aaaanything. Like a secret passageway. Because that passageway over here is not secret. Unlike the other one!

GUILD HQ SCHEMATIC

AUTHOR'S NOTE

Join the Readers' Guild by subscribing to my monthly newsletter to stay up to date on everything happening in the *NYC Questing Guild* universe, including exclusive short stories, discounts, and news.

Sign up at www.jonauerbach.com/back_matter_magic.

ACKNOWLEDGMENTS

What began as a few sentences scribbled on a page in the fall of 2019 while I was sitting in a coffee shop has finally ended as this book you have just read. It took longer than I thought to get here, and there were some expected and unexpected happenings along the way: a global pandemic, two Kickstarters, side stories, and more. But looking back, it was quite the journey, and I wouldn't have had it any other way.

I would like to thank my family and friends for all of their support along this writing journey. Without their help, this book wouldn't have been possible.

- To my mom Sandi and my sister Alissa, for going above and beyond in making this book possible
- To my dad Rich, for first inspiring my love of science fiction and fantasy
- To my friend Brian Clouser, for always listening to my (sometimes) crazy marketing ideas and politely telling me to get back to the writing
- To my friend Brant Englestein for his invaluable story help once again and for believing in Guild

- To my friend (and fellow author) Travis Riddle for his support, camaraderie, and for being the first Kickstarter backer two times in a row
- To David Walters and FanFiAddict for hosting my cover reveal
- To Typo Squad members, Kara L. and Katy M., for their help in making Guild of Magic a pristine read

And finally,

- thank you to my wife Danielle for her continued love, support, encouragement, and so much more.
- thank you to my kids Allison, Robby, and Claire, the ARC of my world.

KICKSTARTER BACKERS

Thanks to the following people
(and those who chose not to be recognized publicly) for backing
and supporting the creation of *Guild of Magic*.

Aaron Jamieson • acolyte • Adam Rossi • Adam A • Adam Kerstin
Adam Nemo • Adriana Raats • Air-Ron • Alex G. • Alex Stott
Alex Weisman • Alex Wrigglesworth • Alexius Serefeas
Algie Lane III • Alok Baikadi • Amanda M.T. • Amelia
Amelia Armstrong • Anas Abusalih • Andrew Godecke
Andrew Kurtzman • Ángel González • Angel Ocampo
Ariel Shapiro • Arsen Yaku • Arthur Ni • Astridd • Austin Hoffey
Author Amy Campbell

B. Garcia-Kindl • B. Plaga • Benita K. • Bentley Searing
Bethany Tomerlin Prince • Bh • Bill McJohn • Brandon Cleland
Brendan Coffey • Brett H Kammerer • Brett R. "Swantz" Swanson
Brian "Smidge" Twomey • Brian Clouser • Bridgette Findley
Bruce Harpham • Bryan Hill

C. Corbin Talley • C.P. Wilson • Caelin B Hill • Caleb Slama
Candy Gordon Geanoules • Carissa F. • Carmen Maria Marin
Carol A. Park • Cedric Gasser • Chad Bowden • Chance Garcia
Chance Garcia • Charles Bergman • Charlie Stickney
Chris Brimmage • Chris Carbone Chris K. • Chris Matthews
Chris Roeszler • Chris Stillwell • Christian Bonilla
Christina Baclawski • Christopher D Shramko
Christopher Froebe • Christopher J Boisvert • Clair Johnson
Claire Ferguson-Smith • Clay Branche • Connor Lee
Corky LaVallee • Cortney Pearson • Cristina Kovacs
Crystal Palumbo • Curtis and Maryrita Steinhour

Dale A Russell • Dan Cagneux • Daniel Dickerson
Daniel Mizrachi and Alissa Auerbach Mizrachi
Danielle Auerbach • Dave Baughman • Dave Cole • David Bobbitt
David Holzborn • Dead Fish Books • Deanna Gibson
Deanna Stanley • Deborah Hedges • DFarziana
Dianne Nicholson • Dipin Nayee • Dominik • Doris Wooding
Doug "Kosh" Williamson • Dragondarium • DramaDude1231D

Eastin DeVerna • Ed • Ed McCutchan • Eleazar "Dezaræl" Jarman
Elise "Warriorjudge" Feldman • Em • Emily Burt • Emily L
Emily Pedersen • Emmanuel Werthenschlag • Erik "Kesnit" Sapp
Erin • Erin Griffin • Eva Jayet

Fatima Fayez • Finn Kuster • Francine Delgado

G Smith • Gabriel Casillas • Gabriel Crnjac • Gabriel Rivers
Gary Anastasio • Gerald P. McDaniel • GhostCat • Greg Bergerson
Guillermo NWDD

Hannah Ormond Yip-Chuck • Harold van Bolhuis

Heather A. McBride • Heim • Hillary Griffin • Honor Vincent

Ibn

J.D.L. Rosell • J.L. Johnson • Jacob H Joseph • Jacob R. Hunter
James Batchelor • James Oliva • Jane Ashcroft • Janette Fletcher
Janine Belsky • Jared Preston • Jason • Jason Bush
Jason Rippentrop • JD Maynard • Jeanna • Jeffrey Belsky
Jenni D Strand • Jennifer L. Pierce • Jeremy & Erin Boquet
Jerome anello • Jess Pagac • Jesse B. • Jessica Richards • Joe Rixman
Joe Wiedman • John Idlor • John "AcesofDeath7" Mullens
John Gilligan • John Iadanza • John Markley • Jonathan Haas
Jonathan Mendonca • Jordan Arnold • Jordan Holt • Joseph Behar
Joshua C. Chadd • Joshua Callahan • Joy Meisel • JPC • Julie Ma
Justin Aaron Gross • Justin Burgess • Justine Bergman

K.L. Smith • Kait Stubbs • Kajtryna • Kara L • Karen M
Karen Tankersley • Kate Ackerman • Kate Sheeran Swed
Katherine R • Katie Dresel • Katie Wasley
Katy Manck - BooksYALove • Kevin BigO Daniels
Kevin Grønberg Poulsen • Kevin Kastelic • Kirasha Urqhart
Kristi Preston Barnes • Kristian Handberg
Kristopher Horatio Mason • Kyanth Inanis • Kyle McCreary
Kyle Oathout • Kyle Wilkinson

Lahman Marcel • Lance Hurst • Larson Steffek
Lawrence Lane and Sofia Sheydvasser • Lee 'Booksnake' Boswell
Lenka Benešová • Leslie Twitchell • Leyna • Liam Byrne
Lisa Cohen • Lord TBR • Louisa Clark • Louise Mc
Lydia Warriner

M.-H. Ayotte • Malfor • Marcel de Jong • Marco "Fuwo" Nowak

Marie Andreas • Marko S • Martin Oblikas
Mary-Michelle Moore • Mat Meillier
Matt and Camille Knepper • Matt Wayne • Matt Widmann
Matteo Carby • Matthea W. Ross • Matthew Siadak
Mattia Gualco • Maurizio Huaylla • McMoogle • Megan N. Quinn
Megyn "Crimson" MacDougall • Melissa Showers
Michael Daniels III • Michael Hayes • Michael J. Sullivan, author
Michael Sadowitz • Michael Yeh • Michał Kabza
Michele Donahue • Miggel • Mihir W • Mike Kenney
Mike Pandolfini • Mikey and Erica Distenfeld • mikolaj
Mitchell McConnell • Monica Kim • Myrddin Starfari

N. Scott Pearson • Nathan Turner • Neal Martin • Neftali Martinez
Neilson Brown • Nicholas Liffert • Nick Long
Nick Mandujano III • Nicolas Lobotsky • Nicole Holloway
NightScribe • NinaMal • Nuvene Lightfoot

Owen Harnew • Owlbear Enclave • Øyvind Nordli

P. H. Solomon • Patrick "Go Sox" Welsh • Paul FS Hinson
Paul Smith • Peter Allen • Phil Williams • Philippe Gauthier
Pierluca Morando • Prasad Nagaraj

Quintin

Rachael Besser and Rafi Spitzer • Rachel Peterson • Randall Fickel
Raphael Bressel • Rebecca Buchanan • Richard Erik Larsen
Richard Novak • RJ Hopkinson • Rob Crosby • Rob Steinberger
Robert Brown • Robert C Flipse • Robert D. White
Robert Zangari • Robian • Rod Cressey • Ronald H. Miller
Roos van Dijk • Rowan Stone • Russell Ventimeglia

Sam Niles Baribeau • Samantha Landström
Sandi and Rich Auerbach • Sandra K Lee • Sarah
Sarah M. Eggleston • Sarah Werfal • Scott R. • Sean M Tardif
Sebastián Vela (Adaby) • Serena Ho • Shakyra Dunn
Shane Heaton • Shannon L Desmond • Shannon VanBergen
Shawna walker • Shelagh McLean • Sheryl R. Hayes
Silvio Krvaric • Simon Dick • Stacy Shuda • Stefke Leuhery
Stephan Bourges • Stephen Ballentine • Stephen Kotowych
Steve Locke • Steven A. Guglich • Steven Hall • Sunny Side Up
Suzy Grem • Sylvia L Foil

T J Zeeman • T. Alan Horne • T. Hise • Tamara Case
Tammy Kissee • Tania • TDK • TenbatsuZ • Thad Watulak
The Pawson Family • The S.K.N.J. Craig Family • Therena Carlin
Thomas G. • Tomas Gronich • Travis M. Riddle
Trinity Blackmoore • Ty Patterson • TY Wong

Udi Kish

Vengent • Vince Martin • Violette L.

WarGrimm123 • Will Allred

Zach Hall • Zachary M • Zachery Nott • Zack Dale

ABOUT
THE AUTHOR

Jon Auerbach's love of fantasy began at the tender age of six, when his parents bought him the classic 1977 animated version of *The Hobbit*.

He hopes to pass on his stories to the next generation, including his kids, who have their own copy of *The Hobbit* that they lovingly call "the Bilbo book."

www.ingramcontent.com/pod-product-compliance
Lightning Source LLC
Chambersburg PA
CBHW061535190726